THE INFERNO

THE INFERNO

DANTE
THE INFERNO

A New Verse Translation by
PETER THORNTON

Arcade Publishing • New York

First North American Paperback Edition 2019

First published by Barbican Press in Great Britain in 2016

Arcade Publishing books may be purchased in bulk at special discounts for sales promotion, corporate gifts, fund-raising, or educational purposes. Special editions can also be created to specifications. For details, contact the Special Sales Department, Arcade Publishing, 307 West 36th Street, 11th Floor, New York, NY 10018 or arcade@skyhorsepublishing.com.

Arcade Publishing® is a registered trademark of Skyhorse Publishing, Inc.®, a Delaware corporation.

Visit our website at www.arcadepub.com.

10 9 8 7 6 5 4 3 2 1

Library of Congress Cataloging-in-Publication Data

Names: Alighieri, Dante, 1265-1321 author. | Thornton, Peter, translator.
Title: The inferno : a new verse translation / Dante Alighieri ; translated
    by Peter Thornton.
Description: First North American edition. | New York, NY : Arcade
    Publishing, 2017. | Originally published in the Great Britan by Barbican
    Press.
Identifiers: LCCN 2016048793 | ISBN 9781628727456 (hardback) |
    ISBN 9781948924221 (paperback) | ISBN 9781628727487 (ebook)
Subjects: Hell—Poetry. | BISACPOETRY / Ancient, Classical & Medieval.
    FICTION / Classics.
Classification: PQ4315.2 .T48 2017 | DDC 851/.1 LC record available at
    https://lccn.loc.gov/2016048793

Cover design by Erin Seaward-Hiatt
Cover illustration: iStockphoto

Printed in the United States of America

FOR DAVID
who died in the late-twentieth-century plague at thirty-five

nel mezzo del cammin di nostra vita

Into themselves eternity at last
changes them
MALLARMÉ VIA AUERBACH

The thundering text, the snivelling commentary
ROBERT GRAVES

Contents

Translator's Preface xi

Inferno 1
CANTO I 3
CANTO II 13
CANTO III 23
CANTO IV 31
CANTO V 40
CANTO VI 50
CANTO VII 57
CANTO VIII 65
CANTO IX 72
CANTO X 80
CANTO XI 88
CANTO XII 96
CANTO XIII 104
CANTO XIV 112
CANTO XV 121
CANTO XVI 130
CANTO XVII 138
CANTO XVIII 146
CANTO XIX 154
CANTO XX 163
CANTO XXI 171
CANTO XXII 179

Canto XXIII 187
Canto XXIV 195
Canto XXV 204
Canto XXVI 213
Canto XXVII 222
Canto XXVIII 230
Canto XXIX 238
Canto XXX 245
Canto XXXI 252
Canto XXXII 259
Canto XXXIII 266
Canto XXXIV 275

Works Cited 283
Biographical Note on Dante 295

Translator's Preface

Translations of *The Divine Comedy* and especially of the *Inferno*, its most popular segment, have multiplied in English over the last thirty years. If I were beginning this translation today I might be too intimidated to proceed; but I began its lengthy "stitching and unstitching" (Yeats) almost thirty years ago, after ceasing to be an academic, in the off-hours of practicing law. The stream of translations testifies to the continued intensity of our culture's engagement with this pre-modern work. The *Comedy* is one of the few works of literature that really is timeless, as reflected in this continuing popularity; and for those who cannot read the original text, this justifies a stream of versions that attempt to make it immediate by giving it a living voice in contemporary English. I think this popularity also testifies to the capaciousness of Dante's text, which lends itself to the interpretation of every sensitive and patient reader. Although I admire some of the translations of the *Inferno* published while I was working on this one, I can only say that none of them quite conveys the effect that the original makes on me.

First-time readers of the *Inferno* are told that it is allegorical. I think it is more useful at the outset to emphasize that it is the most realistic work of fiction that had been written up to that time. It purports to be not fiction but autobiography and everything is told from the point of view of Dante, the character, who is, as near as we can tell, the historical Dante. Although he journeys through hell – certainly not a naturalistic fictional premise – hell turns out be a great deal like the Italy he knew, and he meets people he knew personally or by reputation. His journey takes him through a landscape described in vivid realistic detail, where he meets highly individualized characters who reveal themselves with startling psychological immediacy in dialogue; and his encounters with them are often intensely dramatic. These are the characteristics of the work (along with an approximation of Dante's voice relating them) that this translation tries above all to convey. I try to remain faithful to Dante's text while attempting to capture, or parallel in a different language, some of his poetic effects. Any translation that achieves these aims with a fair degree of success should be welcome.

There are basically two kinds of translations of the *Inferno*. For readers with some knowledge of Italian, a literal prose rendering on the opposite pages from the Italian text can give the sense of Dante's verses, while serving as a trot for those who wish to dip into the original either at points that especially strike them or for a sense of the full poem. That is how I originally read the *Comedy* in the 1960s in Sinclair's translation. For those with no Italian, providing the Italian text seems redundant and the reader would be served better by a verse translation that gives some sense, however approximate, of the poetic power of Dante's work.

Though a literal prose translation can convey Dante' words more or less precisely, by definition it cannot reproduce the essence of the work, which is its poetry. On the other hand, a verse translation cannot depart too far from Dante's words in search of poetic effects, because it invariably turns out that Dante is a better poet than the translator. Any poetic translation must cross back and forth over the border of interpretation, but the translator of the *Comedy* needs to pay close attention to the shifting semantic fields covered by many of Dante's words and phrases as they are modified by context. I do not purport to be a scholar of the Italian language and rely for this purpose on modern commentaries like Sapegno, Bosco/Reggio and Chiavacci Leonardi, and above all on the *Enciclopedia Dantesca*, a stupendous compendium of scholarship that among other things opines on the shade of meaning of each word in Dante's Italian works in every context in which it appears.

For a verse translation, one question is how far to imitate the form of Dante's verse. The *Comedy* is written in hendecasyllables, eleven-syllable lines with feminine endings. The building block of the narrative is a three-line unit, the tercet or terzina. Dante links these units with an interlocking triple-rhyme scheme he invented called terza rima (aba, bcb, cdc, etc.), which helps pull the narrative forward. The most common English rhyme schemes, the couplet and the quatrain, are not appropriate for translating the *Comedy* because they are closed forms, in which the rhymes chime strongly. Adding the third rhyme in the interlocking pattern surprisingly makes the chiming softer; T.S. Eliot thought that the way to capture the effect in English was to alternate unrhymed masculine and feminine endings. I find that having to rhyme (or even meet the much looser requirements of off-rhyme) would make me depart from Dante's words more than I want to; and especially given the soft echoes of terza rima that doesn't seem justified. I use an unrhymed verse that is regular enough to maintain the rolling momentum of the narrative and to sustain and modulate emotion, but flexible enough to accommodate the cadences of contemporary English, especially in dialogue.

This is blank verse, the workhorse of English meters, in the relatively loose modern form intended to accommodate spoken English; but I structure the free flow of traditional blank verse by preserving Dante's tercets, the framework on which his rhetoric is hung. I try to parallel Dante's poetic practice, in part, by imitating the deployment of his syntax over two, three or even more tercets. Dante's sentences do not always begin and end within the boundaries of tercets, but that is his most usual practice; grammatical units of one or two tercets are the most common. Here is an example over two tercets:

> No twang of bowstring ever drove a shaft
>   to hurtle through the air as rapidly
>   as a small skiff I saw came skimming toward us
> across the water at that very moment,
>   steered by a single oarsman, who was shouting
>   from far off, "Now I've got you, wicked soul!"
>
> (Inf. 8.13–18).

Units of three tercets are not uncommon:

> A farmhand, as he sits upon a hill
>   during the season when the one who lights
>   the world least hides his face and at the hour
> in which the fly gives way to the mosquito,
>   sees in the valley numberless fireflies
>   down where he plows, perhaps, or picks the grapes:

with countless flames like that the whole eighth gulch
    flickered, as I became aware at once
    when I arrived where I could see the bottom.

                                                              (Inf. 26.25–33).

Blank verse is also a good medium for refracting the emotion of Dante's dialogue, as when Count Ugolino says,

    "You must be heartless if you feel no sorrow
        now, when you realize what my heart foreboded.
        What do you ever weep for if not this?"

                                                              (Inf. 33.40–42)

or the drama of Dante's encounter with Bocca degli Abati:

    I grabbed his hair then, at the scruff of the neck,
        and said, "You need to tell me your name now
        or you'll be left without a hair back here."
    "Even," he answered, "if you snatch me bald,
        I will not tell you who I am or show you,
        not if you stomp my head a thousand times."

                                                          (Inf. 32.97–102).

    At first reading, it may be better simply to plunge into the narrative and enjoy its artfully varied scenes, the drama of the encounters with multiple memorable characters and Dante's extraordinary gift for surprising images that illuminate a scene like lightning. For a deeper understanding of the *Inferno*, however, some recourse to scholarly materials is necessary and for readers of a translation is most conveniently supplied by notes. At a minimum you need to understand something about the characters Dante meets and the situation, often involving politics, in which their lives were embedded. Beyond that you need some understanding of the philosophy, religion, history and even science of Dante's time, because all of them are incorporated in his vision of hell (and of purgatory and heaven in the following segments of the *Comedy*).

    The need for such explanations is not solely the result of the lapsed centuries, but arises in part from the complexity of Dante's poem. In the generation after Dante's there were commentaries by Dante's son Pietro, Boccaccio and others and a robust commentary tradition has lasted until today. Translation itself is a sort of commentary, because it pins the translator down to what he thinks every phrase means, when opinion about interpreting many of them is a staple of standard Italian commentaries. The notes at the end of each canto of the current translation are designed with the student and the general reader in mind. They are somewhat more detailed than the notes appended to some translations, so as to give some sense of all of the elements listed above; and a reader should peruse them only to the extent they are found helpful.

THE INFERNO

Canto I

When I had reached the middle of our life's
    journey, I came to myself in a dark wood
    with the straight path gone missing. Ah, how painful
a thing it is to tell what that was like,
    that wild, rough and impenetrable wood,   5
    the very thought of which revives my fear!
It is so bitter death is scarcely worse.
    Despite that, to describe the good I found there,
    first I must speak of the other things I saw.
I cannot give a good account of how   10
    I'd entered there, I'd been so full of sleep
    around the time I'd strayed from the right road.
But when I reached the bottom of a hill
    beyond the point at which that valley ended
    that had transfixed my heart with fear, I paused   15
and looking up I noticed that its shoulders
    were clothed already in the rays of the planet
    that leads all travelers straight on every path.
Then was the fear a little quieted
    that had persisted deep inside my heart   20
    all through the night I'd passed in so much trouble.
And as a man emerging from the sea
    to stand upon the shore, gasping for breath,
    turns back and stares at the peril of the water,

in the same way my mind, still fugitive,   25
   turned back to gaze again upon the pass
   that no one yet has ever left alive.
After I'd given my tired body some rest,
   I once again set forth on the deserted
   slope, and my firm foot always was the lower.   30
Just where the slope began to steepen, look!
   There suddenly appeared a leopard, agile
   and very swift, covered with spotted fur;
and it would not depart but stayed before me,
   cutting my progress off to such a point   35
   that many times I turned to go back down.
Morning was now beginning and the sun
   mounted the sky with its companion stars
   from the first day when the creator's love
imparted motion to those things of beauty,   40
   so that the hour of dawn and the soft season
   furnished me grounds to entertain good hope
as to the beast of the parti-colored coat;
   but not enough to save me from the fear
   that seized upon me when I saw a lion.   45
This one appeared to be advancing on me,
   holding his head high and enraged by hunger,
   making the very air appear to tremble.
And after him a wolf, who in her leanness
   looked like she carried every appetite   50
   and has made many live in wretchedness,
caused me such consternation with the fear
   that seemed to emanate from her appearance,
   I lost all hope that I would reach the height.
A man who counts his gains with eager joy   55
   finds all his thoughts turn anxious and despondent
   the day reverses make him face a loss;
the restless beast made my heart sink like that
   as she was lunging at me, step by step
   driving me down to where the sun falls silent.   60

As I was falling back toward the low place,
    before my eyes a figure suddenly
    loomed indistinct in the pervasive dusk.
Seeing him in that vast waste, I cried out,
    "Whoever you may be, have pity on me,   65
    whether you be a shade or a real man."
He answered: "Not a man; man I was once.
    My father and mother came from Lombardy,
    natives of Mantua both, and I was born
in Caesar's time, though in his later years,   70
    and lived in Rome under the worthy Augustus
    during the days of the false and lying gods.
I was a poet and I sang of the righteous
    son of Anchises, who came out from Troy
    after proud Illium had been set ablaze.   75
But why are you returning to such suffering?
    Why not ascend the mountain of delight,
    the origin and ground of every joy?"
"Are you then Virgil? Can you really be
    the spring from which there flows so broad a stream   80
    of eloquence?" I answered him, shame-faced.
"O glory and guiding light of other poets,
    may the long study and the ardent zeal
    with which I parsed your works now recommend me.
You are my teacher and my great authority;   85
    it is from you alone that I have drawn
    the noble style that has secured me honors.
See the beast there that made me turn back down:
    protect me from her, celebrated sage,
    for she makes the beating of my pulses throb."   90
When he perceived that I was shedding tears,
    he answered, "You must take a different route
    if you expect to escape this wilderness,
because the beast that makes you cry for help
    lets none pass on her path, but cuts him off   95
    at every step until at last it kills him;

and her nature is so wicked and perverse
    that her voracity is never sated,
    for feeding only whets her appetite.
Many she's mated with among the living   100
    and will with many more, until the greyhound
    arrives to make her die a painful death.
He will not draw his nourishment from land
    or money, but from wisdom, love and virtue,
    and between felt and felt will he be born.   105
He shall deliver unhappy Italy,
    for which Euryalus and Nisus died
    of wounds, with Turnus and the maid Camilla;
and he shall hunt the wolf from town to town
    till he dispatches her again to hell,   110
    from which primeval envy set her loose.
I judge, then, that it would be best for you
    to follow me, and I will be your guide
    out of this place through an eternal realm,
where you will hear the screeches of despair   115
    and see the ancient spirits condemned to pain,
    as each of them laments the second death;
then you will see the souls that though in fire
    are full of joy because they hope to come,
    whenever it may be, among the blessed.   120
If you would then ascend among these last,
    there is a worthier soul for that than I:
    at my departure I will leave you with her,
because the emperor who reigns up there
    prohibits me from entering his city,   125
    since I was disobedient to his law.
He holds sway everywhere, but there presides;
    there is his citadel and his high throne.
    Ah, fortunate the soul predestined there!"
"Poet," I said to him, "I beg of you,   130
    by that God whom in life you did not know,
    help me escape this evil and still worse:

lead me where you have just now spoken of,

so I may look upon St. Peter's gate

and those whom you declare so sorrowful." 135

Then he set out and I kept close behind him.

Notes

1–60: *The prologue scene.* The poem begins in a shape-shifting landscape that is felt rather than seen clearly and where dreamlike events take place, all in strong contrast with the realistic narration of the remainder of the *Inferno.* The dark wood, the sunlit hill and the three beasts seem at once insubstantial and pregnant with significance, leading most readers to suspect an allegorical intent.

Dante distinguished different modes of allegory. The allegory of the poets was a fiction or "beautiful lie" designed to convey a hidden truth. *Conv.* 2.1.2–4. The allegory of the theologians was the interpretation of the literal events of sacred history as signifiers in the economy of salvation – as Israel's exodus from Egypt signifies our redemption effected by Christ and the soul's conversion from sin by grace. *Epist.* 13.21. C. S. Singleton argued that the normal mode of allegory in the *Divine Comedy* is theological rather than poetic. Singleton 1954, 89–90; accord, Hollander 1969 *passim*; but see Scott 346. In this view, Dante's journey through the afterworlds is presented as autobiography and thus any allegorical significance that emerges results from principles of interpretation rather than composition.

The prologue scene, however, lacks the presentational realism that would allow us to take it as a factual account, which is the precondition for theological allegory. Moreover, the perils that the wood and the beasts portend suggest an externalization of psychological experiences, a typical feature of poetic allegory. Singleton himself compared the scene to Bunyan. Singleton 1954, 13. For a comprehensive discussion of allegory in Dante, see *DE* 24–34.

1–3: Dante is thinking of Isaiah 38:10: "in the midst of my days I shall go to the gates of hell," which the *Glossa Ordinaria* interpreted as the sinner being damned in midlife; but the biblical passage as a whole stresses the Lord's forgiveness. The life of this world has brought Dante the character close to spiritual death, but grace will offer him a different kind of descent to the gates of hell, which will save him.

1: Dante regarded human life as an arch, the high point of which – given the biblical span of threescore and ten (Ps. 89:10) – a man reaches at the age of 35. In the spring of 1300, the fictional date of the *Comedy*, Dante was at the end of his thirty-fifth year, and he was at a turning point in his life, about to embark on the most active phase of his political career.

2: The dark wood is familiar from Christian moral writings. Augustine said that life was a forest full of snares and dangers. *Conf.* 10.35. Dante himself had spoken of "the wood of error of this life." *Conv.* 4.24.12.

8–9: Recalling the sinful past is painful, but Dante must describe his moral crisis to set the stage for the entry of grace into his life, the initiation of the journey to God that will occupy the whole of the *Comedy*.

10–12: Dante cannot explain how he entered the wood of error because his moral sense was numbed by the torpor of sensuality and habit.

13–18: The sunlit hill that rises beyond the dark wood should probably be understood as happiness in this life, represented by the earthly paradise, which we attain by exercising our own powers guided by reason and following the moral and intellectual virtues. *Mon.* 3.16.7. Like the earthly paradise after the fall, however, Dante the character will find the way to it barred by fallen man's dispositions to sin. In his ensuing pilgrimage, he will attain the moral wholeness glimpsed in the hill only at the end of the *Purgatorio*, when he has climbed the mountain that this vision prefigures.

17–18: The "planet" is the sun, which in medieval cosmology was simply one of the moveable stars orbiting earth. The sun that banishes the terrors and errors of the night-time wood is God: "No object of sense in all the world is more worthy of being a figure of God than the sun." *Conv.* 3.12.7.

20: "Deep inside my heart (*nel lago del cor*)": In Galenic physiology, the heart was the seat of fear and the other emotions and was conceived as the reservoir of the vital spirits, which, mingled with blood, carried nourishment throughout the body via the arteries. (Boccaccio: "the heart contains a hollow always abounding in blood, in which, according to some, the vital spirits reside. . . ." *ED* 3.552.)

Richard Lansing notes that *lago* derives from the Latin *lacus*, which in the Vulgate Old Testament is used for the underworld of the dead (in Christian thought the pit of hell) or more generally a place of darkness and despair. Lansing argues that the image underlines the pilgrim's "extreme moral peril," which has brought him close to spiritual death. Lansing 2009, 62–69.

28–30: Dante has seen the right way and attempts to attain it under his own power. Because he is not in a state of grace, however, his attempted ascent of the hill will quickly be checked by the inclinations to sin of his fallen nature. (Dante the character is hereafter called "the pilgrim" (see *DE* 701–03) to distinguish him from Dante the poet although, as Lino Pertile notes, the two are not fully distinct but interlaced. Pertile 2007a, 67–68.)

30: John Freccero illuminates an ancient tradition in which the right foot initiates motion while the left remains fixed. This verse, in which the left foot is always behind, therefore implies that the pilgrim limps. According to a related tradition that speaks of the "feet of the soul," the right foot is the pilgrim's reason, while the left is his will. Both intellect and will are wounded by original sin, the intellect by ignorance and the will by concupiscence, but the will is wounded more severely.

The pilgrim limps because his intellect is not in control of his appetites. Freccero 1986, 33–46.

31–60: The threatening beasts that appear and disappear as in a dream cannot be referred to a straightforward narrative, but the allegorical significance to be attributed to them is controversial. Jeremiah 5:6 describes the punishments the Lord visits on faithless Israel: "a lion out of the wood hath slain them, a wolf in the evening hath spoiled them, a leopard watcheth for their cities."

The 14th century commentators who will figure in these notes – Dante's son Pietro, Benvenuto da Imola, Francesco da Buti, Boccaccio and the author of the Ottimo Commento – all understood by the leopard the vice of lust, by the lion the vice of pride and by the wolf the vice of avarice. (The Renaissance commentator Daniello said those were the three basic vices, as shown by the fact that members of religious orders took the opposite vows of chastity, obedience and poverty.) From the late 19th century on, many critics have instead identified the beasts with the types of sin punished in the three major structural divisions of Dante's hell: sins of incontinence or self-indulgence (the wolf), sins of violence (the lion) and sins of fraud (the leopard). Durling/Martinez; Freccero 1986, 46–54; see generally *DE* 85–89.

31–36: The leopard fits the medieval scheme the least well of the three beasts, and the modern scheme the best. The leopard is linked with fraud in *Inf.* 16.106–08, though the import of that passage is mysterious. Deception is the likely meaning of the leopard's painted hide (see *Inf.* 16.108), as it is the meaning of Geryon's painted sides, chest and back (*Inf.* 17.14–15); and the hypocrites are "painted people" (*Inf.* 23.58).

37–42: The idea that the world was created under the sign of Aries is ancient. See Macrobius 1.21.23. Brunetto Latini cited the belief that March 14 was the first day of creation. *Tresor* 1.6.3.

44–48: The lion fits the medieval and modern schemes equally well. The way he holds his head has been emblematic of pride since ancient times, but the terror he impresses on the very air is equally expressive of violence. Brunetto said that lions were characterized by pride and fierceness. *Tresor* 1.174.4–5.

49–60, 94–102, 109–11: The wolf fits the medieval scheme the best of the three beasts and the modern scheme the least well. Identifying the wolf with sins of incontinence, reflecting lack of self-control, is an intellectual exercise; identifying her with greed is the natural interpretation of her bottomless voracity, which only grows by feeding. See Boyde 2000, 160–61. (Albertus Magnus said wolves never grow fat because they gulp chunks of meat whole without chewing them. *De Animal.* 22.115.) The wolf is identified with greed in *Inf.* 7.8 and *Purg.* 20.10–15; and Aquinas cited Ezechiel comparing the avaricious to wolves. *DE* 76.

Sin has a public as well as a private face for Dante (see, *e.g.*, Ferrante 39), but here only the wolf is expressly treated as a public evil, which a future reformer, the greyhound, will eliminate from the world. Increasingly in the late Middle

Ages, greed (cupidity, avarice) displaced pride as the root of all evil (*radix enim omnium malorum est cupiditas* 1 Tim. 6:10). See Scott 177 and note to *Inf.* 16.73–75. Moreover, if the future reformer is a hoped-for emperor (see note to 101–11), the allegory of greed dovetails with Dante's political philosophy.

61: The pilgrim's attempt to climb the hill has confronted him with parts of his nature that, once free of the wood, he recognizes as subject to evil. This leaves him in a worse state than before, as he verges on despair.

62ff.: *Virgil.* The 14th century commentators believed that Dante's Virgil should be understood as an allegory of reason, but Dante is clearly not working in the mode of personification allegory. His Virgil is very much the historical Virgil as Dante conceived of him, and his character is developed in solid detail. Dante's notion of the historical Virgil, however, is very different from ours. Beginning in late antiquity and continuing through the Middle Ages, Virgil became the reigning genius of culture, endowed with universal wisdom. He was an infallible authority on all branches of learning, from philosophy to natural science. See Curtius 443–45; W.H. Stahl in Macrobius 3–4, 108n. In addition, Dante came to see the Roman empire as the ideal form of civil society and Virgil as its supreme witness. This background explains the pilgrim's calling Virgil a celebrated sage (*Inf.* 1.89) and the sea of all sagacity (*Inf.* 8.7). Nonetheless, it is as a poet that Virgil most inspires Dante's reverence, wins his love and exerts pervasive influence on his work. At the same time, in Dante's high conception of the poet's calling, sage and poet are not entirely different roles.

One of the most original features of the *Comedy* is Dante's choosing as his guide through hell, not the conventional angel, but a pagan poet himself condemned to hell, a figure who will in fact guide him up through purgatory to the earthly paradise. Before Singleton, Erich Auerbach proposed understanding Dante's historical characters through what he called the medieval figural interpretation of history. Auerbach's figuralism is the allegory of the theologians, in which one historical person or event foreshadows another that fulfills it, as the church fathers understood people and events in the Old Testament as announcing the coming of Christ.

In the context of the *Comedy* Auerbach emphasized in particular the aspect of theological allegory called anagogical, which reads things of this earth as prefigurations of eternity. So the earthly life of a historical character foreshadows the full reality that the person will possess in the afterlife. Without ceasing to be the actual people they were, Dante's characters are deracinated from their temporal contexts and become fulfillments of a larger significance. Auerbach thought that for Dante the historical Virgil, as fulfilled in the afterlife, became a figure combining poet, prophet and guide. Auerbach 1944, 68–69. (Virgil was thought a prophet in that his Fourth Eclogue was believed to foretell the coming of Christ.) John Scott suggests that an Aristotelianized Virgil combines for Dante philosophical teaching, the authority of the empire and the genius of Latin poetry. Scott 169–70.

Virgil's wisdom is nonetheless limited because it is unenlightened by Christian faith, and some Dante criticism since the mid-20th century has read the poem as undercutting Virgil's authority at every opportunity and associating him with falseness. There are certainly passages in which Dante emphasizes Virgil's human weaknesses and perplexities, generally reflecting his limitations as a pagan; but this hand has been overplayed. Virgil is ordinarily a trustworthy guide in the *Inferno*, limitations and all. In a Christian worldview, merely human wisdom is inadequate. The Middle Ages, however, believed that in Aristotle and Virgil pagan antiquity had come as close as reason could to discovering principles consistent with Christianity; and Dante appears to have understood Virgil as a bridge between the pagan and Christian eras. See Davis 1957, 123. Grace perfects nature; it does not displace it. *ST* 1.1.8. In addition, Virgil's role as guide will sometimes even require that his knowledge not be limited by his paganism; in *Inf.* 34, for example, he will explain the circumstances of Satan's fall from heaven. See generally *DE* 862–65; see also Hawkins 99–124 and especially Steinberg 82–88, 163–64.

70: Virgil was actually born in 70 BC, when Julius Caesar was still a young man far from supreme power.

72: Virgil's phrase "the false and lying gods" comes from Augustine (*Civ. Dei* 2.29; see also 2.2, 2.10) and reflects the traditional Christian belief that the pagan gods were not human inventions but rather demons preying on human credulity. See Pelikan 1.132.

73–75: For late antiquity and the Middle Ages, the supreme work of literature was Virgil's *Aeneid*, which tells how the upright Aeneas leads a band of Trojans to find a new home after the destruction of Troy. They settle in Italy, where the line of Aeneas will later found Rome; and Virgil's purpose was to glorify the Roman empire.

76–78: Virgil regards the hill as man's natural goal because the moral and intellectual virtues that undergird the earthly paradise are what he understands. The remainder of the canto, however, shows that he is testing the pilgrim by this question. Instructed by heaven, he knows that the pilgrim will mount higher, where he, Virgil, cannot accompany him, and that even to reach the summit of natural happiness the pilgrim must descend through hell.

101–11: *The greyhound.* Dante believed that the natural happiness of man on earth, and not simply his happiness in the next world, is the goal of a just society, in which people can live in freedom and peace. *Mon.* 3.16.1–12; *Conv.* 4.4.1–4. Here Virgil, the representative of the Roman empire – which Dante regarded as the living and divinely ordained form of the just society (*Epist.* 6.2) – is made to prophesy the future fulfillment of this ideal. The prophecy is veiled in mystery and efforts to show that Dante had a specific figure in mind for the greyhound founder on the ambiguity of the text and especially on Virgil's statement that the greyhound has not yet been born in 1300 (*sua nazion sarà* 105). See *ED* 5.908.

More generally, the reformer who will save unhappy Italy – plagued by endless factionalism fueled in part by greed (see *Inf.* 6.74–75) – seems most plausibly to be a future emperor, perhaps considered as a type of Christ in judgment, as Pietro Alighieri thought. Unlike the wolf, the greyhound will not devour land or money, because there is nothing the emperor could covet. *Mon.* 1.11.11–12. The emperor's specific function is to establish justice and – since greed is the great enemy of justice – to suppress greed; hence he will drive the wolf from city after city. See *Mon.* 1.11.12; 1.13.7. Beatrice will say that greed is blighting the world because the imperial throne is empty. *Par.* 27.121–48. Beatrice (*Purg.* 33.34–45) and St. Peter (*Par.* 27.55–63) will also make obscure prophecies of a coming savior characterized with images of the empire (the eagle, Scipio). See *ED* 5.908; Hollander 1969, 181–91; Ferrante 115–19.

103–04: In part the contrast of the greyhound that will not feed on land with the voracious wolf is literal because Pliny (*Nat. Hist.* 8.34.83) and Albertus Magnus (*De Animal.* 22.114) asserted that when hungry the wolf ingests earth.

105: Most early commentators explained this riddle astrologically. L. Olschki argues that the correct astrological interpretation is "under the sign of Gemini," because the twins of the zodiac were depicted wearing conical felt caps. See *ED* 2.835.

106–08: Dante's Virgil creates an image of Italy out of his *Aeneid*, citing as heroes warriors of the Trojan and Latin races who battled each other but are enshrined in the mixed Roman heritage. For the essentially fictional idea of "Italy" in the late Middle Ages, see Larner, 1–4, 38. For Dante it is a cultural and linguistic entity, the historic seat of the universal empire.

117: The pool of fire where sinners are cast is the second death. Apoc. 20:14–15. For them, the death of the soul, which they lament eternally, follows the death of the body.

124: Dante called God "the prince of the universe." *Mon.* 3.16.2.

134: St. Peter's gate appears in *Purg.* 9.76–129, guarded by an angel who is Peter's vicar (*Purg.* 21.54) and holds his keys, because purgatory is the gateway to heaven.

Canto II

The day was fading and the dusky air
  released the creatures that inhabit earth
  from toil; and I alone among them all
steeled myself to confront the grueling contest
  of the long journey and the attacks of pity,   5
  which memory, unerring, will recount.
O Muses, O high genius, help me now.
  O memory, which recorded what I saw,
  here shall you demonstrate your excellence.
"Poet who guide me," I began, "consider   10
  if my abilities are adequate
  before committing me to the arduous passage.
You tell us that the father of Silvius
  ventured before his death to the undying
  world and experienced it in the flesh.   15
But if the foe of evil showed such favor
  to him, considering the great result
  to spring from him, both who and what he was
seem worthy to a man of understanding;
  for he was chosen in the highest heaven   20
  as the progenitor of sacred Rome
and of her empire, which, to speak but truth
  was destined to become the holy place
  where the successor of great Peter sits.

And on the journey you give him credit for   25
    he learned things that would later bring about
    his victory and the mantle of the popes.
The chosen instrument went there afterwards
    to bring back confirmation of our faith,
    starting point on the pathway to salvation.   30
But why would I go there? and by whose warrant?
    Aeneas I am not, nor am I Paul,
    and neither I nor others think me fit.
Thus, if I let you talk me into coming,
    I am afraid the journey may be reckless.   35
    Your wisdom understands more than I say."
Sometimes a man unwills what he has willed
    when second-guessing leads to change of heart,
    until he quite draws back from his beginning:
I was like that upon the darkened slope,   40
    as pondering the matter, I dissolved
    the enterprise begun with such dispatch.
"If I have understood your words correctly,"
    answered the shade of that great-hearted man,
    "your spirit is being sapped by cowardice,   45
which often interposes obstacles,
    making one turn from praiseworthy endeavors
    as glimpsed illusions cause a horse to shy.
To help you shake this fear, I shall explain
    why I have come and what it was I heard   50
    in the first hour I felt compassion for you.
While I remained with the others in suspense
    a lady called me, one so beautiful
    and blessed that I begged for her commands.
The splendor of her eyes surpassed the stars;   55
    and she began, with grave and quiet sweetness,
    speaking in such a voice as angels use:
'O generous and noble Mantuan spirit,
    whose great fame still endures throughout the world
    and shall endure as long as the world itself,   60

my friend, who loves me out of no self-interest,
    finds himself so impeded in his progress
    on the deserted slope that fear has turned him.
I am afraid he may already be
    so lost that I have stirred too late to save him,   65
    according to what I have heard in heaven.
Hurry, and with your polished eloquence
    and anything required to rescue him,
    assist him, so that I may find some comfort.
I who commission you am Beatrice,   70
    come from the place where longing draws me back;
    love made me come, the same that makes me speak.
When I am in the presence of my lord,
    I will commend you frequently to him.'
    Then she fell silent, and I began to answer: 75
'O lady full of the virtues that alone
    elevate humankind above all else
    within the heaven of the least circumference,
so welcome is your charge, had I obeyed
    already it would seem to me too late;   80
    you have but to reveal your will to me.
But tell me why you feel no trepidation
    about descending to this core from those
    wide spaces where you are longing to return.'
'Because you search for greater understanding,   85
    I will explain without delay,' she said,
    'why I am not afraid to come inside here.
Only those things should properly be feared
    which have the capability to harm us,
    and not the others, for they are not dreadful;   90
and God has so transformed me through his grace
    I am not touched by your unhappiness,
    nor can the flames of this great furnace scorch me.
A noble lady in heaven, most distressed
    by the impediment to which I send you   95
    cancels the rigorous sentence there above.

And calling Lucy to her side, this lady
    said to her, "Now your faithful devotee
    needs you and I entrust him to your care."
Lucy, the enemy of every cruelty,   100
    left her and came to where I had my seat
    beside the ancient Rachel. She addressed me:
"Beatrice, true praise of God, why are you not
    supporting him whose love for you was such
    it made him take his leave of the common herd?   105
Can you not hear the anguish of his weeping,
    not see the death confronting him on the torrent
    that leaves the sea itself no room to boast?"
Never was anyone more prompt on earth
    to seize advantage or shun detriment   110
    than I was, when those words had been pronounced,
to leave my seat in heaven and come down here,
    confident in your noble eloquence,
    which brings you honor in which your audience shares.'
When she had finished saying this, I saw   115
    her bright eyes turn, now glistening with tears,
    which made me hasten all the more to come.
And just as she desired, I came to you:
    I saved you from the beast that blocked the path
    leading directly to the beautiful mountain.   120
What is it then? Why, why do you still hold back,
    why entertain such cowardice in your heart,
    why do you have no confidence or courage,
given that three such blessed ladies as these
    advance your interests in the court of heaven,   125
    and my words promise so much good for you?"
As little flowers that were bent and closed
    with night-time chill lift upright on their stems
    and open when the sun irradiates them,
my drooping forces all at once revived   130
    and so much bracing courage rushed to my heart
    that I burst forth, now feeling resolute:

"What great compassion she who helped me showed!
    And you, how generous, who with such dispatch
    obeyed the words of truth she spoke to you!   135
Your speech has wakened in my heart such eager
    desire to come with you that I have now
    returned to my original resolve.
Proceed, for there is but one will between us:
    you are my guide, my teacher and my lord."   140
    Those were my words and when he moved ahead
I started on my risky, arduous journey.

Notes

The first canto of the *Inferno* is an introduction to the *Comedy* as a whole. The second canto is the introduction to the *Inferno* proper, as indicated by the invocation (7–9).

1–6: The confrontation with the beasts has occupied the morning of Good Friday and the discussion with Virgil the afternoon. As darkness falls the pilgrim, isolated from the daily round of nature, prepares to cross the threshold of the dark kingdom.

5: The pilgrim fears being pierced with pity for the damned. This natural emotion, one of the pains that the living experience, must not cloud his understanding of sin and its consequences.

7–9: The invocation addresses the sources of Dante's poem. The Muses provide inspiration. The poet's genius predisposes him to the inspiration and endows him with the power of artistic composition. His memory stores and retrieves the material he will elaborate in verse. See *ED* 3.442. Dante does not seek aid from his memory, but rather expresses confidence in its excellence. Memory's book is already written; now the task of genius is to illuminate it. Dante gives memory two full verses not only to emphasize the factual accuracy of his account, but also because memory was considered the basis of all composition in antiquity and the Middle Ages; the Muses are memory's daughters.

8–9: The modular structure of Dante's afterworlds, with their minutely described locations, seem designed to assure Dante's perfect recall of his extraterrestrial journey. Ancient and medieval arts of memory used architectural mnemonic schemes as "places" to index memories for retrieval. Carruthers 71–79, 144–55 *et passim*. Consistent with the prescriptions of those schemes, Dante's succession of contrasting backgrounds (individualized circles in hell, terraces in purgatory, spheres in heaven) makes it easy to recollect examples of the virtues and vices, together with the rewards and punishments they merit.

13: The father of Silvius was Aeneas, who visits the underworld in *Aen.* 6, an important model for the *Inferno*. Dante believed that Aeneas was a historical figure (see *Mon.* 2.3.6), but leaves the factual status of his journey through Hades open here and in *Par.* 15.25–27.

25–27: In Hades Aeneas learned the glorious imperial future of Rome. This caused his later military victory in the sense that it inspired him with a goal. It caused the papal office and power, symbolized by the pope's mantle, in the sense that Aeneas laid the foundations of the universal empire that the universal church would build on. See Davis 1957, 33–36.

28–30: St. Paul said he was "caught up into the third heaven." 2 Cor. 12:2–4. The *Glossa Ordinaria* took this to mean that Paul saw God directly. See also *ST* 2-2.175.3. The pilgrim will reach this state at the end of the *Paradiso*, the most audacious claim Dante makes for himself.

The *Apocalypse of Paul*, a 3d century apocryphal scripture, recounts Paul's journey through hell, accompanied by an angel. This work, which was largely responsible for the popular idea of hell in Western Christian culture (Elliott 616), was known to the early commentator Buti and contains a number of motifs that appear in the *Inferno*. Dante's reference to "bringing back confirmation of the faith," however, more appropriately describes Paul's journey to heaven.

44–45: Virgil is the shade of a great-souled man (*magnanimo*), an Aristotelian ethical concept that recurs in the *Inferno*. See notes to *Inf.* 3.34–36, 4.112–20. Virgil's diagnosis is that in shrinking from the great mission offered to him, the pilgrim displays the opposite quality of pusillanimity. This does not seem characteristic of the historical Dante, but the narrative represents a universal psychological truth: all sinners shrink from conversion, which demands sacrifice.

52: "In suspense": *i.e.*, in limbo. See note to *Inf.* 4.23–30.

53ff.: Beatrice is the lodestar of Dante's poetic and spiritual life. The story of his love for this Florentine woman some months younger than himself is told in the *Vita Nuova* (*New Life*). Dante first sees her when he is at the end of his ninth year, and his heart says "here is a lord more powerful than me, come to rule over me," while his brain says "here now is your beatitude." *VN* 2. By his own account he never exchanged more than greetings with her. Knowing nothing of her life "between the pantry and the linen chest" (Yeats), he was able to maintain a vision of her as a special revelation of glory, a miracle of nature and grace. See Williams 20; Gilson 57; Foster/Boyde 2.98.

After the death of Beatrice, ten years before the action of the *Comedy* is set, Dante speaks of his having entered into a long period of confusion. He came to love another woman, the *gentile donna*, who pitied his grief for Beatrice. He studied philosophy and began a philosophical treatise, the *Convivio*, in which he claimed the *gentile donna* was only a personification of philosophy. This murky period ends in the dark wood at the beginning of the *Comedy*, which is the story of Beatrice's re-entry into his life.

In the *Comedy* Beatrice never stops being the woman Dante idolized. When she appears, this canto begins to echo Dante's lyrics written in what he called the *dolce stil novo* ("sweet new style"), full of grave tenderness and elevated sentiment. But the young woman of Florence was only, in Auerbach's term, a *figura*, a prefiguration of the fully realized Beatrice of the *Comedy*. This fulfilled Beatrice is one whose eyes continually see God, even in hell, and this enables her to assume a role in the scheme of Dante's salvation, guiding him toward the ultimate reality of which this life is a shadow. Ernst Curtius thought Dante went further than that, giving Beatrice a role "in the objective process of salvation" available to all believers. Curtius 372–73; accord, Bloom 76–77. The medieval commentators got Beatrice's direct knowledge of God backwards when they said that she was a personification of theology, but that formulation served their goal of making Dante look more orthodox than he is.

For a summary of Beatrice's role that stresses implied comparisons between her and Christ, see *DE* 89–95.

55–57: These are typical stilnovist verses. The eyes shining like stars and the voice of an angel are hallmarks of the lady to whom amorous lyrics in this style were addressed. See Barolini 1984, 80. Lino Pertile suggests that the conception of love in *Inf.* 2 has changed by the time Dante reaches the late cantos of the *Paradiso*, "probably about twelve years of exile" later. He suggests that the *stilnovo* "does not survive beyond Purgatory," because the Beatrice whom the pilgrim finds there has transcended this conception. Pertile 2003, 113.

58–60: In classical oratory, the speaker begins by praising his audience to win their goodwill before trying to persuade them. Virgil will use this rhetorical device repeatedly, and some critics think that this shows his pagan falseness. The initial use of the device by Beatrice, however, suggests that the *captatio benevolentiae* is not trickery by flattery, but homage that the speaker owes to one from whom he will ask a favor.

64–66, 69: Beatrice's troubled emotions are not fully consistent with the impassivity of the blessed. See note to 91–93. The contradiction arises because the glorified Beatrice remains the lady of stilnovist lyric, and so one of her idealized characteristics is pity for the lover devoted to her.

67: "Polished eloquence (*parola ornata*)": The current view that this phrase characterizes Virgil's false pagan rhetoric, by contrast with plain Christian truth (despite the fact that Beatrice is praising Virgil for it), is anachronistic. Medieval handbooks regarded ornament as essential to poetic language: "discourse must be decorated." Curtius 71; see *ED* 4.200. Augustine said that eloquence – consisting largely of the skillful use of abundant verbal ornaments – was indifferent between good and evil, and he urged Christians to use it in the service of truth. *De Doctrina Christiana* 4.2–3. Dante himself said that anyone who writes poetry should adorn [*exornare*] it as much as he can. *VE* 2.1.2. By re-using the phrase *parola ornata* for the seductive technique of Jason (*Inf.* 18.91), Dante will acknowledge that art can be used for bad ends. (It is also true that the poetic style of Dante's "comedy" will differ significantly from the uniform high style of the *Aeneid* (which Dante calls Virgil's "tragedy") by including every stylistic register from the high to the humble. See, *e.g.*, Barolini 1998, 281.)

76–81: If Beatrice can speak with the art of a classical orator, Virgil can speak with the courtesy of a medieval lover, expressed in the philosophical-theological refinements of stilnovist poetry. See Jacoff/Stephany 16.

78: The heaven of the least circumference is that of the moon. Dante's earth sits motionless at the center of his universe. Surrounding it are the nine concentric hollow spheres that carry the moving planets and the fixed stars and beyond them the empyrean, the highest heaven.

83: "Core": Hell is underground and its constriction is contrasted with the spacious freedom of the empyrean.

88–90: If Beatrice begins by sounding like a philosopher, Patrick Boyde notes that she is in fact paraphrasing Aristotle. Boyde 1993, 225–26.

91–93: The blessed are impassive, insulated not only from physical pain (Is. 43:2, "when thou shalt walk in the fire, thou shalt not be burnt"), but also from the pain of human passions such as pity. The blessed experience pity only intellectually and thus cannot pity the damned, whose punishment results from divine justice. *ST Suppl.* 94.2. This distinction between intellectual and emotional pity – and the fact that the living are not impassive – is ignored by critics who claim that experiencing pity for the souls in hell is gravely sinful.

94–96: *The Blessed Mother.* A celestial perspective opens up to explain how the actions of *Inferno* 1 have been influenced from heaven. This is the one scene in the *Inferno* that previews the world of the *Paradiso*, but it is modeled on classical epic, where the councils of the gods often intrude on human affairs. Dante is thinking of *Aen.* 1.223–96: after Aeneas and his companions endure a terrible storm at sea, the scene shifts to Olympus, where Venus, the hero's goddess-mother, implores Jove not to allow any interference with the great destiny foretold for her son. Virgil is in turn imitating the scene in *Illiad* 1 where Thetis implores Zeus for the success of her son Achilles, but Virgil transforms the issue from the personal to the universal. Venus is pleading for no less than the future world-empire of Rome.

In Dante, the issue shifts back to the personal; but the personal is universal for Christians when it illustrates the drama of salvation. Instead of a goddess-mother, Dante has the Blessed Mother, who intercedes for us all. *Inferno* 2 is the canto of grace, and the communication of grace was the function of the Virgin Mary and the other saints. See Pelikan 3.159. The 12th century cult of Mary viewed her as the mediatrix between the believer and her Son who pleads the cause of men in heaven. Pelikan 3.168. In *Par.* 33.13–18, St. Bernard will explain that all who seek grace must have recourse to Mary, but that she often goes before the asking.

96: As Buti thought, the rigorous sentence is the pilgrim's damnation, already decreed because "the wages of sin is death." Rom 6:23. In medieval devotion, Mary intervenes to save souls that divine justice has condemned (Sumption 397), though this formulation is theologically problematic. See Fosca 2011. She cancels Dante's sentence by triggering a miraculous eruption of grace into his life. See *Par.* 20.94–96.

97–108: The most striking narratological feature of *Inf.* 2 is the long relay of intermediaries that rescues the pilgrim from the plight of *Inf.* 1. The Virgin acts through her ladies-in-waiting – Lucy, Dante's patron saint, and Beatrice, his love. Through the communion of saints the mediating function of Mary could be extended to a saint for whom a believer had a special devotion. Dante's son Iacopo testified to his father's devotion to St. Lucy (*ED* 3.717); and she will help the pilgrim again in *Purg.* 9.55–63.

This personalized mediation of grace is extended further here. The chain of mediation through the communion of saints serves to validate Beatrice as a surrogate for Mary. Personalizing the process yet further, Beatrice herself does not act directly, but through the medium of Virgil, Dante's poetic idol. Though Virgil is in hell, he forms the final link in the chain of grace that extends back to the Virgin.

103–05: Dante's selfless love for Beatrice ennobled him and led to the poetry of disinterested praise embodied in the canzone *Donne ch'avete intelletto d'amore* ("Ladies who have intelligence of love") (*VN* 19), which brought a new spiritual dimension to the love poems of the common run of poets.

103: All of God's creation praises him by reflecting part of his perfection; by her eminent virtue and beauty Beatrice praises him "truthfully," with an especially bright and steady reflection.

107–08: "Torrent (*fiumana*)": Whatever the significance of the swollen river, it appears to have only a metaphorical existence, like the sea of *Inf.* 1.23–24. Given that the ladies in heaven regard the *fiumana* as something from which the pilgrim must be saved, it seems likely that it carries the Christian significance traditionally attributed to a river as well as the sea – that of this life of temptation, subject to the storms of the passions. Death, on this reading, is the renewed threat of spiritual drowning that the pilgrim escaped in *Inf.* 1.22–27. The sea would thus be unable to boast of being more tempestuous than the river, as Buti and Boccaccio said. Other critics identify the river with the Jordan and even the waters of baptism, in which the sinful self dies. See Scott 186–87; Freccero 1986, 64–69.

115–16: Dante imitates the well-known line from the Venus/Jove scene in the *Aeneid*, in which Venus looks at Jove, "her bright eyes brimming over with tears." *Aen.* 1.228.

127–40: The image of the flowers opening at dawn contrasts with that of creatures retiring at sunset at the beginning of the canto. This is in a sense the most important moment in the *Inferno*, the moment when the pilgrim turns definitively from his self-willed wanderings and surrenders to the promptings of grace, accepting the hard road laid out for him. Virgil's narrative has opened his eyes fully. He now knows that he owes the opportunity to escape his perilous spiritual condition not to any merit of his own but to the intervention of grace occasioned by his devotion to Beatrice. His love for Beatrice becomes his road to God, and it must lead down to hell before ascending to heaven.

133: The Virgin and St. Lucy have now been definitively absorbed into Beatrice.

Canto III

THROUGH ME THE WAY TO SORROW'S CAPITAL,
  THROUGH ME THE WAY TO EVERLASTING PAIN,
  THROUGH ME THE WAY THAT LEADS AMONG THE LOST.
JUSTICE DIRECTED MY GREAT MAKER'S HAND.
  DIVINE OMNIPOTENCE CREATED ME,   5
  TRANSCENDENT WISDOM AND PRIMORDIAL LOVE.
NOTHING WAS MADE BEFORE ME BUT THE THINGS
  THAT LAST FOREVER, AND I LAST FOREVER.
  YOU THAT PASS IN, LEAVE EVERY HOPE BEHIND.
These words I saw in shadowed characters   10
  inscribed above a gate, and looking I said,
  "Master, their meaning fills me with dismay."
And he replied, as someone with experience,
  "Here you must leave behind all second thoughts
  and here all your faint-heartedness must die.   15
Now we have reached the place I told you of,
  where you will see the sufferers who have lost
  the only good in which the mind can rest."
And after he had placed his hand on mine
  and looked encouraging, which gave me comfort,   20
  he brought me into the world that stands apart.
There lamentations, sighs and high-pitched wailing
  reverberated in the starless air,
  so that on hearing them at first I wept.

A babel of languages brutally pronounced, 25
    utterances of pain and shouts of rage,
    loud and faint voices and the slapping of palms
created a confused uproar that swirls
    forever in that timelessly dark air
    the way the sand does when the whirlwind blows. 30
My head encircled by perplexity,
    I asked him, "Master, what is this I hear,
    what people, who seem overcome by grief?"
And he replied, "This pitiful behavior
    is typical of the wretched souls of those 35
    who lived without incurring blame or praise.
Here they are mingled with the craven choir
    of the angels who did not rebel nor keep
    their faith with God, but formed a separate party.
The heavens, so as not to be disfigured, 40
    expel them and deep hell will not admit them
    or else the wicked might have cause to brag."
"Master," I asked him, "what distresses them
    so much it calls forth such loud lamentations?"
    He answered: "I will tell you very briefly. 45
The wretches here can have no hope of death
    and their blind life is so contemptible
    it makes them envy every other fate.
The world lets no report of them survive;
    mercy and justice scorn them; let us speak 50
    no more of them, but look and walk on by."
And as I looked again, I saw a banner
    racing around in a circle, at such a speed
    it seemed that it could tolerate no rest;
and after it there came a line of people 55
    so long that I would never have believed
    that death could have undone so great a number.
After I'd recognized a few among them,
    I saw and knew the shade of him that made
    through cowardice the great renunciation. 60

At once I understood beyond all doubt
　　that these made up the party of the spineless,
　　hateful to God and to his enemies.
These abject creatures, who had never lived,
　　went naked and were stung repeatedly　　　　　　　　65
　　by wasps and stinging flies that swarmed around them,
so that their faces were all streaked with blood
　　that mingled with their tears and fell at their feet
　　where it was harvested by loathsome worms.
And then I looked beyond them and I saw　　　　　　　　70
　　people upon the bank of a broad river,
　　which prompted me to say, "Master, allow me
to know who those may be and what compulsion
　　makes them show so much eagerness to cross,
　　as seems apparent even in this weak light."　　　　　75
"All of these things," he answered, "will be made
　　plain to you when we interrupt our progress
　　upon the dismal shore of the Acheron."
Then with my eyes cast down in shame, for fear
　　that he had found my questioning annoying,　　　　　80
　　I held my tongue until we reached the river.
And suddenly, coming toward us in a boat,
　　there was an old man, his hair white with age,
　　who shouted, "Now you're done for, wicked souls!
Don't even think of ever seeing the sky:　　　　　　　85
　　I come to take you to the other shore
　　amidst eternal darkness, fire and frost.
And you, the living soul there, step aside
　　and separate yourself from these who are dead."
　　Seeing that I did not depart, he added:　　　　　　　90
"Not here – another road and other ports
　　will bring you to the shore for crossing over.
　　A lighter craft than mine must carry you."
My guide addressed him: "Do not vex yourself,
　　Charon, for this is willed where will is one　　　　　95
　　with its fulfillment: ask no more about it."

And from that moment on, the wooly jaws
    of the pilot of the muddy marsh were still,
    while all around his eyes rolled wheels of flame.
But meanwhile those disheartened naked souls   100
    had suddenly changed color when they heard
    those cruel words and began to gnash their teeth.
They cursed God and their fathers and their mothers,
    all of humanity, the place and hour
    and seed of their conception and their birth.   105
Weeping aloud then, all of them assembled
    in a dense crowd upon the evil shore
    that waits for all who have no fear of God.
And with his burning eyes, the demon Charon
    beckons them and collects them all aboard,   110
    smacking his oar on those who don't step lively.
And as the leaves detach themselves in autumn,
    each following the last until the branch
    sees all its clothes upon the ground below,
there the bad seed of Adam at his signal   115
    throw themselves one by one from the high bank,
    the way a falcon comes at its recall.
They go away then over the dark water,
    and before they disembark on the far shore
    again on this one a new crowd has gathered.   120
My gracious teacher said to me, "My son,
    all those who die at enmity with God
    gather together here from every land;
and they feel eagerness to cross the river
    because God's justice puts the spurs to them,   125
    so that their terror changes to desire.
No good soul ever goes across from here;
    and so if Charon has complained of you,
    now you may grasp the import of his words."
He'd scarcely finished when the murky floodplain   130
    trembled with so much violence that the memory
    of my terror leaves me bathed again in sweat.

The tear-soaked land heaved forth a gust of wind
　　that blazed up in a flash of brilliant red,
　　the force of which made all my senses fail;　　　　　　135
and I fell like one seized suddenly by sleep.

Notes

1–9: The gate of hell, the first of many threshold guardians that people the *Inferno*, speaks in the first person.

5–6: Power (being), wisdom (intellect) and love (will) are predicated respectively of the Father, Son and Holy Spirit as they coexist in the unity of the godhead. See *Conv.* 2.5.7–8; Bonaventure 3.5; *ST* 1.27.3.

7–8: The angels, the heavens and prime matter were the first creations; earth, of which hell forms part, was created soon after. *Par.* 29.22–45; Boyde 1981, 242–45. Earth will endure forever, being renewed after the Last Judgment. Apoc. 21:1–7.

12: "Fills me with dismay (*m'è duro*)." Daniello thought the pilgrim was frightened, rather than puzzled, by the inscription, which strengthens the psychology of the following passage.

14–15: In contrast to the damned, who must leave all hope behind, the pilgrim must leave behind all pusillanimity. Aeneas' guide, the Sybil, says, "You need your courage now and your stout heart" (*Aen.* 6.261); but Dante's line is more pointed, because in *Inf.* 2 the pilgrim has exhibited faint-heartedness. Moreover, by enterprising acceptance of his mission now the pilgrim will overcome the sin punished in this vestibule of hell.

18: God is the truth in which every intellect rests. *Par.* 28.108. The reasoning mind can find ultimate satisfaction only in direct knowledge of the first cause, attained in the beatific vision, the end for which man's mind was formed and which the damned have forever lost. The concept is based on the Aristotelian idea that the good of the intellect is truth. *Conv.* 2.13.6; see *Eth.* 6.2 (1139a27–31); *In Eth.* ¶ 1130.

34–42: Virgil's brief comment describes the sinners that early commentators designated as the pusillanimous. The sources of the concept are both biblical and Aristotelian, but the power of the scene that follows derives from Dante's personality. As a man of ardent and ambitious temper who felt himself called to public service, Dante responded forcefully to Aristotle's concept of *magniminitas*, the virtue of the great-souled man who rightly thinks himself capable of great things. *Eth.* 4.3 (1123b1–2). Opposed to this virtue is *pusillanimitas*, the vice of the petty-souled man who wrongly thinks himself incapable of great things. Aristotle thought that such people were motivated by laziness and Aquinas added fear of failure. *Eth.* 4.3 (1125a19–27); *ST* 2–2.133.2. Aquinas held this disposition sinful, comparing it to the servant in the parable who buried in the ground the money he received from his master because he was afraid to trade with it (Matt. 25:14–30). *ST* 2–2.133.1.

Dante's scriptural warrant is Apoc. 3:15–16: "I would that thou wert cold or hot. But because thou art lukewarm, and neither cold nor hot, I will begin to vomit thee out of my mouth." This had inspired a passage in the *Apocalypse of Paul* where the saint sees sinners in a fiery river in hell; and the angel explains that they were neither hot nor cold, meaning they were neither just nor godless. Elliott 633. Richard K. Emmerson notes occurrences of the theme in St. Anselm and Jacopone da Todi. Emmerson 306.

37–39: Despite scholarly references to sketchy ancient and medieval parallels (see *ED* 1.270–71), the idea of the "neutral angels" appears to be essentially Dante's.

52–69: *The contrapasso.* The plight of the pusillanimous introduces the symbolic mode of retribution (in addition to the deprivation of the sight of God, shared by the souls in limbo) that will operate throughout hell, known as the *contrapasso* from *Inf.* 28.142. Its essential principle is that the damned punish themselves. In each circle the punishment that Dante has imagined fits the crime because it is simply the sin itself viewed *sub specie aeternitatis*. As Dante explained in the epistle to Can Grande, the state of souls after death in the *Comedy* represents allegorically the choices that the people made in life through the exercise of free will.

Just as the sinners' spirits are represented as bodies, their spiritual condition is translated into physical form. In the second circle the lustful will be carried away by the gusts of their passions in the form of a tempest; in the eighth the hypocrites will be crushed by the weight of their pious false appearances in the form of capes of gilded lead. The internal choices in which the damned persisted in life have in death become the outward condition of their being, illustrating the law *you become what you do*. Dante's son Pietro understood this; his glosses, although not always convincing, follow the principle that the state of souls in hell is an allegory of their habits in life.

52–54: The banner is the blank standard of the party of those who refuse to take sides. It rushes onward but only in a circle, and the great train of the pusillanimous rush giddily after it.

58–60: *The great renunciation.* The earliest commentators identified this shade as Pope Celestine V and most modern critics agree. (The other major candidate has been Pontius Pilate.) Celestine was revered for his holiness and was canonized some years after the *Inferno* was written. He was an elderly hermit, and his elevation to the papacy in 1294 was widely perceived as a hopeful sign that the church would abandon the worldly power politics pursued by the 13th century popes. Unable to deal with the demands of the office, however, he resigned within five months, to the consternation of the reformers, whose aspirations Dante shared. He was succeeded by Boniface VIII, who attempted to bring the imperial papacy to its zenith. Dante thus thought of Celestine as a man called upon to reform the church but who shirked the great task. See Simonelli 50–56; Scott 8–9.

64: Unlike the other souls in hell, the pusillanimous refused to choose. Because the exercise of the will is the essence of living as a human, their lives consisted of a refusal to live.

65–67: Pietro saw the flies and wasps as a trope for the petty worries and faltering actions of these wretches – the thousand deaths the coward dies.

66: Albertus Magnus distinguished two types of flies, the first of which has a sharp beak that draws blood. *De Animal.* 26.19.

70–120: In describing the souls eager to cross the Acheron, Dante closely follows the scene Aeneas comes upon after crossing the threshold of hell. *Aen.* 6.295–416. In turning the scene to Christian purposes, however, Dante gives a new significance to the details. Virgil's souls are the unburied; they implore Charon to let them cross because, barred from the underworld, they can know no peace. Dante's souls are the damned, who are anxious to cross because divine justice deep within them puts the spurs to them. Their own consciences are the agents of their punishment.

82–99: *Charon.* In ancient Christian tradition, the classical pagan gods were regarded not as fables but as demons, an especially easy transference with the cruel gods of the underworld. While making Charon a demon, Dante reproduces the Charon of the *Aeneid* faithfully, as Pietro noted. Dante's representational art nonetheless retains a distinctive originality. Virgil, and still more Ovid, are fond of detailed physical descriptions; by contrast, Dante selects only the most expressive details and disperses them among action and dialogue for maximum dramatic effect. See *ED* 1.848–49. Dante's Charon exceeds Virgil's in his inflexible cruelty and violence and justifies Michelangelo's imitation of this scene in his Last Judgment, where Charon is simply a Christian devil.

88: The pilgrim's soul still animates his body and thus he can still be saved.

94–96: Virgil's speech is a magical formula, the equivalent of the golden bough in the *Aeneid*, which the Sibyl brandishes when Charon will not take Aeneas across. *Aen.* 6.405–7.

97–99: In the *Aeneid* Charon's eyes are "staring flames." *Aen.* 6.300. Dante energizes the striking image further, the implied dynamism of the wheels of flame around Charon's eyes emphasizing the rigid stillness that strikes the gesticulating and shouting figure upon hearing Virgil's words and signals his acknowledgement of superior power.

112–17: The images of the leaves and the birds come from the *Aeneid*, but Dante puts them to different uses. Virgil's similes are straightforward: the souls Aeneas sees are as numerous as the falling leaves in autumn or the birds that flock south in winter. *Aen.* 6.309–12. Far from picturing the souls as a numberless throng, Dante's similes emphasize each soul's individuality. The damned jump into Charon's boat, each following the last the way one personified leaf after another detaches itself from the branch. Alternatively, responding to Charon's signal, they launch themselves one by one, as a falcon comes to the lure of the trainer. Stressing at once the will of the leaf and the hawk and the compulsion to which they submit, Dante's images convey the plight of the damned soul, responsible for its condition but now powerless to change it.

130–36: By having Charon refuse to carry the pilgrim across the Acheron, Dante has painted himself into a narrative corner. He solves the problem with an earthquake that makes the pilgrim lose consciousness. At *Inf.* 4.1–2 the pilgrim will be awakened by a crash of thunder, surely the one that follows the lightning flash here, showing that his transference is instantaneous and thus remains a mystery.

Ancient science held that earthquakes were caused by winds imprisoned underground (see *Purg.* 21.55–57); they were conceived as subterranean thunderstorms, which explains the red flash here. Pliny said that "a quaking in the earth is nothing other than thundering in a cloud and a fissure nothing other than lightning erupting from an underground wind fighting to get out to freedom. . . . Earthquakes end when the wind finds a vent." *Nat. Hist.* 2.81.192, 2.84.198.

Canto IV

Shattering the deep sleep in my head,
    a heavy crash of thunder made me start
    awake like someone who is roughly roused;
and lurching to my feet I looked around
    with eyes refreshed by rest, staring intently   5
    to gain intelligence of where I was.
I somehow found myself upon the rim
    of hell's great valley, the abyss of sorrows
    that gathers numberless wails into one roar.
The valley is so dark and deep and smoggy,   10
    no matter how my vision plumbed its depths
    I could distinguish absolutely nothing.
"Let us descend into the blind world now,"
    began the poet, who had gone quite pale;
    "I shall go first and you will follow me."   15
But having noticed his complexion change,
    I said, "How can I go when you are fearful,
    who strengthen me when I am wavering?"
"The torment of the people down below
    paints on my face," he answered me, "the pity   20
    that you mistake for fear. But let us go now,
for the long road is pressing us." And while
    he spoke, he entered and he made me enter
    the first of the circles ringing the abyss.

And here, as far as I could judge by listening, 25
    there was no lamentation except sighs
    that caused the everlasting air to quiver,
arising from the grief untouched by pain
    experienced by the numerous large crowds
    of little children and of men and women. 30
My gentle teacher said, "You do not ask
    what spirits are these you see? I want you now
    to understand, before you walk on further,
these did not sin; but any merits of theirs
    did not suffice, because they lacked baptism, 35
    the gateway of the faith that you confess;
and if they lived before the Christian ages
    they did not worship God in the right way;
    and I myself make one among their number.
Through such deficiencies, not actual guilt, 40
    we all are lost, but suffer only in this:
    bereft of hope, we live possessed by longing."
Great sorrow gripped my heart on hearing him
    because I knew of very worthy people
    abiding there, suspended in that limbo. 45
"Instruct me, master, tell me, lord," I said,
    looking for confirmation of the faith
    that overcomes all doubt, "has anyone
left here and then attained to blessedness
    either through his own merit or another's?" 50
    And understanding my veiled reference,
he said, "When I was new in this condition
    I saw the coming of a mighty one
    crowned with a sign of victory. That one led
away from here the shade of our first father, 55
    the shade of Abel his son and that of Noah;
    Moses, obedient giver of the law;
King David and the patriarch Abraham;
    Israel with his father and his sons
    and with Rachel, whom he won with many labors; 60

and many others; all these he made blessed.
　　And I would have you know that prior to these
　　no human soul was brought to its salvation."
And while he spoke we did not leave off walking
　　but passed on through the forest the whole time,　　　　　　65
　　I mean the forest of the thronging spirits.
Our path had led us only a short way
　　from where I slept, when I could see a blaze
　　prevailing over a hemisphere of shadows.
We were some distance from it still, yet not　　　　　　　　　70
　　so far but I could dimly sense the place
　　was tenanted by people worthy of honor.
"You that shed glory on learning and on art,
　　say, who are these that have the honor of being
　　distinguished from the state of the other spirits?"　　　　75
"The honor that surrounds their names," he answered,
　　"resounding still throughout your upper world,
　　wins heaven's favor and thus this privilege."
Just at that point I heard a voice proclaim:
　　"Welcome with honor the illustrious poet;　　　　　　　　80
　　his shade, which had departed, now returns."
After the voice had ceased and fallen silent
　　I saw approaching four majestic shades
　　with looks expressing neither joy nor sadness.
My gentle teacher started to explain:　　　　　　　　　　85
　　"Observe the one who carries sword in hand
　　and goes before the other three as lord:
that one is Homer, the poet without peer;
　　Horace the satirist is the next who comes;
　　the third is Ovid and the fourth is Lucan.　　　　　　　90
Each of them holds in common with myself
　　the name the single voice pronounced and therefore
　　they honor me, and in that they do well."
And so I saw the gathering of the noble
　　academy of the lord of loftiest song　　　　　　　　　95
　　who like an eagle soars above the others.

After they had conversed a while together
　　they turned to me with welcome in their looks,
　　at which I noticed that my teacher smiled;
and then they showed me greater honor still, 100
　　for they included me among their number
　　and I made then a sixth amid such wisdom.
So we walked onward toward the light, while speaking
　　of things about which silence now is fitting,
　　just as was speaking of them where I was. 105
We finally reached the foot of a lordly castle
　　encircled seven times with towering walls
　　defended all around by a goodly stream.
This last we crossed as though it were firm ground;
　　through seven gates I entered with those sages 110
　　and reached a meadow green with fresh spring grass.
Others were there with grave slow-moving gazes
　　and looks conveying great authority;
　　they spoke infrequently, their voices pleasing.
And so we moved aside and took our places 115
　　upon an open, elevated spot
　　flooded with light, where we could see them all.
And there upon a field of green enamel
　　the spirits of the great were shown to me,
　　the sight of whom transports my own soul now. 120
I saw Electra with numerous companions,
　　of whom I recognized Aeneas and Hector
　　and Caesar in arms with his bright raptor's gaze.
I saw Penthesilea and Camilla;
　　and King Latinus on the other side 125
　　was seated with his daughter Lavinia.
I saw the Brutus who drove Tarquin out,
　　Lucretia, Julia, Marcia and Cornelia;
　　and separate from the rest was Saladin.
Then, when I raised my eyes a little further 130
　　I saw the master of those who understand
　　seated among his family of philosophers.

All eyes were fixed on him, all paid him honor;
    among them I saw Socrates and Plato
    in places next to his, before the others;   135
Democritus, who founds the world on chance,
    Thales, Diogenes, Anaxagoras,
    Zeno, Empedocles and Heraclitus.
I saw the expert classifier of simples,
    Dioscorides; I saw Orpheus, Linus,   140
    Cicero, Seneca the moralist;
Euclid the geometer and Ptolemy,
    Galen, Hippocrates and Avicenna,
    Averroes of the great commentary.
I cannot represent them all in full;   145
    my crowded subject drives me at a pace
    that often makes the words fall short of the fact.
The company of six divides in two;
    my wise guide leads me by another path
    out of the quiet into the quivering air;   150
and I arrive where there is not a glimmer.

Notes

8–9: Hell is a vast funneling pit. The multitude of separate sounds of *Inf.* 3.22–28 has blended into the roar of earth's dungeon.

23–30: *Limbo.* Each circle of hell is a ledge inside the crater, forming a ring that supports a class of sinners. The first circle holds the just who died without baptism. In Christian doctrine an upright life cannot save a man without the sanctifying grace conferred by baptism. "Unless a man be born again of water and the spirit, he shall not enter the kingdom of heaven." John 3:5. Even unbaptized infants, who have committed no actual sins, are tainted with the original sin we inherit from Adam and Eve. "In iniquity was I conceived." Ps. 50:7.

29–30: The crowds of men and women show that Dante's limbo will differ sharply from that of mainstream theology. Aquinas assumed that there were no adults in limbo after Jesus freed the biblical patriarchs, because the supposition that an adult could die with only original or venial sin was untenable. See *ST* 1–2.89.7; *Suppl. App.* 1.1.2.

31–42: Dante was troubled that the ancient masters he revered for their wisdom, poetry and moral philosophy were damned by Christian doctrine. His conflicted feelings motivate the theological innovations of including adults as permanent residents of limbo and creating for the ancient worthies a privileged area that replicates Virgil's Elysian Fields in the *Aeneid*.

39: John Scott argues that Virgil's damnation is essential to his vitality as a character in the *Comedy* and keeps him from being a lay figure like the traditional angel guide. Scott 236, 240. Peter Hawkins speaks of the poignancy of Virgil, like Moses at the edge of the promised land he would never enter. Hawkins 108.

42: Although they feel no pain, the souls in Dante's limbo share the doom inscribed on hell's gate: they have no hope. The children in limbo, Aquinas reasoned, do not grieve at being denied heaven, which is beyond their expectation, but are content with the natural perfections with which God endowed them. *ST Suppl. App.* 1.1.2. By contrast, Dante's ancient great ones, though they enjoy in the afterlife all that they could have expected when on earth, experience longing because they are now aware that this is not all.

46–63: *The Harrowing of Hell.* Between his death and resurrection, Jesus descended to hell, where he freed the patriarchs and prophets and led them to heaven. This story, told in "The Descent of Christ into Hell," a 5th or 6th century work incorporated into the apocryphal *Gospel of Nicodemus*, was popular in the Middle Ages. Elliott 185–204. The crucifixion was seen as a battle in which Jesus, man as well as God, vanquished Satan ("Jesus jousting in Piers' armor," *Piers Plowman* 18.19–26; 19.10–14), after which he stormed Satan's stronghold and took Satan's prisoners as spoils of war.

51: Despite the statement that he understood the pilgrim's reference, Virgil appears to speak as an uncomprehending and therefore objective witness to events that a Christian would recognize from their description.

54: The cross is the symbol of Christ's victory over Satan, and Christ is usually depicted in medieval art with a halo inscribed with a cross, hence "crowned with a sign of victory." Others think Dante is referring to the cross-staff with banner that Jesus carries in the mosaic depicting the harrowing of hell in St. Mark's, Venice (c. 1200), illustrating a line from "The Descent of Christ" in which Christ sets his cross in hell as sign of victory. Elliott 203.

67–78: The inhabitants of the light are the great spirits of ancient Greece and Rome, and the word *onore*, "honor," and its derivatives are used five times in regard to them. Dante often repeats thematic words, but the bell never tolls more insistently than here. Aristotle held honor to be the highest of external goods, a reward for virtue, which is an internal good proper to man. *Eth.* 4.3 (1124a1). The ancient worthies possess in perpetuity the reward that human reason grants to virtue and that they expected in life: they have honor.

76–78: Aquinas believed that the damned would have their punishments mitigated for their good deeds in life (*ST Suppl.* 69.7), but Dante goes further. The great spirits who dwell in the light obtain this privilege by reason of the fame with which their names still resound on earth. This is an audacious theological formulation, even though fame is connected in Dante's mind with the exercise of virtue. See note to *Inf.* 15.84–86.

83: The first of the ancient great are the poets and their honor is the undying poetic glory that Dante fervently wished for himself.

86–90: Dante gives pride of place to Homer, whom he did not know even in translation, on the basis of Homer's reputation in antiquity. See *VN* 25.9. In *VE* 2.6.7 Dante recognizes Virgil, Ovid, Lucan and Statius as *regulati poetae*, the canonical poets whose song is founded upon a language and an art with fixed rules, unlike the vernacular and its poetry. These four in effect represent the medieval canon of ancient poetry and are the four to whom Dante was personally most indebted. The pilgrim will meet Statius in purgatory.

98–102: Some critics work overtime to save Dante's modesty here, but as Umberto Bosco and Giovanni Reggio note modesty is not a virtue of the great spirits; and Dante unequivocally classes himself with those who rightly judge themselves worthy of great things.

106–11: Though he is probably imitating the Cyclopean walls that Aeneas passes through to reach the Elysian Fields (*Aen.* 6.628–36), Dante's castle is very medieval. With its seven walls – an "allegory of the poets," a fiction that veils a moral meaning – the castle can be interpreted as the citadel of man's natural perfections, which Aquinas held the souls in limbo enjoyed. The association of virtue with a castle, implying attack and defense, is deeply rooted in medieval tradition, and in *Purg.* 7.34–36 Virgil will explain that the souls in limbo possess all of the virtues except the three theological virtues of faith, hope and charity. Thus the great spirits enjoy the virtues natural to man, in Aquinas's terms the four principal moral virtues (prudence, justice, fortitude and temperance) and the three intellectual virtues (wisdom, science and understanding). See *ST* 1–2.61.1, 2; 1–2.57.2. (Giuseppe Mazzotta prefers the Ottimo's idea that the castle represents philosophy and its walls the seven liberal arts. Mazzotta 1993, 25.)

112–44: Aeneas visits the Elysian Fields, where the spirits of the great disport themselves in green fields in the warlike sports, the dancing and the feasting of earthly life. Dante's spirits are posed in green fields in a serene stasis more characteristic of the Christian imagination. The parallel was understood: St. Antonino, archbishop of Florence in the mid-15th century, condemned Dante for representing the ancient sages as dwelling in the Elysian Fields. See *ED* 1.308–09.

Does Dante's late medieval vision anticipate later humanism? He exhibits some humanistic attitudes in germ, especially in his belief that happiness on earth is worthy in itself (*Mon.* 3.16.7; see Kantorowicz 463–70) and in his privileging of ethics over metaphysics because it assures human happiness. (Etienne Gilson noted how unusual the latter was for the Middle Ages. Gilson 104–05, 111–12.) Dante is nonetheless certainly not a humanist in the proper sense because he lacks the historical and critical perspectives of that movement and his actual knowledge of antiquity was limited in comparison with that of the humanists.

In a more general sense Dante's enthusiasm for antiquity is programmatic, and his assemblage of the ancient great sets the paradigm followed at the height of humanism in Raphael's Vatican frescoes of *The School of Athens* and *Parnassus* (in which Dante appears next to the ancient poets). Even in the absence of faith and grace, Dante valorizes the dignity of human life ordered by the dictates of reason and the grandeur of the human spirit in its notable political, intellectual and moral achievements. At the same time, however, the structure of his poem places these human values firmly in the eschatological framework. The light of human reason is merely a bonfire in the darkness compared to the sun of divine wisdom, of which these souls are forever deprived. See *Purg.* 7.25–27. For a balanced treatment of this subject, see *DE* 172–75.

112–20: Dante's vision of the great spirits is shaped by Aristotle's concept of the great-souled or "magnanimous" man, who is concerned above all with honor. *Eth.* 4.3 (1123b7–1124a20); see *In Eth.* ¶¶ 742–43. The great spirits (other than the poets) are separated into two groups corresponding to the active life and the contemplative life; but Dante also has a more specific program in mind. In *Conv.* 4.3–6 he set himself the goal of establishing the authority of the emperor and the authority of the philosopher, both of which must work in harmony for human life to reach its fullest potential. Dante's first group, paralleling the adumbrations of empire that Aeneas views in the Elysian Fields (*Aen.* 6.756–853), is centered on the Roman empire and its antecedents, and thus on the ideal of universal justice. His second group is centered on moral philosophy as perfected by Aristotle, and thus on the ideal of human life lived according to reason. Together the two groups form the pattern for ordering human life on earth.

121: Electra was the mother of Dardanus, the mythic founder of Troy. She appears here, as in *Mon.* 2.3, as the source from which the Trojan and therefore the Roman people sprang. Dardanus appears in Virgil's Elysian Fields for the same reason. *Aen.* 6.650.

122–23: Hector was the greatest Trojan hero. Providence willed that Aeneas escape Troy's ruin and found the colony in Italy that gave rise to Rome, future seat of empire. Julius Caesar is the climactic figure in this series, descendant of Aeneas and founder of the empire. Caesar's battle-dress shows that the great ones are clothed, consistent with their dignity, unlike any other souls in hell (except the hypocrites in *Inf.* 23, who wear punishing robes).

124–26: Aeneas married Lavinia, daughter of King Latinus, so that the Roman people are descended from both Trojan and Latin sources. Penthesilea and Camilla were warrior maidens representing these two sides of the Roman heritage.

127–28: Tarquin, son of Rome's last king, raped the noblewoman Lucretia, who committed suicide after swearing her husband and his companion Brutus to vengeance. Brutus avenged her by driving out the kings and establishing the republic.

128: Julia was the daughter of Julius Caesar and the wife of Pompey. Marcia was the devoted wife of Cato of Utica. "Cornelia" is likely the second wife of Pompey, whose name is twinned with Marcia's as faithful wives in Lucan. *Phars.* 2.348–49. (Alternatively, she may be the mother of the Gracchi.)

129: Saladin (Salah-ad-Din), the chief Muslim opponent of the crusaders, was a medieval *figura* of *magnaminitas* (see, *e.g.*, *Decam.* 1.3, 10.9), earlier praised by Dante for courtesy and liberality. *Conv.* 4.11.14.

131–35: The master of those who understand is Aristotle, whom Dante called the leading master of the human reason, most worthy of belief. *Conv.* 4.6.7–8. Like the later humanists, Dante privileges moral philosophy (ethics) over metaphysics, because it deals directly with human life. See *Conv.* 2.14; Gilson 104–05. Aristotle holds the central position here because in his *Nicomachean Ethics* he perfected the theory that virtue consists in a mean between the extremes of excess and defect. Socrates and Plato sit nearest him because they were the first to grasp this insight. See *Conv.* 4.6.13–14.

136–37: Democritus stands for indifference to comfort and convention in the pursuit of truth. See *Conv.* 3.14.8. Diogenes the Cynic enjoyed a similar but greater reputation. See *ED* 2.458–59.

137–38: Dante could have learned about these pre-Socratic philosophers from the description of their teachings in Aristotle.

138: Zeno is the founder of Stoicism; the story of his suicide may have made Dante regard him as a *figura* for love of liberty, like Cato. See *ED* 5.1168–69.

140: Aquinas treated Orpheus and Linus as philosophers who represented nature in myths. *Commentary on Aristotle's Metaphysics* ¶ 82.

140, 143: Galen and Hippocrates were the greatest physicians of antiquity. Dioscorides wrote a treatise on the medical uses of plants.

141: Cicero and Seneca appear as moral philosophers.

142: Ptolemy put in its classical form the system of the universe taken for granted between late antiquity and Copernicus, but he was even better known as an astrologer.

143–44: Avicenna (Ibn Sina) and Averroes (Ibn Rushd) were medieval Muslim physicians and philosophers. Averroes' great commentary is his commentary on Aristotle's *De Anima*.

Canto V

So I descended from the first of the circles
   to the second, which encompasses less space
   and much more pain, which goads the souls to groan.
There rises Minos, snarling, horrible;
   there at the entrance he tries all offenses,   5
   judges and sentences by count of coils.
I mean that when the misbegotten soul
   appears before him, it confesses everything,
   and that experienced judge of sin, discerning
the place in hell where it belongs, entwines   10
   his tail around his body the number of times
   that shows the level where he wants it placed.
Crowds of them always stand in front of him;
   they come to judgment, each one in his turn,
   they speak, they listen, and then are flung below.   15
"O you who come to the abode of pain,"
   Minos called out to me when he perceived me,
   pausing in his discharge of his great office,
"be careful how you enter and whom you trust;
   do not be fooled by the broad entryway."   20
     "Why do you keep on growling?" my guide answered.
"Attempt no interference with his destined
   journey, for it is willed where will is one
   with its fulfillment; ask no more about it."

Notes of affliction now begin to reach   25
    my ears, and I have now attained a point
    where a great squall of weeping breaks upon me.
I came to a place in which all light was mute,
    and it bellowed as the sea does in a storm
    beneath the onslaught of conflicting winds.   30
Hell's hurricane, which concedes no respite ever,
    hurtles the spirits with its brutal force;
    tossing and buffeting, it harries them.
And when they come before its devastation
    they shriek, they wail together, they lament   35
    and they scream curses at the power of God.
I realized that the spirits condemned to such
    a torment as this must be the carnal sinners,
    who had subjected reason to desire.
And as the wings of starlings carry them   40
    in a broad, close-packed flock in the cold season,
    the tempest blows those spirits of the damned
at one time here, then there, now up, now down;
    and they are never comforted by hope
    of pain diminishing, much less of rest.   45
And as cranes sing their mournful songs in flight,
    stretching themselves in a long line through the air,
    so I could see approach, emitting groans,
shades borne along upon the turbulence,
    which made me ask him, "Master, who are those,   50
    the people the dark air so punishes?"
"The first of those about whom you desire
    to be informed," my master let me know,
    "was empress over many languages.
She was so broken to the vice of lust   55
    that she made lechery lawful by decree
    to clear the infamy she had incurred.
She is Semiramis, of whom we read
    that she succeeded Ninus, her late husband
    and ruled the lands now governed by the Sultan.   60

The next is she that killed herself for love
    and broke faith with the ashes of Sichaeus;
    and next is the lascivious Cleopatra.
There you see Helen, for whose sake a cycle
    of evil years revolved, and great Achilles   65
    who fought his final combat against love.
See Paris, Tristan . . . ," and he pointed out
    and named for me a multitude of shades
    whom love had separated from our life.
And after I had heard my teacher name   70
    the knights and ladies of old times, great pity
    seized on me and I hardly knew where I was.
"Poet," I ventured, "I would very gladly
    speak with the two of them who move together
    and seem to lie upon the wind so lightly."   75
"Watch for the moment they draw close to us,"
    he said, "and then entreat them by the love
    that carries them along, and they will come."
So when the wind had made them veer our way
    I sent my voice out: "O exhausted souls,   80
    come speak with us, if it is not forbidden."
As doves called back by yearning glide through the air
    down on extended and immobile wings
    to their sweet nest, sustained by their desire,
these two descended from the flock of Dido   85
    and came toward us through the malignant air,
    such was the power of my impassioned cry.
"O gracious and benevolent human creature
    coming through inky air to pay a visit
    to those of us who dyed the world dark red,   90
if he that rules the universe showed favor
    our prayer to him would be to grant you peace,
    because you pity our atrocious torment.
Whatever you may wish to hear or say
    we undertake to tell or listen to   95
    while the wind hushes here, as it is doing.

The town where I was born is situated
 upon the seacoast where the Po comes down,
 leading its tributaries, to find its rest.
Love, quickly kindled in a noble heart,   100
 captured this man with the beauty of the body
 snatched from me – how that happened still afflicts me.
Love, which spares no one who is loved from loving,
 captured me with his beauty so completely
 that as you see, it has not yet released me.   105
Love drew the two of us to the same death.
 Cain's Ring awaits the one who snuffed our lives."
 These were the words that they addressed to us.
When I had listened to those suffering souls,
 I dropped my eyes and held them lowered so long   110
 the poet finally asked, "What are you thinking?"
When I could answer, I said, "Oh, the pity!
 How many tender thoughts and how much longing
 have only brought them to the straits of grief!"
And afterwards I turned to them and spoke;   115
 and I began: "Your sufferings, Francesca,
 cause me to weep for sorrow and for pity.
But tell me, in the time of your soft sighs
 by what sign and in what way did love grant you
 awareness of your hesitant desire?"   120
"There is no greater anguish," she replied,
 "than to recall our happy days amidst
 our misery; and your teacher understands this.
But if you feel such great desire to learn
 the first root of our love, I will rehearse   125
 the tale like one who speaks even while weeping.
We read a book one day to pass the time,
 about how Lancelot was in the grip
 of love; we were alone with no misgivings.
That reading pulled our eyes repeatedly   130
 together and it turned our faces pale;
 but we were vanquished by one passage only.

While we were reading how the famous lover
    kissed, at the last, the long-desired smile,
    this one – from whom I never shall be parted –   135
trembling all over, kissed me on the mouth.
    The book and he that wrote it played the part
    of Galehault: that day we read no further."
And all the while that the one spirit spoke
    these words, the other wept; so that from pity   140
    my senses failed me as it were in death,
and down I fell as a dead body falls.

Notes

2–3: As hell's funnel narrows, each circle is smaller and punishes worse sins.

4–6: Minos, King of Crete in myth, sits in judgment at the entrance of the underworld in *Aen.* 6.431–33. The circles of Dante's hell have entrance guardians drawn from classical literature, which Alison Morgan notes was an innovation in medieval representations of hell. Morgan 57. Often, however, the classical figure is transmogrified. Here Minos assumes the grotesque animal-human form in which the Middle Ages often imagined its devils. His snarling, the ritual play of his tail, and his sarcasm infuse the classical figure with a new vitality derived from popular culture.

9: The judge Minos resembles is the inquisitor, who inspires a terror that makes the sinner babble every detail.

21–24: Virgil brandishes the talismanic formula that quelled Charon. *Inf.* 3.95–96.

25–33: The pilgrim's first impression is aural. The storm begins as a simile intended to explain the infernal noise the pilgrim hears, but then turns out to be quite literal.

30: Aristotle asserted that hurricanes are formed "when some winds are blowing and others fall on them." *Meteorol.* 2.4 (365a2–4).

37–39: The pilgrim deduces the character of the sinners from the nature of their punishment and thus comprehends the symbolic principle of the *contrapasso*. The lustful have disordered their souls by subjecting reason to desire and they have no inner harmony. This moral turbulence is reified in hell, where they are ceaselessly tossed and buffeted by gusts beyond their control that allow them no rest for eternity.

39: Cicero summarized the Greek philosophers: reason and appetite are the two powers of the soul; reason must command and appetite obey. *On Duties* 1.28.101; see *Eth.* 3.12 (1119b1–15). Dante elsewhere compares appetite to a horse and reason to the rider without which the horse cannot go right, no matter how noble its nature. *Conv.* 4.26.6–7. (Cf. Hume's provocative formulation in the *Treatise of Human Nature*: "Reason is and ought only to be the slave of the passions. . . .")

40–41: Pliny said that starlings fly in flocks and wheel in a circular ball. *Nat. Hist.* 10.35; see *De Animal.* 23.140.

46–51: Pliny noted that cranes fly in line, following their leader and keeping together by their cries. *Nat. Hist.* 10.30. The cranes flying in formation are individuals, whereas the starlings were massed in a dense flock. Dante is distinguishing famous and infamous lovers from the mass of the lustful.

52–69: This catalogue of the victims of love finds many parallels in medieval literature. See *ED* 4.305. This is the only part of hell in which women outnumber men, as those who died for love in *Aen.* 6.440–76 are virtually all women.

52–60: Dante paraphrases the early Christian historian Orosius. *Hist. Adv. Pag.* 22–23. Semiramis ruled in wanton Babylon.

61–62: Dido slew herself after Aeneas abandoned her at the command of the gods. In loving him, she broke faith with her late husband Sichaeus to whom she had promised eternal fidelity. See *Aen.* 4.28–29, 553. Elsewhere Dante says that in leaving Dido, Aeneas controlled appetite by reason. *Conv.* 4.26.8.

63: Cleopatra's affairs with Julius Caesar and Mark Antony are seen as the result of wanton lust, rather than as the canny use of sex for political ends.

64–65: Helen of Troy, by deserting her Greek husband to run off with Trojan Paris, gave rise to the Trojan war, which lasted ten years. Dante apparently thought Helen was killed in the sack of Troy. See *ED* 2.651.

65–66: In the works through which the Middle Ages knew the stories of the Trojan war, Achilles falls in love with the Trojan princess Polyxena, and when he goes to tryst with her is slain by Paris. See *ED* 1.38.

67–72: The ancients consumed by pitiless love, whom Virgil consigned to the Mourning Fields (*Aen.* 6.440–76), are here assimilated to the medieval poetic tradition whose central theme was the problematization of love. The great pity the poet feels is not for the named individuals (like the monstrous Semiramis), but for all the "knights and ladies of old times" overcome by fatal passion. The pity is called for by the literary tradition to which these figures belong, but its added intensity comes from the infernal context: love brought them not only tragedy on earth but also eternal damnation. Teodolinda Barolini emphasizes the extent to which Dante's treatment of lust here and in the *Purgatorio* is milder than that usual in medieval vision literature and didactic poetry and focuses on the psychology of desire rather than overt sexual acts. Barolini 2006, 70–73, 332.

67: Paris abducted Helen, and after killing Achilles was himself slain by a poisoned arrow.

67: While Tristan was escorting Iseult to be the bride of his uncle, King Mark, they mistakenly drank a love potion. In some versions of the story, Mark kills Tristan when he discovers their adultery.

74–75: These are Paolo and Francesca. Francesca da Rimini, daughter of the lord of Ravenna, married the capable but crippled Gianciotto Malatesta, son of the lord of Rimini, and had two children by him. The accepted story is that she fell in love with her husband's dashing younger brother Paolo (also married and with children); and that her husband, finding them together, killed them both.

75: Of all the flock, only two form a couple carried together on the storm, which they ride more lightly than the others. Their lightness is ambiguous: either they are tossed more violently by the wind or, as Boccaccio thought, are less wearied by it. The underlying question is whether Paolo and Francesca's eternal linkage aggravates or mitigates their punishment; and the answer, suiting the ambiguity of the image, is that it does both.

82–87: The dove was the bird of Venus. Pliny believed that doves were faithful to their partners for life and did not leave their nests. *Nat. Hist.* 10.52.

90: "Dark red (*sanguigno*)": Francesca refers to all the great lovers, not just herself and Paolo. *Sanguigno*, a dark madder red, alludes to the violent deaths of these sinners betrayed by love, but it is also the color of love. See Mazzoni 1977, 118; *VN* 2 (color of Beatrice's dress).

96: Paolo and Francesca have descended below the level of the tempest, as the dove simile implies. Providence allows them this respite to educate the pilgrim.

97–107, 121–38: Francesca da Rimini is the only major female character in the *Inferno*, and the first example of Dante's ability to render a character with remarkable psychological immediacy. Francesco De Sanctis was not wrong in calling her the first real woman in modern literature. See *DE* 748. Like Dante's Virgil, Francesca has been treated with increasing hostility by some critics since the mid-20th century. As the century grew more permissive in its sexual mores, critics grew more shrill in denouncing Francesca, almost as if they hated the sinner more than the sin. Such critics assume that Dante the poet condemns the pity the pilgrim feels for Francesca and they find the episode otherwise unproblematic.

Textual support for this view is questionable. Dante certainly judges Francesca. The punishment of the second circle is his judgment: she has the eternity of passion with Paolo that she chose for herself, and the pilgrim as well as the poet understands that. But Dante's attitude toward the sinners in hell, as opposed to their sins, is quite nuanced. Pity must not be allowed to cloud the pilgrim's understanding of sin and its condign punishment; but because he intuitively understands the *contrapasso* (37–39), the pity he experiences for some sinners is not a rebellion against God's justice but rather sorrow at what they have made of themselves. The tragedy of the *Inferno* is that people damn themselves despite their better qualities or because of the dark side of those very qualities. The pilgrim first weeps and then faints because his heart is wrenched at seeing the love celebrated by the poets, including himself, leading so directly to damnation. Lino Pertile comments that the pilgrim discovers on his journey how intertwined good and evil can be in all of us. Pertile 2007a, 75–76, 81–82.

97–99: Ravenna lies near the mouth of the Po, which seeks its rest through obliteration in the sea, the rest Francesca is forever denied.

100–107: The tragedies of love experienced by the storied knights and ladies of old times are brought into the present by Francesca's telling her story in the formulas the poets used to describe the origin and the effects of love. In the paradigm of courtly love that some Italian poets derived from the Provençal troubadours, desire is inflamed by beauty and overcomes reason, paralyzing the will. (For the troubadours, see, *e.g.*, Lazar 61–100.) In a culture permeated by an ascetic Christian morality, this naturally was a source of conflict. By having Francesca explain her surrender to passion in these terms, Dante consciously puts in issue this great problematic of medieval poetry. Dante – and here the relation of pilgrim to poet is murky – does not agree with this analysis of love. Nonetheless, this problematic has haunted much of his poetry, and it is not very long since he himself said things very similar to Francesca's formulations.

Teodolinda Barolini's essays on this subject expand on Kenelm Foster and Patrick Boyde's recognition that the view of love expressed in the *Comedy* did not develop in a straight line. See Barolini 2006 and Barolini/Lansing. In *Donne ch'avete* in the *Vita Nuova* Dante developed the sublimated ideal of love for Beatrice that would lead in the *Comedy* to her being a conduit for love of God; but both earlier and much later he expressed different attitudes. In the early canzone *Lo doloroso amor*, love for Beatrice is a painful obsession leading to death, but the poet does not fear damnation because in contemplating her he will not feel the pains of hell. In the canzone *Amor, da che convien*, written around the time Dante is thought to have begun the *Inferno*, the poet experiences passionate love as a tempest against which reason and will are powerless.

The pilgrim's pity for Francesca is thus complicated by a sense that he is complicit in her sin, because she tells her story in his words. Barolini concludes that the evolution of his views up to the writing of the *Inferno* was the result of a long struggle. Barolini 2006, 91. Even now, Dante has transformed rather than abandoned the tradition of courtly love (*e.g.*, Beatrice is another man's wife, an idea that was too shocking for G.A. Scartazzini to accept). The pilgrim is uneasy that the tradition can be understood in the original and ultimately damning sense in which Francesca understands it. He faints at the end of the canto precisely because he recognizes how like Francesca he is. Barolini 2006, 331.

100: This line echoes Dante's sonnet "Amore e 'l cor gentil sono una cosa (*Love and the noble heart are but one thing*)." *VN* 20. In addition to the initial line, Francesca's account of the origin of love in the perception of beauty, by women as well as by men, paraphrases the sonnet. The difference is that the sonnet contains qualifications that enforce the idea of "good, ethical, rational" love, and so lead toward the *Comedy*. Foster/Boyde 2.105. In *Purg.* 18.19 Virgil will generalize the idea: "The soul, which is created quick to love"; but he will make clear that love can lead either to heaven or to hell.

101, 104: It is a commonplace of medieval love poetry that love enters through the eyes; and beauty will still figure importantly in Virgil's analysis of love in *Purg.* 18.27.

103: Dante will not reject this adage of courtly love but rather transform it in *Purg.* 22.10–12: "Love / once lit by virtue, always lights another, / provided that its flame shine openly."

105: Pertile notes that Francesca's line echoes *Aen.* 6.444, where in the underworld doomed lovers (including Dido) mourn because even death does not extinguish the sorrows of love. Pertile suggests that this echo makes Francesca more of a tragic figure than the contemporary consensus allows. Pertile 1999.

107: Francesca predicts that her husband (still alive during the pilgrim's journey in 1300) will end in the lowest circle of hell, in the place reserved for those who kill their kin.

116–17: Emotional pity is not intellectual pity. See note to *Inf.* 2.91–93. Nor is pity for the damned unknown in Christian tradition. In the *Vision of St. Paul* the saint experiences so much pity for the souls in hell that he convinces God to intermit their punishment on Sundays. Elliott 638–39.

118–20: The pilgrim seeks to understand what troubles him – how did such a heightening of the soul so quickly become its debasement? The question is phrased in terms that share Francesca's assumptions: love is the actor and she is acted upon.

121–23: The sentiment is from Boethius. *Cons. Phil.* 2.4.

127–38: The molding of Francesca's conception of love by medieval erotic literature is confirmed by the story of her fall, in which the Old French prose Lancelot Romance is the catalyst of her passion. See Toynbee 1901, 7–37. Paolo and Francesca's reading of the text, with its immediate unleashing of a storm of passion, symbolizes the fated character of their love as Francesca sees it, like the potion that Tristan and Iseult drank. The infernal setting, however, suggests a parody of such a device, because in terms of Christian moral casuistry Paolo and Francesca's reading erotic literature in the seclusion of the castle is a classic occasion of sin.

130–31: The verses echo a well-known passage from Abelard's *The Story of My Misfortunes*, describing his study sessions with Heloise: "love drew our eyes to look on each other more than reading kept them on our texts." Abelard 67.

131: Rule 15 of *The Art of Courtly Love*, a 12th century treatise by Andreas Capellanus, is that the lover turns pale in the presence of his beloved. Capellanus 185.

133–36: In the romance Guinevere finally bestows a kiss on Lancelot and some critics ask why Dante (or Francesca) misrepresents the narrative. See Noakes 1986, 154–55. This post-modern fascination with the misreading of texts bypasses the basic point that the Paolo and Francesca scene deflates romance conventions: the ethereal kiss of the Lancelot Romance (kissing a smile) contrasts with the carnal urgency it incites (kissing on the mouth), which requires Paolo to spark the encounter.

137–38: Gallehault is a powerful knight who brings the lovers together and convinces Guinevere to give Lancelot the kiss. Francesca says the book – and its author – facilitated her adultery in the same way. Paolo Valesio observes that by including the author as an unneeded third term in the metaphor, Dante puts in question his own role as author of this scene. Valesio 71–72. Dante made Paolo and Francesca's story the most celebrated tale of love between those of Tristan and Iseult and Romeo and Juliet, an indication that susceptible readers could take from this scene the compelling description of passion, not the warning with which the context surrounds it. Dante's possible recognition that his anti-romance might be read as a romance – in effect involving the reader as a voyeur in a scene he condemns – would amplify his sense of complicity. In any case, the foregrounding of an interaction between literature and sin puts in issue Dante's own project of furthering his readers' salvation. *Epist.* 13.39; see *DE* 413.

Canto VI

With consciousness returning, which shut down
    before the piteous spectacle of the two
    in-laws that left me stupefied with sorrow,
I see new torments all around me, new
    tormented souls, no matter where I go,   5
    no matter where I turn or where I look.
This is the third of the circles, that of rain,
    abominable, eternal rain, cold, heavy,
    unvarying in character and cadence.
Great hailstones mixed with turbid water and snow   10
    come pouring down through the crepuscular air,
    and the soil absorbing it gives off a stench.
Cerberus, a misshapen, savage monster,
    stands baying like a dog through his three throats
    over the people who lie sunken there.   15
His eyes burn red, his black beard drips with grease,
    his belly bulges and with taloned hands
    he scores the spirits, skins and quarters them.
The rain makes these degraded wretches howl
    like dogs, and they roll over frequently,   20
    trying to shelter one flank with the other.
When Cerberus, the swollen grub, perceived us,
    his mouths gaped and he showed us all his fangs
    and every limb took part in the commotion.

My leader spread each hand to its full span,   25
    gathered up earth and with his fists both full
    he hurled it into those voracious gullets.
As a dog that yelps from craving food falls quiet
    the moment it sets tooth to scrap, absorbed
    completely in the struggle to gulp it down,   30
so did the filthy faces of the demon
    Cerberus, whose continual thunder stuns
    the souls until they wish that they were deaf.
Then we go forward, walking over the shades
    the heavy rain beats down, planting our feet   35
    upon their emptiness that looks like body.
All of those shades lay stretched upon the ground
    except for one that raised himself to sit
    as soon as he observed us pass before him.
"You that are led through hell," he said to me,   40
    "look at me and remember, if you can,
    for you were made before I was unmade."
"Perhaps the torment that you undergo
    has wiped you from my memory," I replied,
    "because it seems to me I've never seen you.   45
But tell me who you are, dispatched to such
    a grievous place to suffer the most loathsome
    of punishments, if not the most severe."
And he: "Your city, which is stuffed with envy
    until the sack is ready to spill over,   50
    held me within its walls in the sunlit life.
Among you citizens I was known as Ciacco;
    and for the ruinous vice of the stuffed gullet,
    as you can see, I languish in the rain.
And I, unhappy soul, am not alone,   55
    for all these bear like punishment for like
    offense." He added not another word.
"Ciacco," I answered, "your affliction weighs
    so heavily on me that I feel like weeping;
    but tell me, if you can, how they will end,   60

the citizens of our divided town,
    if any there are just, and for what reason
    such great dissension has taken it by storm."
"Their lengthy quarrel will at last," he said,
    "erupt in bloodshed, and the rural party   65
    will drive the other out with great oppression.
That party must in turn, however, fall
    within three years, as must the other rise
    by the power of one who is now maneuvering.
Long will those hold their heads high, while they keep   70
    the former down with crushing impositions,
    ignoring their complaints and their resentment.
Two men are just and no one there will listen;
    avarice, pride and envy are the three
    sparks that have made a bonfire out of hearts."   75
And here he made an end of these sad words.
    "I long for you to tell me more," I said,
    "and grant me further speech. Say, Farinata
and Tegghiaio, who were men of such distinction,
    Jacopo Rusticucci, Arrigo, Mosca,   80
    and the others diligent for the common good,
where are they now? Acquaint me with their fates;
    for I am seized by eagerness to know
    if they taste heaven's sweetness or hell's poison."
And he: "They are among the blacker souls;   85
    different offenses weight them toward the bottom:
    there you can see them if you go that far.
But when you have returned to the sweet world,
    bring me, I beg of you, to people's minds.
    I say no more to you, nor will I answer."   90
Turning his gaze to sidelong from direct,
    he stared at me a while, then dropped his head
    and fell headfirst among the rest of the blind.
My leader said to me, "He wakes no more
    until the blast of the angelic trumpet   95
    signals the coming of the rigorous judge;

each will revisit then his wretched tomb
    and repossess his flesh in the same likeness
    and hear the words that echo through eternity."
We walked on, all the while, across the nasty   100
    slush of the shades and the rain with measured steps,
    speaking a little of the life to come;
and I asked therefore, "Master, will these torments
    intensify, once past the general judgment,
    or weaken, or still smart as bad as now?"   105
"Go back to your philosophy," he answered,
    "which holds that a more perfect being feels
    pleasure more keenly; so it is with pain.
Although these cursed souls will never reach
    their true perfection, they can still expect   110
    afterwards to be more complete than now."
We walked around the curve that path describes,
    saying much more that I will not repeat,
    until we reached the point where it descends;
there we found Plutus, the great adversary.   115

Notes

7–12: The third circle. The shades beaten down into the stinking mud by the steady
    downpour are the gluttons. Theirs is a simple but degrading form of intemperance.
13–18: Dante reshaped the image of Cerberus to suit his ends. Cerberus seems at first
    the hell-hound of Virgil and Ovid, baying through his three throats (*Aen.* 6.417;
    Metam. 4.450–51), but he bays *like* a dog. Then he turns out to have a beard and
    hands (although the hands are clawed). Dante's updated Cerberus is a medieval
    demon, anthropomorphic but with some canine features. The plastic vigor with
    which Dante endows him – his burning eyes, his greasy beard, his belly and the
    way he butchers the sinners – saves him from being a cardboard personification
    of gluttony. This effect derives from the kitchen or butcher-shop imagery, which
    signals a low style foreign to Dante's models but appropriate for medieval devils.
14: The three throats of Cerberus suit the demon of gluttony. Aristotle said that
    gluttons delight more in touch than in taste, and he cited a gourmand who wished
    for a throat longer than a crane's. *Eth.* 3.10 (1118a26–1118b1). Ciacco will call
    gluttony the vice of the gullet.

18: Embellishing his scheme of punishment, Dante makes the gluttons the demon's food, skinned and cut up like joints of meat.

25–32: The Sibyl enables Aeneas to slip past Cerberus by feeding it drugged honey-cakes (*Aen.* 6.417–23). Dante consciously vulgarizes the scene. His Cerberus can be distracted by anything at all, because his indiscriminate voracity experiences everything as food.

34–35: Despite the realism of Dante's infernal landscapes, he manipulates details to suit his convenience. Few readers notice at this point that the pilgrim walks between the raindrops.

38–57: Ciacco is the first Florentine the pilgrim meets. He proves to be an intelligent man of sound judgment with a brusque manner, as though he is irritated at being awakened. He appears in *Decam.* 9.8 as a man of wit who, unable to afford his taste for good living, spends his time at the tables of the rich, winning favor by making himself a mordant commentator on society. As with other Dantean characters who appear in the *Decameron*, whether Boccaccio is supplying historical information or writing a sort of fan fiction is open to question.

51: "[T]he sunlit life (*la vita serena*)": Souls in the darkness of hell remember the sweet light (*Inf.* 10.69) of the upper world. Some sinners will be blamed for having been morose in the sweet air the sun exhilarates. *Inf.* 7.121–22. Dante does not share the contempt for this world prevalent in medieval religious writing.

60–75: Questions about Florentine politics enter the *Inferno* for the first time. Bitter and violent factionalism was a constant in the Italian cities. There was a horizontal cleavage between magnates and *popolani* that produced ongoing power struggles. In addition there was a vertical cleavage between supporters of imperial power in Italy, called Ghibellines from the time of Emperor Frederick II in the mid-13th century, and anti-imperialists called Guelfs, who gravitated toward the papacy and its client Charles of Anjou, who defeated Frederick's son Manfred. See Larner 106–22; Waley 117–56. These external allegiances crystallized local hatreds that were independent of them. After the Guelfs triumphed permanently in Florence in 1266, there were about 25 years of peace, the years of Dante's youth. Then the Guelf party split into the Black and White factions, which continued the struggle with equal bitterness. It is this dissension, not yet open combat, that the pilgrim questions Ciacco about. For a good summary of the Florentine history in the background of the *Comedy*, see DE 386–403.

Joan Ferrante argues that in the discussions of Florentine politics and commerce, in the vices of the notable Florentines in hell, and in the image of hell as a fortified city (all coming up in succeeding cantos), Dante has portrayed hell as a corrupt city-state and specifically as Florence. Ferrante 61–75.

60–61: Aeneas hears prophecies in the underworld about the future of Rome (*Aen.* 6.756–807) as the pilgrim does about the future of Florence. Prophetic vision in the dead is not consistent with the opinions of the theologians, an indication of how important it was to Dante as a dramatic effect. Aquinas held that neither angels nor demons nor separated souls know the future except as it can be predicted from causes. *ST* 1.89.3.

64–66: In May 1300 – shortly after the pilgrim's journey through hell – a bloody affray between adherents of the Cerchi and Donati families led to open war in Florence. The party of the Cerchi became the Whites and that of the Donati the Blacks. In 1301 the leading Blacks were exiled, but Dante appears to exaggerate the severity of the Whites' conduct, which was characterized above all by indecision. See *Cron.* 9.39; *ED* 1.622.

65: The Whites are called the rural party because the Cerchi came from the country. Dino Compagni (1.20) said they were of low status but very rich merchants, whereas the Donati were an older family but not so rich. Accord, *Cron.* 9.39.

67–72: Pope Boniface VIII sided with the Blacks. Pretending impartiality, he charged Charles of Valois, the French king's brother, with "pacifying" Florence in 1301. When Charles entered the city in force, he was followed shortly by the exiled Blacks, who effectively assumed control. In January 1302 the White leaders were exiled and their faction never regained power. These were the central events in Dante's political life. See note to *Inf.* 10.79–81.

73: The presence of a few just men in a corrupt city is an Old Testament theme portending disaster for the city. Gen. 18:23–32; Jer. 5:1; Ezech. 14:14–20. Dante probably thought of himself as one of the just men being ignored.

77–84: After Ciacco's condemnation of contemporary Florence, the pilgrim asks him about Florentine leaders of earlier generations. Dante looks back at his youth as a time when the common good was pursued, and he regards even the earlier struggles of the Guelfs and Ghibellines as a time when there was honor on both sides. Although these men are Dante's civic heroes, he does not assume they are saved. Most critics comment that public virtue is not sufficient to save a man, but it is equally important that whether these men are in hell for private vices does not affect Dante's judgment that they were forces for good in Florentine politics.

79–81: Farinata is in the sixth circle (*Inf.* 10) and Tegghiaio and Jacopo Rusticucci in the seventh (*Inf.* 16). "Arrigo" does not appear in the *Comedy*.

80: Mosca is in the eighth circle (*Inf.* 28) for inciting a murder that led to factional violence. Bosco/Reggio attribute his inconsistent appearance as a positive force here to the golden haze Dante throws over past generations in his eagerness to deplore the present.

86: This is a clear statement of the structural theme in the *Inferno* that equates sin with heaviness and virtue with lightness. Aquinas explained that just as bodies have levity or gravity that makes them rise or sink, so souls have merit or demerit; and when the bonds of the flesh are broken, the soul rises to heaven or sinks to hell by its nature. *ST Suppl.* 69.2.

92–94, 100–01: While the gluttons fed the body they starved the soul, submerging spirit in the blind torpor of matter. In the shocking image of the nasty slush, they become indistinguishable from the mud in which they lie.

95–99: The last trump at the end of time will announce the coming of Christ in majesty to pronounce the Last Judgment, at which reward and punishment will be meted out to all who have lived, in contrast to the particular judgment that each of the souls in hell has already experienced at the moment of death.

99: The sentence pronounced against sinners at the Last Judgment (*Depart from me, you cursed, into everlasting fire,* Matt. 25:41) will echo in their minds throughout their eternal punishment.

103–11: After the resurrection of the dead that will accompany the Last Judgment, the torments of the damned will be augmented because the sinners will be punished in their bodies as well as their souls. Because Dante's narrative requires that the pilgrim meet souls who seem as much like the living as possible, he invents a subtle body that the separated soul forms for itself from the circumambient air. *Purg.* 25.88–108. Through this *shade* the soul exercises the powers of sensation as it did when united with its body on earth. This unorthodox construct (for the contrary view see *ST Suppl.* 70.1–3) makes it clear that the damned can suffer the pain of sense, and not just the pain of loss, in the present; less clear is the reasoning here, which means at best that after the resurrection the damned will feel their torments somewhat more vividly in their more robust reconstituted bodies.

106: "Your philosophy" is the philosophy of Aristotle, as interpreted and reconciled with Christian doctrine by the Scholastics, which the pilgrim has studied.

Canto VII

"*Pape Satàn, pape Satàn, aleppe!*"
    Plutus began to cry in a rasping voice;
    and the noble sage, all-knowing, said to me,
to reassure me, "Do not let your fear
    cripple you; for whatever power he has   5
    shall not prevent our going down this cliff."
He swung around then on that swollen face
    and said, "Be silent, you accursed wolf,
    and let your rage consume your guts within!
This journey to the bottom does not lack   10
    a cause, for it is willed on high, where Michael
    exacted vengeance for pride's mutiny."
As sails that are all bellied out with wind
    fall, when the mast snaps, in a tangled heap,
    here that cruel beast collapsed upon the ground.   15
So we descended to the fourth of the hollows,
    proceeding further down the dismal slope
    that bags up all the evil of the universe.
Justice of God! Who crams in all the strange
    torments and punishments I saw before me?   20
    And our sins, why do they so torture us?
The waves around Charybdis break upon
    the others that they meet head-on, and so
    the folk here do, who must dance back and forth.

I saw more people here by far than elsewhere,   25
    on both sides of the circle, howling loudly
    and rolling weights by brute force with their chests.
They crashed together and then upon the spot
    they turned around and rolled them back, while shouting
    "What use is hoarding?" "Where did wasting get you?"   30
So they returned around the gloomy circle
    on either side to the point opposite,
    crying out once again their singsong taunts;
and then, the point attained, each turned again
    through his half circle to the other joust.   35
    And I, who felt as if my heart were pierced,
said to him, "Master, please explain what people
    these are, and whether those upon our left
    with tonsures could have all been clergymen."
"In the first life," he answered, "all of them   40
    squinted so badly in their minds that none
    of them could ever spend in moderation.
Their voices howl it out plainly enough
    each time they reach the two points of the circle
    where opposite offenses separate them.   45
These with no cap of hair upon their crowns
    were clerics – some were even popes and cardinals,
    among whom avarice exceeds itself."
"Master," I ventured, "surely in such a mob
    I should be able to recognize at least   50
    a few that were polluted with these evils."
And he: "You entertain an idle thought:
    the undiscerning life that sullied them
    obscures them now beyond all recognition.
Forever they will come to the two buttings;   55
    these will arise with closed fists from their tombs
    as those will rise up, having taken a haircut.
Wrong giving and wrong keeping took from them
    the beautiful world and set them at this scrimmage:
    I will not waste fine words on such as that.   60

Now you may see, son, the brief mockery
    of the goods entrusted to the power of Fortune,
    over which humankind is always squabbling;
for all the gold there is beneath the moon,
    and all there ever was, could bring no respite   65
    to even one of these exhausted souls."
"Master," I said, "now you must tell me more:
    who is this Fortune that you touched upon,
    the one who clutches the world's goods so tightly?"
"O foolish creatures," he replied, "how great   70
    the ignorance that afflicts you! In this matter
    I will have to spoon-feed you my reasoning.
He whose transcendent wisdom shaped the heavens
    assigned to all of them their guiding spirits
    so each part may shed splendor on each other,   75
apportioning the light in equal measure.
    Likewise, to guide the splendors of the world
    he chose a general administrator,
one that would shift the light goods in due course
    from nation to nation, and from clan to clan,   80
    beyond the power of man's wit to prevent;
and so one people lords it while another
    languishes, all pursuant to her decree,
    which, like a snake in grass, remains concealed.
Human sagacity cannot oppose her,   85
    for she foresees, decides and executes
    her governance as the other gods do theirs.
Her changes never pause: necessity
    compels her to be swift; and thus it happens
    so frequently that men change their condition.   90
This is the one so much reviled by those
    who should in fact most praise her, but instead
    unjustly heap reproach on her and slander.
But in her blessedness she does not hear;
    happy among the other first-born creatures   95
    she turns her sphere and only knows delight.

But now we must descend to greater torment;
    the stars that rose when I was setting out
    already sink and lingering is forbidden."
We crossed the circle to its other edge,   100
    near where a fountainhead was bubbling up
    and spilling into a stream that flowed from it.
The water looked more black than inky purple;
    and we, in company with its turbid flow,
    made our way downward by a difficult path.   105
This dismal little stream, when it has reached
    the bottom of the sinister leaden slopes
    loses itself within the marsh called Styx.
Staring about attentively, I noticed
    mud-covered people in the marsh, all naked   110
    and with resentment showing in their faces.
They battered each other, not with fists alone
    but kicking too and butting heads and chests,
    tearing each other to pieces with their teeth.
"Son," my good master said, "you are seeing now   115
    the souls of those whom anger overcame;
    and I would also have you hold it certain
that underwater there are people who sigh,
    making the surface of the water bubble,
    as you can see wherever your eye turns.   120
Sunk in the mire they say, 'We were morose
    in the sweet air the sun exhilarates,
    bearing a sluggish smoke within our hearts;
now we are sullen here in the black muck.'
    This hymn they have to gurgle in their throats   125
    because they cannot form the words completely."
And so, between dry shore and boggy ground,
    we walked in a great curve round the foul swamp,
    our eyes still on the ones who swallowed mud.
And we arrived at last at the foot of a tower.   130

Notes

1: *"Pape* [two syllables] *Satàn"*: The Ottimo said that on seeing the poets "the father of riches cried out in amazement, lamenting and calling on the aid of his master," Satan.

2: *Plutus/Pluto (Pluto)*. Plutus was the god of wealth, but he was not always clearly distinguished in antiquity from the more important Pluto, king of the underworld. This guardian of the circle of riches is best understood as "the demon of avarice," as Buti called him.

7–9, 15: "Accursed wolf" pairs Plutus with the "ancient she-wolf" of *Purg.* 20.10–15, usually identified with avarice, as well as with the she-wolf of *Inf.* 1.49–51; see also *Par.* 9.132, 27.55.

11–12: Triggered by Plutus's call to Satan, Virgil's reference to the Archangel Michael's defeat of Satan's rebellion in heaven (Apoc. 12:7–9) is one of the instances where it is convenient for his knowledge not to be limited by his status as an ancient pagan.

22–24: The salient feature of the fourth circle will be the complex choreography of the sinners' punishment, of which the pilgrim in his descent has a panoramic view. The Tyrhennian Sea meets the Ionian Sea in the Strait of Messina, between Sicily and Calabria, generating strong tidal currents that were supposed to create the fabled whirlpool Charybdis. Dante imagines the waves crashing against each other as the whirlpool produces a chaotic circular motion. He compares this to the country dance that he ironically imagines the sinners to be performing – the *ridda*, a round dance for many people accompanied by song, in which the dancers changed direction at every stanza. See *ED* 4.920.

22–23: The Strait of Messina was one of the dangers Aeneas had to face, featuring on one side the whirlpool Charybdis and on the other the sea monster Scylla in a cave surrounded by rocks. *Aen.* 3.420–32. Failing to steer between the two, ships would be, as Isidore of Seville said, "either swallowed up or dashed to pieces." *Etym.* 14.6.32. This proverbial dilemma furnishes an apt metaphor for Aristotle's paradigm of virtue as a mean between excess and defect, the master concept of the fourth circle. Gino Casagrande and Christopher Kleinhenz, however, believe Dante intends to limit the scope of the image to Charybdis, noting that it was used by the church fathers as a symbol of avarice. Casagrande 357–59.

27: See *Aen.* 6.616: "others roll a great stone."

38–39: *The tonsure.* A distinctive mark of a Christian religious was that the crown of his head was shaved, a symbol of clerical continence. See Gilson 34 (citing Peter Lombard).

40–45: The two groups are the misers and the spendthrifts, opposed here because they were guilty of opposite sins with respect to possessions. Dante's choreography illustrates Aristotle's definition of virtue as a mean between vices of excess and defect. *Eth.* 2.6 (1107a2–6); see *Conv.* 4.17.7. With respect to money, the virtue is liberality. The miser is excessive in acquiring money and defective in dispensing it, while the spendthrift is the contrary. *Eth.* 2.7 (1107b9–13).

The moral equivalence implied by Dante's symmetry, however, reasserted at *Purg.* 22.31–54, is questionable. Aristotle held that the spendthrift was guilty more of foolishness than of vice. *Eth.* 4.1 (1121a16–30); *In Eth.* ¶ 686–89. In later medieval literature and preaching, avarice was the most reviled of all the capital sins (*see* notes to *Inf.* 16.73–75, 17.34–75), while prodigality was not treated as a sin. Dante has designed the *contrapasso* with the misers in mind. The Ottimo commented that those who pile up treasure do so with great weariness and must then expend great pains to guard it. (He was paraphrasing *Rom. Rose* 5119ff.)

More generally, the Aristotelian construct was not really congruent with Christian morality, which considered virginity and fasting eminently virtuous. (But see *SCG* 3.136 "insensibility"; *Conv.* 4.17.4 "excessive abstinence.") Even Dante's use of the construct here sits uneasily with the Christian ideal of voluntary poverty (for which see *SCG* 3.134–35). (Perhaps recognizing the problem, Aquinas defined parallel sets of moral virtues. Those acquired by habit aim at the good perceived by human reason, while those infused by God aim at the good established by divine law. The mean for the latter virtues is calibrated differently. For example, according to the divine rule the mean in eating is not simply to maintain health but to chastise the body. *ST* 1–2.62–64.)

41: The mental vision of these sinners was never direct; that of the misers squinted to one side and that of the spendthrifts to the other.

38–39, 46–48: The only sinners mentioned on the left – which turns out to be the side of the misers – are priests, bishops, cardinals and popes. The fourth circle thus focuses not simply on avarice but specifically on the avarice of the church hierarchy.

56–57: At the Last Judgment the misers will rise from their graves reflexively clutching at vanished coins. The spendthrifts will rise with their hair cropped, apparently (as in *Purg.* 22.46) because their prodigality leaves them bare of everything.

67–72: Dante makes the pilgrim the straight man to set up Virgil's philosophical explanation of Fortune. The pilgrim holds the naïve view that Fortune is a miser who keeps the world's wealth for herself. Virgil will show that in fact she is the exemplar of liberality.

73–96: The popular image of Fortune turning her wheel of change, derived from Boethius's *Consolation of Philosophy*, haunted the imagination of the Middle Ages, where instability was the norm. Dante, however, alters the popular iconography by creating a cosmic myth of mutability consistent with Christian Aristotelianism. Medieval cosmology held that a series of angelic Intelligences guided the motion of the celestial spheres (see *Conv.* 2.4.2), and Dante makes Fortune the lowest of these Intelligences, guiding the splendors of the world around the earth's globe.

Like the other angels she carries out the divine plan, raising some peoples to greatness. See *Mon.* 2.9.

The project of reconciling the capricious goddess Fortuna with divine providence also came from Boethius, whom Dante here understood more deeply than did the popular culture of his time. From Book 2 of the *Consolation* popular culture derived the moral that the fickleness of Fortune should teach us the vanity of earthly goods. Dante moves beyond this to replace the emphasis on human misery in a world ruled by chance with a vision of a world in which apparently arbitrary natural forces are in fact agents of God's overall plan. Book 4 of the *Consolation* makes a similar leap, demonstrating that fortune is the agent of divine providence, all fortune being intended by God to reward or discipline good people or to punish or correct the bad. (In *Conv.* 4.11.6–12 Dante had expressed the more conventional view of fortune, to which he reverts in *Inf.* 15.93–96 and 30.13–15; see *Par.* 17.22–27.)

77–96: The sphere Fortune turns recalls the emblematic wheel of her popular image but is a far grander conception. The celestial spheres are unchanging. Below the sphere of the moon, by contrast, is the changeable mortal world; this is the sphere of Fortune. As an Intelligence, she is the mistress of mutability, guiding the splendors of the world as they pass around the stationary globe; but the image assimilates mutability to immutable providence.

87: The "other gods" are the other angels who govern the motion of the spheres.

88–90: Dante's mythopoeic image allows him to explain in terms of a natural law the sudden changes of fortune with which medieval literature is obsessed. As the Intelligence of the sphere of earthly splendors, Fortune is compelled to move with uniform swiftness.

91–93: Fortune is reviled by the poor, but they are the ones who should praise her, because, as Boethius says, good fortune chains minds with false goods, while bad fortune frees them by showing the fragility of earthly happiness. *Consol. Phil.* 2.8; see also *Rom. Rose* 4837–4974.

94–96: Boethius's Fortuna laughs at the groans she causes (*Consol. Phil.* 2.1); Dante's simply rejoices with the other angels in carrying out her celestial duties. Like all who share the beatific vision, she is insensible to pain, including the pain of pity. See *Inf.* 2.91–92.

95: The first-born creatures are the angels, Rilke's "dawn-lit crests of all creation."

97–99: Virgil urges speed on his charge, as the Sibyl does on Aeneas. *Aen.* 6.535–39.

100–08: The entire fifth circle consists of the marsh Styx, which surrounds the walled fortress that contains lower hell.

109–20: The wrathful belong among the incontinent of upper hell (see *Inf.* 11.70–90 and note) because in sinning they were overcome by strong passion. They are in the lowest part of upper hell because the acts they committed in passion partook of violence, deliberate acts of which constitute the sin punished in the next region, the first of lower hell. The difficult downward path the poets must negotiate to reach the fifth circle (103–08) indicates the increased gravity of this sin. The punishment of the wrathful according to the law *you become what you do* is scarcely allegorical; brawling is the natural expression of their vice. But the unmotivated viciousness of their conflict and the mud in which they brawl make the scene exemplary.

118–26: The souls say that in life they carried with them a sluggish smoke, which suggests a smoldering resentment that suits Daniello's view that the vice of these souls was a "slow anger." Aristotle and Aquinas distinguished among (1) *choleric* people who anger too easily, and (2) people whose anger endures too long, divided into (a) the *sullen*, who nurse their anger, and (b) the *morose*, who brood on vengeance. *ST* 2–2.158.5; see *Eth.* 4.5 (1126a13–28); *In Eth.* ¶¶ 809–11. Here the choleric souls brawl in the swamp, while the sullen and morose sulk underwater. Alternatively some critics identify these latter souls with the slothful. Some of the critics regard sloth as the opposite of wrath, paralleling the opposition between the misers and the spendthrifts (see Scott 191); others regard sloth as equivalent to sullenness (see *DE* 784–85).

Canto VIII

I must explain, to follow up, that long
    before we reached the foot of the high tower,
    our eyes had travelled to the top of it
because of two small fires we saw placed there,
    to which another flashed an answering signal,   5
    so distant that the eye could scarcely catch it.
And turning toward the sea of all sagacity,
    "What do these say," I asked, "and what response
    does the other fire make? and who has set them?"
"Over the muddy waters," he replied,   10
    "you can already glimpse what is awaited,
    unless the mist of the marsh conceals it from you."
No twang of bowstring ever drove a shaft
    to hurtle through the air as rapidly
    as a small skiff I saw came skimming toward us   15
across the water at that very moment,
    steered by a single oarsman, who was shouting
    from far off, "Now I've got you, wicked soul!"
"Phlegyas, Phlegyas," said my lord, "this time
    your shouting is for nothing; you will have us   20
    no longer than it takes to cross the bog."
And Phlegyas, as he held his anger in,
    looked like a man who hears a nasty trick
    has just been played on him and takes it hard.

My guide stepped down then into that light craft   25
    and made me enter after he was in;
    only with me aboard did it seem burdened.
As soon as we embarked, my guide and I,
    the boat took off; its ancient prow was plowing
    the water deeper than it did with others.   30
While we were navigating the dead channel,
    a mud-caked figure rose before me, saying,
    "And who are you, who come before your hour?"
I shot back: "Though I come, I am not staying.
    But who are you that have become so foul?"   35
    "You see," he said, "that I am one who weeps."
"Remain here with your weeping and your sorrow,
    accursed spirit," I replied, "for now
    in spite of all your filth I recognize you."
He reached out toward the boat then with both hands;   40
    my teacher, though, was ready and pushed him off,
    saying, "Get back there with the other dogs!"
And then he threw his arms around my neck
    and kissed my face and said, "Indignant soul,
    blessed be she who bore you in her womb!   45
That one in life was an overbearing man;
    not one good action graces his memory,
    at which his shade here is consumed with rage.
How many up there now who think themselves
    great kings will wallow here like hogs in slop,   50
    leaving behind them only scathing scorn."
"Master," I said, "I would be very glad
    to see him get a ducking in this soup
    before we've made our way across the lake."
And he replied, "Before the farther shore   55
    comes into view, you shall be satisfied,
    for such desires deserve gratification."
Indeed, a little afterwards I saw him
    treated so brutally by the muddy people
    I still praise God for it and give him thanks.   60

Everyone shouted, "Get Filippo Argenti!"
    and even that hot-tempered Florentine
    spirit attacked himself with his own teeth.
We left him there, and so I say no more
    about him. Now a wailing struck my ears,   65
    making me stare intently ahead of me.
"Son," my good master said, "the city known
    as Dis will presently draw near, with all
    its weighty citizens and defending force."
"Master," I said, "already I make out   70
    distinctly in the valley its minarets,
    as red as if they just had left the forge."
And he replied, "The everlasting fire
    that heats them from within makes them glow red,
    as you will notice in this lower hell."   75
At last we glided into the deep entrenchments
    surrounding the disconsolate capital;
    the walls appeared to me to be of iron.
After we first had come in a wide curve,
    we reached a place at which the boatman cried   80
    loudly, "Get out! The entryway is here."
I saw above the gates a countless number
    of those who rained from heaven. "Who is this,"
    they angrily protested, "who untouched
by death invades the kingdom of the dead?"   85
    Hearing that, my wise teacher made a sign
    that he desired to speak with them in private.
Damping their furious rage somewhat, they said,
    "Come by yourself, and let him go away
    that rashly has intruded on this realm.   90
Let him return alone along his reckless
    road, if he dare; for you will sojourn here,
    who guided him across so dark a land."
Imagine, reader, whether I became
    disheartened at the sound of those accursed   95
    words, for I thought I never should return here.

"O my dear guide, who time and time again
      have kept me safe and rescued me from grave
      dangers that have confronted me, do not
abandon me," I said, "to my destruction;   100
      and if further progress is prohibited,
      let us retrace our steps at once together."
But that lord who had led me there replied,
      "Master your fear, for none can block our passage,
      such is the power of him who granted it.   105
Wait for me here and strengthen your exhausted
      spirit by feeding it with a firm hope,
      for I will not leave you in the underworld."
And so my gentle father goes away,
      abandoning me there to stand uncertain   110
      while Yes and No do battle in my brain.
I could not hear what he proposed to them,
      but when he'd been with them for only a moment
      all of them raced each other back inside.
Those enemies of ours clapped the gates shut   115
      in the face of my master, who remained outside;
      and he turned back to me with halting steps.
He kept his eyes on the ground, his brow was shorn
      of all assurance, and he muttered, sighing,
      "Such as these keep me from the sorrowful houses!"   120
To me he said, "Do not let my distress
      leave you dismayed, for I will win this struggle,
      however they bustle in there to keep us out.
There is nothing new in this effrontery,
      for they displayed it once at a less hidden   125
      gate, one that still remains without a lock.
Above that gate you saw the fatal writing;
      this side of it there now descends the slope,
      passing without a guide through all the circles,
one through whose power the city will be opened."   130

Notes

1–2: This is the only time in the *Inferno* when the narrative backtracks to fill in facts omitted earlier, an omission that allowed Dante to provide a surprise ending for the previous canto.

3–6: An aura of ominous mystery surrounds the first feature of hell that resembles a human structure, an intimation that we are approaching hell's fortified center.

7–12: The dialogue reveals obliquely that unseen watchers in the tower have set the two fires, apparently signaling the arrival of the two poets. An answering signal confirms that the intruders will be attended to. Signal fires atop towers were common in Dante's Italy. See note to *Inf.* 22.7–8.

17–21: Phlegyas is the guardian of the fifth circle, the marsh Styx. He was a king who, enraged at Apollo's seduction of his daughter, set fire to the god's temple at Delphi and was thrust down to Tartarus. See *Aen.* 6.618–20. Here Virgil implies that Phlegyas expected to guard the poets forever, suggesting that his role is to ferry the wrathful to their places in the Styx. Benvenuto thought his function was to ferry souls to Dis. In either case the earlier explanation that Minos flings the soul where he judges it belongs (*Inf.* 5.15) is disregarded when it suits the narrative. The original scheme reappears in *Inf.* 13.96–99, 24.122, 30.95; but at other times characters in hell will assume the poets are walking to their assigned places. *Inf.* 12.61–62; 28.43–45; 33.110–11.

22–24: The vivid description of Phlegyas's irascible nature suggests that a mythological character originally human (like Minos) has evolved into the demon of wrath.

27–30: This detail emphasizing the pilgrim's substantial body is imitated from the description of Aeneas's crossing in Charon's boat. *Aen.* 6.413–14.

33–39: This verbal duel, the pattern of which includes repetition of the antagonist's key phrases, resembles the *tenzone*, in which poets (including Dante) exchanged insult poems. See note to *Inf.* 30.106–29.

33: Buti thought the sinner was implying that the pilgrim had been thrust down to the Styx before his death (see *Inf.* 20.31–36), meaning that he shared the sinner's vice of wrath in a more egregious form.

39: The pilgrim recognizes the sinner as the Florentine Filippo Argenti, who appears in Boccaccio as a tall muscular man who loses his temper on the slightest pretext. *Decam.* 9.8. The early commentators said that Filippo was a personal enemy of Dante's.

43–45: The pilgrim's harsh words might suggest that he was in fact one of the irascible, but Virgil's response signals that the apparent tit-for-tat has been a demonstration of righteous indignation on the pilgrim's part. Many readers have not been convinced. If Filippo was not a personal enemy of Dante's, the assertion of the early commentators to that effect shows that they felt such an explanation was necessary (Bosco/Reggio).

45: Dante goes so far as to compare the pilgrim implicitly to Jesus by having Virgil echo Luke 11:27.

46–51: Virgil may not be giving specific information about Filippo, but simply moralizing on him as an *exemplum* for those who still share his vice. But see note to *Inf.* 10.32.

62–63: Biting oneself is the most extreme manifestation of a mind overthrown by rage. See *Inf.* 12.14–15.

67–69: *The City of Dis.* In this canto and the next, the citadel of hell is treated elaborately as a medieval city-state. Dante is likely thinking of Ovid, who describes the capital of "black Dis" set in the marsh of Styx, where shades throng the forum, the palace and the workshops. *Metam.* 4.434–45. The citizens of this capital are the sinners, weighted by the graver sins that drag them further toward the bottom. See *Inf.* 6.86 and note. The city's garrison is made up of the devils who will defend the gate against the poets.

67–68: Dis is the alternative name of Pluto, and is used in the *Aeneid* to characterize the underworld. *Aen.* 6.127, 269.

70–75: This is the first appearance in hell of fire, which Dante associates with the deliberate sins punished in lower hell.

71: "Minarets." The pilgrim says *meschite*, "mosques," but Buti understood him to be referring to the mosques' minarets: "towers in the style of campaniles that the priests climb to call the people to worship." These would have been the highest points of the skyline. To the medieval imagination, it was fitting that the monuments of the devil's city should be what were considered places of false worship. The mosque image is especially apt here because the first circle within the walls is that of the heretics, among whom the Middle Ages classed Muslims. See note to *Inf.* 28.22–27.

76–77: The inner reaches of the marsh are treated as a defensive moat around Satan's walled city.

78: Dante's City of Dis is based partly on Tartarus, the lowest dungeon of Hades in the *Aeneid*, a fortress circled by a triple wall and a moat of flame, fronted by a high gate with adamantine pillars and a tower of iron, guarded by an unsleeping Fury. *Aen.* 6.548–56. Like the walls of Dante's City of Dis, those of Tartarus enclose a pit. *Aen.* 6.577–79.

82–85: Devils in the form imagined by Christian tradition appear here for the first time. The mythological demons seen until now were compatible with the high poetic style that Dante called "tragic." By contrast, the devils of popular culture, though they may be terrifying, are suited to the lower "comic" style; and their indignation is expressed in a lively and forceful idiom. Not coincidentally, Virgil is for the first time out of his element here.

83: Dante may be thinking of Luke 10:18, where Satan falls from heaven like lightning; the devolution of the image from lightning to rain suits the multitude of minor devils.

94–96: This is the first of Dante's addresses to the reader, which often put us inside the pilgrim's skin at a moment of maximum tension in the narrative.

112–16: The precipitate behavior of the devils is comic in its rudeness. In the medieval drama, devils were frightening but also comic figures. See notes to *Inf.* 21. One of the plays in a cycle of biblical dramas was devoted to the harrowing of hell. There the devils attempt to bar the main gate of hell against Jesus in a parody of an army defending a castle in medieval warfare. See, *e.g.*, "The Harrowing of Hell," Play 37 of the York Corpus Christi Plays.

117–20: Virgil is surprised when the devils are not pacified by what must have been his announcement of his divine warrant. He underestimates the irrational power of Satan's followers to resist divine commands even though it is likely to increase their pain. See *Inf.* 9.94–96.

Virgil's failure to gain entry parallels the inability of the Sibyl to lead Aeneas through Tartarus, after which she simply describes the sins punished there. *Aen.* 6.562ff. The *Aeneid* can afford that because the purpose of Aeneas's journey is fulfilled in the Elysian Fields. By contrast, Dante cannot abort the infernal trek here because the pilgrim must experience every degree of sin and its condign punishment.

121–30: Despite his inability to effect an entry, Virgil remains a seer. He speaks again with confidence, relating his vision of the divine assistance even now hastening to their aid.

125–27: Virgil compares the devils' defense of their territory now with their ancient defiance of Jesus at the harrowing of hell, narrated in the *Gospel of Nicodemus*. See *Inf.* 4.46–63, 12.37–39 and notes. In the prototype for the medieval dramas, the demons secure the brass gates of hell with iron bars; but the bars and gates are smashed and Jesus enters. Elliott 188.

The gates of the City of Dis remain closed because Christ did not come down this far; he descended only to the first circle, from which he led off the righteous. *Inf.* 4.52–61. With the main gate of hell smashed, the devils of popular culture have barricaded themselves behind the gate of lower hell, consistent with their appearing only now.

Canto IX

The pallor cowardice sent forth upon
    my cheeks on seeing my leader turn around
    made his new color hastily retreat.
He stood attentive in a listening posture,
    being unable to project his sight   5
    a great way through the dark air thick with fog.
"Yet we must win this fight," I heard him say,
    "or else . . . but such a one appeared . . . how long
    it seems to take for someone to arrive!"
I saw quite plainly how he'd covered up   10
    what he began to say with what came after,
    words very different from the first in sense;
but nonetheless his words aroused my fears,
    for I extracted from the chopped-off phrase
    a meaning worse, perhaps, than it contained.   15
"Does any among those of the first level,
    whose only punishment is hope cut off,
    ever descend this deep in the dismal crater?"
I posed this question and he answered me:
    "It is exceptional for any of us   20
    to make the journey I am bound upon,
but true it is I once before was down here.
    I had been summoned by the cruel Erichtho,
    who called back shades to the bodies they had left.

My flesh had not been bare of me for long 25
    when she compelled me to pass inside this wall
    and bring a spirit from the circle of Judas.
That is the deepest and the darkest place,
    the farthest from the all-enclosing heaven:
    well do I know the way, so rest assured. 30
This marsh exhaling such a powerful stench
    surrounds on every side the sorrowful city,
    which now we cannot enter unopposed."
What more he said I cannot call to mind,
    for now my eyes had drawn me up entirely 35
    to the high tower's glowing battlements
where instantaneously there had arisen
    three hell-born Furies spattered with dark gore.
    Their forms and attitudes were those of women,
and bright green water-snakes engirdled them; 40
    for hair they had small serpents and horned vipers
    that twisted horribly about their brows.
And he, who recognized at once the handmaids
    that serve the queen of endless lamentation,
    said to me, "Look upon the fierce Erinyes: 45
that is Megaera on the left, Allecto
    is wailing on the right, Tisiphone
    stands in the center." With that, he fell silent.
All of them tore their breasts with their own nails,
    struck themselves with their palms and screamed so loudly 50
    I shrank against the poet out of fear.
"Bring out Medusa – turn him into stone!"
    they all cried, glaring down. "We were too lenient,
    not making Theseus pay for his assault!"
"Turn your back now, and keep your eyes shut tight, 55
    for if they show the Gorgon and you only
    glimpse it, you never would return above."
My teacher gave this warning and himself
    turned me around and, not being satisfied
    with my hands only, with his own as well 60

covered my eyes. You of sound understanding,
  reflect upon the teaching that lies hidden
  beneath the veil of these mysterious verses.
Just then across the swirling muddy waters
  there came a terrifying crash of sound   65
  that caused the shore to shudder on both sides.
It sounded like the roaring of a gale
  grown violent from the clash of heated air streams
  that strikes the forest and with unchecked force
cracks branches, beats them down and sweeps them off;   70
  driving the dust, it passes proudly onward,
  putting the shepherds and animals to flight.
He freed my eyes and said, "Now square your line
  of vision out across the ancient scum
  in the direction where the fumes are sharpest."   75
Frogs will all vanish underneath the water
  just as their enemy the snake appears,
  until they huddle on the mud at the bottom;
I saw a countless number of damned souls
  scatter like that before the approach of one   80
  who in his crossing crossed the Styx dry-soled.
He stroked his left hand frequently before him
  to brush away the thick air from his face,
  and only this nuisance seemed to weary him.
I saw at once that he was sent from heaven   85
  and turned to face my teacher, who made a sign
  that I should hold my peace and bow to him.
How full I thought he looked of indignation!
  He reached the gates and with a little rod
  opened them, and they offered no resistance.   90
"Outcasts of heaven, race despised," he said,
  taking his stand upon the dreadful threshold,
  "where do you find the effrontery you cherish?
Why do you still kick back against the will
  whose purposes can never be aborted   95
  and which has many times increased your pain?

What is the use of butting against the fates?
    Your Cerberus, if you recall, still bears
    his chin and throat rubbed raw for doing that."
Then he turned back along the muddy way   100
    without a word for us; he had the look
    of someone pressed and gnawed at by concerns
other than those of anyone around him;
    and as for us, we walked on toward the city,
    feeling secure now after the holy words.   105
We made our entrance unopposed by any;
    and I, being curious to take a look
    at what might be contained in such a stronghold,
glanced all around as soon as I was in.
    On either hand I see a spacious plain   110
    filled with lamenting and atrocious torment.
At Arles, near where the Rhone flows into marshlands,
    also at Pola, by the Gulf of Carnaro,
    which bathes the border of Italy it encloses,
tombs make the ground uneven everywhere;   115
    they did the same on all sides here, except
    that their condition here was far more bitter,
for flames were scattered all among these tombs
    and made them glow throughout with a red heat
    as great as any craft demands of iron.   120
All of their lids were raised, and from within
    issued excruciating cries of pain,
    clearly produced by wretches under torment.
"Master," I asked him, "who are all the people
    confined within those chests who make themselves 125
    known by their moans of suffering?" And he answered,
"Heresiarchs of every sect lie here,
    together with their followers; and these tombs
    are far more crowded than you might imagine.
Like is ensepulchered with like, and some   130
    monuments burn with greater heat than others."
    And then, when he had turned to the right, we passed
between the torments and the towering ramparts.

Notes

3: Virgil's "new color" is either pallor caused by worry or, as the Ottimo thought, the dull flush of humiliation at his mistreatment by the devils.

7–9: Virgil attempts to reassure himself, but his doubt breaks out in his exclamation of impatience for the messenger who will not only resolve the present difficulty but also confirm the poets' divine mission.

10–15: The device of a soliloquy being overheard and triggering emotional conflict in the hearer is used to fine dramatic effect.

16–30: Dante sometimes accents moments of high tension with humor at his own expense. See notes to *Inf.* 17.85–93, 21.25–30. Here the pilgrim tries naively to be circumspect in questioning Virgil's reliability as a guide; but his motive is as clear to Virgil as it is to us.

22–24: Dante found the witch Erichtho in Lucan; she told fortunes by finding a fresh corpse and calling its spirit back for questioning. The spirit would have the knowledge of the future possessed by the dead, but would not yet have passed too far beyond the world for communication. *Phars.* 6.619–23. Much of Lucan's episode is graphically disgusting and may have granted Dante, as Virgil did not, classical authorization for loathsome imagery in the *Inferno*.

27–29: The ninth circle lies at the bottom of the pit, where Judas is punished. Virgil has thus seen all of hell.

29: The ninth heaven, the *Primum Mobile*, is the outer limit of the physical universe and the source of cosmic motion. *See Conv.* 2.3, 2.14.

38–42: The Furies are infernal goddesses who induce madness in those whom the gods wish to destroy. Virgil's Tisiphone guards the closed gates of lower hell, but she does not stand on the tower; she sits in the doorway, as do Ovid's Furies. *Aen.* 6.552–56, 6.574–75; *Metam.* 4.453–54.

38: The classical Furies are wrapped in bloody robes. *Aen.* 6.555; *Metam.* 4.482.

40: Dante's Furies are engirdled with "hydras," water snakes that Albertus Magnus assigned to the Nile. *De Animal.* 25.2.30. Statius and Virgil associated them with the Furies. *Theb.* 1.113; *Aen.* 7.447.

41: A hundred horned vipers stand up on the head of Statius's Tisiphone. *Theb.* 1.103–04. The Furies of Ovid and Virgil also have snakes for hair, or in their hair. *Aen.* 7.450; *Metam.* 4.454.

43–45: "Erinyes" is a Greek name for the Furies. The "queen of endless lamentation" is Proserpina, wife of Pluto and queen of hell, or the more shadowy Hecate. Both were said to be triple in form, representing the infernal aspect of Luna and Diana. See *Aen.* 4.511; *Phars.* 6.700n.; *Etym.* 8.11.57.

46–48: *Megaera, Allecto, Tisiphone.* Because they relentlessly pursued those guilty of crimes, the Erinyes can be understood as agents of remorse. This was the interpretation of Buti, who commented that "the poets understood that these are they who trouble the minds of sinners who sin through malice." This makes the Furies the appropriate mythological demons to preside over the entrance to lower hell as a whole; the sins of malice breed remorse. *Inf.* 11.52.

52–53: To look upon Medusa's face turned men and beasts to stone. After the hero Perseus cut off her head, he kept it in a bag and it retained its power. See *Metam.* 4.655–62.

54: Theseus agreed to help his friend Pirithoüs abduct Proserpina from hell. See *Aen.* 6.393–97. In *Aen.* 6.617–18 he is condemned to sit in hell forever, but in medieval glosses the story is told with variations in which Theseus escapes. *ED* 5.596.

55–63: Dante's admonition to look beneath the surface of his verses is a formulation usually associated with the allegory of the poets (though seen also in Apoc. 13:18); but he is more likely thinking of a parallel to a moral reading of events in scripture. The mysterious verses in question are surely the preceding lines, most often understood as the threat posed by Medusa. Some critics have associated the threatened petrification with obdurate resistance to the truth – willful blindness – which was the medieval characterization of heresy, the sin punished in the upcoming circle. Others have associated it with the deadening habits of the hardened sinner, which would be appropriate to lower hell as a whole. The Furies, however, are calling for Medusa to complete their work. If they are spirits of remorse, the completion of their work would be despair; and it would be natural for the Gorgon, who hardens men forever, to be the catalyst of the final despair that paralyzes the soul into its sinful posture for eternity. This was the majority view of the 14th century commentators. Aquinas regarded despair as the most dangerous of sins. *ST* 2–2.20.3.

Robert Hollander argues that the mysterious verses are those describing Virgil's covering of the pilgrim's eyes, suggesting that "stoic restraint is not enough to keep a sinner safe from dangerous temptation." Hollander 2013. Less credibly, commentators beginning with Pietro Alighieri have opined that the mysterious verses are those in the upcoming passage about the celestial messenger. See Iannucci 123–33.

56: "[T]he Gorgon (*'l Gorgòn*)": The unusual use of a masculine article with "Gorgon" probably indicates that Dante is referring to Medusa's severed head (see Bosco/Reggio).

64–72: Auerbach used the storm simile to show that Dante was the first vernacular poet to revive the ancient concept of the sublime. Auerbach 1958, 228–33. The simile breathes the high Virgilian air, but the personification of the wind's power is Dante's own and has biblical antecedents appropriate to the messenger of omnipotence. A great wind manifests the divine presence in both the Old and New Testaments. Ezech. 1:4; Acts 2:2.

67–68: Dante characteristically supplies a scientific explanation for the wind's violence. In Aristotle's meteorology, wind is a dry exhalation drawn up from the earth by the sun. *Meteorol.* 2.4 (360a5–16). These exhalations ordinarily flow in definite directions, like rivers (*id.* 360a28–34), and turbulence results from the clash of winds from different quarters, as in *Inf.* 5.29–31. (We would say that air flows across temperature and pressure gradients, and the steeper the gradient the stronger the flow.)

73–74: Dante is again being scientifically precise: he says "direct your optic nerve," meaning an object must arrive in a straight line at the center of the pupil to be seen distinctly and stamp the imaginative faculty, because the cavity along which the visible spirits flow is oriented that way. See *Conv.* 2.9.4–5.

76–80: The Virgilian simile is immediately followed by an equally vivid one in the low style suited to the subject. The juxtaposition of high and low styles is characteristic of the *Inferno* and constitutes a prime distinction between medieval and ancient literary language. See Auerbach 1958 *passim.*

80–99: Pietro and Benvenuto thought that the one sent from heaven was Mercury, the messenger of the gods. Few modern critics believe that Dante's syncretism goes so far; most agree with Buti and the Ottimo that the messenger is an angel. But Pietro's and Benvenuto's perceptions were valid: the messenger is an angel of classicized form who looks a good deal like Mercury.

Milton compares his angel Raphael to Mercury and gives him winged feet (*Paradise Lost* 5.283–85), but Dante goes further. The messenger's wand derives from Mercury's caduceus and his use of it to open the gate is probably imitated from Ovid, where Mercury opens a door with the caduceus (Hollander 2000). The messenger's brushing away the thick air recalls Statius's Mercury returning from the underworld, burdened by its thick air and foul exhalations. *Theb.* 2.2–5. Above all, the messenger refers to Hercules's abduction of Cerberus (see note to 98–99) as though it were an actual event. Buti had trouble explaining how an angel could say this. It requires a reader accustomed to thinking typologically and used to the idea that Hercules's abduction of Cerberus was a prefiguration of Christ's harrowing of hell, the event to which the angel is referring in veiled terms.

91–99: Despite the sublime fanfare of the storm, the angel uses plain speech suited to the stern voice of heaven condemning sin. *Recalcitrate* (kick against 94) recalls the voice of Jesus to St. Paul when he has been struck from his horse: "It hurts you to kick against the goad (*Durum est tibi contra stimulum calcitrare*)," Acts 9:5.

98–99: The last of Hercules's twelve labors was to bring the hell-hound Cerberus to the upper world. He dragged the dog by a chain around its neck. See *Aen.* 6.395–96.

106: The entire threatening phantasmagoria of devils and Furies has vanished like a stage illusion, as demons were thought to do before an exorcist.

112–14: Arles is situated on the Rhone near the marshy area known as the Camargue. It has a Roman cemetery known as Les Alyscamps (The Elysian Fields). Pola, near the southern tip of the Istrian peninsula and divided from the mainland by the Gulf of Carnaro, was also known for Roman ruins.

118–21: Virgil will explain that the sinners entombed here are the heretics. The punishment of fire does not represent this sin symbolically, but is merely the eternal prolongation of the burning at the stake to which heretics were condemned by law. The sentence prescribed in the *Liber Augustalis* of Frederick II is typical: "Committed to the judgment of the flames, they should be burned alive in the sight of the people." Peters 208.

120: The tombs are Roman stone sarcophagi with prism-shaped lids, as can still be seen at Les Alyscamps. The lids are probably propped upright against the sarcophagi, as shown in some depictions of the Resurrection (*e.g.*, *Petites Heures de Jean de Berry*). This would explain the position of the engraved lid the pilgrim deciphers at *Inf.* 11.6–9.

128–29: Aquinas held that the sin of heresy consists not in doctrinal error itself, but in the obdurate maintenance of such error in the face of the revealed truth preached by the Church. *ST* 2–2.11.1, 2. The position of the heretics in the first circle of lower hell corresponds to that of the blameless unbelievers in the first circle of upper hell. When Virgil explains the scheme of hell in *Inf.* 11, he will not mention either limbo or the circle of the heretics, because he is explaining hell in terms of Aristotle's categories of wrong actions. Unbelievers and heretics are guilty of wrong beliefs. (Heresy is nonetheless an exercise of the will. Some critics suggest it is a sin of the intellect rather than the will. See *DE* 869, citing Freccero. But in Aquinas's terms, although unbelief is in the intellect as its subject, like all sin it is in the will as its moving principle. *ST* 2–2.10.2.)

129: *I.e.*, many heretics do not openly avow their unorthodox beliefs. For Bernard of Clairvaux, heretics were crafty and skilled at dissimulation (Peters 85–101); and Bernard Gui's manual for inquisitors is full of tips for ferreting out crypto-heretics. Kirshner and Morrison 304–12.

Canto X

On a secluded path now, tucked away
    between the torments and the city wall,
    my master walks and I come on behind.
"Summit of virtue," I began, "who steer me
    around the godless circles as you please,   5
    speak to me now and satisfy my wishes:
would it be possible to see the people
    lying within the tombs? for all the lids
    are raised and there is no one standing guard."
"All will be shut," he answered, "on the day   10
    when they return here from Jehoshaphat,
    bringing the bodies they have left above.
All of this section forms the cemetery
    of Epicurus and his followers,
    whose creed is that the soul dies with the body.   15
And so the question that you put will soon
    be satisfied in here, as will the other
    desire of which you do not speak to me."
"Best guide," I said, "I do not keep my heart
    hidden from you except by saying little,   20
    which you've just now and earlier encouraged."
"O Tuscan who walk living through the city
    of fire with dignified, respectful words,
    be pleased to linger in this place a while.

The accent of your speech without a doubt 25
  shows you a native of the noble city
  toward which my measures were perhaps too harsh."
This sound came swelling unexpectedly
  out of a sepulcher and made me shrink
  in fear a little closer to my leader. 30
And he: "What are you doing? Turn around
  and look where Farinata has arisen:
  from the waist up you'll make him out in full."
Already I had locked my gaze on his;
  he drew himself erect – chest out, brow lifted 35
  as though he looked on hell with great disdain.
My leader then, with quick encouraging hands,
  pushed me between the tombs in his direction,
  telling me: "Let your words be chosen well."
When I was standing at the foot of his tomb, 40
  he looked at me a while, then with a touch
  of scorn, "Who were your forebears?" he inquired.
And I, for my part eager to comply,
  held nothing back from him but opened all;
  and hearing this, he arched his brows a little, 45
then said, "They were implacable enemies
  to me and to my house and to my party,
  so that not once, but twice, I scattered them."
"They may have been chased out, but they returned
  both times," I answered him, "from every quarter; 50
  that is a skill that yours have not yet learned."
Then in the lidless aperture beside him
  another shade rose up, as far as the chin:
  I think he'd gotten up upon his knees.
He darted looks around me, as if trying 55
  to see if there were someone else with me;
  and when the doubtful hope had flickered out
he said in tears, "If you can walk through this
  blind prison on the strength of a great talent,
  where is my son? and why is he not with you?" 60

"I do not come," I answered, "on my own;
    he that awaits me there leads me this way
    to one perhaps your Guido held in scorn."
His words and the manner of his punishment
    had before this informed me who he was,   65
    the reason my response was so complete.
He stood up suddenly and shouted: "What?
    You said 'he held'? Is he not still alive?
    Does the sweet light no longer strike his eyes?"
Perceiving that I hesitated somewhat   70
    before I answered him, he suddenly
    keeled over backwards and was seen no more.
But that great-hearted one, at whose request
    I first had stopped there, never changed expression
    nor turned his head, nor bent his rigid posture;   75
and taking up our earlier conversation,
    he said, "If they have not yet learned that skill,
    that causes me more torment than this bed.
But you will learn, before the face of her
    that reigns here is relighted fifty times,   80
    how painful that apprenticeship can be.
So may you make it back to the sweet world,
    tell me, why do the people cruelly close
    their hearts against my family in every edict?"
And I: "The havoc and the terrible carnage   85
    that stained the waters of the Arbia red
    cause such prayers to be offered in our temple."
He sighed and shook his head and then he said,
    "There I was not alone, nor certainly
    would I have moved without cause with the others.   90
I was alone, however, when the others
    were all for letting Florence be destroyed –
    the one man to defend her openly."
"Now may your progeny be at peace one day,
    unravel for me," I entreated him,   95
    "the tangle that has snarled my thinking here.

It seems you have prevision, if I gather
    rightly, of things that time is bringing forward,
    but with the present it is otherwise."
"Like one afflicted with farsightedness,   100
    we see the things remote from us," he answered;
    "so far the highest lord yet lends us light.
When things draw near or come to be, our minds
    are useless; and if no one brings us news
    we have no knowledge of conditions on earth.   105
Because of this, as you can understand,
    our knowledge will be totally extinguished
    the moment that the door of the future shuts."
Struck all at once then by my negligence,
    "Please make it clear," I said, "to the one who fell,   110
    his son is numbered yet among the living;
if I was tongue-tied in response just now,
    tell him I was already lost in thought
    about the uncertainty you have resolved."
And now I heard my master calling me back;   115
    I pressed the spirit therefore to describe
    briefly for me the others there with him.
He told me: "Here I lie with a great number:
    Frederick the Second is within and also
    the Cardinal; of the rest I do not speak."   120
With that he sank from sight; I turned my steps
    back to the ancient poet, brooding upon
    the words that seemed to presage ill for me.
He started off and as we walked along,
    "Why do you look so troubled?" he inquired;   125
    and I responded to his question fully.
"Store in your memory all that you have heard
    against yourself," the sage exhorted me.
    "And now attend here," and he raised his finger:
"when you confront the tender shining gaze   130
    of her whose sparkling eyes see everything,
    from her you will learn the journey of your life."

And then he turned his steps again to the left:
> leaving the wall, we headed toward the center
> along a path that ended at a gorge   135
from which a sickening stench rose up to there.

Notes

4–5: "As you please": Contrary to their custom, at *Inf.* 9.132 Virgil began leading the pilgrim to the right, counterclockwise around the sixth circle (perhaps indicating the unusual nature of the heretics' sin). He will resume their usual direction at line 133.

8–12: At the end of time, the bodies of all humans will be resurrected to be reunited with their souls for the Last Judgment and thereafter for their joint reward or punishment. See *Inf.* 6.106–11 and note. The raised tomb-lids parody the traditional iconography of Christ's resurrection, because these sarcophagi stand open like jaws awaiting their prey on judgment day.

11: In Joel 3:2 the valley of Jehoshaphat is the site of the Lord's judgment on the nations that oppressed Israel, identified by Christians with the Last Judgment.

13–15: Epicurus (342–270 BC) was a materialist who taught that the goal of life was avoiding pain. *Conv.* 4.6.11–12. Dante follows tradition in making him the master of those who hold that the soul perishes with the body. See *Etym.* 8.6.15. Accordingly, the *contrapasso* here is that the soul lies in the tomb where the body will join it for eternity.

Although Dante mentions only this pre-Christian philosophy as a heresy, he appears to use the label to refer to contemporary religious skeptics, given that denial of immortality effectively rejects the whole Christian program. This would have included the radical Aristotelians, influenced by Averroes, who questioned belief in personal immortality. See note to 64–65.

In any case, Dante ignores the dissident Christian movements of the Middle Ages. By 1300 the church had experienced a first great wave of dissidence, thrown up by a groundswell of popular piety that rejected the worldly and bureaucratic church and espoused the cause of apostolic poverty. *Inf.* 19 suggests the extent to which Dante was sympathetic to some of these currents of thought.

22–27: The speaker is Farinata degli Uberti, the head of the Ghibelline party in Florence in the generation before Dante's. Born into one of the noblest and richest of Florentine families, Farinata rose to leadership in the 1230s. He defeated and exiled the Florentine Guelfs in 1248 with the help of Frederick II and was in turn exiled with his party ten years later.

In 1260 Farinata was one of the captains of the Ghibelline army that crushingly defeated a larger Florentine force at Montaperti, resulting in another exile of the

Guelfs. The other Ghibelline commanders were in favor of razing Florence, but Farinata opposed the plan and succeeded in saving the city. He died in 1264; in the same year the Ghibellines were again exiled from Florence, and within a few years the power of the party was broken forever. In 1283 Farinata and his wife were declared heretics and their bodies were exhumed as unfit to lie in consecrated ground. The motivation for this was likely political, for the church had tarred the Ghibellines with the brush of heresy. See *DE* 440.

26–27: Farinata expresses a faint and dignified regret for his part in the factional violence that tore apart his beloved Florence, the homeland with which he dealt harshly at Montaperti.

32: Here and in *Inf.* 16 Virgil's function as a knowledgeable guide makes it convenient for him to know by sight and reputation the eminent Florentines of the generation before Dante's.

35–36: By underlining the incongruity of Farinata's attitude in its present setting, line 36 establishes a certain ironic distance from the character, a note not sounded later in the similar description of Jason. *Inf.* 18.85.

41–44: The disdain comes naturally to a member of the old nobility addressing someone inferior in rank. But the motivation for the question is political: faced with a living Florentine, what Farinata most wants to know is whether the man comes from a family of his allies or his enemies. Animated by his own family pride, the pilgrim is eager to declare his allegiance to his clan. He knows that they were Farinata's enemies – that is why Dante emphasizes that he held nothing back.

49–51: The pilgrim cannot let Farinata's remark about his family pass, and the partisan struggle of Florence plays itself out again in hell.

52–60: The second spirit is Cavalcante di Cavalcanti, head of a wealthy magnate family of Florence. A leading Guelf, he was driven into exile by the Ghibelline victories in 1248 and 1260, returned to Florence with the Guelfs after 1266, and in 1267 arranged for his son Guido to marry Farinata's daughter in an attempt to reconcile the factions. He died before 1280. Cavalacante's sudden appearance interrupts the dialogue of the pilgrim and Farinata at its highest pitch, repeating with more force the motif initiated by Farinata's interruption of the pilgrim and Virgil.

58–72: The pathos Cavalcante evokes as a doting father is a deliberate effect, because his questions are modeled on Andromache's questions to Aeneas about Hector. *Aen.* 3.310–12. In contrast to the statuesque pathos of the *Aeneid*, however, Dante's scene has a satirical flavor. Cavalcante's jack-in-the-box movements are grotesque and his obsession with his son is rendered with a touch of caricature.

60: Guido Cavalcanti (c. 1255–1300), some ten years older than Dante, was his good friend and the leading contemporary poet next to Dante himself. When the Guelfs divided into Black and White factions, Guido became an ardent White partisan, attacking Corso Donati, the Black leader. Compagni 1.20. Guido was as noted for his philosophical studies as for his poetry and Boccaccio reports the popular belief that he was trying to prove there is no God. *Decam.* 6.9.

61: *I.e.,* I have not come like Orpheus to appease the dark gods with the power of my art. I am being drawn this way to my salvation by a force outside of myself.

63: Pietro Alighieri and Buti thought that Guido held Virgil in scorn because he preferred philosophy to poetry. Critics today generally conclude that the pilgrim is expressing reservations about Guido's attitude toward Beatrice, who provides a more likely focus for estrangement between the friends than Virgil. As Barolini notes, the concept of love expressed in Guido's most famous poem, *Donna me prega* (*A lady bids me*) is the diametrical opposite of Dante's love for Beatrice. Barolini 1984, 144.

There may be evidence for such an estrangement in Guido's sonnet "I' vegno 'l giorno a te 'nfinite volte (*I come to you a thousand times a day*)," written to Dante after Beatrice's death and reprimanding him for the grief in which he is sunk. See Barolini/Lansing 114, 120, 250. Guido seeks to dispel a loathsome spirit haunting Dante and the sonnet can be read as expressing contempt for Dante's cult of Beatrice. Because she is the lodestone of Dante's poetic life and his spiritual life, such scorn would embrace his whole enterprise of transforming courtly love into the mind's journey to God.

64–65: The speaker's words claimed a relationship to the pilgrim through the speaker's son. The manner of his punishment was that of the Epicureans, and Boccaccio said that both Cavalcante and Guido were notorious Epicureans.

70–71: Boccaccio said that if an idea struck Dante, it was useless to question him because he would not answer until he had completed his train of thought. Smith 44.

73–78: Farinata's marmoreal self-possession reveals not only his indifference to Cavalcante's paternal grief but also his rigid self-control in the face of his own. Because he died in 1264 when the Ghibellines still controlled Florence, Farinata did not know until now about their subsequent defeat and the exile of his family.

75: "That great-hearted one (*quel altro magnanimo*)." The phrase contrasts the self-collected posture and measured speech of Farinata with the shrill questions and jerky movements of Cavalcante. See generally note to *Inf.* 4.112–20.

79–81: The pilgrim's dialogue with Farinata has been a thrust and parry on the subject of exile. Farinata's final retort strikes deep: the pilgrim's own nascent political career will also end in exile. The somber oracular shadings of Farinata's words, however, suggest that after contemplating the long exile of his descendants he speaks more in sorrow than in anger. And the two figures have more in common than the pilgrim knew. His taunt about Farinata's descendants was to return on Dante's own head when his sons were banished from Florence on pain of death on account of their father. See *DE* 373.

Dante's voyage in the afterlife takes place in the spring of 1300, just before the most active phase of his political career began. That June he began serving as one of the six Priors, the governing council of Florence. During his term of office the leaders of the Black and White factions were banished, including Guido Cavalcanti among the Whites. When his term ended, Dante continued to serve the commune and was absent on a mission in November 1301 when the Blacks staged a coup with the backing of the pope and the French. In January 1302 Dante, who had been identified with the Whites, appeared on a list of citizens fined in absentia and banished for two years. Later that year he was condemned in absentia to be burned alive. He never saw Florence again. *DE* 18–19.

79–80: She who reigns in hell is Proserpina, wife of Pluto, like Hecate identified with the infernal aspect of the moon. See note to *Inf.* 9.43–45. Her face will be relighted fifty times in fifty months, the late spring of 1304. That was the period when efforts to secure repatriation of the White exiles failed and Dante lost hope of returning to Florence.

82–84: In successive edicts of amnesty the Uberti were always expressly excluded.

87: *I.e.*, "cause such decrees to issue from our council."

88–93: When the Ghibelline leaders, after their victory at Montaperti, agreed to destroy Florence and reduce it to a village, Farinata stood up and said that "if there were no one but him, he would defend Florence with sword in hand so long as there was breath in his body." The leaders abandoned the plan. *Cron.* 7.81.

97–108: For the knowledge of the future shown by the souls in hell, see note to *Inf.* 6.60–61. We now learn that they cannot see present conditions on earth. See also *Inf.* 16.67–69, 27.25–28.

109–14: The apparently unrelated dialogue on the vision of the damned turns out to illuminate the previous scene. The pilgrim's puzzled hesitation at Cavalcante's ignorance of the present led to Cavalcante's despairing false conclusion.

110–11: Guido was not to remain long among the living. Banished during Dante's priorate in the summer of 1300, he died that August of malaria contracted in his place of exile. It is difficult not to see in the scene with Cavalcante a foreshadowing of Guido's death and perhaps Dante's uneasiness about him.

119: The Emperor Frederick II (1194–1250) was a brilliant polymath, known to contemporaries as *stupor mundi*, the wonder of the world. Dante admired Frederick (see *Conv.* 4.3.6; *VE* 1.12), but he places the emperor among the Epicureans because of his well-known skeptical views toward religion.

120: Ottaviano degli Ubaldini (c. 1210–73) used the high church office he obtained through his Ghibelline family's influence as the base for a political and military career. The early commentators credit him with saying "If there is a soul, I have lost mine a thousand times for the Ghibellines," which may have determined his place among the Epicureans.

132: In the event, Beatrice will delegate this task, which will be performed by Dante's ancestor Cacciaguida in *Par.* 17.

Canto XI

Arrived upon the brink of a steep descent
    formed by a circle of great broken boulders,
    we stood above a crowd in crueler torment;
and overpowered there by the revolting
    stench the deep cavity was sending up,   5
    we found ourselves retreating toward the lid
of a grand sarcophagus, on which I saw
    these words inscribed: "I hold Pope Anastasius,
    the one Photinus drew from the straight path."
"The start of our descent must be delayed   10
    until our sense becomes somewhat accustomed
    to this foul breath and then we will not mind it."
So said my teacher. "Find some substitute,"
    I answered, "so the time may not be lost."
    "As you will see," he said, "I've thought of that."   15
Then he began: "My son, within these boulders
    there are three smaller circles, one below
    the other, like the ones you leave behind.
Though all are filled with damned souls, listen now
    – so later the mere sight may be enough   20
    for you – to how and why each is confined.
Deliberate evil actions, which gain heaven's
    hatred, all aim at some kind of injustice,
    injuring others either by fraud or violence.

But fraud, because it is man's peculiar vice,   25
    offends God more; therefore the fraudulent
    are lower down and greater pain assails them.
The violent fill the whole of the first circle;
    but because violence acts upon three persons,
    three rings compose it and partition it.   30
One may do violence to oneself or God
    or other men, and either in their persons
    or property, as I will show you plainly.
On others violent death and painful wounds
    may be inflicted, and on their possessions   35
    unjust extortion, burning and laying waste;
so the first ring torments in different groups
    all murderers and those who wound in malice,
    together with the looters and the robbers.
One may lay violent hands upon himself   40
    and his possessions; therefore in the second
    ring of the circle are doomed to vain repentance
all who despoil themselves of the world you live in
    and those who dice away and dissipate
    their substance, weeping when they should be joyful.   45
One may do violence to the Deity
    by blasphemy and denial in one's heart
    and by despising nature and her powers;
accordingly, the smallest ring of the circle
    stamps with its seal both Sodom and Cahors   50
    and all who speak of God with heartfelt scorn.
One may use fraud, which always gnaws the conscience,
    against a person who has faith in him
    or one whose purse is empty of such trust.
The latter kind, of course, can only sever   55
    the bond of love that nature generates;
    and thus there nest within the second circle
hypocrites, flatterers and sorcerers,
    thieves, falsifiers and simoniacs,
    grafters and pimps and other filth like that.   60

The other kind of fraud ignores not only
    the love that nature breeds, but the additional
    relation that creates a special trust;
thus in the smallest circle of all, where Dis
    sits at the center of the universe,   65
    all traitors are eternally consumed."
"Master," I said, "your reasoning proceeds
    lucidly and completely analyzes
    these lower depths and those that they contain.
But tell me: those within the oozy marsh,   70
    those the wind drives, those beaten by the rain
    and those who come together with rough tongues,
why are they not, if God is angry with them,
    punished within the bounds of the red city?
    And if he is not, why are they treated so?"   75
"Why does your understanding go astray,
    far from its usual track," he said, "or else
    upon what distant place is your mind gazing?
Have you forgotten, then, the terms with which
    your *Ethics* thoroughly expounds the soul's   80
    three habits that oppose the will of heaven –
incontinence, mad brutishness and malice?
    And how the first of these, incontinence,
    offends God least and merits the least blame?
If you reflect upon that precept closely,   85
    remembering who those others are up there
    who undergo their punishment outside
the walls, it will become quite clear to you
    why they are separate from these wicked ones
    and why God's vengeance smites them with less wrath."   90
"O sun," I said, "that heal all clouded vision,
    you satisfy me so with your solutions
    that wondering pleases me no less than knowing.
Go back a little once again, to where
    you spoke of usury as an offense   95
    against God's goodness, and untie that knot."

"To a discerning mind, philosophy
  makes clear," he said, "in more than one connection,
  how nature takes its course from the divine
intelligence and its activity;   100
  and if you take a good look at your *Physics*,
  not many pages into it you will find
that man's activity takes after nature
  as best it can, as pupil after teacher;
  man's work, then, is God's grandchild, as it were.   105
From work and nature, if you will recall
  the opening of *Genesis*, mankind
  should gain its living and improve its lot;
the usurer, since he takes a different path,
  scorns nature in herself and in her follower   110
  because he puts his faith in something else.
But now I want to move on – follow me.
  The Fish are wriggling over the horizon
  while the Wain hangs above the Northwest Wind,
and our passage down the cliff lies far ahead."   115

Notes

4–9: Pope Anastasius II (died 498) sought a reconciliation with the eastern churches
and received Photinus, a Greek churchman. This ecumenical initiative was resisted
by the Roman clergy, and tradition blamed the pope for welcoming eastern heresy.
See *ED* 1.249–51.

10–15: This canto will proceed in the manner of a philosophical dialogue, a form for
which Dante had models in Cicero, Augustine and Boethius. The discussion will
analyze the plan of hell and the categories of sin punished at the different levels.
Dante's provocative synthesis of ethical concepts and his lapidary formulations
lend distinction to this exposition. The analysis is delivered at the important
threshold between upper and lower hell, and its placement illustrates the cleavage
between them. Offering a guidebook at the outset would have been tedious, and
the simple upper circles have required none; it will be otherwise with the complex
lower circles.

16–49: The first, second and third circles before the poets are the seventh, eighth
and ninth in the general plan of hell.

22–26: The term rendered here as "deliberate evil action" is *malizia*. These acts are performed with "malice" in the sense of a specific intent to harm, the meaning the word still has in the criminal law. Aquinas defined sins of malice as deliberate, knowing choices of evil and held them more grievous than sins of passion because in them the will is more certainly directed to evil. ST 1–2.78.1, 4. Although Dante's Christian scheme is in general consistent with the conceptual framework of Aristotle's *Ethics*, Marc Cogan points out ways in which it differs, *e.g.*, in its focus on individual acts of malice rather than habitual action. Cogan 1–36.

In upper hell, sin was considered in its intrinsic effect of disordering the faculties of the sinner by subjecting reason to the passions. Accordingly, sins were classified by the appetite that the sinner indulged to excess, and the treatment of lust, gluttony, avarice/prodigality, and wrath/sullenness in circles two through five was fairly summary. Consistent with this scheme, the *contrapasso* in upper hell generally followed the principle *you become what you do*. The punishment for disordering the soul is that the disorder is reified as the outward condition of the sinner's being.

By contrast, in lower hell sins will be classified on the basis of their extrinsic effect on the persons and property of other people, the sinner himself, and God. The result will be a greatly expanded treatment, because sinners will be distinguished by their specific actions. The eighth circle alone will occupy thirteen cantos, more than the first six circles combined, and will consist of ten subdivisions, some of which hold several different types of sinners. Consistent with this scheme, the *contrapasso* in lower hell will often follow a second principle: *what you do to others, you do to yourself*. You cannot wound others without wounding your soul (see, *e.g.*, *Macbeth*); and the corresponding wounds are reified in hell.

Often prominent in these lower circles is Dante's concern with how sin affects society. Sins of violence destroy the peace in which the just society can flourish and sins of fraud destroy the trust and brotherly love on which the cohesion of the just society depends. See Scott 192–93; Ferrante *passim*.

23: Aristotle said that justice was virtue considered not in relation to oneself but to others. *Eth.* 5.1 (1129b25–1130a13). The unjust or evil man inflicts injury on others by deliberate choice. *Eth.* 5.8 (1135b25–1136a4). Cogan argues that Dante restricts Aristotle's analysis of vice to the vice of injustice. Cogan 12–13.

24–27: "Fraud or violence (*forza o fraude*)." Dante's judgment of the relative evil of violence and fraud probably comes from Cicero, who held both unworthy of man but fraud more loathsome. *On Duties* 1.13.41.

It is unlikely that Dante is simply espousing the aristocratic preference for the bully over the sneak. But his judgment is not easy to reconcile with the overall scheme of hell because it appears to be based on the sin's effect of disordering the sinner's soul (the criterion of upper hell) instead of the magnitude of harm to the victim (which should be the criterion of lower hell). Aquinas held that although sins against one's neighbor disorder the sinner as well, their gravity depends on the injury they inflict on the victim. ST 2–2.34.4, 73.3. The murderer commits a greater injury than the thief and is accordingly punished more harshly under any rational legal system.

The calculations of fraud, however, use reason not to seek the truth but to obscure it, and thus pervert the noblest and distinctively human power of the soul, by which we participate in the divine nature. See *Conv.* 3.2.14–16. Some such rationale apparently causes Dante to consider fraud worse than violence. But there is no blinking the fact that his intellectualized scheme judges swindlers (*e.g.*, alchemists *Inf.* 29.109–20) to be worse than mass murderers (*e.g.*, Ezzolino da Romano *Inf.* 12.110). It is true, as Ferrante and Scott emphasize, that fraud undermines the trust and good will necessary for society to function. But it would be difficult to argue, in Dante's time or in ours, that systemic corruption is more destructive of a society than endemic violence.

29–33: Aquinas asserted that all sinful acts are directed to God, to oneself or to one's neighbor. *ST* 1–2.72.4. Dante's articulation of the principle only in relation to the sins of the seventh circle – together with his lawyerly distinction between offenses against the person and the property of each victim – shows his determination to impose conceptual unity on the disparate acts that he considers sins of violence.

45: The straightforward explanation is that these squanderers become sorrowful when they run through their money. More fundamentally, however, the life of frenzied dissipation that wastes one's substance is a species of despair.

47: Blasphemy does violence to God in his person. Dante distinguishes between inward denial and outward speech based on it, as Aquinas does. *ST* 2–2.13.1.

48–50: Sodom and Cahors. The sin of Sodom (*i.e.*, sodomy) and the sin of Cahors (*i.e.*, usury) do violence to what belongs to God. *See* note to 94–111. Cahors, a town in southern France, had become proverbial for its usurers; Boccaccio said usurers were commonly called men of Cahors.

52: Fraud is committed in the full glare of consciousness, with reason as its accomplice; and the conscience thus cannot escape its memory.

53–54: Defrauding a stranger severs only the tie of common humanity. Much more serious is the betrayal of trust created by a natural relationship like blood kinship or a voluntary one like vassalage or marriage.

55–60: The eighth circle will consist of ten concentric gulches in each of which a species of fraud is punished. Virgil names eight of the species here, not in the order in which they will appear. This brief and incomplete sketch may indicate that when he wrote the eleventh canto Dante had not yet developed his plans for the eighth and ninth circles as fully as those for the seventh.

64–65: "Dis," the classical god of the underworld, is used here and in *Inf.* 12.39, 34.20 for Satan.

70–90: The pilgrim recognizes that although Virgil has given a thorough account of the sins of malice punished in lower hell, he has not explained how the sins punished in the upper circles differ from these. Virgil responds with Aristotle's distinction: the incontinent man does not *choose* evil, but falls into it because he yields to his passions; the man who acts with malice deliberately chooses evil. *Eth.* 7.8 (1150a29–32); *In Eth.* ¶¶ 1422–23.

Because the structuring principle of upper hell is the innate tendencies to sin of our fallen nature, the actual transgressions of the sinners in the upper circles do not differentiate their positions within the circles. Having been seduced into irrational actions, the sinners are better represented by their ruling passions. By contrast, the structuring principle of lower hell is the specific evil actions deliberately chosen by the sinners, which will assign specific places to them. The capital sins remain in the background, however, as motives for the particular sins of malice.

79–82: At lines 81–82 Virgil paraphrases the opening of Book 7 of the *Ethics*: "Three kinds of moral states are to be avoided: vice, incontinence and brutishness [in the Latin translation, *malitia, incontinentia et bestialitas*]." The terms Dante uses are *malizia, incontinenza* and *matta bestialitade*. Virgil goes on to answer the pilgrim's question about those outside the walls by invoking Aristotle's distinction between incontinence and malice, never returning to brutishness. This third term has been much debated, largely because Dante's scheme of hell is not really tripartite. Rather it proceeds by repeated division of the latter term of a series of dichotomies. First he divides sins into those of incontinence and malice, based on Aristotle. Then he divides sins of malice into those of force and fraud, based on Cicero. Finally, he divides sins of fraud into those of simple fraud and treachery, probably based on the values of medieval society, in which personal loyalty was the cement of the social order.

82: Aristotle held that *bestialitas* is a disposition in which the appetite is perverted by disease, barbarism or habituation, leading to unnatural acts like cannibalism. *Eth.* 7.5 (1148b19–31); *In Eth.* ¶¶ 1372–74. Accordingly, identifying "mad brutishness" with one of the major divisions of sin in Dante's hell would not be consistent with Aristotle, who regarded brutishness as an outlier in the classification of human behaviors. If brutishness plays a role in lower hell, it appears to be that of an additional depravity that can crop up in any of the lower circles.

Dante's use of the world *bestial* ("brutish") to characterize people typically implies the behavior of wild animals. (1) the Minotaur (seventh circle), who is literally half beast, is described in the periphrasis "brutish wrath" (*ira bestial*), and his crazed subhuman ferocity represents "mad brutishness" in a direct manner. *Inf.* 12.33. (2) Vanni Fucci (eighth circle) describes himself as a "beast" who chose a "brutish life" (*vita bestial*) because he was a man of blood and wrath. *Inf.* 24.124–26, 129. (3) Ugolino (ninth circle) presents a "beastly image" (*segno bestial*) because he is gnawing at the brains of his enemy. *Inf.* 32.133. Cannibalism was one of the actions Aristotle identified as *bestialitas*.

The natural expression of brutishness thus appears related to violence. See, *e.g.*, Cogan 293–96. Relating it to fraud, whether simple or treacherous, is more difficult because Dante regards fraud as peculiarly human, a conscious perversion of reason. Although Fucci and Ugolino are damned among the fraudulent and treacherous, their brutishness is not what placed them there. But see Francesco Mazzoni (Mazzoni 1986, 167–210) and Alfred A. Triolo (Triolo 150–65), who identify bestiality with treacherous fraud.

94–111: The medieval reasoning that groups blasphemy with same-sex relations and lending money at interest is recondite. As blasphemy constitutes violence against God, same-sex relations constitute violence against nature, God's child; and moneylending at interest constitutes violence against both nature and human industry, which is nature's child and thus God's grandchild.

In *Physics* 2.2 (194a21) Aristotle states as an assumption that art imitates nature. On the idea of sex between males as a sin against nature, see notes to *Inf.* 14–16. Lending money at interest violates nature because money does not multiply naturally, like animals, which follow God's injunction in Gen. 1:22, 28. Lending at interest violates industry because the moneylender does not earn his bread through labor, producing an article of value like the farmer or the craftsman, as God ordained both before and after the fall. Gen. 2:15, 3:19; see notes to *Inf.* 17.

112–15: Virgil can always tell time by the stars in the cavern of hell; the time is now a few hours before dawn. Dante personifies the signs of the zodiac as Ovid does (*Metam.* 2.171–77, 195–200); as Pisces comes over the eastern horizon, the twinkling of its stars becomes the glitter on the scales of the wriggling fish.

114: "The Wain (*'l Carro*)." Charles's Wain or the Plough (the Big Dipper in the U.S.) is made up of the seven brightest stars in the Great Bear.

Canto XII

The place where we arrived for climbing down
    the bank was steep, and what was there besides
    made it a place that all eyes would avoid.
As the great landslide that once struck the Adige
    upon its flank this side of Trent – set off   5
    by an earthquake, it may be, or else erosion –
tumbled the mountainside as far as the plain
    down from the summit where the ground gave way,
    and made a kind of path for one above:
so here the gorge fell steeply away before us,   10
    and on the upper edge of the ruined cliff
    we found the shame of Crete, which was conceived
within the decoy cow, lying stretched out;
    he, when he noticed us, began to bite
    himself like one consumed within by rage.   15
My sage then shouted at him, "Do you think
    you see the Duke of Athens here, perhaps,
    who brought you death once in the upper world?
Off with you, beast! for this one has not come
    instructed by your sister, but is merely   20
    passing here to observe your punishment."
A bull that's broken free of its restraints
    just as it has received the killing stroke
    cannot advance, but plunges right and left:

I saw the Minotaur behave like that. 25
    Alert, my guide called, "Run now for the pass –
    go down at once, while the fury is upon him."
And down we made our way upon the rubble
    of broken rock, which shifted frequently
    under my feet from the unaccustomed weight. 30
While I went on in thought, he said, "Perhaps
    you wonder at this landslide, over which
    the bestial rage I just put down stands guard.
Now you should know that on the first occasion
    when I descended here to lower hell, 35
    these walls of rock had not yet fallen down.
But it was shortly, if my memory serves,
    before the coming of the one who took
    from Dis the great spoils of the highest circle,
that this deep, stinking chasm everywhere 40
    shook with such force, I thought the universe
    was feeling love, through whose power some believe
the world has many times returned to chaos;
    and in that moment all these ancient cliffs
    collapsed in ruin like this, both here and elsewhere. 45
But fix your gaze below, for now the river
    of blood is drawing near, in which are boiling
    all those who injured others through their violence."
O blind rapacity and frenzied rage
    that goad us on in this brief life, then bathe us 50
    so horribly in the eternal one!
I saw a broad canal that curved in an arc
    and seemed the one that holds the entire plain
    in its embrace, from what my guide had said;
between this and the foot of the embankment 55
    ran centaurs armed with arrows in single file,
    the way they once went hunting in the world.
Seeing us coming down, they stopped abruptly
    and three of them detached themselves from the troop,
    with arrows already chosen for their bows; 60

one shouted from afar, "You that descend
  the slope, what sentence are you going to?
  Tell us from there, or else I draw my bow."
My master said, "Our answer will be given
  to Chiron when we stand beside him there;   65
  you always – to your harm – have acted rashly."
He nudged me then and said, "That one is Nessus,
  who died because of Deianira's beauty
  and for his death exacted his own vengeance.
And there in the middle, brooding on his chest,   70
  great Chiron stands, who reared the young Achilles;
  the other is Pholus, who was full of wrath.
Around the moat they gallop in their thousands,
  shooting at any soul that drags itself
  further above the blood than its guilt allots."   75
Now we were drawing close to those swift beasts.
  Chiron took up a shaft and with the notch
  he pushed his full beard back along his jaws;
and when he had uncovered his great mouth
  he said to his companions, "Have you noticed   80
  the one in back is moving what he touches?
That is not usual with the feet of the dead."
  My leader, who by now was at his chest
  where the two natures join together, answered,
"He is indeed alive, and thus completely   85
  alone, so I must show him the dark valley;
  necessity, not pleasure, drives us on.
The one who gave me this unusual charge
  came to me fresh from singing Alleluias;
  he is no robber, I no thieving spirit.   90
But by the power through which my steps advance
  along a route so nearly impassible,
  lend one of yours to bear us company,
one that can show us where to ford the stream
  and carry this one over on his back,   95
  for he is no spirit that can go through the air."

And Chiron turned to his right and said to Nessus,
    "Go back and guide them, then; and if you chance
    upon another troop, make them steer clear."
Then we went on with our reliable guide   100
    along the border of the crimson seethe
    where the boiled sinners gave off piercing shrieks.
There I saw people who were eyebrow-deep;
    and the burly centaur said, "Those are the tyrants,
    who plunged their hands in blood and seized possessions.   105
The tears flow there for pitiless inflictions;
    Alexander is there, and the cruel Dionysius
    whose gift to Sicily was years of pain.
The forehead there from which such black hair grows
    is Ezzelino's, and that other blond one   110
    Obizzo of Este's, who in truth was slain
by his unnatural son in the upper world."
    I turned then to the poet and he said,
    "Let him be first with you for now, me second."
A little further on the centaur halted   115
    before a group that could be seen emerging
    down to the throat from the boiling stream. He showed us
a shade that stood alone, off to one side,
    and said, "That one cut open, in God's presence,
    the heart that still drips blood above the Thames."   120
Then I saw people who were holding their heads
    and their entire chests above the stream;
    and there were many of these I recognized.
And so, a little at a time, the blood
    grew shallow, till it only cooked their feet;   125
    and here was the place for us to ford the moat.
"Just as in this direction you observe
    the boiling stream grow shallow gradually,"
    the centaur said to us, "I'd have you know
that in the other, just as gradually,   130
    it pushes down its bed, till it rejoins
    the place where tyranny is made to groan.

And there the justice of the Lord torments
    the infamous Attila, a scourge on earth,
    and also Pyrrhus and Sextus; and it milks   135
eternally the tears unlocked by the boiling
    from Rinier da Corneto and Rinier Pazzo,
    who caused such depredations on the roads."
Then he turned back and crossed the shallows again.

Notes

1–10: The height of the bank dramatizes how much worse the sins of violence are than those of self-indulgence.

4–9: This is the great rock-fall known as the Slavini di Marco on the Adige between Trent and Verona. Statius similarly offers alternative explanations of a landslide. *Theb.* 7.744–49.

11–15: Pasiphaë, wife of King Minos of Crete (*Inf.* 5.4–20), fell in love with a bull and concealed herself within a wooden cow to attract him. Of this union was born the Minotaur, half-man and half-beast. To hide his shame, Minos constructed the Labyrinth, where the Minotaur fed on a yearly tribute of Athenian youths and maidens released in the passages from which none could find escape.

    The slaughterhouse simile used to describe the Minotaur's plunging suggests that Dante visualized it as a bull with a human head, the opposite of our image but one seen in medieval art. See Doob, plate 18.

17–20: Theseus was chosen by lot for inclusion among the youths sent to feed the Minotaur. Ariadne, daughter of King Minos, fell in love with him and gave him a ball of pitch and a ball of thread. Theseus threw the ball of pitch into the Minotaur's maw, disabling its jaws, and dispatched it with his dagger. Then he found his way out of the Labyrinth by following the thread he had unrolled on his way in.

31–45: Virgil explains the landslide by bearing witness to a biblical event he does not himself understand. The earthquake he describes took place at the moment of Christ's death on the cross. Matt. 27:51. Virgil gives the time of the event by reference to the harrowing of hell that he witnessed. See *Inf.* 4.46–63 and note. He then explains the earthquake by the theory of the Greek philosopher Empedocles, who posited cosmic cycles of attraction and repulsion among particles of the four elements. Empedocles called these polarities Love and Hate. See Aristotle, *Metaphysics* 1.4, 3.4 (985a21-b4, 1000a24-b13); Aquinas, *Commentary on Aristotle's Metaphysics* ¶¶ 109–11, 473–78.

    Virgil points to a higher truth that he does not understand, because in medieval thought the earthquake resulted from the sympathetic convulsion of nature at the death of its creator. The *Glossa Ordinaria* on Matt. 27:51 says: "All the elements bear witness to the crucifixion of their Lord. The earth moves because it cannot stand to bear its Lord hanging from the cross." In some medieval depictions of the crucifixion there is a crouched figure labeled *Terra* upon whom the cross rests.

46–51: The river is the fiery Phlegethon, one of the four rivers of the classical hell. *Inf.* 14.130–35. Macrobius, who read the classical myths as moral allegories, interpreted the Phlegethon as "the fires of our angers and desires." Macrobius 1.10.11. By contrast, Dante's river consists of the hot blood the violent have shed and in which they steep forever. Here rapacity and rage are merely the initiating conditions for these crimes. The punishment consists of the violence done to others recoiling on the self.

55–57: Reflecting their half-animal nature, the centaurs were represented in classical literature as creatures of violent passions. Invited to a human wedding, they tried to rape the bride, starting a battle. The centaur Chiron, however, was wise and noble and was entrusted with rearing the boy Achilles. Like other guardians, the centaurs are not only punishing human sinners but are themselves being punished for the same sin, though Dante rather seems to forget that here (Bosco/Reggio). Pietro Alighieri said that Dante intended the centaurs to represent the *condottieri*, the mercenary captains who served the bloody ambitions of the Italian tyrants in life and now supervise their punishment after death.

61–63, 67–69: Attempting to carry off Hercules's bride Deianira, Nessus was killed by Hercules's poisoned arrow. Dying, the centaur gave her the tunic stained with his poisoned blood, telling her it would be a love charm. When Deianira gave it to her husband, it stuck to him, making his blood boil and eating his flesh.

70–71, 77–81: A warrior in his youth, Chiron became a bucolic sage, skilled in medicine and the lyre. Chiron's observant thoughtfulness is shown by his absent-minded gesture with the arrow, followed by his shrewd remark.

100–12: The most striking feature of the punishment of violence is its stillness, despite the shrieks Dante mentions. This remote quality accords with the lack of affect the pilgrim shows here. Although the sinners are grouped together, each is immobile, mute and isolated in his suffering, like no other sinners except those encased in ice at the bottom of hell.

107: Dionysius the Elder was the tyrant of Syracuse in Sicily for many years (405–367 BC); his cruelty was legendary among the ancients.

107: The majority of commentators, medieval and modern, (Daniello is an exception) take "Alexander" to be Alexander the Great. In pairing "Alexander and cruel Dionysius," however, Dante was probably just using a pre-packaged citation for tyranny. Cicero linked Dionysius and Alexander of Pherae, a 4th century BC tyrant of Thessaly notorious for his cruelty, as tyrants (*On Duties* 2.7.25); and Brunetto Latini cited this passage in his advice to rulers. *Tresor* 2.119.6. In *Conv.* 4.11.14 Dante takes the common medieval view of Alexander the Great as an exemplar of liberality.

109–10: Ezzelino III da Romano (1194–1259) was for many years the chief supporter of the imperial cause in northern Italy. Villani called him "the cruelest and most feared tyrant there ever was among Christians" and asserted that he burned 11,000 Paduans alive. *Cron.* 7.72.

110–12: Obizzo of Este supported the Guelf party and Charles of Anjou and had a reputation for cruelty. There was a rumor that he was smothered with a pillow by his son, which Nessus confirms. *ED* 2.749.

115–17: These are the murderers, less culpable than the tyrants, who were guilty of slaughter on a massive scale.

118–20: The figure that stands apart, indicating the horror of his crime, is Guy de Montfort, whose father Simon led the rebels in the Barons' War (1263–67) against Henry III of England. When Simon was killed in battle, his body was dragged through the mud by the hair. Guy then took service with Charles of Anjou in Italy. At mass, during the elevation of the host, Guy stabbed to death Prince Henry, nephew of Henry III, and dragged the body out of the church by the hair in revenge for his father. *Cron.* 8.39.

120: Villani said that Henry's heart was preserved in a golden casket on London Bridge. *Cron.* 8.39. Buti and the Ottimo said that a statue of Henry held the golden container in its hand. Both stories reflect the fact that in the 13th century separate interment of the body, the heart and the entrails of royal persons had become common. See Duby 170–71. Henry's heart continues to drip blood because his murder has not been avenged.

121–25: Graduated immersion, signifying degrees of culpability, is a common feature of visions of hell. In the *Apocalypse of Paul* the saint sees a boiling river in which people are immersed up to the knees, others up to the navel, others up to the lips or the hair. Elliott 633. In the version of "St. Patrick's Purgatory" in *The Golden Legend* (1.195), there are trenches filled with molten metal in which sinners are immersed to depths ranging from one of their feet to above their eyes. The ninth circle (*Inf.* 32–34) will feature graduated immersion in ice.

133–38: None of these sinners are tyrants. The first are cruel conquerors, who fall short of that ultimate depth because they slaughtered foreigners, not their own subjects. (Alexander the Great would belong here, if anywhere.) Nessus then mentions those nearer to him in the shallower reaches, where robbers by sea and land are punished.

134: Attila, king of the Huns, invaded Europe from the Asian steppe in the 5th century. His contemporary title of *flagellum Dei*, "the scourge of God," suggests the terror he inspired.

135: Most commentators think Dante means Pyrrhus of Epirus, the Greek king who fought Rome in the third century BC. Orosius, however, did not tax Pyrrhus with cruelty, and Dante elsewhere stressed his nobility. *Hist. Adv. Pag.* 4.1–2; *Mon.* 2.9. Dante probably means Pyrrhus son of Achilles, whose cruelty in the sack of

Troy is emphasized in the *Aeneid* and who offered human sacrifice, which the Ottimo named the first among his sins.

135: Sextus, the son of Pompey the Great, took to piracy after his father's defeat. Lucan said that he defiled his father's naval triumphs. *Phars.* 6.420–22.

137–38: Rinier da Corneto was a 13th century highwayman who infested the marshy Maremma area. Rinier Pazzo was a Ghibelline leader, probably placed here for attacking the party of a Spanish bishop on the highway; the bishop died of his wounds.

Canto XIII

Nessus had not yet reached the other side
    when we were moving forward into a wood
    in which there was no sign of any path.
The foliage was not green but black in color,
    the limbs not smooth and straight, but gnarled and twisted,   5
    with no fruit growing there, but poisoned thorns.
Wild beasts that hate the cultivated fields
    could find no bramble growth as thick or prickly
    between Corneto and the Cècina.
There the repulsive Harpies make their nests,   10
    who drove the Trojans from the Strophades
    with dire predictions of their future loss.
They have broad wings and human necks and faces,
    their feet are clawed and their great bellies feathered;
    atop the weird trees they make mournful cries.   15
"Before you enter deeper," my good master
    began explaining, "know that you are now
    within the second ring and will remain there
until you reach the abominable sands.
    Look around closely therefore – you will witness   20
    things that would steal belief from my account."
I heard moans issuing from all around us
    yet could not see who might be making them;
    and so I stopped, lost in bewilderment.

I think he must have thought that I was thinking 25
    that all these voices coming through the scrub
    were those of people that were hidden from us,
because my teacher said, "If you snap off
    a little twig from any of these bushes,
    your present train of thought will be curtailed." 30
I therefore put my hand out just before me
    and plucked a little shoot from a great thorn bush;
    and at once the stub cried out, "Why do you break me?"
Then, as its end turned dark with seeping blood,
    it started in again: "Why do you tear me? 35
    Are you so lacking in all sense of pity?
Once we were men and now we are spiny shrubs,
    but your unfeeling hand might well have shown
    more pity had we been the souls of snakes."
As a green branch that has been set ablaze 40
    at one end starts to drip sap from the other
    and hisses through it as the air escapes,
so from the broken stub there came together
    both words and blood, at which I let the tip
    drop, and I stood there like a man aghast. 45
"Had he been able to believe before,
    O injured spirit," my sage answered him,
    "what he'd experienced only in my verses,
never would he have raised his hand against you;
    but since the fact was not to be believed, 50
    I had to prompt the act that grieves me too.
But tell him who you were, so he in partial
    recompense can revive your fame in the world
    above, where he is permitted to return."
And the stub: "You lure me so with gentle words, 55
    I cannot hold my peace; be not annoyed
    if I remain ensnared a while in talk.
I am the one who once held both the keys
    to Frederick's heart and who so smoothly turned them,
    both locking and unlocking, I excluded 60

everyone, almost, from his confidence;
  faithfully I fulfilled my glorious office,
  losing my sleep for it and then my life.
The prostitute that never turns away
  her shameless gaze from Caesar's residence   65
  – ruin anywhere, but especially at courts –
inflamed the hearts of everyone against me;
  and they, once flaming, so inflamed Augustus
  my happy honors turned to sad misfortune.
And so my spirit in a scornful mood,   70
  thinking it could escape from scorn through death,
  caused me to be unjust toward my just self.
I swear to you by the unnatural roots
  of this shrub that I never broke the faith
  I owed my lord, so worthy of all honor.   75
Should one of you return to the upper world,
  revive my memory, which is now still lying
  prostrate beneath the blows that envy dealt it."
The poet waited a while, then said to me,
  "Since he falls silent, do not lose the chance,   80
  but speak and ask whatever else you wish."
"You ask again," I said, "about whatever
  you think will satisfy my needs; for I
  could not, such pity presses on my heart."
So he began afresh: "As you desire   85
  what you request may freely be performed,
  incarcerated spirit, may it please you
to tell us further how the soul becomes
  bound in these knots; and tell us, if you can,
  if any are ever loosened from these limbs."   90
At this the stub blew gustily, then the wind
  transformed itself into a voice. I heard:
  "Your questions will receive a prompt response.
After the savage soul departs the body
  from which its own act has uprooted it,   95
  Minos remits it to the seventh circle.

It lands in the woods, nor is there any spot
     selected for it; but wherever chance
     flings it, it sprouts the way a grain of spelt does.
It grows to be a shoot, then a wild shrub,   100
     and then the Harpies feed upon its leaves,
     bringing it pain, and for the pain a vent.
We will return like the others to our cast-offs,
     but not to put them on, for keeping what
     we have stolen from ourselves would not be just.   105
Here we will lug them, and everywhere throughout
     the mournful grove our bodies will be hung,
     each on the bush of its implacable shade."
We were still there, attentive to the stub,
     thinking that there was more it wished to tell us,   110
     when we were startled by a rising clamor,
the way a hunter is who knows the boar
     and its pursuers are drawing near his blind
     because he hears the hounds and the rustling branches.
And suddenly two appeared upon our left,   115
     naked and scratched and fleeing at such a speed
     they tore the tangled branches of the wood.
"Hurry," the one in front cried, "hurry, death!"
     The other, aware that he was lagging badly,
     shouted, "Your legs were not so lively, Lano,   120
during that sporting match beside the Toppo!"
     And then, perhaps because his breath was failing,
     he made a cluster of himself and a bush.
And now behind them I could hear the woods
     full of black bitches, ravenous and swift   125
     as greyhounds that have just been loosed from the chain.
They set their teeth in the one that now was crouching
     and tore him into pieces, shred by shred,
     and afterwards bore off those suffering limbs.
My guide then took me by the hand and led me   130
     up to the bush, which had begun to weep
     uselessly through its many bleeding fractures.

"O Jacopo da Santo Andrea," it said,
    "what good was it to use me for a screen?
    Am I to blame for your unholy life?"   135
My teacher asked, when he had stopped above it,
    "Who were you once, who now blow plaintive speech
    along with blood through all your broken tips?"
It answered us, "O souls who have arrived
    to witness the disgraceful mutilation   140
    that has so stripped my leaves away from me,
heap them about the base of this poor shrub.
    Mine was the city that exchanged for John
    the Baptist her first patron, who for that
will always use his art to bring her grief;   145
    and were it not that on the bridge across
    the Arno there remains some image of him,
the city fathers who rebuilt the town
    upon the ashes left by Attila
    would have performed their labor to no purpose.   150
I made my house a gallows for myself."

Notes

4–15: The poets have entered not a forest of tall trees, but a thick growth of prickly
bushes of a height about as tall as a man.

4–6, 10: Dante negates the idealized forest of medieval poetry point by point.
Here no fresh green foliage of a May morning on trees filled with sweetly
singing birds. See, *e.g.*, *Rom. Rose* 45–102. Instead the pilgrim finds stunted
thorn trees with black leaves – dark with the blood that fills them and, as Buti
suggested, poisons the thorns – and twisted arthritic limbs, the foul nesting
places of revolting bird-women who make lugubrious cries.

7–9: The town of Corneto and the little river Cecina defined the southern and
northern boundaries of the Maremma, the swampy coastal area of Tuscany.

10–15: When Aeneas and his companions land on a deserted island, they slaughter
animals for a feast on the beach. Swooping down suddenly, the screeching Harpies
plunder and foul the banquet. When the Trojans attack them, the chief Harpy
prophesies that after landing in Italy they will suffer starvation for their wrong to
the bird-women. *Aen.* 3.219–57; see 6.289.

16–19: The pilgrim is now in the weird wood, which punishes those who committed violence against their own persons or goods.

22–45: The scene is based on *Aen.* 3.22–68, as Dante acknowledges at line 48. Seeking a branch to deck the altar for sacrifice, Aeneas approaches a mound grown with saplings. When he tears shoots from the ground they drip black blood and a groan comes from the mound: "Why mangle an unlucky man, Aeneas?" It is the voice of Polydorus, son of King Priam, treacherously murdered with spears that have grown into the thicket above him. Dante makes the bleeding shrub itself the body of the dead person from whom the voice issues. This gives his horror a more intimate thrill than Virgil's. The shocking eruption of blood and speech reveals the shrubs as monstrous souls that have rejected their humanity, resulting in a grotesque transformation of the self.

Thomas Peterson notes two additional parallels in Ovid: Daphne turns into a laurel tree when pursued by Apollo (*Metam.* 1.548–67); and after the fall of Phaeton his sisters, the Heliades, weep until they turn into trees. *Metam.* 2.340–66. Peterson notes, however, that unlike Ovid's characters Piero is not transformed from a human into a tree; rather his soul is trapped in a new vegetative body. In Ovid the mother of the Heliades, trying to arrest the transformation, breaks off twigs that drip blood and make a daughter cry out; but unlike with Piero, this is a transitional state. Peterson 206.

22–23: The moans seem to be coming from everywhere because they are issuing from multiple branch tips. See 101–02.

28–35: Justin Steinberg suggests that the disturbing effect of this passage reflects anxieties in Dante's time about the judicial use of torture to extract a confession from the accused. Steinberg 74.

55–78: Piero della Vigna was for over twenty years the closest advisor of the Emperor Frederick II. Employed in the imperial chancery, he exercised considerable legal, administrative and diplomatic influence. One of his chief claims to fame was the elaborate artifice of the Latin prose style in which he drafted the imperial diplomatic correspondence and in particular the pamphlets that urged Frederick's cause in his long struggle with the papacy.

In 1249, after many years in power, Piero was deprived of all offices, imprisoned and blinded. Tradition says that he committed suicide by beating his brains out against the walls of his cell. It is plausible that, as Dante believed, the emperor, grown suspicious in the final years of his reign, was turned against Piero by courtiers jealous of his ascendancy. Pietro and Buti said that chief among the false rumors spread about him was that he had revealed the emperor's secrets to the pope. In addition, Piero had used his long years in power to accumulate considerable wealth, something Frederick desperately needed in those years. See Abulafia 401–04.

55–72: Piero delivers an oration filled with rhetorical figures in a florid style meant to characterize him as the master of artificial Latin elegance. He toys with words, playing on "scornful/scorn" and "just/unjust," and he scores a triple play on "inflamed."

Piero clings tenaciously to his self-image as a loyal vassal, never blaming the emperor but only the courtiers who spread rumors about him. He never understands that the hatred of the courtiers was the predictable result of his excluding everyone else from the emperor's confidence, but Dante makes it clear through Piero's image of the keys. Buti said that Piero "did with the emperor what he wanted and how he wanted."

64: The prostitute is a personification of envy.

70–72: Piero's conclusion that he was unjust to himself echoes the description of the suicides in *Inf.* 11.22–24. Dante followed Augustine in this, as against Aristotle and Aquinas, who held that one cannot be unjust toward oneself. *Eth.* 5.11 (1138a4-b14); *ST* 2–2.58.2. Augustine said that the more innocent the suicide was of any offense the more guilty his self-murder was, and he charged with cowardice those who, like Piero, could not bear the false censure of the world. *Civ. Dei* 1.17, 22. Although suicide was an honorable death in Roman culture, Christianity has always had a particular horror of the ultimate sin of Judas. Aquinas regarded suicide as worse than murder. *ST* 2–2.64.5.

82–84: The pilgrim's lively sympathy for Piero della Vigna may arise from Dante's feeling a certain intellectual fellowship. Piero was the 13th century's chief literary apologist for the independent rights of the empire, and he developed arguments that Dante would use in Book 3 of *Monarchy*.

94–102: Piero answers Virgil's first question, how the soul becomes bound in the thorn bushes. The details of the narrative emphasize the condign punishment of the *contrapasso*. Once the savage spirit removes itself from the natural order, providence no longer cares for it and chance governs its fate. Minos hurls the spirit, which lands at random in the wood, where it sprouts wild and becomes part of the sterile bramble growth. The rhetorical mannerisms of Piero's previous speech fall away here because his personality is no longer the focus; he becomes simply a reliable witness to a feature of hell.

103–08: Piero answers Virgil's second question, whether any of the suicides gets free of its vegetable body. After the Last Judgment the dead are reunited to their bodies, which thereafter share in their glory or their punishment. But the condign punishment of the suicide requires that he *not* inhabit again the body of which he violently deprived himself. His resurrected body, therefore, will continue to be his victim, hanging from the infernal thorn bush that is the new form of his savage spirit. This final vision, with its unmistakable evocation of Judas hanging himself from a dead tree – a common theme in medieval art – is the apogee of horror of the whole episode and the full development of the *contrapasso*.

115–29: In five tercets Dante creates a fully realized scene of rapid action and shouted exclamations, in the strongest possible contrast with the immobility and sententious discourse of the previous scene.

115–21: These are the squanderers, destroyers of their own property. *See Inf.* 11.44. Dante's collocation of these extravagant wastrels with the suicides is consistent with Aristotle, who regarded the squanderer's wasting of his substance as a lesser form of suicide, since life depends on possession of substance. *Eth.* 4.1 (1119b33–1120a3). The difference between these sinners and the spendthrifts of *Inf.* 7 lies in Dante's distinction between self-indulgence and malice. The squanderers do not give in to a desire for pleasure, but act willfully and with a perverse violence in dissipating their material possessions. (When the motive was religious, however, as in St. Francis's theatrical gesture of stripping himself naked in public, self-impoverishment was considered saintly.)

118–21: Lano da Siena was a rich young man said to belong to the "Spendthrift Club" of Siena, made up of youths determined to consume their fortunes conspicuously. See note to *Inf.* 29.130. He joined a Sienese military expedition in 1228. Ambushed at a ford in the river Toppo, the Sienese troops broke and fled; Lano was one of the casualties.

119–29: Jacopo da Sant' Andrea was a wealthy Paduan of the early 13th century, who ran through his large fortune quickly and died in poverty.

124–29: The infernal hunt is a theme of medieval literature, but it is usually a punishment for wrongs in love. See *ED* 5.72. Here the sinners are reified as the fortunes they recklessly scattered and are scattered in turn by being torn piece from piece.

137–38: The anonymous Florentine speaks with dozens of voices issuing from the broken ends of his branches, which depersonalizes him.

139–42: The bush's outrage at the public spectacle that has been made of it and its plea for the return of its leaves are both comic and pathetic. The twin values of propriety and property that they imply suggest that the speaker is a character from the high bourgeoisie.

143–50: The superstition that the suicide recounts – that Florence's internecine warfare was the ancient war god's revenge for replacing him with John the Baptist as civic patron – was given large play by Villani, who recorded the belief that Charlemagne could never have rebuilt the city after its destruction by barbarians unless an ancient statue of Mars had been drawn from the Arno and placed on the site of the Ponte Vecchio. *Cron.* 2.5, 2.23, 3.1, 4.1.

148–49: The speaker confuses Totila the Goth, who besieged Florence in 542, with the earlier and more famous Attila the Hun, who never came that far south (though Dante appears to identify Totila in this connection in *VE* 2.6.4).

Canto XIV

Compelled by my affection for my birthplace,
    I gathered up the scattered leaves and gave them
    back to him, who by now had lost his voice.
Soon we approached the boundary where the second
    ring is divided from the third, and there   5
    one sees a terrible exercise of justice.
To render comprehensible these sights
    not seen before, I must explain we'd reached
    a plain that banishes every plant from its bed.
Around it the suffering forest forms a garland,   10
    as does the moat of sorrow around that;
    and there at the very edge we came to a halt.
The ground consisted of a deep, dry sand
    of the same composition as the dunes
    that bore the imprint once of Cato's feet.   15
Avenging justice of the Lord, how greatly
    you should be feared by everyone who reads
    the things that stood revealed before my eyes!
Numerous groups of naked souls I saw,
    all of whom wept most wretchedly, and it seemed   20
    that different sentences were imposed upon them.
Some of them lay on their backs upon the ground,
    another group was sitting huddled up,
    another walked about in ceaseless motion.

Most numerous by far were those who wandered,   25
    and least the ones who lay beneath the torment,
    but theirs the tongues most loosed in lamentation.
Over the whole expanse of sand large flakes
    of fire were raining down, descending slowly
    like snowflakes in a windless mountain valley.   30
Once Alexander in the torrid zone
    of India chanced to see above his army
    flames that descended to the earth intact;
he promptly issued orders that his troops
    should stamp upon the ground, more easily   35
    to quench the fires while they were isolated.
The eternal fire was coming down like that,
    making the sand ignite, the way that tinder
    does beneath steel and therefore doubling the pain.
There never came a pause in the leaping dance   40
    their wretched hands performed, now here, now there,
    brushing away from them the freshest burning.
"Master," I asked him, "you who overcome
    all obstacles, except when those hard demons
    came swarming out against us at the gate,   45
who is that great one who appears to ignore
    the fire and lies contemptuous and grim,
    as if the rain were causing him no torment?"
At that point, he himself, who had perceived
    that I was questioning my guide about him,   50
    cried out, "What I was living, I am dead.
Though Jove wear out his armorer, from whom
    he seized the pointed lightning in his wrath
    upon that last day when he struck me down;
though he wear out a team of them in shifts,   55
    in Mongibello at the blackened forge,
    crying 'Help, help, good Vulcan!' in his need,
as he did once upon the field at Phlegra;
    and though he strike me with his gathered might,
    still would he not have joy of his revenge!"   60

And then my gentle guide spoke out, more vehemently
    than I had ever heard him speak before:
    "Know, Capaneus, by the very fact
your pride has not died down, you bear the greater
    punishment; for no suffering could match   65
    your rage except the torment of your fury."
Then he turned back to me, his face now calm:
    "That one," he said, "was one of the seven kings
    besieging Thebes; he had contempt for God
and seems to have it yet, seems to despise him;   70
    but as I said to him, his scornful ravings
    are fitting decorations for his chest.
Now walk behind me and be very careful
    not to set foot upon the burning sand,
    but always let your steps hug the wood closely."   75
Going in silence then, we reached the place
    at which a stream comes gushing from the forest,
    so red it makes me shudder even now.
Like the stream that issues from the Bulicame,
    which sinful women share among themselves,   80
    the stream here took its course across the sand.
Its bed and both its banks were made of stone
    and stone embankments ran on either side,
    from which I gathered that our path lay there.
"Of all the other things that I have tried   85
    to show you since we entered by the gate
    whose threshold never is denied to any,
nothing your eyes have seen has been so worthy
    to be remarked on as the present stream,
    which quenches all the flaming sparks above it."   90
These were the words my leader spoke, and I
    at once entreated him to let me have
    the food that he had made me hungry for.
"In the middle of the sea there lies a land
    fallen in ruin," he said, "whose name is Crete,   95
    under whose king the world was innocent once.

A mountain rises there whose name was Ida,
    rejoicing once in leafy boughs and streams;
    now it is desolate, like an ancient ruin.
Rhea once chose it as her infant son's   100
    securest cradle, and to hide him better
    she made them raise a clamor when he cried.
Erect within the mountain stands, gigantic,
    an old man with his back turned toward Damietta,
    gazing at Rome as if it were his mirror.   105
His head is modeled in pure gold, his chest
    and arms are fashioned out of solid silver,
    then he is made of bronze as far as the fork;
from there on down the rest is all good iron
    save the left foot, which is of fired clay;   110
    on that he leans more heavily than the other.
Each of these parts except the gold is cracked
    by a great fissure dripping tears, which gather
    and penetrate the cavern's floor. Their course
plunges from rock to rock to reach this valley;   115
    they form the Acheron, Styx and Phlegethon
    and then proceed below through this slim channel
until, arrived where nothing can sink lower,
    they form Cocytus; what that pool is like
    I shall not tell you here, for you will see it."   120
I put a question: "If the present stream
    flows from our world like that, why is it first
    appearing to us in this borderland?"
"You know the place is circular," he answered,
    "and though you now have come a good long way 125
    down toward the bottom, always turning left,
you have not yet revolved through the full circle;
    and for that reason, if something new appears
    it should not bring amazement to your face."
I again: "Master, where are Phlegethon   130
    and Lethe? for the last you do not mention,
    whereas the first, you say, comes from this rain."

"In all your questions, certainly, you please me,"

he answered, "but the boiling of the red

water should put to rest one that you ask. 135

You will see Lethe, but beyond this ditch,

up where the spirits go to wash themselves

when their repented sins have been removed."

Then he said, "Now the time has come to leave

the wood; take care to follow in my steps. 140

The embankments form a path, for they are not

burning, and over them all flames are quenched."

Notes

3: The bush loses its voice as the wounds opened by the dogs close up again.

9: The sandy plain that banishes growing things from its bed reifies what Dante sees as the sin of the sodomites (see below), who banish reproductive sexuality from their beds.

13–15: Cato led an army across Libya during the civil war between Caesar and Pompey. *Phars.* 9.371–949.

19–24: Dante gives a panoramic view of the punishments of the third ring, most of which, as the subsequent narrative makes clear, the pilgrim could not actually see from the edge of the wood. The sinners lying on their backs are the blasphemers, the violent against God, who will appear in this canto. Those wandering without stopping are the sodomites, the violent against nature, who will appear in *Inf.* 15–16. Those huddled up are the usurers, the violent against nature and art, who will appear in *Inf.* 17.

Richard Lansing has shown that the imagery of the three rings of the circle of violence forms a coherent scheme illustrating the progressive degeneration of the sinners in the rings. The presence of the centaurs in the first ring associates the violent against others with a descent from rational nature to animal nature; the punishment of the violent against self in the second ring marks a further descent to vegetative nature; and here the sterile plain and the rain of fire images a final descent to mineral and elemental nature. Lansing 1981.

25: The sodomites are far more numerous than the usurers, implying that Dante thought sex between males was more common than moneylending in Florence, a city of moneylenders. Michael Rocke's detailed study of Florentine judicial records beginning about a century after Dante's time documents the extreme prevalence of the practice. In the late 15th century a majority of the male population of

Florence was formally implicated at one time or another. Rocke 115, 146. (For the use of the term "sodomite" here, see note to *Inf.* 15.16–21.)

26–27: The blasphemers, who committed violence with their tongues, are still the most vocal because they suffer the worst punishment of the third ring, forced to lie on their backs facing the fire.

28–39: The rain of fire reproduces the judgment of God on the cities of the plain in Genesis 19:24–25: "And the Lord rained upon Sodom and Gomorrha brimstone and fire from the Lord out of heaven," destroying the cities "and all things that spring from the earth." Raining down is contrary to the nature of fire; and contrary to natural rain, which makes the earth fertile, the infernal rain makes it sterile. An unnatural world surrounds those who have rejected nature. In addition, burning alive was the most common punishment for sodomy in medieval statutes. Brundage 534.

28–30: Dante echoes a line by Guido Cavalcanti, who included "white snow falling with no wind" in a list of things his mistress surpassed in beauty. But Dante puts Cavalcanti's simple gallantry to complex use; not for the last time (see *Inf.* 26.25–33) an image of natural beauty makes the torments of the damned more poignant. Divine justice is unhurried, impersonal and, to the disinterested eye, beautiful.

31–36: Dante took from Albertus Magnus an episode from the letter supposedly sent to Aristotle from Alexander the Great in India. Alexander had his men stamp down a snowfall so it did not bury their camp. Albert remembered it as fire falling from the air, but the original showed through in his description of the fire falling like snow. See *ED* 1.118.

46–72: One of the Seven Against Thebes, Capaneus is a larger-than-life figure in Statius's *Thebaid*. Scaling the walls of Thebes and challenging Jove to combat, he is struck by Jove's thunderbolt but faces heaven defiantly until he slides smoking down the wall. *Theb.* 10.837–939. Statius's admiration for his titan lingers in the defiant rhetoric of Capaneus here, but Virgil's remarks convey Dante's judgment. Capaneus's ruling passion is an insane presumption. See *Eth.* 4.3 (1123b25–26); *In Eth.* ¶ 744.

55–57: Revolting against the gods, the giants stormed their citadel on Mt. Olympus, near which the valley of Phlegra lies. Mongibello is Mt. Etna in Sicily. Statius repeatedly compares Capaneus to the giants assaulting Olympus. *Theb.* 10.849–52, 909–10; 11.7–8.

77–78: The stream is red because it is the off-flow of the river of blood of *Inf.* 12.

79–81: The Bulicame was a hot sulfur spring near Viterbo, long a local attraction. See *Cron.* 2.14. Brothels grew up near it and Benvenuto said the prostitutes diverted portions of the stream to their houses for use in hot baths. These were a common feature of brothels. See *Rom. Rose* 10,095–10,118; Fossier 10.

88–89: The rest of the canto, which explains the source and course of the rivers of hell, provides the basis for this surprising judgment.

94–99: Virgil's explanation of the stream begins with the origins of human history as understood in antiquity. He describes Crete, now in ruins, as the ancient center of the reign of Saturn, the king under whom the earliest men lived in the age of primal innocence before the reign of the Olympian gods. In Ovid's version of the Golden Age, men lived in peace and ate the fruits of the earth without either hunting or farming; then came the succeeding ages of silver, bronze and iron, each more corrupt than the last. *Metam.* 1.89–150. Dante's choice of Crete as the setting of the Golden Age and his description of it depend on *Aen.* 3.104–05, 121–23.

100–02: Because it was foretold that Saturn's wife Rhea would bear a son who would dethrone his father, Saturn devoured each of her children at birth. When Jupiter was born, Rhea gave Saturn a stone wrapped in blankets and hid the baby on Mt. Ida. Whenever he cried, she had her followers make a loud noise to mask the sound. Ovid, *Fasti* 4.197–214.

103–20: *The Old Man of Crete.* Three tercets (103–11) describe an ancient monumental statue of an old man inside Mt. Ida, composed of disparate materials. Three more (112–20) describe how the statue is riven by a crack that drips tears and how these plunge through the mountain to reach the cavity of hell, becoming the infernal rivers named in classical poetry. Description of allegorical works of art, already popularized by *The Romance of the Rose* (129–462), was to become a major structural device in the *Purgatorio* and enjoy a wide vogue in later poetry (*e.g.*, Boccaccio, Ariosto, Spenser).

The Old Man's appearance requires the reader to conflate two texts. The statue comes from King Nebuchadnezzar's dream: "The head of this statue was of fine gold, but the breast and the arms of silver, the belly and thighs of bronze, the legs iron and the feet part iron and part clay." Dan. 2:31–35. The parallel between the increasingly base materials of the statue and Ovid's successive ages of gold, silver, bronze and iron underlies the statue's significance as a figure of man in history, degenerating from original vigor and innocence to eventual debility and corruption.

Dante's original contribution is the great fissure that runs through the entire statue except its golden head. Superimposing this flaw on the original schema of decline is not redundant because the biblical-classical schema does not symbolize the central moral fact of original sin, which is responsible for the decline. For Dante the Golden Age is merely a poetic figure of which the reality is Eden. See *Purg.* 28.139–41. The statue is cracked because human nature has been flawed since the fall. The Old Man embodies the grandeur and misery of man without faith and grace. The tears that drip down the crack are man's age-old lament for his own fallen condition. The four rivers of hell turn out to be the steady seep of human misery, the condition of our nature alienated from God by sin.

103–04: The size of the statue and the age of its subject illustrate a progressive human decline throughout history, as much physical as moral. The belief that Adamic man had been gigantic of stature (see Gen. 6:4) was confirmed by periodic discoveries of dinosaur fossils. Pliny mentioned the discovery of giant human remains within a mountain on Crete (*Nat. Hist.* 7.16), perhaps the spark of Dante's conception. Augustine cited Pliny as an expert on the subject. *Civ. Dei* 15.9. The belief that the lives of the first men were measured in centuries arose from the accounts of the biblical patriarchs. Our current short life-span, like our current puny stature, demonstrates, as Pietro commented, that nature is exhausted in the last age of the world.

104–05: The prophet Daniel interpreted Nebuchadnezzar's dream as portending a succession of four empires. Dan. 2:38–45. In patristic and medieval interpretations, the first was Babylon and the last was Rome, which would continue until the end of history. Kantorowicz 292; see *Hist. Adv. Pag.* 2.1; *Civ. Dei* 18.2. Pietro explained that the Old Man turns his back upon Damietta – then an important port at the mouth of the Nile – because behind it lies Babylon, which has already fallen. The Old Man stares at Rome because it is the destined seat of both empire and church, and hence the mirror of man in history.

110–11: Pietro's view that the foot of clay represents the hierarchy of the church is generally accepted, with the corollary that the iron foot represents the empire. The Old Man leans most of his weight on the foot of clay because the church has usurped the powers of the empire.

112–13: Although the stratification of the statue is to be understood diachronically as progressive degeneration, the crack is to be understood synchronically as the effects of original sin on fallen man. It illustrates the "wounds of nature," the impairment of the powers of the soul caused by the fall. The crack widens as it descends through four powers because the fall becomes more obvious in our lower nature. Aquinas said that man's reason (here probably associated with the silver) suffered the wound of ignorance; his will (the bronze) the wound of malice; his irascible appetite (the iron) the wound of weakness; and his concupiscible appetite (the clay) the wound of concupiscence. *ST* 1–2.85.3; see note to *Inf.* 1.30. The unimpaired gold perhaps represents the freedom man still possesses, despite the impairment of his will, to accept God's freely offered grace. See *ED* 5.903.

115–20: References to the rivers of hell, common in classical poetry, entered Christian accounts as early as the 3d century *Apocalypse of Paul*. In Dante's hell, as Virgil explains here, the four rivers make up a single watercourse, sourced from the tears of the Old Man, which reappears in different forms at different levels. Dante, for whom science was part of poetry, has made of the vague classical references a consistent hydrodynamic system.

Acheron circles inside the gates and separates hell from the upper world (*Inf.* 3.71), as it does in *Aen.* 6.295. Each of the other rivers occupies one of the main divisions of hell (incontinence, violence and fraud) and provides part of its punishments. Styx rises in the fourth circle and becomes a vast marsh (see *Aen.* 6.323) surrounding the City of Dis; in it the wrathful and slothful are punished. *Inf.* 7.100–08. Phlegethon forms the outer boundary of the circle of violence, steeping tyrants and murderers in boiling blood. *Inf.* 12.46–54. The present stream flows from Phlegethon through the suffering forest, and after crossing the burning plain it will fall in a great cascade into the circles of fraud, where its waters will collect in Cocytus, a frozen lake at the bottom of hell in which the traitors are embedded. *Inf.* 32.22–36.

Canto XV

One of the stony rims now bears us onward
    and the stream's vapor casts a shade below,
    shielding the banks and the water from the fire.
Between Wissant and Bruges the men of Flanders,
    under the threat of tides that surge upon them,   5
    build barriers to make the sea retreat,
just as the Paduans do along the Brenta
    for the protection of their town and castles
    before Carinthia's mountains feel the heat;
here the embankments were of like construction,   10
    except the architect, whoever he was,
    had made them neither as high nor thick as those.
Already we had come so far from the wood
    I could no longer have distinguished where
    it was if I had turned around to look,   15
when we encountered a company of souls
    walking beside the embankment. Each of them
    was peering at us as one might at evening
peer at another under the new moon,
    each sharpening his frown in our direction   20
    as an old tailor does at his needle's eye.
Standing inspection by that company,
    I saw that I was recognized by one
    who caught my hem and cried out, "What a wonder!"

And when his arm came reaching out toward me,   25
    I searched his scorched expression with my eyes
    in order that the burnt face might not block
my memory from recognizing him.
    Bending, I reached my hand down toward his face
    and said to him, "Are you here, Ser Brunetto?"   30
And he then: "O my son, be not displeased
    if for a little way Brunetto Latini
    turns back with you and lets the file go on."
"I beg you to," I said, "with all my heart,
    and if you'd rather I take a seat with you,   35
    I will, if he I travel with approves."
"O son," he said, "whoever of this company
    stops for a moment, lies for a hundred years
    and cannot shield himself when the flames strike.
Therefore go on, and I will walk at your skirts,   40
    and then I must rejoin my band, who go
    lamenting their eternal punishment."
I did not dare descend from my raised path
    to walk beside him, but I kept my head
    bowed down like one who walks with reverence.   45
"What fortune," he began, "or destiny
    leads you down here before your final day?
    And who is the other, showing you the path?"
"Above, where life is lighted by the sun,
    I lost my way," I answered, "in a valley   50
    before my time of life attained its prime,
and I left it only yesterday at dawn;
    as I was turning back there, he appeared
    and now he leads me home along this road."
"If you keep following your star," he said,   55
    "you will not fail to reach a glorious port,
    if I saw clearly in the happy life;
and if I had not met an untimely death
    I would have lent your work my full support
    because I saw the heavens so favored you.   60

But that ungrateful and malicious people
    come down in ancient time from Fiesole,
    who still hold stubbornly to rock and mountain,
will naturally become your enemy
    because you do the right thing: the sweet fig   65
    cannot bear fruit among the sour sorbs.
The world's age-old tradition calls them blind;
    they are a grasping, envious, stiff-necked people –
    watch that you be not sullied with their ways.
Such is the honor your future holds in store,   70
    both factions will be ravenous for you;
    the grass, though, will be distant from the goat.
Let the cattle of Fiesole make fodder
    out of each other and not graze the plant,
    if one still sprouts among their stable droppings,   75
in which the holy seed shall rise again
    of the Romans who remained within the city
    after it had become a nest of vice."
"If everything I prayed for had been granted,
    you would not yet have been," I said to him,   80
    "sent into exile from humanity.
My memory is stamped – and now it grieves me –
    with your dear figure, kind and fatherly,
    teaching me now and again while you were living
the way a man may make himself immortal;   85
    how dear to me that memory is my tongue,
    as long as I shall live, must testify.
I write down what you tell me of my future
    and save it to be glossed with another text
    by a lady who will know how, if I reach her.   90
I want to make one thing quite clear to you:
    provided that my conscience does not chide me,
    I am prepared for any whim of Fortune.
My ears become accustomed to such forecasts;
    let Fortune, therefore, turn her wheel however   95
    she likes, and let the peasant swing his mattock."

And just then I could see my teacher's right
profile as he turned back and looked at me
and then said, "A good listener remembers."
I nonetheless walked on in conversation 100
with Ser Brunetto, and I asked about
his associates of greatest rank and fame.
"Some it is well to know about," he said,
"of the others it is proper to be silent,
for the time would be too short for so much talk. 105
Know in a word that all of them were clerics
or great and celebrated men of letters,
polluted in the world with the same sin.
There Priscian wanders with the wretched crowd,
Francesco d'Accorso too; and you could see, 110
if you had any desire for such scurf,
the bishop whom the servant of the servants
transferred from the Arno to the Bacchiglione,
where he soon left his sinfully strained sinews.
More I would tell you, but this talk, this escort 115
can last no longer for ahead I see
another dust cloud rising from the sand:
people are coming with whom I must not be.
To you I entrust my *Treasury*, in which
I am still alive, and more I do not ask." 120
Once he had turned, he looked like one of those
who run the Green Cloth footrace at Verona
through the surrounding fields; and of them all
he looked to be the winner, not the loser.

Notes

4–6: Wissant and Bruges, important medieval ports for Florentine merchants, marked
the western and eastern limits of Flanders. Systematic dikes were built there in
the 12th and 13th centuries and would have been a notable work in Dante's time.
7–9: I.e., Padua's river, the Brenta, rises in the Alps, and the Paduans reinforce its
banks before spring melts the Alpine snows.

12: The embankment's height is somewhat less than a man's.

16–21: The approaching sinners are the sodomites, the term that conveys the medieval judgment of men who have sex with other males. Foucault's dictum that the sodomite of former times was a person who committed certain acts, while the homosexual of modern discourse is a certain type of person, has been controversial among writers on homosexuality. Foucault 43; see, *e.g.*, Crompton 174–75. But understood as describing a cultural paradigm, it appears sound. Some medieval texts recognize that there are men who prefer their own sex (even humorously, as in *Decam.* 1.1 and 5.10). The uniform judgment of the culture, however, was that men who repeatedly engaged in same-sex relations were simply habitual sinners, guilty of the vice against nature, not persons with a certain sexual orientation.

In addition to the cultural paradigm, there is the question of the facts on the ground. Rocke's study of judicial records of sodomy in late medieval and early modern Florence shows not only the extreme prevalence of the practice, but also a distinctive profile of activity. In the age-old Mediterranean tradition, the overwhelming preponderance of such arrangements involved a dominant man (to whom alone the term "sodomite" applied) and a submissive boy, usually between the ages of thirteen and eighteen. Today such practices generally would be considered sexual predation or prostitution rather than the norm of gay sex. Often enough this was not an exclusive taste for the men, but provided a convenient sexual outlet before marriage (men usually did not marry before thirty) or an additional outlet after marriage. Rocke 14, 88, 96, 110, 112, 116, 162 *et passim*. This profile would appear to fit Dante's sodomites in *Inf.* 15–16. Much of the modern commentary on these characters is anachronistic, derived from 20th century stereotypes about homosexuals.

23–30: Brunetto Latini (c. 1220–94) composed official documents for the first Guelf commune of Florence in the 1250s. When the Ghibellines seized power he went into exile and wrote his *Treasury* (*Li Livres dou Tresor*), the first medieval encyclopedia in the vernacular (French) and the first to reflect the emphasis on rhetoric, ethics and politics that would later characterize humanism. In the second Guelf commune Brunetto served as chancellor and public orator. Villani said, "He was the master who first began to refine the Florentines, to make them perceive how to speak well and know how to guide and govern our republic in accordance with the art of politics." *Cron.* 9.10; see Najemy 1994, 34, 38–39.

Brunetto was married and had children; he condemned sodomites (*Tresor* 2.33, 40) and other than this canto there is no evidence of his having been one. Some have argued that he must have had a contemporary reputation as a sodomite, but the pilgrim's amazement at meeting him indicates the fictional premise that Dante is revealing something he only learned in hell. Dante is sometimes castigated for blackening Brunetto's reputation; but given the prevalence of the practice in Florence, where at least somewhat later a majority of the adult male population was charged with sodomy, the allegations about Brunetto and the admired statesmen of *Inf.* 16 may not have been as shocking as critics generally assume. See Rocke 115, 146. The allegation certainly did not compromise their masculinity. See Rocke 110. Lower in hell, sinners will try to keep their identities concealed. *Inf.* 18, 24, 27. By contrast, Brunetto and the three Florentine sodomites of *Inf.* 16 ask the pilgrim to keep their memory alive. Justin Steinberg notes that sodomy incurred legal *infamia*, but so did adultery (Steinberg 17); and Boccaccio treated both comically in parallel (see *Decam.* 5.10, where husband and wife both get what they want from a youth).

The keynote of these meetings is the pilgrim's matter-of-fact attitude toward the transgressions of these sinners. The sin of Brunetto and the three Florentines merits the rain of fire, but as in the case of Farinata, the sin does not determine Dante's attitude toward them. His estimate of their characters is far larger than the sins they are expiating. A man may be damned for a private sin without ceasing to be a public-spirited man, admirable for political integrity and civic virtue. Dante's unblinking vision finds expression in the fully human portrait within the eschatalogical frame.

26–28: Brunetto's burnt face makes recognition difficult and in *Inf.* 16.29, 35 the three Florentines are blackened, raw and singed hairless. The symbolic principle of Dante's *contrapasso* that acts here is suggested in the *Glossa Ordinaria* on Gen. 19:24–25 (the destruction of Sodom): "Those that burned with the stench of flesh toward perverse desires should have perished by right in sulfur and flame. Thus they learned from just punishment what they had done from unjust desire." Divine punishment is the reification of the sin itself: as the sodomites burned on earth with unnatural lust, they burn in hell with unnatural fire. See note to *Inf.* 14.28–39.

31–36: Unsure of the pilgrim's reaction, Brunetto humbly asks his old protégé to be allowed to spend a few minutes with him. The pilgrim shows exquisite courtesy, assuring his old mentor that nothing has changed between them.

37–42: The inability of the sodomites to rest resembles that of the lustful in *Inf.* 5, but instead of being helplessly tossed on gusts of passion, they roam the sterile plain as though purposefully. Pietro Alighieri said this was because on earth they were unable to remain within the bounds of nature in their restless search for strange ways of life.

46–47: Brunetto echoes Deiphobus (*Aen.* 6.531–34), who asks Aeneas what chance or destiny has brought him to the underworld.

55–78: Brunetto's forecast of the pilgrim's destiny, though shadowed by adversity, is a message of comfort and hope from the only soul in hell whom the pilgrim loved on earth. The scene echoes the meeting of Aeneas with his father Anchises in the underworld. *Aen.* 6.679–892. Anchises foretells his son's glorious destiny, as Brunetto does his adoptive son's. Anchises prepares Aeneas for the war he must fight in Italy; Brunetto prepares the pilgrim for the crisis of his political career.

Dante's term of office on the governing council of Florence began a few months after his fictional meeting with Brunetto, and it led to his exile two years later.

Dante never mentions his own father, but he has Brunetto twice call him "son" and the pilgrim echoes the idea. Adoptive fatherhood was a political institution in ancient Rome, where a powerful man would legally adopt a younger one who was his ally and would become his successor. Brunetto gives the pilgrim his blessing to succeed to his own respected place in Florentine cultural and political life, a process that he regrets not being able to influence in person. Dante, whom Brunetto calls the holy seed of the Romans, follows him in breathing new life into the ancient legacies of rhetoric, which inspires men to right action, and governance, which creates justice in the state. This is to be Dante's glorious destiny, one in which learning and literature are not clearly distinguished from politics. Dante will be the new Cicero as much as the new Virgil.

This scene at the center of the *Inferno* will be completed by the pilgrim's meeting with his ancestor, a more complete father figure, at the center of the *Paradiso*. But see Freccero, who argues that one cannot imagine a more radical rejection of Brunetto as a father figure than charging him with sodomy. Freccero 1991, 66.

61–69, 73–78: Brunetto's *Tresor* (1.36) blamed the perpetual wars among the Florentines, which resulted in his own exile, on the ancient revolt in which Catiline and his followers, after being put down by Cicero, fled to the hill town of Fiesole. The town was subjugated by a Roman army, which built Florence on the plain below. Villani explained that the city was populated by a mixture of Fiesolans and Romans, and commented that it was no wonder if the Florentines were always at war and dissension among themselves, given that they descended from "two peoples so opposite, hostile and divergent in habits as the Romans, noble and virtuous, and the Fiesolans, boorish and harsh in war." *Cron.* 2.1. Dante's Brunetto follows the same line but emphasizes that only a small minority, including Dante and implicitly himself, descend from the ancient Romans. Given this implacable hostility, Brunetto's exile foreshadows Dante's.

65–66: Cf. the lily among thorns and the apple tree among the trees of the woods in Song of Songs 2:2–3.

70–78: Dante's fortune holds great honor in store because he will dedicate his genius to serving the public good rather than the power of a party. This will make both parties hungry for his ruin; the Blacks will exile him and the behavior of the White exiles will cause him to break with them in disgust, earning their hatred. Neither party, however, will succeed in destroying him.

76: The "holy seed" within the tree (Isai. 6:13) was the prophet Isaiah's image for the saving remnant of the devastated people of God, identified in the *Glossa Ordinaria* with the twelve apostles. Dante uses the image to sanctify the theme of the "noble seed" (*Inf.* 26.60) saved from the fall of Troy and destined to found the universal empire, of which he is the cultural heir and political supporter.

84–86: Brunetto taught Dante, Pietro explained, that by acquiring knowledge and virtue a man immortalizes himself in this world and gains an imperishable name. Brunetto himself said that after the death of a worthy man "the renown which remains of his good works makes it seem as if he is alive." *Tresor* 2.120; see Davis 1957, 87–90.

88–90: The pilgrim inscribes Brunetto's prophecy in the book of memory and will keep it (along with Farinata's) until he reaches the scholar who can explain it. He assumes this will be Beatrice, but she will delegate the task to his ancestor Cacciaguida.

91–96: The pilgrim confronts the dark prophecies of his future with a principle Dante articulated in the *Convivio* (4.10.7–8): the trivial goods controlled by Fortune's caprice can neither confer nor take away nobility, and a man of rectitude does not change with their changes.

95–96: The sense appears to be "let the world go on its usual course, oblivious of honor." In yoking Fortune with her wheel to the peasant with his mattock, the pilgrim treats her with contempt. In a lyric Dante accepts the gift of exile as an honor. Foster/Boyde No. 81.

97–99: Most commentators think Virgil is praising the pilgrim for noting down Brunetto's prophecy. It would be satisfying to think that he is chiding the pilgrim for not remembering his own recent strictures on those who insult Fortune because they fail to recognize her as the agent of divine providence. *Inf.* 7.70–72, 91–93. But the pilgrim does not understand that providence has chosen exile as the refiner's fire from which the great destiny foretold for him will emerge, though in an altered form. This will be revealed to him only in *Par.* 17. See Najemy 2007, 238.

101–08: The pilgrim asks Brunetto about the people being punished with him as sodomites. Following the intellectual scheme of the theologians, Dante treats sodomy not as a species of lust but, as Aquinas put it, as a violation of nature itself and hence a direct affront to God the author of nature. *ST* 2–2.154.12. By contrast, in *Purg.* 26.25–90 homosexual and heterosexual sins of lust are treated as precise counterparts and the sinners seem equal in numbers. Some critics have wondered whether Dante's attitude had changed by the time he wrote the *Purgatorio*. But these contrasting treatments of sodomy correspond to the different schemes of Dante's hell and purgatory. Lower hell is a prison where the punishments are calibrated to specific crimes – in this case acts that violate nature. Purgatory is a hospital where the cures are adapted to the maladies of the soul – in this case lust.

106–08: The assumption that sodomy was especially prevalent among clerics and in the schools and universities was common in the Middle Ages. Curtius 113–17; Boswell 187. Peter Damian's apocalyptic warnings of epidemic sodomy focus entirely on the clergy, and Alain de Lille's *Complaint of Nature* on the learned.

109: The early medieval grammarian Priscian was one of the two authorities on this all-important subject in the Middle Ages (the other, Donatus, appears in the *Paradiso*). He was taken as the type of the schoolmaster, and as the early commentators noted sodomy was associated with the schools.

110: Francesco d'Accorso (c. 1225–94) was the most famous jurist of his day.

110–14: Andrea de' Mozzi, bishop of Florence, was litigious and ignored a papal order, the probable cause of his transfer to Vicenza, where he died within a year. (The Arno and the Bacchiglione are the rivers of Florence and Vicenza.) See *ED* 3.1051–52. None of this explains why he is singled out for Dante's contempt here.

112: The papal title "servant of the servants of God," current since at least the time of Gregory the Great, is here used ironically of the proud and imperial pontiff Boniface VIII.

114: The phrase *mal protesi nervi* was explained by Buti as a sarcastic reference to Mozzi's sexual practices: "that is, the sinews of the virile member that he had used wrongly, in that he had used it against nature."

118: As the heretics are segregated by sect (*Inf.* 9.130), Buti commented that the sodomites are segregated by their station in life. The approaching cohort consists of soldiers and statesmen.

121–24: Dante refers to an annual footrace held in Verona. The winner received a length of green cloth and the loser was given a rooster as part of a ritual of mockery. The Ottimo said the runners were naked, which would give added point to the comparison.

Canto XVI

Now I had come where one could hear the distant
    rumble of water falling to the circle
    below, which sounded like the drone of beehives,
when three shades separated in a group,
    all running, from a company that was passing   5
    under the terrible torment of the rain.
They came in our direction, each of them crying,
    "Stop for a moment, you who by your dress
    seem to have come from our degenerate city."
Alas, what wounds I saw upon their bodies,   10
    both old and recent, branded by the flames!
    Even the memory saddens me again.
Hearing their cries, my teacher checked his pace,
    and then he turned to me: "Wait now," he said,
    "for these should be received with courtesy.   15
And were it not the nature of this place
    to dart down flames, I would consider haste
    to be more suitable for you than them."
After we paused, they took up once again
    their old lament, and catching up with us   20
    the three arranged themselves to form a wheel.
In the way that champions do, when naked and oiled
    they look for holds by which to gain advantage
    before a blow or bruise has been exchanged,

these three were circling as they kept their gazes   25
    locked upon me, which made their necks revolve
    in the reverse direction to their feet.
Then: "If this wretched waste of yielding sand,
    together with our blackened and skinned features,
    brings scorn upon ourselves and our petitions,"   30
one of them said, "then let our reputations
    make you inclined to tell us who you are
    that walk through hell immune on living feet.
The one whose footprints you can see me tread,
    though now he wanders naked and singed hairless,   35
    was a man of higher rank than you suppose:
this grandson of the virtuous Gualdrada
    bore the name Guido Guerra and in life
    accomplished much with counsel and with arms.
The one whose feet are trampling the sand behind me   40
    is Tegghiaio Aldobrandi, whose advice
    should have been welcomed in the upper world.
And I who have been placed with them in torment
    was Jacopo Rusticucci, and past doubt
    more than all else my shrew of a wife has hurt me."   45
If I had been protected from the fire
    I would have thrown myself down there among them,
    and I believe my teacher would have allowed it;
but since I would have gotten scorched and burned,
    fear overcame the rush of sympathy   50
    that made me yearn to clasp them in my arms.
Then I began, "It was not scorn but sorrow
    that struck my heart at seeing you like this,
    sorrow too great to shed in a short time,
from the first moment that my master here   55
    made a remark from which I understood
    that those who came were men such as yourselves.
Coming from your own city, all my life
    I fondly heard and fondly told again
    your honored names and memorable deeds.   60

I leave the bitterness and journey toward
    the sweet fruit promised by my truthful guide;
    but I must plunge, before that, to hell's core."
"Now may your soul sustain your body yet
    for many years," he answered me again,   65
    "and may your fame still shine when you are gone,
tell us: do noble manners and high merit
    still flourish in our city as they did,
    or have they now forsaken it completely?
For Guglielmo Borsiere, who has suffered   70
    a short time with us and goes there with our
    companions, troubles us much with his reports."
"Florence! The new men and their overnight
    enrichment have spawned arrogance and excess
    within you, and you weep for it already!"   75
I cried these words out with my face uplifted;
    and the three took this for my reply and stared
    at one another like men before the truth.
"If other times," they said, "it costs so little
    to satisfy another, how fortunate   80
    you are if you can speak your mind like that!
And so may you escape from these dark regions,
    returning to behold once more the stars
    in beauty, when it gladdens you to say
'I once was there,' then speak of us to people."   85
    And after that they broke the wheel apart
    and in their flight their swift legs seemed like wings.
You could not even have pronounced *Amen*
    as quickly as they disappeared; and therefore
    my teacher judged that it was time to leave.   90
I followed, and we'd gone but a short distance
    before the roar of the water came so near
    we scarcely could have heard each other speak.
Of all the rivers from Mount Viso eastward
    along the left slope of the Apennines,   95
    the first to take an independent course

is called the Quietwater in the hills
    before it empties into its lower bed
    and, that name left behind below Forlì,
comes thundering down above San Benedetto   100
    dell'Alpe, where it falls in one great leap
    a distance that should take a thousand steps;
so here we came upon the stream's dark water
    thundering down a precipice so loudly
    it would have deafened us in a short while.   105
I had a rope I'd tied around my waist,
    and earlier I had thought of using it
    to snare the leopard with the painted hide.
After I had unwrapped the entire length,
    following the directions of my guide,   110
    I handed it over, rolled and tangled up;
and taking it, he turned toward his right side,
    and casting out some distance from the edge
    he flung it down the bottomless ravine.
"Something unseen till now must surely answer,"   115
    I said within myself, "to this strange signal
    my teacher follows with his eye so closely."
Ah, how much prudence we should exercise
    with those who can not only see our actions
    but with their understanding read our thoughts! 120
"Soon now," he said to me, "there will arise
    what I await and your daydream imagines;
    soon it will be revealed before your eyes."
A man should seal his lips as long as he can
    upon a truth that wears the face of a lie,   125
    for through no fault of his it brings him shame;
but I cannot keep silence here: I swear
    upon the verses of this Comedy,
    reader – may it not lack for lasting favor –
that I could see through that thick murky air   130
    a shape come swimming up that would have struck
    even the most courageous heart with awe,

moving the way a seaman, surfacing

after he's dived to free an anchor snagged

on a reef or something else the sea conceals, 135

comes stretching upward, drawing in his feet.

Notes

3–5: The company of soldiers and statesmen that was seen as an approaching dust-cloud has now drawn even with Virgil and the pilgrim, but it passes a good deal further from the dike than Brunetto's.

7–9: The three sinners recognize the pilgrim by his Florentine costume, as Farinata did by his Florentine speech, and come running for news. Boccaccio said that each city had its distinctive mode of dress.

10–12: Dante provides a telescopic close-up of the sinners' wounds – the pilgrim could not actually see the figures in this detail yet – to set the affective context for the scene that follows.

13–18: Virgil provides a basis for the pity Dante expressed at lines 10–12 by establishing the respect due the approaching sinners. These Florentines were men of signal accomplishments, conspicuous for the nobility of their public conduct, whatever their private failings. To no other figure in hell except Ulysses does Virgil accord such respect. Robert Hollander notes with surprise that Dante treats these three Florentines with greater respect than any other figures in hell except those in limbo. Hollander 1996.

21–27: The strange and dramatic postures of the three sinners are explained by the situation. The terms of their punishment forbid them to remain still, yet they want to keep their attention focused on the pilgrim so as to hear his news. They therefore wheel about in a circle, each one rotating his head so as to keep his gaze fixed on the pilgrim even when wheeling away from him.

22–25: A champion was a substitute fighter in the medieval trial by combat, but Dante is applying the term to a classical archetype. The "naked and oiled" champions recall the companions of Aeneas stripped and slicked with oil engaging in wrestling matches. *Aen.* 3.281–82. The detail of the wrestlers sizing each other up before coming to grips is realistic, but Statius described wrestlers in the same way. *Theb.* 6.760–64. Dante is imagining ancient heroes and calling them "champions" much as he calls them "knights" (*Inf.* 5.71) and as he uses another phrase for the trial by combat to describe the contest of Hercules and Antaeus. *Mon.* 2.7.9–10. Comparing the three sinners to Virgilian athletes gives them dignity, and the question of their dignity versus their abasement becomes the overt theme of the following passage.

34–39: Count Guido Guerra VI (c. 1220–72) belonged to the Conti Guidi, for centuries the most important feudal house of Tuscany. Guido was the military leader of the Tuscan Guelfs in the climactic phase of their struggle with the Ghibellines. He was defeated by Farinata at Montaperti in 1260 and exiled. He gave decisive aid to Charles of Anjou in the defeat of Frederick II's son Manfred in 1266 and returned in triumph to restore Guelf rule in Florence. For Tuscan Guelfs of Dante's generation, he would have been remembered as the man on the white horse.

37: Gualdrada dei Ravignani, born into one of the great Florentine families, married Count Guido Guerra IV about 1180. Her reputation for virtue is reflected in the story told by Villani that she refused to let the emperor kiss her, declaring that that would be the prerogative of her husband alone. *Cron.* 6.37.

40–42: Tegghiaio Aldobrandi was a leading politician in the first Guelf commune in Florence in the mid-13th century. The advice that should have been valued was his advice to the Florentines to wait out the summer of 1260, after which the Ghibellines would be weakened by the departure of their allied German cavalry. See *Cron.* 7.77. Rejection of this advice led to the Florentine military disaster at Montaperti, where Aldobrandi nonetheless was one of the Florentine captains.

43–45: Jacopo Rusticucci was Aldobrandi's ally in Guelf politics in Florence and held office under the first Guelf commune. The pilgrim asked Ciacco about both of them as worthy men whose fate he wished to know. *Inf.* 6.79–81.

45: As with the sinners in *Inf.* 15, nothing in the biographies of these three supports the allegation of sodomy. Jacopo's elliptical remark is the one time a sinner in either canto alludes to his sin. It comports with the evidence that a significant minority of men incriminated for sodomy were married. See Rocke 120–22. Jacopo's implication appears to be that he turned to adolescent boys for the tenderness he could not get from his shrewish wife.

54–55: Grief enters swiftly like a knife, but departs little by little like leaves falling from a tree.

67: "Noble manners and high merit." The formula *cortesia e valor* goes back to the troubadours and here evokes a civilized ideal of public life consistent with Brunetto's but with a more aristocratic emphasis. See *ED* 1.872 and Chiavacci Leonardi; see also Larner 96–99 on favored terms for aristocratic values.

70: Guglielmo Borsiere appears in one of Boccaccio's stories as a worthy man, well dressed and well spoken. *Decam.* 1.8.

73–75: Dante's judgment on Florence cuts to the root of the important economic forces transforming his society. Dante's Florence was a boom town that from the mid-13th century had increasingly become a center of manufacturing, commerce and banking. As people flocked in from the countryside, the city's population, about 50,000 in 1200, reached almost 100,000 by 1300. Waley 21. Power shifted from the landed aristocracy to the financial and commercial bourgeoisie, leading to greatly increased social mobility.

Dante regards these new social forces, which were to render irrelevant his ideal of an unchanging Christendom co-managed by pope and emperor, simply as manifestations of greed. Greed is the chief obstacle to social justice, and the emperor's chief duty is to restrain it. *Conv.* 4.4.1–4; *Mon.* 1.13.7. The pilgrim's judgment here is that the quick profits of greedy upstarts have made them arrogant, which has fomented the unending violence for which Florence weeps. Dante was not alone in this judgment. Dino Campagni (1.1) described the Florentines as "proud and contentious and rich with unlawful profits." Huizenga remarks that whereas pride had been regarded as the foremost sin in the feudal period, by the later Middle Ages, when the increasing circulation of money had changed the conditions of power and a new class could satisfy its ambition by accumulating wealth, greed became the predominant sin in people's imaginations. Hatred of the rich, especially of the new rich, was general. Huizenga 27–28; see also Scott 177.

Lino Pertile reminds us that what Dante is rejecting is the dynamic, enterprising society that was emerging in Florence and would open the way to the Renaissance and advocating instead a static aristocratic structure believed to be ordained by God, in which all change is degeneration. Pertile 1997, 6, 13–16.

76: Lifting his face upward, the pilgrim makes the public gesture of a prophet, who calls on heaven to witness the truth of his judgment on his people.

79–85: The three sinners are praising the pilgrim's boldness in speaking out against public abuses and are asking him to keep their memory alive because he shares their civic ideals (Chiavacci Leonardi). This request to be remembered stands out among the others in the *Inferno* for its Virgilian note of noble pathos.

91–135: The pilgrim will spend the rest of *Inf.* 16 reaching the edge of the lower pit. In sharp contrast with the preceding scenes, this journey veers toward the fantastical, mythopoeic end of the *Inferno*'s range and becomes eerie and suspenseful.

94–105: This simile provides a waterfall on earth as a reference for the noise level the pilgrim experiences at the waterfall in hell. Lines 94–99 do not contribute to this purpose, but giving geographic specificity to the earthly term of the comparison reinforces the reality of its infernal counterpart. Theodore Cachey finds a further significance in the simile. The circle of violence opens and closes with images of violent nature: the earthquake simile of *Inf.* 12.1–13 and here the simile of the thundering waterfall, marking the boundary to the region of fraud. Cachey 332.

94–96: Mt. Viso rises in the Alps near the French border. All the rivers between Mt. Viso and Dante's river, the Montone, run into the Po, whereas in Dante's time the Montone ran directly into the Adriatic.

97–99: The Acquacheta ("Quietwater") is actually a tributary of the Montone.

100: San Benedetto dell'Alpe was a Benedictine monastery along the road from Forlì and near the cascade of the Acquacheta, as Dante specifies.

106–17: Virgil is calling from the depths Geryon, the guardian monster of the circle of fraud below. Without benefit of explanation, the pilgrim recognizes that the mysterious ritual Virgil performs is a summoning charm, and he is tense with expectation of some fantastic creature unseen as yet. Commentators assume that the rope carries an allegorical significance, but they do not agree on what that might be, largely because the available clues – the rope's potential use to snare the leopard and its use as bait for Geryon – are open-ended.

The surprising information that the pilgrim intended to use the rope to capture the leopard (*Inf.* 1.31–36) leads critics who associate the leopard with lust, or more generally with sins of self-indulgence, to identify the rope with self-discipline or temperance. Such a meaning would be traditional, as when St. Francis exchanged his leather belt for a rope, a sign of asceticism. *Gold. Leg.* 2.221; see *Inf.* 27.92–93. This reading fails to explain, however, why throwing the rope over the ledge attracts Geryon.

The early commentators thought the rope symbolized fraud itself. The rope's being wound and knotted resembles the coils of the monster and the circlets painted on his skin. See *Inf.* 17.14–17 and note. Virgil could thus be using a symbol of fraud to decoy Geryon to a supposed sinner destined for the eighth circle. That would explain Geryon's sulkiness when he is cheated of his prey. *Inf.* 17.127–36. This reading may also be consistent with the pilgrim's intention to take the leopard with the rope if the leopard represents fraud, a common modern interpretation. See note to *Inf.* 1.31–60. Susan Noakes suggests that the rope itself is transformed into Geryon. Noakes 1998, 221.

124–27: Dante seeks to bolster credibility for the special effect he will spring at the opening of the next canto by admitting that the account is incredible. He reinforces his position as a common-sense observer of the fabulous, one who will risk being called a liar because the force of what he saw compels him to speak.

125: Brunetto Latini had used the same phrase, urging the prudent man to withhold judgment in doubtful situations because "truth often wears the face of a lie (*la verités a maintes fois face de mençoigne*), while a lie is dressed in the appearance of truth." *Tresor* 2.58.3. Brunetto's reciprocal formula will be cunningly echoed here, because the truth that wears the face of a lie will be Dante's account of Geryon, who will prove to be a lie that wears the face of the truth.

128: This is the first time Dante has called his work a comedy; he will do so again at *Inf.* 21.2. (The epithet "divine" was not added until the 16th century.) In the epistle to Can Grande, Dante defined his work as a comedy because it was a poetic narrative that began in misery and ended in prosperity (starting in hell and ending in heaven) and it was written in an informal, colloquial style in the vernacular. *Epist.* 13.31. These conservative principles, however, relate uncertainly to the *Comedy.* In particular, the *Comedy* contains characters from the highest to the lowest status and similarly embraces every level of style and use of language, contrary to the inherited norms Dante cites. Critics have suggested, however, that by Dante's time the term comedy signified the most inclusive and flexible of the poetic genres and therefore best accommodated the originality of his poem. See *DE* 180–81, 184–87.

Canto XVII

"Look now upon the beast with the barbed tail,
    who crosses mountains, breaks through walls and weapons!
    Behold the one whose stench infects the world!"
Even as he began to speak, my guide
    was making signs for it to come ashore   5
    near where the masonry we'd walked on ended.
And that obscene embodiment of fraud
    approached until it beached its head and body,
    but did not draw its tail up onto the bank.
It had the countenance of an honest man,   10
    so gracious in the appearance it conveyed,
    with all the rest belonging to a serpent;
its two forepaws were furry to the armpits,
    its back, its chest and both its sides were painted
    with interlaced designs of knots and circlets.   15
No Turks or Tartars ever used more colors
    to form the ground or figure for their textiles,
    nor did Arachne's weaving blend such hues.
As river barges lie upon the banks,
    partly in water and partly on the land,   20
    and as up north among the gluttonous Germans
the beaver settles down to lay its siege,
    before us the evil animal lay poised
    upon the rim of stone that girds the sand;

and wriggling in the void, its length of tail   25
   twisted up overhead the poisoned fork
   that, as upon a scorpion's, armed its tip.
"Now it is necessary for our path
   to turn aside a little," said my teacher,
   "toward that malevolent creature perching there."   30
Then we descended on the right hand side
   and took ten steps along the very brink,
   so keeping well away from the sand and the flames.
When we had reached the beast I noticed, somewhat
   further beyond it on the sand, some people   35
   seated upon the edge of empty space.
And there my teacher said to me, "Go now,
   view their condition, so that you may take
   the full experience of this ring with you.
But let your conversation there be brief;   40
   till your return I shall confer with this one
   to gain for us the loan of his strong shoulders."
And so, still further on the uttermost edge
   of the seventh circle, all alone I went
   and came where those unhappy people sat.   45
Their grief came bursting from their eyes; their hands
   shielded them now on one side, now the other
   against the burning air and the burning sand,
much the way dogs will do in summertime,
   now with their snouts and now with their hind paws,   50
   when fleas or gnats or horseflies bite at them.
And when I turned my gaze upon the faces
   of some on whom the painful fire was falling,
   I did not recognize any; but I noticed
that from the neck of each a bag was hanging,   55
   each with its special color and insignia,
   and they appeared to feast their eyes on these.
Then as I came among them looking about,
   upon a yellow pouch I saw a figure
   in blue that had a lion's shape and posture.   60

My gaze then rolling further on, I saw
    another pouch as red as blood, and whiter
    than butter was the goose displayed upon it.
One of the shades, whose bag was white and bore
    the image of a gravid sow in blue,   65
    said to me, "What's your business in this pit?
Leave us alone – and since you're still alive
    remember this: my neighbor Vitaliano
    will take his seat upon my left side here.
I am the only Paduan in this crowd   70
    of Florentines, and they often make my ears
    ring with their shouting: 'Let him come, the peerless
knight who will bring the bag with the three goats!'"
    He stretched his mouth and stuck his tongue far out,
    the way an ox does when it licks its nose.   75
And I, afraid a longer stay would vex
    the one who'd cautioned me to keep it brief,
    turned back and left those weary souls behind.
I found my leader mounted up already
    upon the back of that ferocious creature.   80
    From there he told me, "Now be strong and daring;
from here on we descend by steps like these.
    Climb up in front – I want to be in the middle
    in order that its tail may do no harm."
During the shivering stage of quartan fever   85
    your nails turn blue and you begin to tremble
    all over if you only look at shade:
I was like that reacting to his words;
    but shame was yet more threatening, which can make
    a servant brave before his valiant lord.   90
I took my seat upon those monstrous shoulders,
    wanting to say – my voice, though, would not come
    the way I meant it to – "Be sure to hold me."
But he who'd come to my relief before
    in other dangers clasped me in his arms   95
    once I had mounted and supported me.

"Geryon, shove off now," he said, "and make
   your wheelings wide, descending gradually;
   be mindful of your unaccustomed burden."
It moved off in the same way that a boat does,   100
   backing and backing as it leaves its berth;
   and when it felt it had complete free play
it turned, reversing tail in place of chest,
   and stretching it, made motions like an eel,
   while gathering in the air with both its paws.   105
I think that Phaeton could have felt no greater
   fear in the moment when he dropped the reins,
   scorching the sky as you can still observe,
nor the unlucky Icarus when he felt
   his sides unfeathering from the melting wax   110
   and heard his father shouting, "You're off course!"
than I felt when I saw myself surrounded
   by nothing but thin air on every side,
   with every sight extinguished but the beast.
Slowly, slowly, it goes swimming on;   115
   it wheels and sinks, but I can only tell
   by the wind against my face and from below.
And now upon my right I heard the torrent
   making a terrifying roar beneath us,
   which made me thrust my head out to look down.   120
Then I was still more fearful of tumbling off,
   for I could make out fires and hear great weeping;
   and trembling, I gripped the tighter with my knees.
Then I could gauge our circling and descent,
   as earlier I could not, by the great torments   125
   that started drawing near on every side.
A falcon that has long been on the wing
   and sighted neither lure nor bird will cause
   the falconer to cry, "Oh no, you're dropping!"
by sinking wearily through a hundred wheelings   130
   back where it swiftly rose and will alight
   far from its master, sullen and resentful.

Geryon likewise set us on the bottom,

    right at the foot of the sheer wall of rock,

    and once he was unburdened of our persons   135

vanished the way an arrow leaves the bowstring.

Notes

1–3: The arrival from the depths is Geryon, the demon of fraud and guardian of the eighth circle. Against fraud natural defenses and human fortifications and weapons are of no use; Pietro noted that the fraud of the wooden horse had breached the walls of Troy.

7–27: As the allegorical description of Geryon progresses from head to tail, the monster changes aspect, his nature fully realized only at the end. The bland human face on the body of a serpent is an image well known in medieval art, where Satan was represented as taking the form of a serpent with a maiden's face when he tempted Eve. Pietro connected his father's description of Geryon with this image of Satan. Langland described Satan in the garden as a "lizard with a lady visage." *Piers Plowman* 18.337.

13: The furry clawed forelegs are probably those of a lion, evoking another medieval iconographical equivalent. The manticore, which appeared in the bestiaries, was a composite creature with a man's face, a lion's body and a scorpion's tail; it fed on human flesh. See *Tresor* 1.192; *Nat. Hist.* 8.30.

14–17: The knots and little wheels painted on the monster are perhaps a reminiscence of the geometric complexity of Islamic design, known from trade with Turks and Tartars. They symbolize the winding subterfuges of fraud, an association thought fitting for the art of people believed to be traitors to the true faith. See note to *Inf.* 28.22–27. The profusion of hues figures the manifest allurements of deceit and may also allude to the hypnotic powers of serpents, like the scitalis, described by Brunetto as "so well spotted with clear and shining colors that people flock willingly to look at it as it approaches them." *Tresor* 1.142.

18: Arachne, a great weaver, challenged a goddess to a contest in which she wove a masterpiece of bright colors subtly modulated like the rainbow. *Metam.* 6.1–145.

19–27: Geryon presents its guileless human face, while leaving in the void its scorpion tail, ever poised to strike, with its double barb symbolizing the duplicity of fraud. In this, the monster also recalls the locusts of Apoc. 9:7–10, which are composite beasts whose parts include men's faces and the tails of scorpions. Chaucer, who had never seen a scorpion, concluded that it was an animal that approached its victim with a deceiving face while preparing to sting with its tail. Merchant's Tale 2058–59.

21–22: Pietro explained the belief that the beaver sat on the bank and fished with its tail. Agitating the fatty tail in the water would release oily drops that attracted fish, which the beaver would turn around quickly to catch.

28–30: The Ottimo explained that the path to fraud is not direct but twisting.

34–75: *The usurers.* Dante never expressly identifies the sin of those who sit beside the void, but he indicates it clearly by reference to medieval iconography. The pilgrim's impression of these people is dominated by the bags hanging from their necks, which appear to absorb their attention and their very identities. A square flat bag hanging from the neck is a standard attribute of one of the damned souls in a Last Judgment on a cathedral tympanum (*e.g.*, Rheims, Laon, Chartres), and its presence here would have identified these sinners as "usurers," that is, moneylenders or bankers. The bags are moneybags, tools of the lender's trade, and they hang from his neck to display his sin.

By decree of Pope Urban III in 1187, usury consisted of charging any interest for providing a loan. LeGoff 1990, 26. Moral concern with lending at interest was intense from the 12th to the 14th centuries, the period that saw the birth of early capitalism, with the rise of commerce and credit and a great increase in the amount of money in circulation. Lending at interest became a big business and was increasingly decried as gravely sinful. Moneylenders were supposed to be excommunicated and denied Christian burial, but they appear to have been tolerated when they stayed within commonly accepted interest rates. These rates were very high compared with those of more developed economies; in Florence rates were generally between 20 and 30 percent. LeGoff 1990, 35–36, 70–71.

46–51: The restless motion of the hands trying to brush away the flames was previously noted for the sinners of the seventh circle. *Inf.* 14.40–42. The simile of the dogs here, however, introduces the pungent realism of Dante's comic style and indicates that the pilgrim will feel no sympathy for these sinners.

57: The disjunction between the usurers' preoccupation and the place in which they find themselves is grimly comic. They sit beside the void for eternity as they did behind their counters, their eyes fixed gloatingly on the moneybags to which they persist in attributing supreme value.

58–73: The pilgrim claims not to recognize any of the sinners, thus consigning them to the anonymity of the misers and spendthrifts of *Inf.* 7; but the insignias on their moneybags identify them as members of banking families, all but one Florentine. The social level that the family crests imply indicates that these usurers were merchant bankers rather than simple moneylenders. Florence was one of the leading centers in which the techniques of modern banking were developed, and by 1300 Florentine bankers carried on an important international business, employing agents in all the major trading centers of Europe.

This episode continues the condemnation of Florence's sudden wealth – much of which came from banking – pronounced by the pilgrim in *Inf.* 16. Dante feels contempt for the "new men," the rising bourgeois who were being knighted, like the Scrovegni; but the focus of his satire here is on the old nobility who were becoming moneymen, like the Obriachi. (In *Par.* 16 Dante's ancestor Cacciaguida will lambaste the Florentine aristocracy for intermarrying with commercial bourgeois.) The escutcheons that once stood for the *cortesia e valor* (*Inf.* 16.67) of the noble families are now no more than corporate logos that the bankers' eyes caress only because they mark the ownership of sacks of coin. This bourgeois obsession is the opposite of the liberality that Dante held to be essential to nobility. See Conv. 4.13, 4.17.

59–60: The first bag bears the arms – *on a field or, a lion rampant azure* – of the Gianfigliazzi, a prominent Guelf family of Florence.

62–63: The arms on the second bag – *on a field gules, a goose argent* – are those of the Obriachi, an old and powerful Ghibelline family of Florence with extensive banking operations.

64–73: The speaker's bag bears the arms – *on a field argent, a gravid sow azure* – of the Scrovegni of Padua. The speaker is Reginaldo degli Scrovegni, one of the most successful bankers of the late 13th century. He addresses the pilgrim with the abruptness and arrogance of a man whose success in business has given him a high self-regard.

68–69: The early commentators identified this character as Vitaliano del Dente, Reginaldo's son-in-law. Reginaldo not only savors the prospect of his relative's damnation but also awaits him as an ally against the foolish Florentines.

72–73: The colleague whom the Florentines expect is Giovanni Buiamonti. His bag will bear the arms – *on a field or, three goats sable* – of his family, which had banking interests extending from Florence to France. Buiamonti, who held office in Florence and was knighted, is clearly *il cavalier sovranno* to the Florentine usurers only because of the scale on which he conducts usury. This is the satiric punch-line of the episode, driving home the point that money-grubbing is incompatible with nobility.

74–75: The simile of the ox, which closes the episode of the usurers, echoes the simile of the scratching dogs, which opened it. In between, the usurers are shadowy backgrounds on which the vivid bags are superimposed like masks, making the sinners undergo a Circean transformation into the lion, goose, pig and goats of their logos.

85–93: The pilgrim is everyman, whose reactions guide the reader's response to the horrors of hell. Although his fear of demons is rational rather than cowardly, the physical symptoms of fear are always comical to a detached observer. See *Inf.* 21.25–30 and note.

97: *Geryon.* One of Hercules' exploits was to kill Geryon and take his great herd of cattle. Ovid and Virgil do not attempt to describe Geryon, but merely refer to him as "triple" or "three-bodied." *Heroides* 9.91–92; *Aen.* 8.202. Dante has updated this "tripleness" through the popular medieval imagery of composite monsters.

100–36: Geryon swims slowly through the air in a wide descending spiral, another figure for the toils of fraud. Dante makes the composite beast move in a convincingly plastic manner, first backing out from the shore in a last appearance of the boat imagery, then swimming through the thick air, combining the techniques of an eel with those of a mammal. The imaginative tour de force, however, is Dante's persuasive evocation of flying through the air – a harrowing experience that no one had ever had – by summoning one after another the pilgrim's precise tactile, auditory and finally visual sensations as he descends slowly.

106–08: Allowed to drive the chariot of the sun by his father, the sun god, Phaeton was unable to control the fiery horses and grew giddy when he looked down. He dropped the reins, and the horses of the sun bolted from their courses, setting fire to the sky. *Metam.* 2.1–324.

108: Phaeton's scorched track is the Milky Way. In his philosophical writing, Dante had rejected this explanation of the galaxy "influenced by the fable of Phaeton," preferring the explanation that the galaxy is a band of stars too small to distinguish. *Conv.* 2.14.

109–11: Daedalus, imprisoned with his young son Icarus in the Cretan labyrinth he had created, designed wings of feathers held together by wax. They flew out of the labyrinth, but in the intoxication of flight Icarus ignored his father's warning to "hold a middle course." As he flew too near the sun the wax of his wings melted and he fell into the sea. *Metam.* 8.183–235.

127–32: The falcon's hunting technique is to "stoop," or fall from a height, upon another bird. A trained falcon was supposed to stay aloft until it saw prey to stoop on or until the falconer called it back by whirling a lure, made of birds' wings on an armature attached to a cord. Dante's falcon tires before either happens and descends in a series of slow wheels through the air.

Canto XVIII

Hell has a region known as Devil's Gulches,
    entirely formed from iron-colored rock
    like the encircling rampart of the cliffs.
Dead in the center of that evil space
    there yawns a very wide deep well, whose features   5
    I shall account for at the proper time,
so the remaining belt between this well
    and the base of the rocky wall is circular,
    its floor divided up into ten valleys.
When moats are looped outside of other moats   10
    around a castle to defend its walls,
    the ground they occupy displays a pattern
configured like the one these valleys formed;
    and just as from the gate of such a fortress
    small bridges lead across to the outer bank,   15
down here stone ridges ran from the cliff's base
    and spanned the banks and ditches up to the well,
    which cut them off and gathered them together.
Shaken from Geryon's back, it was this place
    in which we found ourselves; and then the poet   20
    set out upon the left and I behind him.
I saw upon my right new anguish, torments
    not seen before, strange torturers wielding whips,
    for spectacles like these filled the first gulch.

Down on the bottom naked sinners walked,   25
    approaching on our side but on the other
    pacing our progress though with longer strides,
as the Romans in the year of the Jubilee,
    because of the great crowds, devised a method
    for making people cross the Tiber bridge   30
so that on one side everybody faced
    the castle and proceeded toward St. Peter's,
    while on the other side they faced the hill.
Scattered upon the dark rock on both sides
    I saw horned demons standing with great whips,   35
    who struck the sinners cruelly from behind.
Ah, how they made them lift their heels up high
    at the first lash! for there was none among them
    who waited for a second or a third.
My eyes, as I was walking, chanced upon   40
    the eyes of one of them; and I exclaimed
    at once, "I know I've seen that face before!"
And so I stopped to make him out more clearly;
    my kindly leader halted too and even
    permitted me to go a short way back.   45
The one beneath the lash thought he could hide
    by lowering his face; it did not help,
    for I called out, "You there, that drop your eyes:
unless the face you're wearing lies about you,
    your name's Venèdico Caccianemico.   50
    But what has landed you in such hot sauce?"
"Unwillingly I say it," he replied,
    "but your plain speech, which makes me once again
    remember the old world, compels my answer.
I it was who induced Ghisolabella   55
    to satisfy the marquis's desires,
    however they now tell the sordid tale.
Nor am I the only Bolognese who weeps here;
    the place is so well stocked with us, in fact,
    that fewer tongues now learn our dialect term   60

for *yes* between the Sàvena and the Reno;
    and if you want convincing evidence
    of that, recall our avaricious hearts."
As he was saying this, a demon struck him
    with a leather whip and said, "Get moving, pimp!   65
    There are no women here to play your tricks on."
I joined my guide again and after that
    it took us only a few more steps to reach
    a rocky ridge projecting from the cliffs.
This we were able easily to mount,   70
    and turning right upon its jagged spine,
    we left behind those everlasting circuits.
When we had climbed above the opening
    through which they pass as they are whipped along,
    my leader said, "Stop here, and let the gaze   75
of the remaining misbegotten wretches
    confront you, those whose faces you have not
    yet seen because they walked in our direction."
From the old bridge we gazed upon the line
    advancing toward us on the other side,   80
    who were likewise driven onward by the lash.
And my good master said, without my asking,
    "See the commanding figure who approaches,
    seeming to shed no tears despite the pain:
how like a king he carries himself still!   85
    That one is Jason: cunning and courageous,
    he carried off the fleece as spoil from Colchis.
His journey took him past the Isle of Lemnos
    after its women, bold and pitiless,
    had put their males to death to the last man.   90
There he deceived the young Hypsipyle
    with amorous looks and artful words, the girl
    who had deceived the other women first.
There, solitary and with child, he left her;
    and that offense condemns him to this torment,   95
    by which Medea is avenged as well.

With him go all who practice such deceit;
    and let that be enough for you to know
    of this first valley and those between its teeth."
Now we had reached the point where the narrow path   100
    crosses the second bank and makes it serve
    as the abutment for another arch.
There we heard people uttering smothered groans
    in the other gulch and snorting through their snouts
    and slapping open palms against themselves.   105
The banks were thickly overgrown with mold
    formed where the exhalation from below
    stuck to them, irritating eyes and nose.
The bottom is so deep there is no place
    to view it from unless you climb the arch   110
    to where its rocky back heaves up the highest.
We climbed it, and from there I made out people
    down in the ditch, immersed in excrement
    that looked as though it came from earth's latrines.
While searching with my eyes down there, I noticed   115
    someone whose head was so befouled by shit
    you could not tell if he were priest or layman.
"Why do you stare so greedily at me,"
    he yelled, "when all the rest are just as foul?"
    "Because," I answered, "if my memory serves,   120
I used to see you with dry hair. You're surely
    Alessio Interminelli of Lucca.
    That's why I look at you more than at them."
To which he answered, drumming on his dome,
    "The flatteries of which no surfeit ever   125
    made my tongue gag have plunged me into this."
And afterwards my leader said, "Now stretch
    your line of sight a little further forward
    until you get a good look at the face
of the filthy slut with the disheveled hair   130
    scratching herself with shit-caked fingernails,
    squatting one moment and standing up the next.

That one is Thaïs: she is the prostitute
   who when her patron asked 'Have I deserved
   your gratitude?' replied 'Eternally!'   135
And with that sight, we've had enough of this."

Notes

1–18: Halfway through the *Inferno*, the opening of canto 18 lays out the terrain
   of the eighth circle that the poets will traverse for the next 13 cantos. This
   description is based on the aerial view the pilgrim could only have obtained
   from Geryon's back: ten concentric circular canyons in the gray rock, intersected
   by spurs of the same rock arranged like the spokes of a wheel. The modular
   structure of these gulches – as Gothic as a row of niches on a cathedral
   façade – with each gulch holding a different category of sinner, articulates
   an anatomy of the species of fraud.

1: *Devil's Gulches.* Dante's name for the whole circle is *Malebolge*, "Evil purses," each
   gulch being a *bolgia*, a pouch, though Dante also calls them valleys and ditches.

10–18: The simile of the castle and its moats continues the imagery of lower hell
   as Satan's fortress. The city of Dis and the eighth and ninth circles within it can
   be entered only by crossing formidable barriers. In each case the poets need help
   to cross and are confronted by a guardian castle. In *Inf.* 8 the castle was literal;
   here it is metaphorical. Dante interprets the gulches as the outer defense works
   of the central pit that, as will appear, contains the ninth circle and constitutes
   Satan's final stronghold – his donjon as well as his dungeon – which the pilgrim
   will see bristling with towers in *Inf.* 31.

20–21: The poets proceed clockwise, as they do throughout hell. They turn left and
   walk along a circular ledge inside the cliffs, with the first of the gulches yawning
   below them on the right. (Freccero 1986, 72–75 explains why turning to the left
   results in clockwise circulation in the *Inferno*.)

28–33: A contemporary public event helped early readers visualize the novelty of
   regimented two-way traffic. In 1300 Boniface VIII declared the first jubilee year,
   and his offer of a plenary indulgence to pilgrims who came to Rome brought great
   crowds from all over Europe. See *Cron.* 9.36. The bridge that leads over the Tiber
   to St. Peter's would have been continually thronged, and a barrier was erected to
   separate the streams going to and from the basilica. Crossing toward St. Peter's, they
   faced Hadrian's tomb, known since the Middle Ages as the Castel' Sant' Angelo;
   crossing in the other direction, they faced a hill known as Mount Giordano.

34–39: The two files of sinners are driven by lashes in the same fashion but in
   opposite directions because they are guilty of similar but in a sense opposite sins.

The sinners on the outside are pimps and those on the inside are seducers. The seducers persuaded women to serve their pleasure before abandoning them, while the pimps persuaded women to serve the pleasure of others for their profit. The appropriateness of whipping to this gulch is legal rather than symbolic. Whipping was a common punishment for morals offenses, and Sapegno notes that it was decreed for pimps in several communal statutes.

34–36: Traditional medieval devils previously appeared in *Inf.* 8, guarding the castle at the entrance of lower hell. Only in the eighth circle do they appear in their traditional role of torturers.

37–39: This exclamation expresses not commiseration (as in *Inf.* 16.10–12) but sarcasm; Dante enjoys his gibe at the expense of the damned. This note will be common in Devil's Gulches, as will the low comic style appropriate to medieval devils and to Dante's contempt for these sinners.

46–54: Most of the sinners of the first seven circles have besought the pilgrim to keep their names alive in the upper world. But fraud operates by concealing itself, and most sinners in the eighth and ninth circles want the secret of their crimes to perish with them. The pilgrim pins the sinner to the floor of the gulch with his own name, making revelation of the sin part of fraud's punishment.

51: The pilgrim's mocking "hot sauce" is a kitchen metaphor for the sting of the lash.

50–57: The sinner attempting to hide his face, whom the pilgrim treats so contemptuously, was an important man who served as *podestà* of several cities. Venedico Caccianemico was born into a leading Guelf family of Bologna and in the city's factional struggles was a lifelong supporter of Obizzo d'Este, Marquis of Ferrara. *ED* 1.740. Venedico implies that his confession (which is not confirmed by other sources) would have been a surprise to contemporaries, because a different version of the story was in circulation.

58–63: So far all the moral castigation has been reserved for Florence. Beginning here, residents of other cities will appear who exemplify vices for which Dante holds their citizens proverbial.

60–61: The local color includes the fact that in Bolognese dialect the word for "yes" was *sipa* (variant of *sia*) instead of the standard *sì*. The rivers Reno and Sàvena flow on either side of Bologna.

83–96: The king of Colchis in the Crimea promised Jason the golden fleece of a magical ram that hung in a wood if he could perform three impossible tasks. Jason succeeded with the help of the king's daughter Medea, a powerful witch who fell in love with him. *Metam.* 7.1–158.

83–87: The low-comedy mode of the previous scene is abandoned for the elevated language in which Virgil gives his due to an ancient hero. Unlike the raving blasphemer Capaneus (*Inf.* 14.46–72), Jason is accorded a touch of grandeur for refusing to acknowledge that eternal punishment can break his spirit.

88–93: Venus made the women of the island of Lemnos repulsive to their men. Swearing revenge, the women put their sleeping fathers, husbands, brothers and sons to the sword. Only the king's daughter, Hypsipyle, broke faith and helped her father escape the island. *Theb.* 5.29–325.

91–96: On their way to Colchis, Jason and his companions stopped at Lemnos shortly after the slaughter of the males and, welcomed by the women, set about repopulating the island. Jason took Hypsipyle for himself. One day on Jason's orders the men took off again on their mission. *Theb.* 5.335–485; Ovid, *Heriodes* 6. Arrived in Colchis, Jason became Medea's lover to gain her help, but abandoned her in turn when it became expedient. *Heroides* 12.

Dante follows a tradition in which the Jason-Hypsipyle and Jason-Medea stories served as *exempla* of seduction and abandonment. Ovid's *Heroides* included both stories and his format emphasized the plight of the victim, as Dante does. *The Romance of the Rose* 13,229–264 included the Jason-Medea story among similar *exempla*; and Dante paraphrased this passage in *Fiore* 161.

99: The walls of the gulch are imagined as jaws with teeth that grasp the sinners, a reminiscence of the hell-mouth of medieval art and drama, in which the entrance to hell was pictured as Satan's mouth devouring sinners.

100–14: *The second gulch.* The sinners at the bottom of the deep trench are the flatterers. For those who never gagged on nauseating flattery, living at the bottom of a cesspool is an eternal lesson in disgust. The punishment reifies the moral state to which these people debased themselves and elaborates in allegory the gross images in which popular speech still expresses its attitude toward flatterers. Contrary to commentators who think the flatterers are standing in their own excrement (e.g., Pagliaro 626), line 14 suggests it is that of the world they flattered, as the popular expressions imply. Zygmunt Baranski notes the precedents for Dante's scatological language in Christian religious writing. Baranski 2003, 266–67.

Dante's conception of flattery was influenced by Cicero's *De Amicitia*, whose treatment of the subject was standard in the Middle Ages. Cicero held that flattery harms friendship, which should be based on truth. Flattery debases the flatterer because it is unworthy of a free man, let alone a friend; and it debases the person flattered because he becomes a dupe. *De Amicitia* 24–26. Aquinas too regarded flattery largely as an offense to friendship. *ST* 2–2.115.1–2. The ancient and medieval authors generally did not articulate what appears today as the signal danger of flattery: it isolates powerful people in a feedback loop that amplifies their worst tendencies. Tyrants create flatterers but flatterers also create tyrants.

105: The gulch's inhabitants slap their bodies in sign of grief, as the Furies do in *Inf.* 9.50.

115–36: Nothing concrete is known about Alessio Interminelli. Benvenuto said that he "could not utter a word that he did not season with the oil of flattery; he anointed everyone, he licked everyone, even the meanest hired servants." The comment may be no more than an amplification of the text. In social terms, a man who flatters even the humble may merit contempt for his cringing servility.

Eth. 4.3 (1124b31–1125a2); *In Eth.* ¶ 776. In moral terms, however, the man who simply tries to please is not especially blameworthy. *ST* 2–2.115.1–2.

125–26: Like Venedico's punishment, Alessio's is conveyed comically through a kitchen metaphor, but this one is richer, sliding between the functions of the tongue as organ of speech and organ of taste. See *ED* 5.461. Baranski argues that Dante groups the flatterers with the pimps and seducers because they all abused the gift of speech, and that he places both first in the eighth gulch because false speech is emblematic of the sins of fraud. Baranski 2003, 269–72.

117: You could not tell whether his crown showed white from having been shaved in the clerical tonsure. See *Inf.* 7.38–39 and note.

118: "Greedily" continues the kitchen metaphors and repeats the motif of the pilgrim staring at the sinner, culminating in the public revelation of the sinner's identity.

127–35: The sinners of the second gulch balance those of the first. In both cases the pilgrim contemptuously exposes a contemporary, after which Virgil moralizes on a figure of the ancient world. The figure of Thaïs comes from a Latin comedy by Terence, but Dante misattributes the lines he cites. The braggart captain Thraso, having sent the parasite Gnatho with a present to the courtesan Thaïs, asks him, "Does Thaïs really send me great thanks?" Gnatho replies, "Prodigious!" *The Eunuch* 391–92. Dante was not recalling the scene from Terence directly, because the citation came pre-selected as an example of flattery by exaggeration in Cicero. *De Amicitia* 26.98.

Her name alone would have made clear to a medieval reader that Thaïs was a prostitute. Originating with a celebrated courtesan of ancient Greece, "Thaïs" became a type-name for a prostitute in antiquity, and this use continued in the Middle Ages. There is a St. Thaïs, a reformed prostitute, in *The Golden Legend*. The figure was coarsened and expressly portrayed as a flatterer in a tale contained in a popular collection attributed to Aesop. *ED* 5.510; *DE* 811.

Canto XIX

O Simon Magus! O you wretched tribe
    who follow him and driven by your greed
    have dared to prostitute the things of God,
which ought to be the brides of holiness,
    for gold and silver! Now for you the trumpet   5
    must sound, for you inhabit the third gulch.
We had already climbed, at the succeeding
    tomb, to the ridge's highest point, which hangs
    directly over the middle of the trench.
O wisdom supreme, how great the art you show   10
    in heaven, on earth and in the evil world,
    how just the dispensations of your power!
I saw that all along the bottom and sides
    of the gulch the dusky rock was full of holes,
    all the same size and circular in shape.   15
They looked to me no narrower nor wider
    than those inside my beautiful St. John's
    designed as places for performing baptisms,
one of which, not so many years ago,
    I broke because a boy was drowning in it;   20
    and let that be my seal to set men straight.
Out of the mouth of every hole protruded
    a sinner's feet and the portion of his legs
    up to the thighs, with the remainder hidden.

The soles of every sinner were afire, 25
    causing his legs to twitch so violently
    that ropes or twisted vines would have been snapped.
The way that flames on oily substances
    will only play across the very surface,
    so these did from the heels as far as the toes. 30
"Who is the one who shows his torment, Master,
    by squirming more than any of his companions,"
    I asked, "and whom a redder flame is licking?"
"If you wish it, I will carry you," he answered,
    "down by the easier slope, where you can learn 35
    from him about himself and his misdeeds."
"You are my lord, I wish it if it pleases
    you," I said, "for you know I always follow
    your choice and know what I leave unexpressed."
Then we went out on top of the fourth bank 40
    and turning left descended to the gulch's
    floor, where the space between the holes was meager.
My kindly master carried me on his hip
    and only set me down before the cavity
    of the one who was complaining with his shanks. 45
"Whoever you may be that stand top downwards,
    unhappy soul embedded like a post,
    say something, if you can," I started out.
I stood like a friar hearing the confession
    made by a faithless assassin when already 50
    planted, who calls him back to put off death.
And he shouted: "Are you standing there already,
    Boniface, are you standing there already?
    The writing lied to me by several years.
Already glutted with the wealth for which 55
    you did not fear to trick the beautiful lady
    into a marriage, only to do her violence?"
I stood there feeling like the butt of a joke,
    the way that people do who fail to grasp
    what's said to them and cannot find an answer. 60

Then Virgil prompted, "Tell him right away:
    'I'm not the one – the one you think I am,'"
    and I delivered the suggested answer.
At that the spirit's feet began to twist;
    then sighing, in a voice that now held tears,   65
    "What do you want, then," he replied, "from me?
If knowing who I am is so important
    to you that you've come running down the bank,
    know that I once was clothed in the great mantle.
Truly I was the she-bear's son: I hungered   70
    so to promote the cubs that up above
    great wealth and here myself I pocketed.
Below my head are driven all the other
    popes who preceded me in simony,
    flattened within the fissures of the rock.   75
I too will fall down there on the arrival
    of my successor, whom I thought you were
    when I addressed you with my hasty question.
He will be planted here with crimson feet, though,
    a shorter time than mine have cooked already   80
    as I've been standing upside down like this;
for after him will come a lawless shepherd
    out of the West, whose actions will be yet
    more foul, one fit to cover both of us.
He'll be a second Jason, of whom we read   85
    in *Machabees*; and just as his king proved
    compliant, so will he that reigns in France."
Perhaps at that point I became too reckless,
    for I began to answer in this strain:
    "Tell me, what was the quantity of treasure   90
Our Lord demanded that St. Peter pay
    before he made him the keeper of the keys?
    Surely his sole request was 'Follow me.'
Neither did Peter nor the rest take gold
    or silver from Matthias, chosen by lot   95
    to fill the place the wicked soul had lost.

Stay there, for you deserve your punishment;
    and take good care of all the ill-gotten cash
    that roused your bravery against King Charles.
And if my reverence for the supreme keys   100
    of which you once were the custodian
    in the happy life did not prohibit it,
the language I would use would be still stronger,
    because your avarice corrupts the world,
    trampling the just and raising up the crooked.   105
It was you shepherds the Evangelist
    anticipated when he saw the woman
    seated upon the waters, whoring with kings –
the one who had been born with seven heads
    and from ten horns got vigorous support   110
    so long as virtue gave her spouse delight.
You've made yourselves a god of gold and silver:
    how are you different from idolaters
    but that they pray to one and you a hundred?
Ah Constantine, what evils have been born,   115
    not out of your conversion, but the dowry
    the first rich pope accepted from your hand!"
And all the while I sang this tune for him,
    he must have felt the bite of wrath or conscience,
    because his feet were thrashing wildly about.   120
I feel quite sure, though, that my guide was pleased,
    for he kept listening with a contented
    look to the sound of those true words I spoke.
In consequence he caught me up in his arms,
    and after he had lifted me to his chest   125
    he climbed back up the path that he'd come down;
nor did he tire of clasping me to himself
    before he'd carried me to the top of the arch
    that crosses from the fourth bank to the fifth.
On that he laid his burden gently down,   130
    gently, because the ridge's rugged steepness
    would have made passage difficult for goats.
From there another valley lay revealed.

Notes

1–6: This solemn address sounds the note of Dante's apocalyptic mode, in which he passes judgment on the evils of his time. Gabriel will blow his trumpet to signal the Last Judgment, when the sins of all will be made manifest.

1: Seeing that converts received the Holy Spirit when the apostles laid hands on them, Simon Magus offered the apostles money for their power. St. Peter answered: "Keep thy money to thyself, to perish with thee, because thou hast thought that the gifts of God may be purchased with money." Acts 8:9–24.

2–6: From Simon's name derives "simony," defined by Aquinas as the buying and selling of spiritual things. *ST* 2–2.100.1. The chief objects of such commerce in the Middle Ages were bishoprics, which were positions of wealth and power, and benefices, which were guaranteed incomes. In popular usage "simony" more generally signifies prelates' use of their positions to accumulate wealth, and the sweep of the concept in *Inf*. 19 will be similarly broad. Dante will express the outrage of the late medieval public at the spectacle of a papacy more devoted to church revenues than to spiritual ministry, and he will go on to attack the legitimacy of the popes' temporal power itself.

16–18: "My beautiful St. John's" is Dante's nostalgic reference to the Baptistery of Florence. The overt point of the comparison between the holes and the baptismal fonts is the diameter of their apertures, but there is also a covert correspondence: the font of salvation becomes the dry well of damnation for those who have prostituted the things of God for money.

19–21: Dante's solemn assertion of his purpose suggests that he is defending himself from an imputation of sacrilege in breaking the font. He is implicitly offering the same defense for this canto, where he also does violence to the outward form of a consecrated thing in the name of the values the thing is supposed to serve. See Sinclair.

22–30: The sinners' posture in the holes recalls the boy stuck in the font – for an adult not only dangerous but also ridiculous. Their head-in-the-ground position reifies their absorption in earthly things in life, and forms the first part of the *contrapasso* of the third gulch. Pietro Alighieri quoted a gloss on Ezechiel 7:19: "For simony casts a man's head down into darkness and lights up the soles of his feet with the fire of cupidity." Giotto's Last Judgment in the Arena Chapel shows sinners in hell with their legs protruding from a communal hole in the rock.

The flames licking the sinners' soles suggest the tongues of flame that descended on the heads of the apostles at Pentecost (Acts 2:1–4), the outward image of the Holy Spirit that filled them. It was the power they inherited from the apostles of communicating the Spirit, through holy orders in particular, that the simoniacal prelates sold. The persistence of the Holy Spirit's image in a vengeful form on the soles instead of the crown – signifying the simoniacs' perversion of the Spirit's gifts – forms the second part of the *contrappaso*. The finely observed detail of flames on oily substances suggests the anointing with chrism in baptism, confirmation and holy orders (Durling/Martinez); and it reinforces the reversal of head and feet, since it is the head that is anointed in those sacraments.

31–33: The pilgrim's attention is drawn at once to a sinner whose punishment declares, by the intensity of the flames and the exaggerated writhing they induce, that he is the chief of the simoniacs. Aquinas said that simony was worst in a pope, "since the higher a man's position, the greater is his sin." *ST* 2–2.100.2.

35: The farther bank of every gulch is lower than the nearer one because the whole of Devil's Gulches funnels down toward a central well. The farther bank is also less steep.

40–45: The poets cross over the third gulch to the fourth bank beyond it, then turn left onto the top of that bank; turning left again, they descend into the third gulch. Virgil carries the pilgrim all the way because the footing is perilous, the holes reducing the remaining ground to a network.

45: The black comedy suggested by the initial picture of the sinners stuffed into the holes is confirmed here, where the sinner's emotions are expressed through his legs, and it becomes apparent that the substitution of feet for head is a satiric trope.

46–48: The pilgrim's demeanor is demure but his phrase is mocking. The pope's position parodies the martyrdom of St. Peter, the first pope, who was crucified head downwards because he said he was unworthy to die like his master.

49–54: The speaker is Pope Nicholas III, dead for 20 years in 1300 when the pilgrim visits hell. The reigning pope was then Boniface VIII, Dante's great enemy, whose scheming in Florentine politics was responsible for Dante's life-long exile. In this satirical set-up, the pilgrim need not say a word against Boniface because the pope's damnation is predicted, with the foreknowledge of the damned, by his predecessor in simony.

Condemnation of worldly popes was in the air in the early 14th century. Writings probably originating with the Spiritual Franciscans held Boniface VIII to be an evil hypocrite. The Spiritual Ubertino da Casale's *Arbor Vitae Crucifixae Jesu*, which Dante knew, identified Boniface with the mystical Antichrist. Bernard McGinn in *Apocalpytic Spirituality* 153–55.

49–51: Hired killers in Dante's Florence were executed by being buried alive, head downward. The hit-man in Dante's simile has been stuffed headfirst into a hole, and before the executioners can fill in the dirt around him, he calls the friar back to put off death for a few minutes by offering to betray his principal. See *ED* 1.420, 4.417.

54: Nicholas is probably not referring to an actual writing, but to the book of the future in which the damned can read more or less clearly. See *Inf.* 10.97–108. Boniface died in 1303.

55–57: The beautiful lady Boniface tricked into marrying him is the church. The story went that when Boniface was a cardinal he manipulated the previous pope, the unworldly Celestine V, into abdicating after five months in office. *See Inf.* 3.58–60 and note. Villani claimed that he then cut a political deal with the ruler of Naples, who controlled many cardinals' votes. *Cron.* 9.5–6. After he was pope, Boniface forced the church into prostitution, selling her to the highest bidder (Buti). Villani said that Boniface claimed everything belonging to the church was his by right. *Cron.* 9.6; see also 9.64.

56–57: This matrimonial trope was common in the writings of canonists and theologians, deriving ultimately from St. Paul. Eph. 5:25–27; see Kantorowicz 212n., 215n.; see also Bosco/Reggio.

66–72: The great mantle signifies the dignity of the papal office. See *Inf.* 2.27. Nicholas belonged to the Orsini family, long one of the most powerful in Rome, and the references to bears play on his family name (*orsini*, bear cubs); a bear appeared in the family arms. Villani said that Nicholas "was among the first, if not the first, pope at whose court simony was openly practiced on behalf of his relatives." *Cron.* 8.54.

72: "Pocketed." Nicholas makes a sardonic joke at his own expense. Peter told Simon Magus that he would be damned along with his money, but for Nicholas the simoniacs symbolically *become* the money they got by prostituting the church; as they stuffed this money into their purses, they are stuffed into hellish purses contrived in the rock.

73–75: This is the hole of the popes. When a new pope is thrown into it (see *Inf.* 5.15), he drives his predecessor further down, which has the same effect on earlier popes down the chain. As time passes, the popes are wedged ever more tightly and deeply into the cracks of the rock, being flattened out in the process. They symbolically devolve from money in a purse to veins of gold and silver in the rock. (Michael Sherberg thinks that at this point they become coins, which bear flattened images. Sherberg 15.)

79–87: Nicholas's feet have been cooking for 20 years when the pilgrim visits him in 1300. Boniface will die in 1303, and his feet will cook for only 11 years, because he will be replaced in the hole in 1314 by his successor in simony, Pope Clement V. Clement is called a lawless shepherd "out of the West" because he was a Gascon and Archbishop of Bordeaux. Villani claimed that Philip IV of France promised to use his influence to get Clement elected pope if Clement would give him a share of church revenues. *Cron.* 9.80. Clement never went to Rome after his election but settled in Avignon, under the thumb of Philip.

79: The red feet allude ironically to the pope's red slippers (Pézard), which were taken as symbolic of his office. See *Cron.* 8.54. Originally part of the imperial insignia, they reflected the papal claim to imperial power in the West. Ferrante 29; see note to 115–17.

85–87: Jason bribed the Hellenistic ruler of Palestine to make him the Jewish high priest. 2 Mach. 4:7–10. Villani called Clement "a man very greedy for money and a simoniac at whose court all benefices were for sale." *Cron.* 10.59.

88: Dante's doubt as to whether his indignation carried him beyond just measure in the invective that follows serves to excuse its heat and to remind the reader that Dante is not a rebel against the pope's spiritual authority.

90–93: In Matt. 16:15–19 Peter affirms his faith in the divine mission of Jesus, who says, "I will give to thee the keys of the kingdom of heaven." In Matt. 4:19 Jesus first sees Peter and his brother fishing and tells them to follow him.

94–96: Matthias was chosen by lot the fill the place of the twelfth apostle, vacated by the death of Judas. Acts. 1:15–26.

98–99: The pilgrim echoes St. Peter's words to Simon Magus. Dante is probably referring to a current story about Nicholas III and Charles of Anjou, the French king of Sicily and Naples. In 1282 resentment at Charles's harsh rule erupted in the revolt of the Sicilian Vespers, which drove the French from the island. The popular account implicated the pope in a conspiracy to foment the rebellion after receiving a bribe from the Byzantine emperor. See *Cron.* 8.57.

100–117: Building up to his apostrophe to Constantine, the pilgrim implicitly passes judgment on the long-running struggle between the papacy and the empire for control of Western Europe. Dante argued in *Monarchy* that the Holy Roman Emperor was endowed by God with universal temporal power, just as the pope was with universal spiritual power, spheres that should be kept separate. The pilgrim's tirade here denounces the pope's becoming a territorial sovereign, amassing great wealth and pretending to the status of a universal monarch able to appoint and depose tributary kings.

In the end neither empire nor papacy could sustain its claims. Whereas in the East the emperor became pope, in the West both pope and emperor tried to become emperor and both failed. The empire was institutionally weak and depended on charismatic leaders like Otto the Great or Frederick II. With Frederick's death in 1250 the empire was effectively reduced to a German feudal primacy. During the long struggle, however, the church lost credibility as a spiritual institution, having become increasingly a political and financial one. The papacy's theocratic pretensions ended with the death of Boniface VIII in 1303, followed a few years later by the "Babylonian captivity" of the popes in France. Albert Russell Ascoli notes that in contrast to Dante's *Monarchy*, *Inf.* 19 and the *Comedy* as a whole "stress the utter contemporary failure" of both institutions in Dante's time. Ascoli 171.

106–11: Dante identifies the corrupt church leaders ("you shepherds") with "the great harlot who sitteth upon many waters, with whom the kings of the earth have committed fornication." Apoc. 17:1–2. She is seated upon a scarlet beast with seven heads and ten horns, which are explained as seven mountains and ten kings. Apoc. 17:3, 9, 12. Interpretation of imagery from the Apocalypse is often difficult and Dante multiplies the difficulties. The beast does not appear in this passage; the puzzle is that Dante gives its seven heads and ten horns to the great whore and interprets them *in bono* as her attributes at a time before she was corrupt, when her spouse followed virtue.

The great whore was originally identified with the Roman empire persecuting the early church, but by Dante's time she was being used as a figure for the corrupt contemporary church in the denunciations of the "carnal church" by the Spiritual

Franciscans, with whom this passage strikes a chord. The traditional interpretation of this passage takes the church's spouse as the pope (see line 57 and note) and reasons that before papal simony the seven heads and ten horns of the early church were the seven sacraments and the ten commandments, the embodiments of the new dispensation of grace and the old dispensation of law. (Problem: the seven heads and ten horns are explained differently in Apoc. 17 and they clearly mean something different in *Purg.* 32.142–47.)

Charles T. Davis offers an alternative interpretation in which the great whore is Rome rather than the church, the seven heads being the seven hills of Rome and the ten horns kings who paid her fealty in the early days (per Apoc. 17:9, 12). The spouse is then not the pope but the emperor, who followed virtue until Constantine disastrously moved eastward and granted Rome to the popes, leading to the corruption condemned in *Inf.* 19. Davis 1998, 269–72; see *DE* 755, Davis 1957, 222–26. (Problem: lines 106–08 identify the great whore with "you shepherds" and lines 56–57 identify the spouse with the pope.)

Ronald B. Herzman suggests tht the pilgrim's growth from ignorance to spiritual vision is a theme sometimes more explicit than implied and that in such instances apocalyptic imagery is most evident. He finds that is true above all in this canto, where the pilgrim denounces the degenerate papacy in apocalyptic terms that foreshadow the evils of the last days. Herzman 409–10.

112–14: The Israelites in their idolatry worshipped a single golden calf, while the prelates seek to worship as many images graven on gold and silver as they can. "Of their silver and gold they have made idols unto themselves." Hosea 8:4.

115–17: The pilgrim reaches the root of the matter: the evils of the worldly church can be traced to the moment when the pope assumed the powers of an earthly monarch. The Donation of Constantine, forged by the papal chancellery, purported to be a decree given by Constantine when he moved the seat of the empire from Rome to Byzantium. In it the emperor grants to the papacy the imperial power in the Western empire and authorizes the pope to wear the imperial insignia.

Dante believed in the authenticity of this document, which was not debunked until the Renaissance, but he deplored it, asserting that Constantine had no power to give away the empire's rights, nor did the church have power to accept them. *Mon.* 3.10. The medieval jurists were of the same opinion. Kantorowicz 177; see also *Piers Plowman* 15.559–60. The temporal power of the church will be attacked further in *Purg.* 16.106–14, 127–29; and in *Par.* 20.55–60 Constantine will recognize the harm he caused.

Canto XX

Now a strange punishment must fill my lines,
    furnishing matter for the twentieth canto
    of this first book, which deals with those below.
I was by this time thoroughly prepared
    to scrutinize the floor that lay revealed   5
    below us, which was bathed in tears of anguish;
and I saw people approach around the curving
    valley in silence, weeping, and at the pace
    adopted in this world by church processions.
And when my gaze fell lower, it appeared   10
    that all of them were amazingly contorted
    between the chin and the springing of the chest,
for each one's face was twisted toward his kidneys;
    and they were walking backwards of necessity,
    for they had been deprived of forward vision.   15
Sometimes, perhaps, paralysis produces
    a patient so completely wrenched around,
    but I've not seen it nor believe it likely.
May God permit you, reader, to draw profit
    from what you read, imagine for yourself   20
    whether I kept my eyes from getting wet,
observing at close range our human form
    so far distorted that the tears from the eyes
    showered the buttocks, running down the cleft.

I wept indeed as I leaned on a projection   25
    of the flinty ridge, until my guide addressed me:
    "Are you still acting like the other fools?
Here pity can survive only by dying;
    for who could be more impious than a man
    who thinks he can constrain God's providence?   30
Lift up your head, lift it and see the one
    whom the earth opened under, with the Thebans
    watching, which made them shout: 'Amphiaraus,
where are you rushing off to? Quitting the fight?'
    He never paused from plunging into the pit   35
    till he reached Minos, who snags everyone.
See how he's made a chest of his shoulder blades:
    because he wished to see too far ahead
    he looks behind and backwards makes his way.
Look at Tiresias, who changed his shape,   40
    becoming a woman after being a man,
    all of his members having been transformed,
and who was then required once more to strike
    the twining serpent couple with his staff
    before recovering his masculine plumage.   45
He that backs up to that one's belly bears
    the name of Arruns, and in Luni's mountains,
    tilled by the Carrarese who live below them,
he had a cave in the white marble in which
    he lived and where for gazing on the stars   50
    and sea he had an unobstructed view.
She that approaches covering up her breasts,
    hidden from view now, with her streaming tresses,
    and has her hairy parts in back of her,
was Manto, who went wandering all through many   55
    lands and then settled down where I was born,
    a tale I want you briefly to hear from me.
After her father had departed from life
    and Bacchus' city was reduced to slavery,
    she roamed throughout the world for a long time.   60

Above in beautiful Italy lies a lake
    they call Benaco, at the foot of the Alps
    that close in Germany beyond the Tyrol.
A thousand springs and more must bathe the region
    of Garda, Val Camonica and the Alps   65
    with water whose flow ceases in that lake.
Out in the middle lies a spot at which
    the shepherds of Verona, Trent and Brescia
    could give their blessing if they made the journey.
Peschiera sits, a strong and handsome fortress   70
    confronting the men of Bergamo and Brescia,
    at the low point of the surrounding shore.
There of necessity overflows whatever
    cannot remain within Benaco's lap,
    and forms a river running through green meadows.   75
Once it begins to run, the water is now
    no longer called Benaco, but the Mincio,
    down to Govèrnolo, where it joins the Po.
A short way through its course it comes upon
    low ground where it spreads out and forms a marsh,   80
    a place sometimes unhealthy in the summer.
There the cruel virgin, as she passed that way,
    discovered land surrounded by the marsh,
    uncultivated, uninhabited.
There, to escape all human company,   85
    she settled with her servants, there she practiced
    her arts and lived and left her empty corpse.
Later the people living scattered about
    assembled there because it was secure,
    having the marsh on every side of it.   90
They built the city over those dead bones
    and after her that first had chosen the place
    they called it Mantua, needing no other omen.
Once were the people it held more numerous,
    before the foolishness of Casalodi   95
    was taken in by Pinamonte's trick.

And therefore I adjure you, if you ever
  hear of a different origin of my city,
  not to allow a lie to defraud the truth."
"Master," I said, "your explanation sounds   100
  so certain and I find it so convincing,
  the rest will be to me but burnt-out embers.
But tell me whether you can recognize
  any worth noting among those approaching,
  for that is all my mind keeps coming back to."   105
And he replied, "The one whose beard is spilling
  down from his cheeks across his dusky shoulders
  was – when all Greece was emptied of its males
till there was scarcely one to fill a cradle –
  an augur: he and Calchas chose the moment   110
  for the first cable to be cut at Aulis.
Eurypylus is his name, and so my high
  tragedy sings about him in a certain
  passage, as you know well, who know the whole.
The other, with so little on his ribs,   115
  was Michael Scott, who knew as well as any
  the hocus-pocus used in magic frauds.
There you see Guido Bonatti, there Asdente,
  who wishes now that he had stuck to leather
  and thread, but his repentence comes too late;   120
there the sad women who left needle, shuttle
  and spindle and went in for telling fortunes
  and weaving spells with herbs and images.
But come along – Cain with his thorns already
  touches the boundary of the hemispheres   125
  and dips into the waves beyond Seville,
and last night the moon's disk was round already;
  you should remember it, for more than once
  it did you less than harm in the deep woods."
And as he spoke to me we went along.   130

Notes

2–3: "canto . . . book (*canzon*)": Zygmunt Baranski notes that both the terms *canto* for one of the minor divisions of the *Comedy* and *canzon* for one of its major divisions (later *cantica*) were unusual; in particular *canzone* was a term for a lyric poem. He also notes that the early commentators substituted the familiar classical terms chapter and book. Baranski 1995, 7–11. (These latter at least avoid confusion.)

7–9: In a procession, the faithful chant supplications to God and his saints as they walk, and the relevance of this image can be seen only in retrospect. These people are the diviners – soothsayers and astrologers. Divining was an important priestly function in ancient paganism and this grotesque parody of a Christian procession mocks the futility of these false prophets.

10–24: The wrenching around of the sinners' heads explains their silence; their walking backwards explains their slow shuffle. The diviners are in the eighth circle of hell because "with a deceitful fraud they forecast the future to men." *ST* 2–2.95.1, citing Isidore, *Etym.* 8.9. The *contrapasso* of this fourth gulch, however, punishes their sincere attempt to force God's plan for the future by seeing "too far ahead" (38); here, as retribution, they can only see backward. Richard Kay, however, argues that the sin of the diviners was that, "having discovered the will of God from the study of the heavens, they attempted to evade it." Kay 1994, 275.

19–30: The pilgrim has previously, without rebuke, expressed sympathy for the damned – Francesca, Ciacco, Piero della Vigna, the Florentine sodomites – but this is the first time he has expressed pity in the eighth circle. He will do so only once more and will be rebuked again. *Inf.* 29.1–7. Virgil here accuses the pilgrim of deploring God's punishment of the diviners. But the pilgrim does not yet know who these people are and he is not feeling compassion for them individually, as in the earlier incidents. He is moved to pity and terror by the spectacle of the human form hideously transmogrified, evincing the degradation wrought by sin. The excess of Virgil's vehemence may betray Dante's uneasiness about Virgil's medieval reputation as a magician. Benvenuto thought Virgil's tone was that of a man who had overcome his own failings in this regard.

29–30: Virgil expresses the Christian view of divination, not that of his culture.

31–56: The first group of diviners consists of three priests and a priestess of the ancient religion, and a final ancient priest will lead the second group. All are taken from Dante's favorite authors – Virgil, Statius, Lucan and Ovid. Divination was close to the core of classical culture. Even Cicero, who repudiated it intellectually, favored its retention in the rituals of the state (*De Divinatione* 2.12), and the poets invested it with cultural prestige. To negate this tradition, Dante demeans the diviners by describing them in gross physical terms and where necessary rewriting his classical poetic sources.

31–39: Amphiaraus was one of the Seven who besieged Thebes. Statius makes him a warrior-priest who foresees in the flight of birds the defeat of the Seven and his own death. *Theb.* 3.460–551. Apollo allows him to dominate the battle before the ground opens before him and he drives his chariot down to Hades. *Theb.* 7.690–8.133. Cicero said he was honored as a god after his death. *De Divinatione* 1.40. Because this treatment did not serve Dante's purpose, he interpolated the incident of the Thebans watching from the walls and taunting Amphiaraus, making the scene more like an Old Testament *exemplum* of the fate of a false prophet.

40–45: Tiresias of Thebes saw two snakes coupling and struck them with his staff, whereupon he was changed into a woman; repeating the act seven years later, he was changed back to a man. *Metam.* 3.322–31. He appears in Statius as the seer of Thebes, reading the entrails to predict the defeat of the Seven. *Theb.* 4.406–645.

45: I.e., a man's beard.

46–51: Arruns is an Etruscan soothsayer in Lucan. When strange portents are seen in Rome, he reads the entrails and predicts the horrors of the civil war to come. *Phars.* 1.585–638.

52–55: In describing Manto in particular Dante insists on degrading physical details. The loose tresses were characteristic of a prophetess inspired by divine frenzy.

56–57: Virgil's birthplace was Mantua.

58–59: Manto's father was Tiresias. After the war of the Seven, Thebes ("Bacchus' city") was ruled by the tyrant Creon.

61–78: This passage is remarkable for its description of an actual landscape, unlike the descriptions of ideal places conventional in Latin poetry (*e.g.*, that shady grove in the heat of the day). Dante's approach is more scientific than picturesque: he describes nature's dynamic processes rather than its physical appearance. The spine of the passage is an explanation of the hydrography of a delimited region in northeast Italy. Benaco is the modern Lake Garda, which extends north and south in an Alpine valley. Dante sketches the lake's watershed in the Alps to its north, from Garda on the eastern shore to Valcamonica appreciably to the west. The thousand springs are the Alpine streams that feed the lake and come to rest in its basin before overflowing at the lowest point on the lake shore to form the Mincio River, which eventually empties into the Po.

70–72: Peschiera was a castle at the southeast corner of Lake Garda that the Scaligers, lords of Verona to the east, had recently fortified against the forces of Bergamo and Brescia to the west.

79–81: Having completed his description of the regional flows, Dante backtracks to focus on a spot not far below the lake, where the river, flowing into a broad depression, spreads out and slows, forming a marsh.

82–93, 97–99: Remarkably, Dante makes Virgil give an account of the founding of Mantua that contradicts the one in the *Aeneid*. There Manto was not a virgin, but the mother of Ocnus, who founded the city and named it for her. *Aen.* 10.198–203. The vehemence of Virgil's denunciation of other accounts as false makes it likely that the contradiction is deliberate on Dante's part. His revisionist account may be part of an unavowed strategy to refute the medieval tradition that Virgil was a magician and thus a potential denizen of the fourth gulch himself. (In the *sortes Vergilianae* people opened the *Aeneid* at random as a method of divination.) Dante's version concedes that Virgil's town was named for Manto. It makes clear, however, that the town was not founded by her or her son, but by unrelated settlers who chose the site for its defensibility, and who did not even use the traditional augury in naming it. (To complicate matters further, in *Purg.* 22.113 Manto is said to be in limbo with Virgil.)

93: In the ancient world, the founding and naming of a city were matters on which the gods were to be consulted through augury. See Livy 1.6.

94–96: Count Alberto da Casalodi, lord of Mantua, and his aristocratic party were unpopular. He accepted the advice of the scheming Pinamonte de' Buonaccorsi and forced many nobles to leave the city. With Casalodi stripped of support, Pinamonte led a popular uprising that exiled him and either killed or exiled the leading families.

106–23: The second group of diviners includes well-known astrologers and prophets of the Middle Ages, who are given more summary treatment. There was widespread interest in divination in the late Middle Ages, as indicated by the existence of popular how-to books in the vernacular. Kiekhefer 60, 64.

106–14: Eurypylus is briefly mentioned in *Aen.* 2.114–19, but does not play the role of augur described here. Unlike the passage about Manto, this is probably a case of Dante nodding.

108–11: Greece was emptied of men because they had been recruited for the Trojan war and were waiting in the harbor at Aulis for the signal to sail.

112–13: "My high tragedy" is the *Aeneid*. Dante held that tragedy was poetry in the highest style, fit only for the expression of the noblest subject matter. *VE* 2.4.5–7.

115–18: The medieval astrologers Michael Scott and Guido Bonatti represent a different subspecies of fraud from that of the ancient soothsayers. All claims to know the future in itself – as opposed to predicting future events such as eclipses through causation – usurp what belongs to God alone. See *ST* 2–2.95.1. The ancient diviners fraudulently claimed to be divinely inspired priests, using indifferent things – the entrails of sacrificed animals, the flight of birds – as occult signs of future events.

By contrast, the contemporary astrologers claimed they practiced science, not religion. The Middle Ages did not distinguish between astronomy and astrology. All medieval thinkers, Dante as well as Aquinas, believed that many things were influenced by the stars; but Dante and Aquinas were clear that the stars do not control and thus cannot predict the actions of individuals. *Purg.* 16.67–81; *ST* 2–2.95.5. Astrologers like Scott and Bonatti asserted that the stars could predict all things. Their claims thus went beyond the proper bounds of astrology, and if they did not invoke demons directly, their procedures invited the involvement of demons. See *ST* 2–2.95.5.

115–17: Michael Scott (c.1175–1225), an eminent scholar, spent his later years as court astrologer to Frederick II. By Dante's time he shared with Virgil, Albertus Magnus and Roger Bacon the reputation of having been a great magician.

118: Guido Bonatti (c.1220–c.1300), astrologer to Guido da Montefeltro (*Inf.* 27), wrote a treatise that held the astrologer knows all things past, present and future, because he knows the motions of the heavens and the effects they produce. Kiekhefer 129.

118–20: Master Benvenuto (c.1220–c.1290), known as Asdente ("Toothless") because of his large crooked teeth, was a shoemaker. Although illiterate, he was versed in the apocalyptic writings of Joachim of Fiore and other prophetic literature. His activity as seer seems to have consisted mainly in interpreting those texts. See *ED* 1.591–92. As such he was symptomatic of the mystical reforming piety that swept the lower classes in the wake of Joachim and the Spiritual Franciscans.

121–23: The anonymous crowd represents the lowest social stratum of the divinatory and magical arts, the local wise women who have functioned in all times as healers, fortune tellers and purveyors of love charms and spells to harm enemies. These lines are the first overt reference to witchcraft, as opposed to divination, but the two were not always easily separable. Dante's early plans for the fourth gulch may not have focused on divination; in *Inf.* 11.58 Virgil described its inhabitants as those who cast spells.

123: Herbs were used as amulets to ward off evil. Images were used in sympathetic magic, as by sticking pins in them to harm enemies. See Horace, *Satires* 1.8.

124: The Middle Ages and later times read the shadows on the moon as Cain (the original man in the moon) bearing a faggot of thorns on his back, representing his unworthy sacrifice in Gen. 4:3–5. See *A Midsummer Night's Dream*, 5.1.242–64.

125–26: Seville was the conventional edge of the hemisphere of land, so the moon is crossing the boundary to the hemisphere of water and setting in the ocean. Telling time by the moon is tricky, but commentators agree that moonset here indicates about 6 a.m. on Holy Saturday.

128–29: As in *Inf.* 16.106–08, the reference to the events of *Inf.* 1 points outside the frame of the picture we have been given of them. See *Purg.* 23.118–20.

Canto XXI

And so from bridge to bridge, speaking of things
    with which my comedy is not concerned,
    we made our way; and when we reached the summit
we paused to get a view of the next chasm
    of Devil's Gulches with its useless weeping;   5
    and I saw it was astonishingly dark.
As in the Arsenal of the Venetians
    the viscous pitch boils in the wintertime
    to caulk their leaky ships – for in that season
no one can sail and they refit instead: 10
    some work on a new ship, while others plug
    the ribs of one that's weathered many voyages;
one hammers on the bow and one on the stern;
    others shape oars, and others yet twine cordage,
    while someone patches up the jib and mainsail –   15
so through divine art here, and not through fire,
    deep, sluggish pitch was boiling down below
    and sticking everywhere against the bank.
I saw this, but within it I saw nothing
    but the bubbles that the boiling caused to rise,   20
    which made the mass swell up and then deflate.
While I was staring down there, all intent,
    my leader cried out suddenly, "Look out!
Look out!" and pulled me over to his side.

I turned around like someone all agog   25
    to see the danger that he must escape,
    who, seeing it, becomes so panic-stricken

that even while he looks he is running away;
    for when I turned, I saw a pitch-black devil
    come scampering up the ridge in back of us.   30

Ah, how ferocious his expression was!
    How fierce I thought he looked in all his movements,
    so light upon his feet, with wings outspread!

One of his shoulders, which was high and sharp,
    was loaded with both haunches of a sinner,   35
    the tendons of whose heels his claws gripped fast.

He shouted from our bridge, "Hey, Nastyclaws!
    Guess what – another alderman from Lucca!
    Put this one under, and I'll go back for more

to the same place, where there's no lack of them.   40
    There everyone takes bribes except Bonturo,
    and money quickly changes No to Yes."

He flung him over the edge and then turned back
    along the stony ridge; no unchained mastiff
    has ever showed such haste pursuing a thief.   45

The sinner plunged and surfaced backside up;
    and the demons hidden underneath the bridge
    all yelled, "The Holy Face can't help you now!

Here they don't swim the way you do in the Serchio –
    unless you want to learn what scratching feels like,   50
    be careful not to show above the pitch."

And then with numberless hooks they tore at him,
    saying, "Your footwork should be undercover,
    so grab these, if you can, in secrecy."

They looked like kitchen boys the cook appoints   55
    to keep the meat from floating in a cauldron
    by plunging it with long forks in the broth.

"So that your presence," my good master said,
    "may not be obvious to them, crouch down
    behind an outcrop offering you some shelter;   60

and however rough the treatment I receive,
    take no alarm – I understand these things,
    for I was once before in such a scrimmage."
With that he passed beyond the head of the bridge;
    but when he reached the top of the sixth bank   65
    he had to summon his full self-possession.
With all the furious uproar with which dogs
    come rushing out upon a homeless man,
    making him stop in his tracks and beg from there,
out swarmed the demons from beneath the bridge   70
    and turned their whole array of hooks against him.
    But he cried out, "None of you play your tricks!
Before you snag me with your grappling hooks
    send someone forward, let him hear me out,
    and then you can confer on gaffing me."   75
All of them shouted, "Nastytail should go!"
    They held their line while one of them came forward,
    muttering, "I don't see how this will help him."
"Think a bit, Nastytail," my teacher said,
    "would I be standing here in front of you,   80
    proof until now against all opposition,
unless God willed and fate were favorable?
    Let us pass safely, for by heaven's decree
    I guide another on this arduous journey."
At this his insolence was so abashed   85
    he let the hook he carried fall at his feet
    and said to the others, "Well, nobody hurt him."
My leader then addressed me: "You that wait,
    squatting behind a prominence on the bridge,
    you may return to me in safety now."   90
Hearing that, I arose and went to him
    quickly; and all the devils crowded forward,
    making me fear that they would break the truce.

So I once saw the soldiers coming out
 under the white flag from Caprona cringe,   95
 seeing themselves among so many enemies.
I drew up close to my guide and shrank against him
 with my whole person, never letting my eyes
 leave their expressions, which were less than kind.
Their hooks began to sag toward me – "You want me   100
 to scratch his back?" one demon asked another,
 to which the other said, "Yeah, let him have it!"
But the head demon, still engaged in talk
 with him who led me, sharply turned around
 and ordered, "Easy, easy there, Rapscallion!"   105
Then he addressed us: "You can make no further
 progress along this ridge, for the sixth arch
 lies all in fragments on the floor of the gulch.
If you are still determined to go forward,
 walk out along the top of this wall of rock;   110
 nearby another ridge affords a passage.
Yesterday – it was five hours later than this –
 marked the twelve-hundred-sixty-sixth year's end
 since the destruction of the roadway here.
In fact, I'm sending a patrol that way   115
 to see if any are hanging out to dry;
 go with them, they will not cause any trouble.
Hellkite and Hotfoot, front and center now,
 and you too, Dandydog" – he started issuing
 orders – "and Frizzlebeard will lead the squad.   120
Dogscratcher, you go too, and Salamander
 and Porker armed with tusks and Dragonbreath,
 with Scalawag and crazy Rubynose.
Go reconnoiter around the boiling glue;
 see that these two get safely to the ridge   125
 that goes unbroken over all the dens."
"Ah, master, what is this I hear," I said.
 "Let us go on alone without an escort
 if you can find the way, for I want none.

If you have been observant as usual,   130
    you must have noticed how they grind their teeth
    and how their eyebrows threaten us with harm."
"I do not want you to be afraid," he said.
    "Leave them to gnash their teeth at will, they're only
    grimacing at the boiling sufferers."   135
They made a flanking turn on the left bank;
    but first each stuck his tongue between his teeth,
    pointing it at their corporal in salute,
at which he made a trumpet of his rump.

Notes

2: Dante's reaffirmation that his poem is a comedy (*see* note to *Inf.* 16.128) contrasts with Virgil's calling his a "high tragedy." *Inf.* 20.113.

7–15: Venice was the first great sea power in Europe and its state shipyard, the Arsenal, was a major industrial complex of the time. In addition to serving as a depot for arms and naval stores, it had docks for shipbuilding and repair and shops for fabricating sails, oars and ironwork. See Lane 163–64. Dante describes different trades – shipwrights, caulkers (who work with boiling pitch), sail-makers, oar-makers and rope-makers – working together in a scene of animated bustle.

  The formal basis for his simile is the presence of boiling pitch in both the fifth gulch and the Arsenal. The apparently superfluous details of the Arsenal, however, indirectly evoke an image, common in medieval art, of hell as a workshop of pain, where smirking devils work on the damned with tongs or pour molten metal down their throats. In the 12th century *Vision of Tundale* the pilgrim visiting hell goes through a foundry and workshops where the demons are metal workers and the souls of the damned are the metal. Gardiner 172–73.

16: On earth God's art works through nature (see *Inf.* 11.97–100; *Mon.* 2.2.2); in hell God's art produces effects unmediated by nature.

25–30: This canto and the next will be an unprecedented comic interlude. Dante begins here by heightening the drama of the moment with humor at his own expense, making the pilgrim experience an exaggerated fear. When he turns around to see his danger, his body reacts before his mind and his feet start running away while his eyes are still looking backwards in horror – a comic gesture revived in our time as a stock device of animated cartoons.

34–36: A grotesque devil with a naked sinner slung over his shoulders in similar fashion appears on the south façade of Chartres. Benvenuto commented that the devil is like a butcher carrying a slaughtered animal to be skinned and sold. Christopher Kleinhenz suggests that the image parodies the representation of Christ as the Good Shepherd with the lost sheep across his shoulders. Kleinhenz 330.

37: The Nastyclaws (*Malebranche*) are the platoon of devils that guards the fifth gulch. In a narrative that extends over cantos 21, 22 and the first third of 23, the popular devils of medieval art and drama appear. The mixture of terror and farce they introduce sets these cantos apart.

Manuscript illuminations and cathedral sculpture show a richly imagined variety of demons, often with composite human and animal features. The animal features include the tails, horns, claws and batwings that have come down to us. Medieval devils are often hairy and they are gray or black. In the art of the illuminators, they are comic grotesques, smirking and capering as they torture sinners.

Devils were a standard part of popular entertainment. Villani described a pageant mounted in Florence in 1304 that represented hell, with local men impersonating demons "horrible to see." *Cron.* 9.70. In the biblical dramas of the Middle Ages devils were the clowns, the humor all the more effective because they were still terrifying. See Russell 259. The effect is similar here. The Nastyclaws engage in vulgar buffoonery, especially at the end of canto 21; but their cruelty is nonetheless frightening, never more so than when they use jokes to heighten the sinners' agony.

38–42: Buti identified Dante's alderman as Martin Bottaio, a major figure in the government of Lucca who died, according to Buti, in 1300, between Good Friday and Holy Saturday, a few hours before the time of the present scene. The exception the devil makes for Bonturo Dati is sarcastic. Dante means that Dati had many of the municipal offices in his control and sold them to the highest bidder. A colleague of Martin Bottaio, Dati was a leader of the democratic party in Lucca and achieved great influence there in the early 14th century. See *ED* 2.319–20.

41: The sinners of the fifth gulch are the "barrators" or grafters. Barratry is the selling of civil offices, as simony (*Inf.* 19) is the selling of ecclesiastical offices. Throughout the Middle Ages, it was common for someone who wanted a post to pay an official who could see to it that he was appointed. More generally, barratry includes an official's acceptance of a bribe to decide legal proceedings or otherwise use his office in someone's favor. Pietro Alighieri described barrators as officials who, corrupted by money, pervert justice. He explained that the pitch represents allegorically the barrators' grasping and tenacious greed.

46–48: The sinner surfaces face down and the demons mockingly pretend to think he is trying to bow or genuflect before the Holy Face (*Santo Volto*), a Romanesque crucifix in the cathedral of Lucca. Famous all over Europe (see *Piers Plowman* 6.100), the Santo Volto was a cult object prayed to, as Benvenuto noted, in time of need. The devils' taunt thus means: "There is no Holy Face (to bow to) here." (Others think the sinner emerges with his face smeared with pitch and the devils mockingly compare him to the Santo Volto, which is made of dark wood.)

52–54: Graft, as Pietro emphasized, is *secret* corruption, so the devils taunt the alderman further on that theme. The rules of this place should suit him fine, they suggest, because he must do his dance entirely under the black pitch. Then as they score him with their hooks they dare him to grab them under cover, the way he was accustomed to taking bribes.

52: *Hooks.* In the Last Judgment on the west front of the cathedral of Bourges the chief devil carries a forked iron hook that has been inserted into the stone sculpture.

55–57: Dante invokes the popular medieval image of hell as a kitchen where the devils cook sinners in a great boiling cauldron, as seen in many manuscript illuminations and in cathedral sculptures (*e.g,* Rheims, Bourges). A cauldron of boiling pitch is a feature of an 11th century vision of St. Patrick's Purgatory. Gardiner 141. Kitchen humor is a frequent theme of medieval low comedy. Curtius 431–35; see notes to *Inf.* 18.

76–78: The demons are vividly characterized throughout as a platoon of mercenaries. Nastytail is their sergeant, a "plausible rascally official" (Sinclair), and Frizzlebeard, who will appear later, is his corporal. If the condottieri are treated with a certain dignity under the guise of centaurs in *Inf.* 12, the foot-soldiers they captained are drawn with unforgettable grossness and brutality in this canto and the next. A parallel distinction between the leading devils and the infernal rank and file, with the low comedy allotted to the latter, occurs in some medieval dramas. See Russell 260.

90–104: Nowhere else in the *Inferno* is the pilgrim threatened so directly by the forces of hell as here. The devils attempt to punish him as they would a corrupt official, and it is difficult not to think in this connection of the decisive event of Dante's life. After the coup of the Black Guelfs in Florence in 1301 (see note to *Inf.* 10.79–81), Dante was banished and fined. The crimes that he and his fellow aldermen of 1300 were charged with included peculation in public office. Later that year he was condemned *in absentia* to be burnt, and the sentence kept him an exile from his native city for the rest of his life.

We need not take the charge seriously. When power changed hands in the endless factional violence that plagued the Italian city-states, the victors regularly charged their predecessors with taking bribes or looting the public treasury. Dante does not deign to defend himself from the charge, but he may be laughing at it. He casts the pilgrim as the intended victim of the devils who punish graft and shows him terrified of their brutality; but in the end the devils are incompetent and are powerless to hurt him.

94–96: Dante mentions his presence at the siege of Caprona, a Pisan fort captured by the Guelfs of Florence and Lucca in 1289. He reverses the perspective and imagines himself here as one of the captives he witnessed as a victor.

112–16: The time is the morning of Holy Saturday in 1300, which is 1266 years after the crucifixion, which caused the earthquake in hell. See *Inf.* 12.31–45.

Nastytail's circumstantial account of the correct date makes his story plausible, but in fact the earthquake destroyed all the bridges over the sixth gulch. The safe-conduct that he gives the poets is accordingly issued with a wink to his men.

104, 107–23: Dante's names for the twelve Nastyclaws that we meet – Malacoda, Scarmiglione, Alichino, Calcabrina, Cagnazzo, Barbariccia, Libicocco, Draghinazzo, Ciriatto, Graffiacane, Farfarello and Rubicante – are comic and grotesque. Innumerable popular names of minor devils were current in the Middle Ages in Italian, French, English and German. See Russell 66. Dante's coinages, a number of which refer to physical characteristics associated with devils, belong to that tradition of popular demonology.

127–35: The pilgrim's outburst appears to continue his comic fear; but as the next canto will show, he has correctly assessed the situation in which the poets find themselves. Virgil, the representative of rational humanistic culture uninstructed by Christian faith, underestimates the irrational malice of the devils.

136–39: On the bank beyond the fifth gulch, the devils turn left at the broken bridge, following the spiral course the poets have taken down the cone of hell. First they face their squad leader and perform a cheeky parody of a military salute, which signals their complicity in the trap Nastytail has laid for the poets. Frizzlebeard's acknowledgement of the salute in kind, which gives the signal to begin marching, is a piece of clowning standard in the repertoire of the stage devils. (Pope reused the image in *The Dunciad* 4.71: "And now had Fame's posterior trumpet blown.")

Canto XXII

I've seen, in my time, a troop of cavalry
   break camp and mount a charge and stand inspection
   and sometimes beat retreat to save their skins;
men of Arezzo, I've seen flying squadrons
   crossing your land; and I've seen raiding parties,   5
   running of jousts, combat in tournaments,
sometimes accompanied by drums or trumpets,
   sometimes by bells or by a castle's signal,
   in short by every sign, our own or foreign;
but never have I seen troops, horse or foot,   10
   set forth nor ship set sail by star or landmark
   to a wind instrument as strange as that.
We traveled on with those ten demons now –
   ferocious company! But the saying goes,
   with saints in church, with rascals in the tavern.   15
All my attention focused on the pitch
   to take in every detail of the gulch
   and of the people being scalded in it.
As dolphins sometimes leap and arch their backs
   to give a sign to sailors, warning them   20
   they must exert themselves to save their ship,
so, to relieve the pain, from time to time
   one of the sinners here would show his back
   and quick as lightning hide himself again.

And as at the edge of the water in a ditch 25
  frogs squat with just their snouts above the surface,
  keeping their feet and bulging middles hidden,
so here the sinners squatted on both banks;
  but at the approach of Frizzlebeard, like frogs
  they disappeared beneath the boiling pitch. 30
I saw – and now my heart still makes me shudder –
  one of them wait too long, as it will happen
  that one frog stays behind while another dives;
and Dogscratcher, who was standing closest to him
  managed to hook him by his pitch-smeared hair 35
  and dragged him up – it seemed to me an otter.
(I'd learned the names of all of them by now,
  because when they were picked I'd paid attention
  and noted afterwards what each was called.)
"Hey Rubynose, make sure you get your nails 40
  under his skin so you can peel it off!"
  all those accursed creatures called at once.
And I said, "Master, see if you can learn
  who that unlucky wretch may be, who's fallen
  into the clutches of his adversaries." 45
My leader then drew close beside the man
  and asked where he was from, to which he answered:
  "My birthplace was the kingdom of Navarre.
My mother put me in service to a lord
  because she'd had me by a profligate 50
  who wasted first his fortune and then himself.
Later I joined the brave King Thibaut's household
  and I began to peddle influence there,
  the bill for which I am settling in this heat."
Then Porker, from whose mouth a tusk stuck out 55
  on either side, like those on a wild boar,
  let him find out how one of them could rip.
The mouse had come among some evil cats;
  but Frizzlebeard enclosed him in his arms,
  saying, "Stand back, while I get hold of him." 60

Turning to face my teacher, "Anything else
    you want to know from him," he said, "ask now,
    before another of them tears him apart."
"Tell us," my guide resumed, "among the other
    sinners, do you know anyone from Italy   65
    under the pitch?" "I left behind just now,"
he answered, "someone who lived very near there.
    If only I were still back under cover
    with him, I wouldn't fear their hooks and claws!"
Then Salamander – shouting, "We've been far   70
    too patient!" – hooked him by the upper arm
    and pulling, tore a muscle free from it.
Dragonbreath also was ready to take a swipe,
    down by his legs; but at that point their corporal
    swung round and gave them both a glowering look.   75
After they all had settled down a bit,
    the sinner staring all the while at his wound,
    my guide was quick to put another question:
"And who was this companion that you left
    – unluckily, as you say – to come to shore?"   80
    "Friar Gomita," he answered, "from Gallura,
a vessel made for every sort of swindle,
    who, when he held his master's enemies,
    dealt with them in a way that made them grateful.
He 'took their cash and quietly released them,'   85
    to quote him; and in other business too
    he was no small-time grafter, but a kingpin.
Here he associates with Don Michael Zanche
    from Logodoro; and their tongues are never
    tired of gossiping about Sardinia.   90
Oh my, look how that other one is gnashing
    his teeth! I'd tell you more, but I'm afraid
    that one is getting set to scratch my dandruff!"
Their high commander turned, saw Scalawag
    rolling his eyeballs, on the point of striking,   95
    and barked an order: "Back, malignant bird!"

"If you would like to see or hear Italians,"
    resumed the frightened sinner after a while,
    "I will make Tuscans come and Lombards too;
but have the Nastyclaws stand back a bit   100
    so they will have no cause to fear reprisals.
    Then I, remaining in this very spot,
all by myself will make a dozen surface
    with just a whistle, which is the 'all clear'
    we give whenever one of us gets out."   105
Hearing this, Dandydog stuck up his snout,
    shaking his head, and growled, "It's just a clever
    trick he's thought up so he can dive back in!"
But he possessed a good supply of snares:
    "Too clever would I be by half," he answered,   110
    "procuring greater torments for my friends!"
Hellkite could not resist, and setting himself
    against the others, challenged him: "You jump,
    you'll find me after you – not galloping,
but swooping down on my wings above the pitch.   115
    We'll leave the crest and hide behind the bank;
    let's see if you alone can beat us all."
Reader, you now will hear of a strange sport:
    all of them turned their eyes to the other side,
    he first that had expressed the most resistance.   120
The Navarrese was quick to seize his chance:
    he braced his feet on the ground, and in that instant
    he leaped and freed himself from their commander.
Each of them felt a pang of guilt at this,
    he most who was the cause of the mistake,   125
    making him take to the air and yell, "I've got you!"
Not that it did him any good, for wings
    could not outdistance fear; the one went under,
    the other, lifting up his chest in flight,
swerved upwards; so a duck will suddenly   130
    dive under when the falcon draws too near,
    while he swoops up, disgruntled and defeated.

Hotfoot, infuriated by the prank,
    went flying just behind him in the hope
    the other would escape, so he could start   135
a brawl; and when the grafter disappeared
    he turned his claws at once upon his comrade
    and came to grips with him above the pitch.
But the other also was a full-grown hawk,
    well able to claw back, and both together   140
    fell in the middle of the boiling pool.
The heat immediately unclenched the pair,
    but now they had no way of getting out,
    their wings were so agglutinate. Frizzlebeard,
unhappy like the rest of them, gave orders   145
    for four of them to fly to the other bank,
    all with their grappling hooks, and very quickly
from all sides they alighted at their posts;
    they stretched their hooks to reach the duo stuck
    in birdlime, both now cooked within the crust.   150
We went on, leaving them in that imbroglio.

Notes

1–12: Cantos 24, 27 and 30 will begin with extended similes in the epic tradition. Here Dante introduces the comedy of canto 22 by parodying this practice in mock heroic style. The catalogue of military signals elaborates on the reversal of expected signs in fraud's kingdom, initiated by the petty officer's salute at the end of canto 21 – a conventional insult responding to his men's conventional gesture of insubordination. (Unknown to the pilgrim, these gestures amount to a conspiratorial wink at the poets' status as dupes of the planned attack.)

4–5: Florence and its Guelf allies defeated Arezzo and its Ghibelline allies at Campaldino in 1289. Dante, then 23 or 24, is believed to have been among the light cavalry of the Guelf vanguard. It would have been later in the same campaign that he saw the surrender at Caprona. *Inf.* 21.94–96.

6: What Dante means by a tournament, as opposed to a joust, is a melee, with two mock armies in an open field.

7–8: In addition to the drums and trumpets we would expect, bells were common military signals. A bell mounted on the painted war carriage called the *carroccio* was struck with a hammer to signal an attack. Bells in a town could give offensive or defensive signals. See *Cron*. 7.75; 8.131. Buti explained that signals from a fort would be given with smoke by day and fire by night. See *Inf*. 8.1–6.

11: A coasting ship would sail by landmarks, such as headlands; but for deep-water sailing, it was necessary to steer by the stars (Buti).

12: "Wind instrument." Dante's *cennamella* is the shawm, a medieval woodwind with a piercing nasal tone. Because of its shrillness, it was used chiefly outdoors, especially in military bands.

19–21: Brunetto Latini said that sailors know a storm is coming when they see dolphins, the fastest of sea-creatures, "fleeing through the sea and flipping over in their flight, as if the thunder were chasing them." *Tresor* 1.134; see *Etym*. 12.6.11; *Pericles* 2.1.24.

25–36: As the pilgrim stares down from the high bank, the distance evaporates and we see the sinners huddling in the pitch in close-up. Frizzlebeard and Dogscratcher enter the frame down at the shore and hook the sinner, then all three are up on the bank-top with no indication of a scene change.

36: Covered with black pitch that slicks down his hair, the sinner looks like an otter with sleek wet fur. (Otters were hunted with dogs. *Tresor* 1.184.) Animal imagery, pervasive in this canto for both the sinners and the demons, is appropriate to the low comic style and gives a view from the outside, excluding sympathy for the sinners on the part of the pilgrim or Dante.

43–54: Early commentators gave the grafter the name Ciampòlo (*i.e.*, Jean-Paul). All of his speeches are intended to give the visitors what they want to hear, but his matter-of-fact statements about his father's vices and his own life and punishment in hell incidentally reveal a hard-boiled yet engaging personality.

48: Navarre in the 13th century was a small kingdom in the Pyrenees. The French counts of Champagne (the line of King Thibaut, below) succeeded to the throne in the 13th century.

52: Thibaut II (1235–70) married the daughter of St. Louis of France and died returning from a crusade.

61–69: This canto is unique in the *Inferno* in consisting of a single, fully dramatized scene, and Dante's disposition and timing of the interrelated dialogue and action is masterful. The poets are only spectators, their involvement limited to the clever use the corrupt courtier from Navarre makes of them. They are like distinguished visitors being given a tour of a prison by the jailors, who stop torturing the prisoners long enough to make them answer the visitors' questions. Recognizing this, Ciampolo attempts to pique the poets' curiosity while suggesting he is unable to satisfy it as long as the demons are threatening him so closely. The cat-and-mouse game alternates dialogue with bursts of violence; but the violence tails off from the attacks at lines 55–57 and 70–72 to the thwarted attacks at lines 73–75 and 94–96 as Ciampolo, no simple mouse, gains leverage on the situation with his tongue.

81–87: Gallura was one of the administrative divisions of Sardinia and Dante's friend Nino Visconti was its Judge, or governor. According to the early commentators, Friar Gomita was Nino's deputy and took advantage of his position to sell government jobs. Nino did not act on complaints about him until he found out that Gomita had let prisoners escape for a bribe; at that point Nino had him hanged.

88–90: Michael Zanche (c. 1210–70) was a noble of Sardinia, where Logodoro was another district. The early commentators said that he became Nino Visconti's chancellor after Friar Gomita and that he enriched himself in that position more than Gomita had. Modern historians have discredited the story.

97–117: In outline, the story of the tricky demons tricked by the sinner is easy enough to follow, but multiple ambiguities pervade the details. Ciampolo's story is plausible, but has he invented the whistle? At the least, he has planted two lures in his proposal: in addition to promising the poets more interviews, he teases the demons with the prospect of more victims. His talk is a *lacciuolo* (109), a snare to catch birds; the quarry is now hunting the birds of prey.

The demons, however, are not taken in by the ploy; Dandydog sees it is just a trick to make them stand back so Ciampolo can jump. The exposed trick nonetheless succeeds, because at least Hellkite cannot resist the challenge it presents. But Hellkite's outburst also raises questions. He says the demons will hide behind the bank on the far side of the gulch, but the demons have no power to leave the fifth gulch. *Inf.* 23.55–57.

99: "Tuscans or Lombards." Ciampolo has recognized that Virgil is a Lombard and Dante a Tuscan. (Cf. *Inf.* 27.20–21 for Virgil's Lombard dialect; *Inf.* 10.22–23, 23.76, 33.10–12 for the pilgrim's Tuscan speech and 16.8–9 for his Florentine dress.) Such a submerged detail, perhaps recognized only after multiple readings, heightens the illusion of extra-textual reality.

118–32: The questions multiply as the "strange sport" begins. Why do the demons turn away from Ciampolo to look over the far side of the bank on which they are standing? Do their eyes automatically turn where Hellkite proposes they hide? Why is Dandydog, who has sniffed out the trick, the first to go along? Does he, like Hellkite, find the challenge irresistible? Or is he, anticipating Hotfoot, hoping Ciampolo will escape so he can pin the blame on Hellkite? Do the others fall in with a plot against one of their own? With such layers of bad faith underlying everyone's words and actions, the narrative becomes indeterminate.

124–25: The demons feel guilty when Ciampolo escapes because tormenting sinners who get out of the boiling pitch is not only their pleasure but also their military duty. They disobeyed God in heaven but their malice serves him faithfully in hell.

128–30: To see this maneuver executed, look at the little lamenting angel in the center of Giotto's Deposition from the Cross in the Arena Chapel.

133–50: Ciampolo's stratagem was a snare that caught Hellkite. The intervention of Hotfoot springs the birdcatcher's other favorite trap, birdlime, a viscous coating smeared on twigs. Hellkite and Hotfoot are caught in boiling glue and cannot extricate themselves. The observation that they are cooked within the crust marks the final turning of the tables, because it echoes the kitchen metaphor of *Inf.* 21.55–57, where the demons fork the alderman in the pitch like kitchen-boys keeping the meat in a pot from floating. The demons are now meat pies.

139–41: Hawks and larger raptors do in fact grapple, locking their feet and whirling in a vertically oriented plane as they fall. They usually separate not long before they strike the earth or water below. Older literature ascribes the behavior to courtship (cf. Walt Whitman, "The Dalliance of the Eagles") but the extensive study by R.E. Simmons and J.M. Mendelsohn shows that it usually results from territorial aggression.

Canto XXIII

Silent, alone, without our escorts now
    we went on, one in front and one behind,
    the way Franciscans walk along the roads.
The brawl we'd seen made one of Aesop's fables
    come to the surface of my thoughts, the one   5
    that tells the story of the frog and the mouse;
for *sure* is no more similar to *certain*
    than these two incidents, if you compare
    attentively the way they start and finish.
And as one thought will burst forth from another,   10
    later another thought was born from this one
    that made my earlier alarm redouble.
This was my thought: "Because of us these demons
    were tricked and hurt and made to look like fools
    in a way that I imagine must be galling.   15
When rage is coiled in evil nature's skein
    they will be after us, more pitiless
    than a hound whose jaws are snapping at a rabbit."
When I could feel my hair stand up from fear
    while I was staring backward all intent,   20
    I spoke up: "Master, if you cannot hide
both of us quickly, I fear the Nastyclaws.
    They are behind us now, and I so clearly
    picture them I can almost hear them coming."

And he: "If I were made of silvered glass   25
    I'd catch your outer image no more quickly
    than I am gathering your inner one.
Just now your thoughts had come among my own;
    they had the bearing and the look of mine,
    and so from both I have formed a single plan.   30
If the right bank slopes gradually enough
    to ease our passage down the farther gulch,
    we can escape the chase that we imagine."
He had not finished telling me this plan
    when I could see them coming, wings outspread,   35
    not far behind, intent on seizing us.
All of a sudden my leader snatched me up
    the way a mother, wakened by an uproar
    and catching sight of fire blazing around her,
snatches her baby up and does not stop   40
    even to throw a shift on, more concerned
    for him than for herself, but rushes out;
and plunging from the rim of the stony bank
    he slid, his back against the sloping rock-face
    that forms one boundary of the gulch beyond.   45
Never did water race along a sluice
    to turn the great wheel of a water mill,
    even when it was rushing on the paddles,
as rapidly as my master slid straight down
    that wall, while carrying me upon his chest   50
    as if I were his child, not his companion.
His feet had scarcely touched the bed of the gulch
    when they appeared above us on the crest;
    but now they were no longer to be feared,
for the high providence that appointed them   55
    its ministers within the fifth of the ditches
    withholds from them all power of leaving it.
Down there we came upon a painted people
    that walked their rounds with slow and halting steps,
    weeping and seeming broken by exhaustion.   60

They all wore robes of the most ample cut,
    like those that are made at Cluny for the monks,
    with cowls that fell down low above their eyes.
Outside these cloaks are gilt, so they are dazzling;
    but inside they are all of lead, whose weight   65
    makes those imposed by Frederick seem like straw.
Ah, weary vestments for eternity!
    Turning again, as usual to our left,
    we walked with them, attentive to their tears;
but weighed down as they were, these tired people   70
    advanced so slowly that we found ourselves
    with every step among new company.
And so I said to my leader, "Cast your eyes
    about you as you walk and try to find
    somebody known by name or by achievement."   75
And one that recognized my Tuscan speech
    cried out when we had passed, "Restrain your pace,
    you that go running through the dusky air!
I may perhaps provide what you are seeking."
    At that my leader turned and said, "Wait here   80
    and then move on, matching your pace to his."
I stopped and noticed two of them whose eyes
    revealed the great haste in their minds to join me,
    though the load slowed them and the narrow road.
When they caught up with us, they stared askance   85
    for a long time at me, without a word;
    then turning toward each other, they remarked,
"The way his throat moves, that one seems alive;
    and if they are dead, what privilege lets them go
    without the covering of the heavy stole?"   90
And then to me: "O Tuscan, come among
    the assembly of the somber hypocrites,
    do not disdain to tell us who you are."
I answered, "I was born and I grew up
    in the great town upon the beautiful Arno,   95
    and this is the body I have always had.

But who are you, whose sorrow I can see
  trickle so freely down your cheeks? What manner
  of punishment is yours that shines so brightly?"
One of them said, "The saffron cloaks are made   100
  of lead of such a thickness that the weights
  placed on the scales cause them to squeak like this.
We were both Jolly Friars from Bologna,
  I Catalano and he Loderingo;
  we were appointed by your city jointly,   105
the way a single man had usually been,
  to keep the peace; how well we did our job
  can still be seen in the Gardingo quarter."
"O brothers," I began to say, "your evils . . ."
  but broke off, for there rushed upon my sight   110
  one crucified with three stakes on the ground.
Then he saw me and his entire body
  contorted and he puffed sighs through his beard;
  and brother Catalano, noticing this,
remarked, "The staked-out soul you're staring at   115
  advised the Pharisees it was expedient
  one man be made to suffer for the people.
Naked he lies, stretched out across the path
  as you observe, where he is made to feel
  how much each weighs as each is passing over.   120
Within this trench his father-in-law endures
  the same pain, with the others of the council
  that proved a seed of evil for the Jews."
Then I saw Virgil lost in astonishment
  over the one who lay there stretched on the cross   125
  so shamefully in the eternal exile.
Then he addressed the friar in these words:
  "Be pleased to tell us, if it is permitted,
  whether some opening on the right affords
a passage by which we two could emerge   130
  without obliging some of the black angels
  to come and lift us from the floor of the gulch."

"Nearer than you are hoping," he replied,
    "a rib of rock springs out from the circling cliffs
    and passes over all the cruel ravines   135
except for this one, where its arch lies shattered,
    allowing you to clamber up the rubble
    that slopes against the bank and heaps the bottom."
My guide remained some time with his head bowed,
    then said, "A bad account of this affair   140
    we got from him back there who hooks the sinners."
"I heard once in Bologna," said the friar,
    "among the devil's many other vices,
    he is a liar and the father of lies."
My leader walked away then with long strides,   145
    his countenance somewhat clouded by vexation;
    so I too parted from those burdened souls,
and followed in the prints of the dear feet.

Notes

1–3: The poets' solitary walk provides only a moment's lull before the scherzo of the devils concludes, but their slow and silent progress foreshadows the demeanor of the damned they will meet in this canto.

3: The Anonimo commented that it was the custom of the Franciscans to walk with the one in authority in front and the other following behind.

4–9: The fable was apparently one of the best known of those attributed to Aesop in the Middle Ages; Benvenuto said it was included in selections from Aesop taught in schools. A mouse who wanted to cross a river asked a frog for a ride. The frog tied the mouse to his leg and when they were in the middle of the river, he dived to drown the mouse. A kite saw the struggling mouse and swooped, getting the frog as well because of the string. The close parallel Dante asserts is anything but obvious, and commentators have produced conflicting interpretations.

37–51: In Dante's practice, two extended similes generally illuminate different aspects of the action. Here the first simile focuses on Virgil's parental solicitude and the second on the rushing speed of the descent.

47: "Water mill." Dante's *molin terragno* is a mill with a paddle-wheel on land near a stream. His phrase distinguishes such land-based mills from those mounted on barges in a river or moored under the arches of a bridge, which, as Benvenuto noted, were common on the Po. Water mills became the widespread industrial technology of medieval Europe. See Gimpel 1–23.

58–67: Dante gives a thorough description of the inhabitants of the sixth gulch, but only at line 92 will the pilgrim learn that these are the hypocrites.

61–63: For centuries the Benedictine abbey of Cluny in Burgundy was the leading monastery of Europe. Cluny was a wealthy foundation and the monks' habits were unusually ample. On top of the monastic scapulary habit with its hood, Cluniacs wore a long pleated robe. Goetz 103. St. Bernard of Clairvaux mocked the habits for being luxurious and inconsistent with monastic austerity.

64–67: The explanation of the cloaks reflects the poet's knowledge, not the pilgrim's, and we end this passage knowing how the sinners are punished but not why. In hindsight, the gilding of base metal is an obvious trope for false appearances. Dante probably accepted a spurious etymology of the period that derived the word "hypocrite" from Greek roots signifying a gilded surface. *ED* 3.511. Again in hindsight, it is the leaden inside of the robes that imposes the specific punishment of the sixth gulch – eternal exhaustion resulting from the unremitting burden of maintaining false appearances. Following the first law of the *contrapasso, what you do, you become*, the slow pace, the sadness, the tears – the sort of appearances the hypocrites assumed to simulate sober and penitent virtue – are enforced on them forever by the leaden monastic habits.

65–66: Early commentators asserted that Frederick II executed traitors by having them covered in a cloak of lead and put in a cauldron, so that the lead would melt as the victim boiled. Dante may have accepted the story, for which there is no evidence; but Frederick's alleged punishment did not depend on weight.

70–72, 77–78: Dante emphasizes the slow progress of the burdened souls by juxtaposing opposite points of view. First the pilgrim notices that he and Virgil walk among them as though they went through a waxworks. Then one of the souls catches sight of the poets sprinting through the crowd of pedestrians and calls after them.

85–86: The shades are required to look sidelong at the pilgrim because they cannot move their heads within the rigid confines of their metal cowls. But the oblique glance of the hypocrites is also the revealing gesture of a devious mind.

92–108: The pilgrim learns that these sinners are the hypocrites. Hypocrisy received a distinctive emphasis in the teaching of Jesus. He condemned the outward show of piety of the Pharisees, whom he accused of following the letter of the law but neglecting its spirit of justice and mercy. Matt. 23:23. His calling them whitewashed tombs (Matt. 23:27) is echoed in Dante's "painted people." Aquinas defined hypocrisy as a lie told by outward signs in which the sinner simulates the person of a just man. *ST* 2–2.111.1–2.

Dante follows medieval anticlerical satire in taking false piety among the clergy as the exemplary form of hypocrisy. The sinners wear a parody of monastic robes and the two whom the pilgrim meets are friars. The economic success of the monks and later of the friars undercut their claim to be Christ's poor and furnished medieval satire with a strong example of the gospel paradigm of hypocrisy as false piety. In Dante's adaptation of the *Romance of the Rose* Falsembiante (Faux-Semblant) is a friar who reveals the wealth the friars have amassed under the semblance of pious poverty. *Fiore* 89. Here the gilded cloaks allude to this popular motif and the friars the pilgrim meets reveal their own hypocrisy.

92–93: The unusually long interval between the description of the hypocrites and the revelation of their sin may reflect its hidden nature and the medieval convention that they are known through self-revelation (in addition to Faux-Semblant, cf. Chaucer's Pardoner).

92: "Somber (*triste*)" recalls Jesus's injunction: "when you fast, be not as the hypocrites, sad (*triste*)." Matt. 6:16.

100–02: Catalano, the speaker, has a gift for cryptic utterances. Here he is thinking of a scale with two pans hanging from a balance beam. When excessive weight is placed in the pans, the beam squeaks as it moves. So, as the great weight of the iron maidens tips back and forth in the progress of the hypocrites, the suffering souls groan and sob. The souls are thus reduced to the condition of human scales eternally measuring the weight of their own hypocrisy.

100: "Saffron (*rance*)." Yellow was the only color not favored for clothing in the Middle Ages (Piponnier 60) and often had sinister associations (Pleij 77–79; see Huizinga 272). It was sometimes a badge of infamy: in many areas Jews, Muslims, heretics and witches had to wear yellow patches on their clothing (Pleij 79), while reprieved heretics had to wear yellow crosses (Peters 204). Judas often wears yellow in the art of the period. In the supreme example of hypocrisy, when Giotto's Judas in the Arena chapel gives Jesus the kiss of betrayal, he envelops him in his yellow cloak.

103–08: Catalano de' Malavolti and Loderingo degli Andalò were both born into noble Bolognese families around 1210. Both joined the religious and military order of the Knights of the Blessed Virgin, whose mission included making peace between the warring factions in the Italian cities. Because the order was free of the usual restrictions (some members could marry and bear arms), it was known as the Jolly Friars (*frati godenti*).

In 1266 the two jointly held the office of *podestà* in Florence. Their mission to make peace between Guelfs and Ghibellines was supposed to be furthered by one's being a Guelf and the other a Ghibelline. The Ghibelline cause, however, was fatally wounded on the battlefield in that year. The pope was eager to overthrow Ghibelline rule in Florence and Catalano and Loderingo acted as tools of papal policy. With the government backing the Guelfs, the Ghibellines fled the city and their houses were torn down.

107–08: The Gardingo, an old tower, was located near the site later occupied by the Palazzo Vecchio. In 1266 the houses of the Uberti clan (see *Inf.* 10) in the vicinity were torn down and in 1300 their ruins still bore mute witness to what Dante regards as the hypocrisy of Catalano and Loderingo.

110–13: For his climactic example of hypocrisy, Dante returns to the gospel. The figure, as Catalano will explain, is that of Caiaphas, the High Priest who advised that Jesus be put to death. His crucifixion is the most literal example of the second law of the *contrapasso: what you do to others, you do to yourself.*

111: Caiaphas is crucified with three stakes – one through each hand and one through his crossed feet. In the 13th century the crucified Christ began to be represented in this fashion, replacing an earlier scheme with four nails. Link 37–38.

112–13: Caiaphas manifests dismay at seeing the pilgrim, apparently because he recognizes that the pilgrim is alive and can report his humiliation to the living.

115–23: When the chief priests and the Pharisees conferred on what to do about Jesus, given that he performed many miracles, threatening to win the people's faith, Caiaphas said it was expedient "that one man should die for the people," speaking a greater truth than he understood. John 11:47–50.

The punishment of Caiaphas, his father-in-law Annas (see John 18:13) and the others of the council is heavier than that of the other hypocrites. Like them, they are made into human scales; but they must measure the weight of all the other hypocrites, who walk over them, because in justifying deicide their hypocrisy has been universal.

126: Dante calls hell the everlasting exile by contrast with earth, the temporary exile from heaven, our true homeland. See Heb. 11:13–14. Virgil will use the same phrase of himself in *Purg.* 21.18.

142–44: In this fine touch, we see Catalano practicing his vice, mocking Virgil under cover of a pious platitude. ("[T]he devil . . . is a liar and the father thereof." John 8:44.)

Canto XXIV

In the year's youthful season, when the sun
    douses his hair beneath Aquarius
    and nights are shrinking to the length of days,
and when the frost transcribes upon the ground
    a faithful duplicate of her white sister,   5
    but with a pen whose point is quickly blunted,
the countryman whose feed is running short
    gets up and looks outside, and when he sees
    the fields all shining white, he slaps his hip,
goes back inside and paces up and down   10
    grumbling, like a poor wretch at his wits' end;
    then, going back out, he gathers hope again,
seeing the face of nature quite transformed
    in those few moments; and he takes his crook
    and drives his little flock of sheep to pasture.   15
My master left me equally dismayed,
    seeing the clouds so hang upon his brow,
    and just as soon the hurt was remedied;
for when we reached the bridge's ruins, my leader
    turned to me, on his face the gentle look   20
    that I had first observed below the mountain.
After examining the ruins attentively
    and coming inwardly to some decision,
    he spread his arms, clasped me and lifted me.

And like a man who plans ahead while working   25
   and always seems prepared before the event,
   while he was boosting me to reach the summit
of some great boulder he would scan the next
   projection, saying, "Now grab hold of that one,
   but test it first, to see if it will bear you."   30
This was no road for one who wore the cloak,
   for he and I – he light, I boosted up –
   could barely climb from handhold up to handhold.
And had the bank on that side not been lower
   than on the other, I cannot speak for him,   35
   but I would surely have been overcome.
But since the whole of Devil's Gulches funnels
   into the opening of the deepest pit,
   each of the valleys is so situated
that one bank must sink lower than the other,   40
   and in the end we made it up to the point
   where the last block of stone had broken off.
When I got up there, all the air was squeezed
   out of my lungs and I could go no further,
   but sank to a seat as soon as I arrived.   45
"Now you must rouse yourself," my teacher said.
   "No one wins fame by lounging upon cushions
   or lying under a coverlet; and one
who spends his life without obtaining that
   leaves the same traces after him on earth   50
   as smoke in the air or foam upon the water.
Get up then, overcome your loss of breath
   by strength of soul, invincible in all
   unless it sink beneath the body's weight.
Having left these behind is not enough: 55
   there is a longer ladder we must climb.
   Act for your own good if you understand me."
I stood then, making show of having gotten
   my wind again, more than I felt, and said,
   "Go on, for I feel strong and confident."   60

Upward we made our way along the ridge
    and found it craggy, narrow and difficult,
    very much steeper than the previous one.
Not to seem faint, I talked while I was walking,
    at which a voice arose from the next trench,   65
    one that had difficulty forming words.
I do not know what it said, though I already
    stood at the top of the arch that crosses there;
    but the speaker seemed to me to be in motion.
I leaned far over, but my living eyes   70
    could not arrive at the bottom through the gloom.
    "Master," this made me say, "let us press on
to the other belt and there climb down the wall;
    for now I hear but cannot understand,
    and look below but can distinguish nothing."   75
He answered, "I will give you no response
    except by action, for a fair request
    ought to be followed by the deed in silence."
So we descended at the bridge's head,
    on the side where it adjoins the eighth of the banks,   80
    and then before my eyes the gulch lay open:
in it I saw a horrifying mass
    of writhing snakes, and in such monstrous shapes
    the memory still can make my blood run cold.
Let Libya boast no longer of her sands;   85
    for though she hatches javelin snakes, two-headed
    serpents, pharaeas, cenchri and chelydri,
she never yet could show such multitudes
    of noxious pests, nor Ethiopia
    nor the land the other side of the Red Sea.   90
Amid this cruel and desolating plenty
    people were running, naked, terrified,
    no hope of hiding place or heliotrope;
their hands were bound behind their backs with snakes,
    the heads and tails of which were thrusting out   95
    along their sides and tied in knots before them.

And look! one of the serpents hurled itself
    at someone near our bank and skewered him
    right where the neck attaches to the shoulders.
Quicker than pen has ever formed an O   100
    or I, he caught on fire and was consumed
    and could not help, transformed to ash, but fall;
and when he lay dispersed upon the ground
    the dust spontaneously came back together,
    at once reconstituting him the same.   105
(The phoenix dies and is reborn like that
    at the approach of its five-hundredth year,
    as the great scholars all attest; throughout
its life it feeds on neither plants nor seeds
    but only tears of frankincense and balsam,   110
    while myrrh and spikenard form its final shroud.)
And like a man who falls, not knowing how
    – whether a demon's power pulls him down
    or a blockage that impedes his vital functions –
and getting up again, stares all about,   115
    bewildered by the agony he has suffered,
    and as he looks around him, heaves a sigh:
such was the sinner after he arose.
    How stern and rigorous is the power of God,
    that pours its vengeance down in strokes like these!   120
My leader asked him who he was. He answered,
    "I rained down, not so long ago, from Tuscany
    into this savage maw. Mule that I was,
I chose an animal's life and not a man's.
    My name is Vanni Fucci, called The Beast: 125
    for me Pistoia was a fitting den."
"Tell him," I said to my guide, "not to slip off,
    and ask what crime has cast him down so far,
    for I knew him as a man of blood and rage."
And the sinner, who had heard, did not dissemble   130
    but turned to face me with his full attention,
    his features coloring up in sullen shame.

"Having you catch me in the misery
  you see," he said then, "causes me more pain
  than being taken from the other life.   135
Now I cannot refuse to answer you:
  I have been thrust this deep because I stole
  the gleaming treasures of the sacristy,
though someone else was falsely blamed for it.
  But to prevent your gloating upon this   140
  if ever you emerge from the dark regions,
open your ears and hear what I foretell.
  Pistoia first grows thin from losing Blacks,
  then Florence changes parties and regimes.
Mars draws a dry and fiery exhalation   145
  from Val di Magra, wrapped in swirling clouds,
  and in a furious and violent storm
battle will rage above Campo Piceno,
  until a blinding flash tears through the clouds –
  one that will strike the heart of every White.   150
And I have told you this to cause you pain."

Notes

1–21: Seeing the consternation of his protector in this hostile environment, the
  pilgrim is anxious; but Virgil quickly recovers, and the return of his kind manner
  comforts his protégé. In the pastoral simile that conveys the pilgrim's rapid change
  from fear to joy, a shepherd mistakes the frost of an early spring morning for
  snow and fears his sheep will starve in a lingering winter. Signs can be deceptive;
  here the deceptions arise not from fraud but from misreading signs in light of the
  reader's fears.

1–2: From ancient times the sun's rays were identified with Apollo's streaming
  golden hair. See *Aen.* 9.638 and ancient Greek coinage. Aquarius is probably
  imagined as pouring water from an urn, the traditional image, as in the
  contemporary *Hours of Henry VII*. The sun is in Aquarius from January 21
  to February 21, and the sun "tempers" his hair (*i crin . . . tempra*) under
  its shower because his rays are reduced then. With the advancing season,
  however, Apollo's hair will emerge brighter from its dousing under Aquarius,
  as steel is strengthened by tempering, including the plunge in cold water.

3: Under Aquarius the nights are diminishing toward the vernal equinox, when they will equal the daylight hours.

4–6: The image comes from the scriptorium: the frost copies the outward form of her sister the snow, but does so with a pen that is soon blunt because the frost melts as soon as the sun is touches it.

43–60: Critics have remarked on the disproportion between the pilgrim's sitting down for a moment to regain his breath and the lengthy exhortation this evokes from Virgil, who pulls out all the stops of classical rhetoric. But Virgil acts in the manner of a master who uses trivial everyday events as teaching tools. As to his teaching, Virgil speaks from the limited perspective of an ancient pagan, for whom honorable fame, the reward for virtue, is the highest good. But Dante's own susceptibility to that last infirmity of noble mind should not be underestimated.

76–78: Modern readers are often contemptuous of Virgil's using so many words to say he will not use any words; but it belongs to his function as an ancient sage to express sententious wisdom, highly prized in the Middle Ages and long afterward.

82–90: Snakes are a traditional feature of the punishments of hell. In the *Vision of St. Paul* the apostle sees sinners in hell with dragons coiled around their necks, shoulders and feet. Elliott 636. (For dragons as serpents, see *Etym.* 12.4.4.) In "St. Patrick's Purgatory" the visionary sees sinners in hell lying on their backs while fiery serpents coil around their necks, arms and bodies. Gardiner 140. Snakes twining in and out among the bodies of the damned are common in Romanesque church sculpture and also appear in the great marble relief of the Last Judgment that was being carved on the façade of the Orvieto cathedral while the *Comedy* was being written.

85–90: Dante read about the fabulous serpents of Libya in Lucan, where Cato's army encounters them in its march across the Sahara. *Phars.* 9.700–33. Lucan describes the *chelydrus*, which leaves a smoking track as it glides along; the *cenchris*, which moves in a straight line; the *amphisbaena*, which moves toward either of its two heads; the *jaculus* (*jaculum* = javelin), which can fly; and the *parias* (Dante's *pharaea*), which rears up as it moves and plows a track with its tail. Although Dante regarded these serpents as monstrosities, he probably did not think of them as fables. Two of them appear in Pliny (*Nat. Hist.* 8.35.85), and all of them appear in Isidore (*Etym.* 12.4) and Albertus Magnus. *De Animal.* 25.14ff.

90: I.e., Arabia. Dante says "above" the Red Sea because medieval world maps placed East at the top.

91–96: The sinners in the seventh gulch are the thieves, and the Middle Ages connected the slithering of snakes with the stealth of thieves. Isidore said that the serpent is so called because it slinks (*serpit*), not in the open but secretly (*Etym.* 12.4.3); and Pietro Alighieri added that thieves pilfer others' goods by stealth, creeping around walls like snakes. As the sinners run terrified through the writhing mass of snakes the "pickers and stealers" (*Hamlet*) with which they sinned are restrained and thus unable to perform their other function of warding off harm.

93: "Heliotrope." The parallel with "hiding place" suggests that Dante is not referring to the heliotrope plant, said to be an antidote for snake venom (*Nat. Hist.* 22.29.59), but rather to the heliotrope stone, which in connection with the plant was claimed to confer invisibility. *Nat. Hist.* 37.60.75. Pliny, however, followed verbatim by Isidore (*Etym.* 16.7.12), regarded this as a fable for the credulous, so that even the hope would be illusory. See *Decam.* 8.3.

97–102: Like one of Lucan's javelin snakes, the infernal serpent hurls itself through the air and pierces the sinner at the base of the neck. Its incendiary effect, however, is Dante's invention; Lucan's snake killed simply by piercing. *Phars.* 9.822–27.

100–01: Another image from the scriptorium. The Ottimo's and Buti's claim that *i* and *o* were written more quickly than any other letters is unlikely. In most of the book hand scripts of the period, the angular *o* would have taken longer to write than the *l*. Dante may have chosen the letters, as commentators have suggested, because they form the word *io*, "I." In less time than it would take to write either letter of the pronoun of self-identification, the sinner's identity is gone.

106–11: Although the phoenix simile aptly mirrors the destruction and reconstitution of the sinner, it reads like an academic footnote; and in fact Dante lifts whole phrases from Ovid. *Metam.* 15.391–407. (The implied incineration of the phoenix, however, is a post-Ovidian development.) Worse, the exotic glamor of the phoenix appears wildly inappropriate to the snake-infested horror of the seventh gulch.

Is it relevant that the phoenix image has a long allegorical history? Though Dante would have had no reason to doubt the reality of the phoenix, its story had from early Christian times been read as an allegory of the death and resurrection of Jesus. Common to Lactantius, Augustine and others, this theme is also found in the Physiologus, whence it descended to the medieval bestiaries. See Hassig 72–83. This connection is consistent with the cultural cachet of the image, but it seems to make the simile all the more inappropriate here.

In fact, however, the implied comparison of the sinner to Christ justifies the simile as an infernal parody. The punishment of the thieves follows the second law of the *contrapasso – what you do to others, you do to yourself*. Here the thief's human identity, all he retains, is stolen from him repeatedly by the gulch's monstrous serpents, and the worst of it is that he is continually resurrected to suffer the theft eternally.

112–17: This simile conveys the bewilderment with which the sinner arises from his metamorphosis. He appears to have epilepsy, or falling sickness, as Pietro noted. Dante gives both religious and medical explanations for his symptoms. (1) Luke 9:42, where a boy was possessed by a devil that "threw him down" was authority for attributing epilepsy to demonic possession. A 13th century English illustration shows a man being cured of epilepsy as a devil is ejected through his mouth. Clanchy, plate 20. (2) As Buti explained, when an accumulation of humors or their gross vapors blocks the passages that lead from the heart to the brain (*i.e.*, the arteries through which the blood and the vital spirits essential to life were supposed to pass), a man falls down unconscious. See Siraisi 107–09.

121–39: Vanni Fucci, an illegitimate son (hence a "mule") of a leading family in Pistoia, was a violent Black Guelf partisan. In 1289 he murdered a prominent White of Pistoia and later led an armed attack on the family of the White governor and joined in burning and sacking the houses of Whites in the city. Probably in 1295, he and accomplices burglarized the sacristy of the rich San Iacopo chapel in the cathedral of Pistoia. They hid the stolen objects in a notary's house, and an innocent man was imprisoned for the crime. It was apparently Fucci himself, now safe in the mountains, who let it be known where the loot was. In consequence the notary was tried instead of the innocent man, and Fucci was also condemned. There is no evidence he was brought to justice. *ED* 5.878–79.

128–29: The pilgrim asserts that he knew Fucci personally, and Fucci will soon recognize him. Knowing the sinner as a man of violence, the pilgrim would expect to see him in the seventh circle. In Dante's intellectualized scheme of hell, thieves are placed further down than robbers because fraud is intrinsically more corruptive than violence of man's essential faculty of reason. For Aquinas, theft was sinful in two ways: it offends against justice in taking what belongs to another, and it involves guile or fraud, which is sinful in itself. *ST* 2–2.66.5. Aquinas sensibly concluded, however, that robbery is worse than theft because of its effects on the victim, who is more injured by violence than by fraud. *ST* 2–2.66.9.

130–39: By 1300 the pilgrim should have been aware of Fucci's part in the notorious burglary, but having the thief confess the crime to his political enemy with bitter resentment is far more dramatic. Fucci's freely made confession that his life was no better than an animal's was a cynical boast that concealed his rage at having lived such a life. His pride is touched, however, when he is forced to allow someone from back home to discover that the man of violence was also a thief. Aquinas pointed out that men in general are more ashamed of theft than of robbery. *ST* 2–2.66.9.

143–51: Knowing that the pilgrim is allied with the White Guelfs, Fucci takes revenge for his humiliation by revealing that the Whites will be defeated and dispersed in the coming years. As is usual with prophecies, the substance of the prediction is coded in metaphor.

143: In 1301 the Whites of Pistoia chased out the Blacks and pulled down their houses. *Cron.* 9.45.

144: Also in 1301, Pope Boniface VIII, unhappy with the White ascendancy in Florence, sent Charles of Valois there with his French cavalry, ostensibly as a peacemaker. Charles immediately allowed the Blacks to return and his soldiers stood aside while the Blacks rioted, looting the houses and shops of the Whites. *Cron.* 9.49. When Charles left, the Blacks were in control, and the Whites, including Dante, were exiled.

145–50: Fucci goes on to predict the final rout of the Whites. By 1305 they had been defeated all over Tuscany except Pistoia, where they retained control. The

Blacks of Florence and Lucca under Moroello Malaspina besieged Pistoia and in 1306 the city surrendered after almost a year. This is conveyed through an elaborate thunderstorm metaphor: the planet of the war-god draws up an exhalation (Malaspina), which it heats and dries, from Val di Magra (Malaspina's territory). The dry exhalation is surrounded by clouds of cold, moist vapor (the forces of the Whites). The hot and cold elements clash in a violent thunderstorm over Campo Piceno near Pistoia (the siege of the city) and the dry exhalation tears through the clouds with a flash of lightning (Malaspina defeats the Whites). The physics of the thunderstorm is based on Aristotle. See *Meteorol.* 10.9 (369a10–369b10).

145: Mars both acts as a physical cause of the storm and serves as a portent of political disaster. Dante explained in *Conv.* 2.13.21–22 that Mars dries and heats things, which is why it looks enflamed with color, and that these exhalations sometimes catch fire, which "signifies the death of kings and change of kingdoms."

151: As Dante knows when he writes this canto, by 1306 he will become disillusioned with the Whites and will constitute himself "a party of one." *Par.* 17.61–69. He will become an admirer of the Malaspina family (see *Purg.* 8.121–32) and a friend of a Moroello Malaspina who may be the individual referred to here. See *ED* 3.781–82; *DE* 628–29.

Canto XXV

After he said these words, the thief raised both
    his fists, with which he made the fig, and shouted:
    "Take that, God, for I aim it straight at you!"
From that time on, the snakes became my friends,
    for now one coiled itself around his neck   5
    as if to say, "I want no more from you."
Another curled around his arms and bound
    them up once more and twined itself in front
    so tightly that he could not even twitch.
Pistoia, ah Pistoia, why not order   10
    that you be burnt to ash and cease to be,
    now that in crime you have surpassed your founders?
Through all the gloomy circles of hell I saw
    no other spirit so arrogant toward God,
    not him that tumbled down the wall at Thebes.   15
He fled without another word; just then
    I saw a centaur coming, full of rage,
    shouting, "Where is he, the defiant one?"
I do not think Maremma itself contains
    as many snakes as crawled upon his back   20
    up to the point at which our shape begins.
Upon his shoulders, just behind the nape,
    there lay a dragon with its wings outspread,
    setting ablaze all those whom it encountered.

"That one," my teacher said to me, "is Cacus; 25
  beneath the boulders of Mount Aventine
  his slaughters often made a lake of blood.
His road is not the one his brothers travel
  because he rustled cattle cunningly
  from the great herd he found in his environs; 30
for that his villainous deeds were ended under
  the club of Hercules, which dealt perhaps
  a hundred blows, of which he felt not ten."
While he was saying this, the centaur galloped
  past and three spirits came along below us, 35
  of whom my guide and I were unaware
until they called to us, "Who are you two?"
  Hearing that, we broke off our conversation
  and focused our attention all on them.
I did not recognize them, but it happened, 40
  as often happens for whatever reason,
  one of them had to use another's name,
saying, "Now where has Cianfa wandered off to?"
  At that, to make my guide remain attentive,
  I laid my finger from my chin to my nose. 45
Reader, if you are now slow to believe
  what I will tell, it would not be surprising:
  I scarcely credit what I saw myself.
As I looked closely at them, suddenly
  a serpent with six legs sprang up upon 50
  one of them, fastening on him everywhere.
It wrapped its middle pair of legs around
  his belly and with its forelegs gripped his arms,
  then sank a fang in either of his cheeks;
it splayed its hind legs out upon his thighs 55
  and thrust its tail between them, stretching it
  behind him up along his lower back.
Ivy has never twined about a tree
  as closely as that horrifying creature
  twisted its own around the other's limbs; 60

and then they fused together like hot wax,
    mingling their colors until neither one
    seemed to be any longer what it was,
the way a flame advances over paper,
    spreading before itself a brownish tinge,   65
    not black as yet, while the white dies away.
Both of the others watched him and they each
    cried out, "Ah me, Agnello, how you change!
    Look, you are neither single now nor double."
When the two heads had coalesced in one   70
    two physiognomies appeared to us,
    commingled in one face where two were lost.
Two arms took shape from four appendages;
    the thighs and calves, the belly and the chest
    turned into body parts not seen before.   75
All former features now obliterated,
    the monstrous shape resembled both and neither,
    and in that state it lumbered slowly off.
And as a lizard, when it changes hedges
    under the heavy lash of the dog days' heat,   80
    flashes like lightning if it cross the lane,
here there appeared now, streaking toward the bellies
    of the other two, a fiery little serpent,
    black as a peppercorn and furious;
darting at one of them, it struck the part   85
    from which our earliest nourishment is drawn;
    then it fell down, stretched out in front of him.
The one it pierced looked at it but said nothing;
    he simply stood immobilized and yawned
    as if assailed by sleep or by a fever.   90
He and the serpent stared at one another;
    thick smoke began to billow from his wound
    and the other's mouth, and the smoke came together.
Let Lucan now fall silent, where he mentions
    wretched Sabellus and Nasidius,   95
    and wait to see the shot that I let fly.

Let Ovid speak no more of Arethusa
    nor Cadmus either; if in verse he changed
    one to a spring and the other to a snake,
I do not envy him, because he never   100
    transformed two natures face to face, until
    both forms were ready to exchange their matter.
They answered one another by this rule:
    the serpent's tail divided in a fork,
    he that was wounded pressed his feet together.   105
His shins at first and then his thighs adhered
    each to the other, so that in a moment
    no seam could be detected where they joined.
The cloven tail assumed the conformation
    the other side was losing, and its skin   110
    grew supple while his hardened over there.
I saw his arms retract within the armpits
    and both the stubby forelegs of the beast
    lengthen proportionately as those shortened.
Twisted together then, its two hind feet   115
    became the member that a man conceals,
    while the wretch sprouted two of them from his.
And while the smoke was veiling each of them
    in a new color and causing hair to sprout
    on one side as it vanished on the other,   120
one of them stood, the other fell to the ground;
    but neither turned away the ruthless lamps
    beneath which snout and face began to change.
The one that stood retracted snout toward temples
    and from the excess matter gathered there   125
    the ears emerged from the now hollow cheeks;
the surplus that remained in place, instead
    of flowing back, became the face's nose
    and the lips thickened to the proper size.
The one that lay thrust out nose, mouth and jaws   130
    to form a snout, retracting ears inside
    the head the way a snail draws in its horns;

the tongue that had been formed for speech when whole
    divided and the other's tongue, once forked,
    closed up now; and at that point the smoke stopped.   135
The shade that had become an animal
    fled through the valley, hissing as it went,
    and the other, as he spoke, spat after it,
then turned his brand new back upon it, saying
    to the other shade, "Now let's see Buoso crawl,   140
    as I did, on all fours along the track."
I saw the ballast of the seventh hold
    thus change and interchange; and if my pen
    has botched this, let the novelty excuse it.
And though my vision may have been a bit   145
    confused, my mind somewhat disoriented,
    they could not flee the scene so unobserved
but that I made out plainly Puccio the Gimp,
    the only member of the three who came
    earlier who was not transformed; the other   150
was he for whom you weep, Gaville, still.

Notes

1–15: Because he has just regained his human form, Fucci's hands are temporarily free, a condition soon remedied. His gesture of impotent rage makes the pilgrim regard him as worse than Capaneus the blasphemer. *Inf.* 14.51–60. In Dante's intellectual scheme of hell, theft is more wicked than blasphemy, but Dante's real judgments do not always follow his scheme.

1–3: The fig (*fica*) is made by brandishing the fist with the thumb protruding between the index and middle fingers. Fucci uses this ancient gesture of sexual symbolism as an obscene insult.

10–12: Dante had no reason to love Pistoia, birthplace of the Black/White Guelf factionalism that plagued his life, and he urges that the city impose on itself the punishment that its son Vanni Fucci endures in hell. Pistoia's founders, whose wickedness the city that bred Fucci now surpasses, were supposed to be the followers of the Roman conspirator Catiline. *Cron.* 1.32.

17–24: The centaur Cacus with a fire-breathing dragon perched on his shoulders comes from Dante's creative misreading of Virgil. *Aen.* 8.190–267. Virgil's Cacus is a man-eating, fire-breathing giant, but Dante apparently understood Virgil's description of his humanoid form (*semihominis*) as meaning half man and half beast, a description that the centaur fits. Belching flame was natural to Virgil's giant, who was a son of Vulcan, but not to a centaur. Dante therefore updated the image by giving the flames a source – the dragon – understood as natural by his audience. The medieval dragon appears in art as a rather small creature with a crested head on a serpentine neck, a body with wings and two clawed feet, and a long serpentine tail.

18: Context suggests that Cacus is looking for Fucci, but Bosco/Reggio note that elsewhere only devils punish sinners in the eighth circle; and Cacus is here being punished as a thief.

19–20: The Tuscan Maremma was a swampy area on the coast. Buti said it so abounded in snakes that a monastery there was abandoned on that account.

25–33: Cacus was, like Fucci, a creature of rage and blood who turned to theft. When Hercules drove a great herd by his cave, Cacus stole prize cattle from it by night, dragging them backwards by their tails so there would be no footprints leading there. *Aen.* 8.201–12. Hearing a heifer low in the cave, Hercules dislodged boulders to get at Cacus, throttling him until the eyes burst from his head. *Aen.* 8.213–61. Dante substitutes the version in which Hercules kills Cacus with his club, found in Livy and Ovid. Livy 1.7; *Fasti* 1.543–78.

35–45: The three thieves who approach are not running terrified through snakes with their hands bound like those in *Inf.* 24, but rather appear to conduct a casual conversation as they stroll. Some commentators suggest that different types of thieves are subject to different punishments. When such differentiation occurs, however, as in the tenth gulch in *Inf.* 30, Dante makes the punitive scheme plain. Here the general form of punishment has served its allegorical function and recedes into the background.

40–45: Although the pilgrim does not recognize the three shades, he is alerted by the name Cianfa to the fact that they are Florentines. Cianfa was identified by the early commentators as a member of the leading Donati family who died before 1289.

50–78: The first transformation of canto 25, in which a serpent leaps on a sinner, grips him with its legs while biting him, and embraces him until their bodies merge in a single perverted form, is a vision out of the medieval hell elaborated with the aid of Ovid. In the depiction of hell on the mosaic ceiling of the Baptistery of Florence, which Dante would have known, a whole series of creatures like giant lizards or salamanders climb on sinners and cling to them while they bite them. There are many similar depictions in French church sculptures. See Weir/Jerman 58–79.

Dante develops this popular image by drawing on the learned resource of the Ovidian metamorphosis. In the legend of Hermaphroditus, the water-nymph Salmacis loves a cold youth and embraces him when he goes swimming. When she prays never to be separated from him, the gods merge them into a single body with one face and one form. *Metam.* 4.285–388. Dante's ivy simile is taken directly from Ovid's passage. Dante, however, repurposes the Ovidian metamorphosis to convey the horror that accompanies the loss of personal identity. He dramatizes the assimilation of the self by a predatory evil, an effect foreign to Ovid because it depends on the Christian psychology of guilt and retribution. Thomas Peterson argues that in the *Inferno* Dante exploits Ovid's vivid descriptions of change as a natural process but uses them as figurations of Christian eschatology, a tension that Peterson labels parody. Peterson 203–05; see also Cioffi 77–100.

50: No six-legged serpents were known to medieval zoology, so this is an instance of the monstrous forms of the infernal serpents. Medieval serpents included not only legless snakes, but also dragons, which had two legs, and salamanders and lizards, which had four (*De Animal.* 25.25, 25.31, 25.38), though Isidore and Albertus Magnus stipulated that lizards were not true serpents. *Etym.* 12.4.3; *De Animal.* 25.1. The serpent in the garden in Genesis was sometimes represented as a dragon (*e.g.*, the bronze doors of St. Michael, Hildesheim).

64–66: This serpent is apparently black, like the one that will appear next, and the brownish tinge results from melting its color into the victim's. Paper, made from flax and hemp, had only begun to be manufactured in Italy in Dante's lifetime.

67–69: The early commentators identified the victim as Agnello Brunelleschi, a member of a distinguished Ghibelline family of Florence who is not known from contemporary records.

70–72: Dante was not the only contemporary artist to experiment with the horror of two faces lost in one. A fresco in the transept of the lower basilica of San Francesco in Assisi contains a startling image of the hanged Judas, his dead face a mask through which his soul appears with a fiendish expression.

79–93: The second transformation of this canto follows the first without a break. The little serpent that races toward the two remaining shades is *acceso*, which many commentators take to mean "inflamed with wrath," consistent with the medieval view of serpents as aggressive and irascible creatures. *See De Animal.* 25.11.

Instead of the nourishment a human fetus would receive through the umbilicus, the victim receives the venom that makes him a serpent. The victim's yawning, followed by the smoke that pours from his wound and the serpent's mouth, corresponds to Isidore's explanation that because snake venom is cold it merely stupefies the victim at first, but that after it warms in the body it sets the victim on fire and quickly destroys him. *Etym.* 12.4.41. Lucan's Aulus is bitten by a serpent whose venom burns him up internally, yet he feels nothing at first. *Phars.* 9.737–60.

94–102: Dante challenges comparison with two of his classical models, Lucan and Ovid. In the passage from Lucan, Roman soldiers are bitten by the serpents of Libya: Sabellus liquefies, Nasidius bloats fantastically. *Phars.* 9.762–810. Both are simple physical changes, but Lucan analyzes them as a succession of symptoms that shows the working of the venom. Ovid's Cadmus (*Metam.* 3.1–137) turns into a great serpent, and Dante follows some of Ovid's stages – the skin hardening, the man falling and his legs adhering and finally his tongue splitting and hissing – but in more granular detail.

Dante's claim to superiority is technical: the Ovidian metamorphosis involves a person transformed into an animal or feature of the landscape, rather than Dante's double transformation in which two beings exchange identities. In Dante's allegory, the soul, having voluntarily persisted in evil, cannot arrest its involuntary transformation into a horrible alien form that manifests the evil. (A similar fate awaits Milton's Satan in *Paradise Lost* 10.511–18.)

97: Arethusa was a wood-nymph who, pursued by the river god Alpheus, was transformed into a spring. *Metam.* 5.572–641.

104–35: Like Ovid's Cadmus, Dante's sinner turns into a serpent beginning with the feet and ending with the head. The process only gradually reaches the seat of reason, and the tongue is the final detail because speech is the index of rationality.

119: The one becoming a serpent darkens, the one becoming a man lightens.

122–23: The two exchange faces under the ruthless glare of their twin sets of lantern-eyes, which indicates that the man's eyes are already those of a serpent. In medieval zoology, serpents' eyes shine like lanterns or candles or burning coals. *Etym.* 12.4.21; *Tresor* 1.139; *De Animal.* 25.9. The glowing eyes express the hatred of the creatures for each other.

136–41: Dante springs the most surprising twist of this macabre scene: the serpent turned man is an acquaintance of the man turned serpent. He has stolen the latter's human shape and forced him to assume his own serpent's shape. The thieves are condemned to steal the limited number of human shapes from each other in a dreary eternal game of musical bodies. This final transformation conveys Dante's most developed concept for the seventh gulch, which combines both forms of the *contrapasso*: the thief remains what he has made himself, stealing for eternity, but surrounded by other thieves as he is, he is also the eternal victim of theft, as his human identity is repeatedly stolen from him.

140: "Buoso" is probably Buoso dei Donati, a Florentine noble from the generation before Dante's, like the other thieves in this canto (not the Buoso of *Inf.* 30.44). The snake turned man is Francesco "Squinty" Cavalcanti, another member of a leading Florentine family. Only after learning the secret of the second transformation can we look back to the first and realize that the serpent that attacked Agnello was in fact Cianfa, the missing member of the party.

138: Cavalcanti acts on the ancient belief that human saliva is poisonous to snakes. See *Nat. Hist.* 7.2.15; *De Animal.* 22.12; *Tresor* 1.137. Because of the identification of Satan with the serpent in Genesis, the desert fathers used to drive demons away by spitting at them, and the practice continued in the Middle Ages. See Russell 90, 126.

142–43: The gulch is the hold of a ship, whose ballast would ordinarily be broken crockery or other refuse; but in this hold the refuse swarms and pullulates, as human identities migrate back and forth from serpent to human shapes.

148–50: Puccio "Gimpy" Galigai came from a noble Florentine family of Ghibelline allegiance.

151: Francesco Cavalcanti was killed in the village of Gaville, but the village weeps on his account only because his relatives massacred the inhabitants in revenge.

Canto XXVI

Florence, you should be proud, you are so great
    your wings are beating over land and sea
    and your name spreads throughout the depths of hell!
Five of your finest citizens I found
    among the thieves, which makes me feel ashamed   5
    and does not shed much honor upon you.
But if as morning nears we dream the truth,
    shortly you will experience what Prato,
    not to say others, so desires for you.
If it had come, it would not be too soon.   10
    Then let it happen, since it must! No doubt
    it will depress me more the more I age.
We left our perch. My leader climbed back up
    the stairs that earlier had turned us pale
    in climbing down and drew me after him;   15
as we pursued our solitary path
    among the rocky outcrops of the ridge,
    the foot could make no way without the hand.
I grieved then and I grieve now once again,
    turning my mind to what I saw, and more   20
    than usual I must rein my talent in
lest it should run where virtue does not lead it;
    so if a favoring star or something better
    gave me this gift, I may not cheat myself.

A farmhand, as he sits upon a hill   25
    during the season when the one who lights
    the world least hides his face and at the hour
in which the fly gives way to the mosquito,
    sees in the valley numberless fireflies
    down where he plows, perhaps, or picks the grapes: 30
with countless flames like that the whole eighth gulch
    flickered, as I became aware at once
    when I arrived where I could see the bottom.
And as the one who was avenged by bears
    watched while Elijah's chariot left the ground,   35
    the rearing horses rising up to heaven,
but when he followed it by eye could not
    distinguish anything besides the flame
    alone, arising like a wisp of cloud,
in the same way each flame was moving through   40
    the gulch's throat, absconding with a sinner,
    and each of them concealed what it had stolen.
I stood up straight upon the bridge to see,
    and if I had not grasped a jutting rock
    I would have tumbled down without a push.   45
My leader, seeing how intent I was,
    said to me, "There are spirits within those flames,
    each shrouded in the element that burns him."
"Master," I answered, "hearing you explain it
    makes me more sure, but I already thought   50
    it must be so and wished to ask: who comes
within the flame whose tip is cleft in two,
    as though it rose above the pyre on which
    Eteocles was laid beside his brother?"
He answered, "There Ulysses is tormented   55
    with Diomedes; there they bear God's vengeance
    together as they once provoked his wrath.
Within their flame they expiate with groans
    the ambush of the horse that breached the gate
    through which the noble seed of Rome went forth.   60

There they bewail the trickery that makes
    Deïdamia in death still mourn Achilles,
    and there they pay for the Palladium's theft."
"If they can speak within those lights," I said,
    "I beg you, master, and will fervently   65
    repeat it so it counts for a thousand pleas,
not to deny my wish to linger here
    until the horned flame comes this way; you see
    how in my longing I am bending toward it."
He answered, "I consider your request   70
    praiseworthy and will grant what you have asked;
    see to it, though, that you restrain your tongue.
Let me do all the questioning, for I know
    what you desire from them and they, perhaps,
    since they were Greeks, might hear your words with scorn."   75
And when the flame had come so near to us
    my guide concluded that the time and place
    were opportune, I heard him make this speech:
"Hear me, you that go double in one fire:
    if I earned any claim on you in life,   80
    if I earned any claim, be it small or great,
up where I once composed the noble verses,
    do not move on, but let the one of you
    lost on a voyage tell where he went to die."
The greater horn upon the ancient flame   85
    began to toss and make a muffled roar,
    as if agitated by a gust of wind;
wagging its tip then back and forth, as though
    it were a tongue that uttered words, it threw
    beyond itself a voice that said, "When I   90
took leave of Circe, who'd inveigled me
    for longer than a year beside Gaëta
    (before Aeneas gave the place that name),
no tenderness for my son, nor any reverence
    for my aged father, nor the love I owed   95
    Penelope, which would have made her happy,

could overcome the eagerness that burned
    within me for experience of the world
    and of the weaknesses and worth of men.
So I put forth upon the open sea   100
    with only a single galley and the little
    company that had not deserted me.
One coast I saw and the other, up to Spain,
    up to Morocco, and Sardinia
    and the other islands that sea washes round.   105
I and my shipmates had grown old and slow
    before we reached the narrow neck of sea
    where Hercules erected his twin landmarks
to warn men not to venture any further;
    upon my right, Seville now fell behind,   110
    Ceuta had disappeared upon my left.
'Brothers,' I said, 'that through a hundred thousand
    dangers have finally reached the farthest West,
    on the remaining watch – how soon it will
be over – that our senses have to stand,   115
    do not refuse now to experience,
    in the sun's wake, the world devoid of men.
Recall your origins: you were created
    not to live unaware like animals,
    but to seek knowledge and pursue the right.'   120
I made my comrades keen about the voyage
    to such a point, with this brief exhortation,
    that I could hardly then have held them back;
and with our stern now pointed toward the morning
    we made our oars the wings for our mad flight,   125
    continuously bearing further to port.
The night already gazed on all the stars
    of the other pole, with those of our pole now
    so low they did not rise from the ocean's plain.
Five times the light on the moon's underside   130
    had been extinguished and five times relighted
    since we had entered on the arduous voyage,

when there arose to view a mountain, dark
  in the distance, that appeared to me to tower
  higher than any I had seen before.   135
Then we rejoiced, but joy soon turned to weeping;
  for out of that new land a whirlwind arose
  and bearing down upon us, struck our bow.
Three times it spun us around in swirling waters
  and on the fourth it lifted the stern high,   140
  plunging the prow down, as another pleased,
until above us the sea closed again."

Notes

1–12: This ironic apostrophe to Florence extends Dante's attack on Florentine corruption, begun in *Inf.* 16, to the city's power beyond its boundaries. The Florentines encountered in the last gulch prompt the conclusion that the violence and greed that fuel Florence's expanding power also make its well-born citizens thieves, so that the pilgrim has just met the vanguard of the Florentine empire in the seventh gulch.

1–2: An inscription on a 13th century municipal building, the Palazzo del Popolo, boasts that Florence "possesses the sea and the land and the whole earth. . . ."

7: Whether dreams foretell the future is a commonplace of medieval literature (discussed by a hen and a rooster in Chaucer); it was answered affirmatively by a great authority on the question, Macrobius's *Commentary on the Dream of Scipio* (as the rooster points out). Toward morning dreams "begin to feel the truth and stir of day" (Tennyson) and Ovid assumed they were more likely to come true. *Heroides* 19.195–96; see Horace, *Satires* 1.10.33. In *Purg.* 9.16–18 the pilgrim will have a dream at dawn, "when our mind, more a pilgrim from the flesh / and not so much preoccupied by cares / becomes almost prophetic in its visions." See also *Purg.* 27.92–93; *Conv.* 2.8.13.

8–9: The neighboring town of Prato, whose desire is for disaster to befall Florence, reflects Tuscan resentment of the regional ambitions the apostrophe glances at. Prato was under Florentine control and nominally loyal; the other cities referred to may wish even worse for Florence. The disaster Dante foresees is not known, but in Epistle 7 he asked the Emperor Henry VII, whom he regarded as a political savior, to punish Florence.

19–24: Dante's warning to himself to rein his genius in has always been a crux. Older critics tended to focus on the pilgrim's presence in the gulch of the false counselors. Dante in exile hobnobbed with princes and died on an embassy; and critics concluded he was referring to the moral perils of politics. More recent critics tend to focus on the figure of Ulysses in this canto, which leads them to conclude that Dante is expressing his deep-seated unease about the audacity of his poetic journey in the afterworld and warning himself to avoid the folly of Ulysses's last voyage. See Barolini 1992, 52. Giuseppe Mazzotta thinks that the warning indicates caution about Dante's self-appointed role as a prophet denouncing Florence, as in the previous passage. Mazzotta 1998, 355.

23: The favoring stars that endowed Dante with his gifts are his zodiac sign of Gemini (see *Par.* 22.112–23) and the something better is grace.

25–33: The first simile stresses the innumerable flickering lights in the darkness of the gulch. As in *Inf.* 14.28–30, the operation of divine justice in hell, viewed objectively, resembles the beauty of nature.

26–28: *I.e.,* a summer evening.

34–42: As the first simile gives the pilgrim's initial impression, the second gives his understanding of it. Although he can see only separate flames moving away through the gulch, he concludes that each must contain a sinner, concealing (and thereby "stealing") him. We will learn that these are tongues of flame, the formal *contrapasso* for either false counsel, the sin traditionally thought to be punished in this gulch, or simply deceit effectuated through speech.

34–39: The prophet Elisha saw his mentor Elijah carried to heaven in a fiery chariot. Later some boys laughed at the bald Elisha and bears rushed out of the forest and mauled forty-two of them. 4 Kings 2:11, 2:23–24. In Giotto's version of Elijah's assumption in the Arena Chapel, the horse rears up to climb the sky, just as in Dante's.

51–54: In the war of the Seven Against Thebes, the brothers Eteocles and Polynices killed each other. When their bodies were placed on the same pyre, the fire divided and fought against itself. *Theb.* 12.429–32.

55–63: Ulysses and Diomedes, Greek heroes in the war against Troy, accomplished feats without which the city could not be conquered. Their exploits depended on guile and in all of them Ulysses was the moving intelligence. In the *Aeneid* Ulysses is proverbial among the Trojans for treachery, and Donatus said that his nature was always deceitful. Here his role as the senior partner is indicated by his being the greater horn on the flame.

58–63: Three exploits condemn the pair to the eighth gulch. (1) Ulysses contrived the stratagem of the Trojan horse, which "breached the gate" of Troy through which Aeneas, "the noble seed of Rome," went forth to found the eternal city. (2) Ulysses and Diomedes tricked the young Achilles into joining the Trojan war. Dressed as a girl by his mother and hidden among the daughters of a king to keep him from the war, Achilles had an affair with Deidamia, the eldest daughter. Ulysses hid weapons among female finery presented as a gift, and the boy gave himself away when he eagerly seized them. (3) In a midnight raid, Ulysses and

Diomedes stole the Palladium, an ancient image of Athena on which the safety of Troy depended.

The sinners in the eighth gulch have traditionally been identified as false counselors, a category clearly appropriate to Guido da Montefeltro in the next canto and in fact articulated by a devil as the reason for Guido's damnation. *Inf.* 27.115–16. The three actions for which Ulysses and Diomedes are expressly being punished create a problem with this identification because their relation to false counsel, as opposed to deceit in general, is less than obvious. More recent critics (reviving the conclusion of Benvenuto) have suggested that the sin of the eighth gulch should simply be characterized as guile. See *DE* 420, 423.

64–69: Ulysses is the first character from antiquity, other than Virgil himself, to speak in the *Comedy*, and the pilgrim's ardent longing to hear recalls his exaltation in the presence of the ancient great in *Inf.* 4.118–20.

90–142: The last voyage of Ulysses is of Dante's imagining, and Pietro Alighieri suggested it was a *figmentum*, because it differed from the account of Ulysses' death known to the Middle Ages through Dictys Cretensis. The narrative reveals not the craftiness of Ulysses, but rather his insatiable thirst for knowledge of the world and the ways of men. Cicero had illustrated man's innate love of knowledge (the opening theme of Dante's *Convivio*) by the story of Ulysses having himself bound to the mast so he could hear the song of the sirens, while the crew rowed on, their ears stuffed with wax. *De Finibus* 5.18.

Moved, as Tennyson was, by the heroism of Ulysses's voyage into the unknown, recounted in stirring rhetoric that may betray admiration on Dante's part (and perhaps by modern sympathy for the image of man interrogating nature for its secrets), Mario Fubini and others refuse to acknowledge that the canto concludes with a moral condemnation of the voyage. See *ED* 5.803–09. Seeking a consistent interpretation of the seventh gulch, Giorgio Padoan and others take the view that Ulysses dupes his crew into the unheard-of feat, providing an example of the false counsel for which he is punished. *Ibid.* Neither view is ultimately persuasive. Ulysses uses no fraud to stoke his comrades' enthusiasm, though Dante surely disapproves of the voyage he persuades them to take. Such old salts would have known about the Pillars of Hercules as well as he did. His conception of virtue and wisdom – for him essentially courage and prudence – is the limited one of fallen man; but there is no reason to find him insincere in urging this ideal as a motive. Fubini is right to insist that Ulysses's last voyage is not the act for which he has been damned. See note to 58–63.

It is difficult for Fubini to explain, however, why Ulysses calls his voyage a "mad flight." The characterization is confirmed when the pilgrim looks down from heaven and sees "the mad track of Ulysses." *Par.* 27.82–83. Fubini argues that Dante could not seriously have thought that the Pillars of Hercules posed a moral prohibition. But Dante often conflates classical mythology with Christian doctrine, and in the geography of the *Comedy* the Pillars of Hercules do in fact mark the limit of the mortal world. Beyond them lies only the *terra incognita* sighted by Ulysses, which, as we will eventually learn, is the mountain of purgatory with the terrestrial paradise at its top, from which mankind was banished at Adam's fall. The only way to reach purgatory is to die in a state of grace, possible only after Jesus saved mankind. The *Purgatorio* will show that the souls of the saved are ferried to the mountain of purgatory by an angel along a route similar to that taken by Ulysses. Boyde 2000, 235. The mad flight of Ulysses thus resembles the folly of Phaeton in trespassing on divine limitations imposed on human kind. In a legend well known in the Middle Ages Alexander the Great attempts to see the ends of the earth. He descends in a diving bell to the bottom of the sea, marches to the edge of the world in a realm of mist and darkness and ascends to the heavens in a basket carried by great birds. Each time he is turned back with a warning that such ambition is not fit for mortals, and he resolves to stop attempting the impossible. Stoneman 117–23.

In the end, Dante uses Ulysses to explore in the mode of tragedy one of his characteristic preoccupations – the spiritual fate of the great of antiquity. Ulysses has the heroism of the Stoic philosopher, reflected in the grave and unimpassioned tones, devoid of all boasting or complaint, in which he relates his fatal venture. In the absence of revelation and grace, however, the great man is more prone than others to rely on himself and fail to pay reverence to a higher power. In referring to his mad flight and recognizing the hand of God in the tempest that sank him, Ulysses now recognizes that his undertaking was presumptuous. Since his voyage was a quest for knowledge, this amounts to recognizing that reliance on the unaided human reason cannot attain ultimate truth. The pursuit of the transcendent in disregard of man's natural dependence on God leads the hero to drown in the vastness of a creation whose beauty he appreciates but whose meaning remains closed to him.

The *DE* 842–47 puts the arguments of critics for and against Ulysses in perspective.

103–11: After cruising the north and south coasts of the western Mediterranean, Ulysses has reached the Strait of Gibraltar. The peaks on either side were known in antiquity as the Pillars of Hercules and were regarded as forming the boundaries of the known world. Seville in Spain and Ceuta in Morocco were the conventional outposts at land's end; Villani referred to the strait as the Strait of Seville and Ceuta. *Cron.* 1.4.

112–20: As Pietro pointed out, when Ulysses challenges his shipmates to follow the sun to the antipodes, they will necessarily visit an uninhabited hemisphere. Augustine had pronounced it absurd to believe that men had sailed to the other side of the world. *Civ. Dei* 16.9.

126: Ulysses is carried ever further to port, across the equator and eventually to the mountain of purgatory deep in the hemisphere of water, the antipodes of Jerusalem.

127–29: The description of the stars of the other hemisphere coming into view while those of our pole dip below the sea powerfully evokes the strangeness of Ulysses' voyage. In classical poetry the Bears (Ursa Major and Ursa Minor) never dip in the ocean. Virgil, *Georgics* 1.246; see Foster/Boyde No. 89.28–29, *Purg.* 30.1–2, *Par.* 13.7–9. Macrobius explained why our position on the globe hides from us the stars of the south polar region. Macrobius 1.16. Because the pole star has sunk, Ulysses has nothing to steer by.

Canto XXVII

The flame had straightened up again and steadied
    because it said no more and had gone off
    with the permission of the gentle poet,
when now another flame that came behind it
    made our attention focus on its tip,   5
    from which an incoherent noise emerged.
As the Sicilian bull, the one that bellowed
    first with the groans – it was poetic justice –
    of the artificer whose file had shaped it,
was made to bellow with its victim's voice,   10
    so that in spite of being made of brass
    it seemed that it was being pierced by pain,
here the unhappy words, when they could find
    no vent or pathway through the fire at first,
    were changed into the language of the fire.   15
But afterwards, when they had found their way
    up to the tip, to which they gave the quiver
    imparted by the tongue as they were passing,
we heard this: "You toward whom I aim my voice
    and who just now were speaking Lombard, saying   20
    'Go now, for I will stir you up no further,'
do not be too impatient, though perhaps
    I come a little late, to stop and talk.
    I have the patience, you see, and I am burning!

If you fell into this blind world just now   25
    out of the sweet Italian land from which
    I carry all my guilt down here, tell me,
are they at war or peace now in Romagna?
    For I was from the hills between Urbino
    and the high saddle whence the Tiber springs."   30
While I was still bent over looking below
    my leader gave me a nudge in the side and said,
    "You be the spokesman; this one is Italian."
I had the answer on my tongue already
    and so I began to speak without delay: 35
    "O spirit who remain concealed down there,
know your Romagna is not and never was
    lacking for war within her tyrants' hearts,
    but when I left there was no open conflict.
Ravenna has not changed for many years: 40
    the eagle of Polenta nestles it
    and also covers Cervia with its wings.
The city that endured the lengthy siege
    and turned the Frenchmen into a bloody heap
    finds itself under the green claws today.   45
The mastiffs of Verrucchio, old and young,
    who were such brutal wardens for Montagna,
    gnaw to the marrow in their usual way.
The lion cub of the white den, who changes
    parties the way the seasons change, controls   50
    the towns on the Lamone and Santerno.
The town whose flank the Savio sluices down,
    lying between the mountain and the plain,
    lives between liberty and one-man rule.
Now, I entreat you, tell us who you are;   55
    be no more grudging than I was with you
    and let your name still show the world its face."
After the fire had roared a little while
    in its habitual way, its pointed tip
    tossed here and there and then breathed forth these words: 60

"If I believed that I was answering
    someone who could return to the world again,
    this flame would toss no longer; but because
nobody yet, if what I hear is true,
    has made it back alive there from this depth,   65
    I fear no infamy in answering you.
I was a soldier, then a Franciscan friar –
    garbed in the habit, I thought to make amends;
    and my intent would have been realized,
but for the high priest – may perdition take him! –   70
    who set me at my old sins once again.
    I want to tell you how and why it happened.
So long as I informed the flesh and bone
    my mother gave me, my accomplishments
    were not those of the lion, but the fox.   75
Covert maneuvers, subtle stratagems,
    I knew them all and used them with such art
    my reputation reached the ends of the earth.
Then, when I saw my course had carried me
    into the time of life when everyone   80
    should reef his sails and gather in his tackle,
what once had pleased me filled me with regret;
    repenting and confessing I became
    a friar and – wretched me! – it would have served.
The prince of the new Pharisees, who then   85
    was busy making war near the Lateran
    – and mind you, not on Saracens or Jews,
for every enemy of his was Christian,
    and none had played a part in Acre's fall
    or traded in the lands the Sultan rules –   90
did not respect his own exalted office
    and ordination or the belt of rope
    I wore that used to make its wearers thin.
As Constantine, to cure his leprosy,
    summoned Sylvester out of Mount Soracte,   95
    so this one sought me out as his physician,

to cure him of the fever of his pride.
    He asked for my advice and I was silent
    because his words seemed those of a drunken man.
'Harbor no fear,' he said then, 'in your heart;   100
    I absolve you in advance, if you but give me
    a hint how I may level Palestrina.
I, as you know, possess the power to lock,
    as well as unlock heaven, for the keys
    the last pope did not care about are two.'   105
These weighty arguments drove me to the point
    where silence seemed the greater of two evils.
    'Father,' I said, 'since you are cleansing me
of that sin into which I now must fall,
    make promises for longer than you keep them   110
    and you will be victorious on your throne.'
Saint Francis came for me when I was dead,
    but one of the black cherubim rebuked him:
    'Do me no wrong by taking what is mine.
This one must go below among my lackeys   115
    for counseling how to perpetrate a fraud;
    since that day I have never left his side,
for none can be absolved without repentance
    and no one can repent and will at once,
    for nature tolerates no contradictions.'   120
Oh wretched me! My eyes were rudely opened
    when he took hold of me and said, 'Perhaps
    you did not realize I was versed in logic.'
He carried me to Minos, who first wrapped
    his tail eight times around his scaly back,   125
    then bit it in great fury and announced:
'This one belongs within the thieving fire.'
    Here where you see me, therefore, I am lost
    and robed like this, I walk and eat my heart out."
When it had brought its tale to this conclusion,   130
    the flame moved off from us still sorrowing,
    twisting and tossing its pointed horn about.

And we continued onward, I and my guide,

  along the ridge as far as the next arch,

  which spans the trench where wages are disbursed   135

to those who earn their loads by disuniting.

Notes

7–12: Perillus fashioned for the tyrant Phalaris a hollow brass bull with a trapdoor. When prisoners were roasted within, their screams would be magnified by the hollow chamber and so provide the bull's bellowing. Phalaris tested the invention on Perillus, and Orosius commented that though Phalaris was unjust, he punished Perillus justly. *Hist Adv. Pag.* 1.20; see Ovid, *Art of Love* 1.653–56.

In Dante's usual manner, the simile offers more than the physical comparison that is its ostensible point, furnishing an apt image of the fate of those who give wicked advice to rulers. As such it foreshadows the downfall of Guido da Montefeltro, the shade trapped inside the flame, whose attempts to speak are being compared to the bellowing of the bronze bull. Richard Lansing notes that Guido and Perillus are both inventors in the service of unscrupulous authorities and each is ironically and justly undone by their inventions. Lansing 1976, 62–64.

19–30: The speaker is Guido da Montefeltro, one of the great leaders of the Ghibellines in the 13th century, called by Villani "the wisest and most subtle man of war in his time in Italy." *Cron.* 8.80. In the 1270s, when the popes attempted to incorporate Romagna, a region of east central Italy, into the papal states, Guido led the anti-papal resistance as captain of the people at Forlì and won a series of victories over the Guelf forces. In 1281 the pope sent a joint French and Italian army against him, and by the mid-1280s the papal forces controlled most of Romagna. Reconciled to the church in his seventies, Guido became a Franciscan in 1296, living an austere penitential life during his remaining two years. Dante elsewhere praised the wisdom that Guido, "the very noble Italian," showed in old age. *Conv.* 4.28.

19–21: Virgil was from Mantua in what later became Lombardy, and his regional speech is rendered in a dialect word (*istra*, now). Dante believed that the historical Virgil had spoken an ancient Italian vernacular distinct from Latin, which had been a secondary, learned language in his time as it was in Dante's own. See *VE* 1.1.3–4; Shaw 216, Scott 18, 36, 41–42.

The plebian phrase differs markedly from the lofty language in which Virgil addressed Ulysses in the previous canto. Lino Pertile argues that this is an inartful attempt to transition from Ulysses to Guido – making Virgil sound Lombard gives the Lombard Guido an incentive to address him. Pertile 2007b.

28: Guido wants to know the outcome of the peace negotiations still pending between the Guelfs and Ghibellines of Romagna at his death in 1298. Peace was concluded the following year and the pilgrim's answer will describe the status quo in 1300.

36–54: In five tercets using largely heraldic imagery, the pilgrim describes the contemporary political situation of seven cities in Romagna.

40–42: The first city is Ravenna, and the eagle is Guido da Polenta the Elder, who gained the lordship of the city through a coup in 1275 and later brought Cervia under his control as well. The eagle appeared in the family's coat of arms, and despite the pilgrim's opening jab about the tyrants of Romagna, the image of Guido the Elder sheltering the two cities is benign. His grandson, Guido the Younger, was to become Dante's host in the final years of the poet's life. *ED* 4.580–81.

43–45: The third city is Forlì, which in 1300 was under the power of Scarpetta degli Ordelaffi. The claws, suggesting a more negative judgment than the last heraldic image, come from his coat of arms, which showed the forepart of a lion in green.

43–44: Guido da Montefeltro won a victory when Forlì was besieged by the pope's French and Italian army. While the French cavalry entered the city by one gate, Guido exited by another and defeated the remaining papal force outside. The French were looting the city when Guido reentered and, taking them by surprise, slaughtered them. *Cron.* 8.81.

46–48: The fourth city is Rimini, seized in a coup in 1295 by Malatesta da Verruchio and his son Malatestino; the dog image suggests their cruelty. Their takeover of Rimini was resisted by Montagna dei Parcitadi, whom they threw into prison, where Malatestino murdered him. *ED* 4.961–62.

49–51: Next come Faenza and Imola, both under the control of Maghinardo Pagani (whose arms were a blue lion in a white field). Villani said that he was a Ghibelline at home in Romagna but supported the Florentines as a Guelf against their enemies, whether Guelf or Ghibelline. *Cron.* 8.149.

52–54: The final town is Cesena. The pilgrim's description reflects a certain fluidity in the city's political situation in which communal and authoritarian influences came and went. See *ED* 1.927.

61–66: Guido cannot see the pilgrim and so does not realize that he is alive, and he has failed to draw that conclusion from the pilgrim's suggestion that his response will help his name resist the attack of time. In what follows, Guido will not reveal his name but his account of his career, together with his coming from Romagna, would have made his identity clear to early readers, as it does to the pilgrim.

73: In the metaphysics of Aristotle and Aquinas, an individual substance is a union of matter (potency) and form (act); the rational human soul, which survives death, is the form that animates the otherwise inert matter of the body during life.

85–111: The modern prince of the hypocritical Pharisees is Pope Boniface VIII; the epithet originated in the anti-papal polemic of the Spiritual Franciscans. *ED* 3.14. The Christians on whom Boniface was making war were the Colonna family, a powerful Roman clan, headed in Boniface's time by two cardinals. Angered by their lack of respect and nursing dynastic ambitions of his own, Boniface excommunicated the whole clan in 1297 and began tearing down their palaces in Rome. When the Colonna and their allies fought back, Boniface decreed an indulgence for all who would join a crusade against them; Florence sent 600 men.

The Colonna had a stronghold at Palestrina, some 25 miles outside Rome; because of its location on a hill and its strong walls, it withstood siege for more than a year. In 1298 the city agreed to surrender upon Boniface's promise to spare it and to restore the honors of the Colonna. Contrary to his promise, he razed Palestrina and built a new town on the plain below called Papal City. *ED* 4.260–61. Modern historians do not accept the story that Guido advised Boniface in this treachery.

86–90: Boniface's local wars were unrelated to the defense of Christianity, the accepted reason for a crusade. Having discovered their power to marshal the military forces of Europe in the crusades for the Holy Land, the popes began turning them against targets closer to home, from heretics in the south of France to the imperial dynasty in southern Italy. Boniface's declaration of a crusade against his personal enemies marks the nadir of this development.

86: St. John Lateran is the pope's cathedral church as bishop of Rome and the ordinary papal residence was nearby at this time.

89–90: Acre, the last stronghold of the crusaders in Palestine, was conquered by the Mameluke Sultan of Egypt in 1291. The pope attempted to raise a new crusade and pronounced a general excommunication against any Christian who traded with the Sultan's lands, but the European states had no further interest in such military adventures and the commercial powers, especially Venice, ignored the ban on trade.

94–95: In a legend from The Donation of Constantine (see note to *Inf.* 19.115–17), elaborated in *The Golden Legend* (1.64–65), Constantine persecutes the Christians and Pope Sylvester goes into hiding on Mt. Soracte. When Constantine is punished with leprosy, he sends for Sylvester. He is converted, and when he goes down into the baptismal water he arises cured.

100–11: Guido presents himself as a man more sinned against than sinning. In two important respects the poem endorses this view. First, Guido's view of Boniface is certainly Dante's, and Boniface is the real villain of this canto. Dante in fact uses Guido to mount his most devastating attack on his great enemy. Second, there is no reason to impugn Guido's late-life conversion. Some modern critics suggest that his retreat to a monastery was insincere because it was for him a mere means to an end. But repenting and confessing in old age for the specific end of saving one's soul is well sanctioned by Christian tradition. Guido's metaphor of reaching the time of life when a man should reef his sails simply repeats the language Dante used in praising Guido's conduct in *Conv.* 4.28.

All the same, it is difficult to read this canto as presenting a tragedy. Guido is especially bitter about his downfall because it is a case of the trickster tricked.

Guido's long practice of the wiles of diplomacy had led him to believe that even heaven could be won by striking equivocal bargains. He knows he is committing a sin, but thinks that Boniface's bargain will spare him the consequences. In a believing world, however, no diplomat can match the wiles of an unscrupulous pope, and Boniface obtains Guido's advice on how to double-cross his enemies by double-crossing Guido to his damnation. Boniface's inducement consists of a carrot and a stick. The carrot is a false promise of absolution in advance, which, as the devil will cogently explain, is meaningless. The stick, conveyed in the reference to the two keys figuratively given by Christ to St. Peter (Matt. 16–19), is an implied threat to excommunicate Guido if he does not accede to the pope's wishes. The use of excommunication for political ends, as Boniface had shown with the Colonna, had become common. Guido had been excommunicated twice for his campaigns against the papal armies. Even Dante's attack on Boniface in *Inf.* 19 pales beside this scathing portrait of the pope.

105: The previous pope, who Boniface contemptuously says did not care about the keys, was Celestine V, "who made the great refusal." *Inf.* 3.60. Contemporary rumor said that Boniface pressured Celestine into abdicating.

112–23: A guardian angel or patron saint contesting the possession of a soul with a devil at the moment of death was a stock theme of popular preaching. The scholastic reasoning that the sarcastic devil engages in, which demonstrates how Guido was taken in by Boniface, is a fine touch, illustrating the adage that the devil is well-versed in theology. *Purgatorio* 5.85–129 will form a contrast with this scene. There Guido's son, mortally wounded in battle, calls on the Virgin and the devil who comes for him is forestalled by an angel.

127: For "thieving," see *Inf.* 26.40–42.

Canto XXVIII

Could anyone, though not constrained by meter,
    fully describe the carnage I now saw,
    even if he kept going over the tale?
Every tongue surely would fall short of it,
    because our language and our cognitive   5
    capacity could not contain so much.
Even if all the men were brought together
    who suffered as their blood was spilling out
    upon the fateful soil of Southern Italy –
from Trojan conquests to the lengthy war   10
    in which the spoil of rings was piled so high
    (as Livy writes, in whom is found no error)
to those whose suffering came from wounds received
    fighting against Robert Guiscard to those
    whose bones today are still heaped near Ceprano,   15
where Southerners betrayed their king, and strew
    the field at Tagliacozzo where the old
    Alardo gained the victory without weapons –
and if they all exhibited their gashed
    and lopped-off limbs, it still would be no match   20
    for the foul sights on view in the ninth gulch.
No barrel missing one of its bottom boards
    could gape more widely than the shade I saw
    split from the chin to where the gut breaks wind:

his entrails hung between his legs; his heart,   25
    his lungs and liver showed, with the foul bag
    that turns what is swallowed into excrement.
While I was staring at him in amazement
    he noticed me and spread his chest with his hands.
    "See how I pull myself apart," he said;   30
"behold Muhammad's mutilated hulk!
    Before me, weeping, goes Alì, his face
    laid open from the hairline to the chin.
And all the rest you see here were in life
    sowers of discord and division of faith,   35
    for which they pay by being carved like this.
A devil waits back there to garnish us
    in this ferocious fashion, as he puts
    each member of the crowd to the sword's edge
each time we go around the track of tears,   40
    because the wounds heal over by themselves
    before we come in front of him once more.
But who are you that loiter on the ridge,
    perhaps to put off going to the sentence
    that was adjudged upon your own confession?"   45
"Death has not reached him yet," my master answered,
    "nor is he led to torment by his guilt;
    rather, to give him full experience,
I who am dead have been required to lead him
    from circle down to circle throughout hell.   50
    This is as true as I am speaking to you."
A multitude of spirits, on hearing this,
    stopped in the trench and stood to stare at me,
    forgetting the pain in their astonishment.
"Be sure then that you tell Brother Dolcino   55
    to stock enough provisions, you who soon
    may see the sun, unless he wants to join me
shortly down here, so that the snow's blockade
    does not hand victory to the Novarese,
    which otherwise would not be lightly won."   60

Having already raised his foot to go,
    Muhammad tossed this last remark at me,
    then set his foot upon the ground and left.
Another one, whose throat had been cut open,
    whose nose was chopped off right below his brows   65
    and who was left with only a single ear,
had stopped and stared at me in wonderment
    with all the others, but he first among them
    opened his windpipe, which showed through all red,
and said, "You, sir, whom guilt has not condemned   70
    and whom I saw above in Italy once
    unless a close resemblance has misled me,
if you return to see the gentle plain
    that slopes from Vercelli down toward Marcabò,
    let your thoughts turn to Pier da Medicina.   75
And let the two chief men of Fano, Master
    Guido and Master Angiolello, know
    – unless our foresight here is an illusion –
both will be dumped in sacks from their ship's bow,
    weighted with stones, near La Cattòlica   80
    as treacherously planned by a cruel tyrant.
Between the islands of Majorca and Cyprus
    Neptune has never seen so great a crime
    committed, not by pirates nor by Greeks.
That traitor, who sees only with one eye   85
    and who controls the city someone now
    here with me wishes he had never seen,
will summon both of them to meet with him
    and then arrange it so they need no prayer
    or vow to steer them past Focara's wind."   90
"Point out your neighbor," I said, "and tell me why,
    if you would have me bring back news of you,
    he is bitter about having seen that city."
He placed his hand upon the jaw of one
    of his companions, forcing his mouth open.   95
    "This is the one," he cried, "and he says nothing.

Banished from Rome, this one suppressed the doubts
    of Caesar by advising that delay
    always brings loss to him who is prepared."
Oh what dismay I read in his appearance, 100
    this Curio, with the tongue cut from his throat,
    he who had shown such boldness in his speech!
Another one, whose hands were both chopped off,
    raising his stumps up high in the dark air
    so that the blood befouled his face, cried out, 105
"Remember Mosca also, who once said
    – unhappily – 'a thing once done is finished,'
    planting a seed of evil for the Tuscans."
"And bringing death to your own line," I added,
    at which, with sorrow piling upon sorrow, 110
    he wandered off like someone crazed with grief.
But I remained to gaze upon the crowd,
    and I saw something I would be afraid
    to vouch for on my own, without more proof,
were I not reassured by my clear conscience, 115
    the faithful friend that fortifies a man
    armored with knowledge of his honesty.
I know I saw – I seem to see it still –
    a headless trunk that walked around, no different
    from all the others of that sorry band. 120
It grasped the severed head by its long hair
    and swung it like a lantern in its hand;
    and the head looked up at us and said, "Oh me!"
Out of itself it made itself a lamp,
    and they were two in one and one in two; 125
    how this could be, he knows who so disposes.
When it was standing right below the bridge
    it raised its arm, lifting the head up high
    to make its words approach us, and we heard:
"Look now upon a dreadful punishment, 130
    you that still breathing come to view the dead;
    judge whether any other be as great.

And know, that you may take back news of me,
    I am Bertran de Born, the one who gave
    evil encouragement to the Young King.   135
Father and son I set against each other;
    Achitophel did nothing more with David
    and Absalom through his evil instigations.
Since I divided those so closely joined,
    I now must carry my own brain, alas!   140
    divided from its source within this stump.
So you may see in me just retribution."

Notes

1–21: To evoke the carnage of the ninth gulch, Dante begins with a resounding catalogue of ancient and medieval battles, whose melancholy grandeur does not disguise the fact that mangled bodies are the most tangible result of division and discord. The passage is an amplified echo of a lament attributed to the troubadour Bertran de Born, who will appear in this canto.

7–12: Dante assembles those maimed in battles fought in Southern Italy from ancient times to his own youth. First come the early battles fought by the Romans (called Trojans because of their descent from Aeneas) to extend their power throughout Italy. Then comes the second war with Hannibal, in which, after the annihilation of a Roman army at Cannae, Livy recounts that Hannibal's brother poured out before the Carthaginian senate bushels of gold rings taken from Roman nobles. Livy 23.11–12.

13–14: Dante recalls the battles fought by the Norman Robert Guiscard for control of Sicily and Southern Italy in the mid-11th century, chiefly against Byzantines and Arabs.

15–18: Finally come the two battles in Dante's own day in which Charles of Anjou defeated the descendants of the Emperor Frederick II, putting an end to imperial rule in Italy.

Ceparano, on the Liri River, marked the frontier of the southern kingdom subject to Frederick's son Manfred. In 1266 Charles crossed there unopposed on his way to defeat Manfred. In Villani's telling, the southern nobles betrayed Manfred by letting Charles cross. *Cron.* 8.5.

Two years later at Tagliacozzo, the army of Manfred's nephew Conradin was defeated by a smaller force under Charles because Erard de Valery ("old Alardo") convinced Charles to hold part of his army in reserve so as to sweep down on Conradin's troops after they had become disorganized by their initial success.

22–27: The depiction of Muhammad is one of the most shocking passages in the *Inferno* and its meaning is not easy for a modern reader to grasp. Medieval Christian scholars were baffled by a religion in which they recognized the monotheistic God and familiar figures from the Old Testament, but all presented in a form that seemed bizarre to them. The only way they could explain it to themselves was to classify Muhammad as a heretic. See Southern 38–39. Bogus biographies of Muhammad, such as one in Villani's chronicle, were ginned up to fit this conclusion. *Cron.* 3.8.

Dante probably accepted that Muhammad was a heretic, but did not place him in the sixth circle, where heretics are punished for their wrong belief considered in its effect on the sinner. Here sin is considered in its effect on others, and Muhammad is punished for division in the faith: splitting Christendom by breaking off the Holy Land, North Africa and, still in Dante's time, part of Spain. His horrifying punishment reifies this schism.

32–33: Ali was Muhammad's son-in-law and his complementary wound completes Muhammad's punishment. His death in a civil war and the passing of power to the Umayyad caliphate in Damascus began the division between Sunni and Shia. Dante may intend Ali to stand for sectarian division leading to subdivision, but it is not clear that he knew this history.

55–63: The theme of division is carried out in Muhammad's interrupted syntax and in his gesture of uttering his last sentence in the midst of a step. Other examples of interrupted syntax occur throughout the canto.

55–60: Brother Dolcino was the leader of a sect known as the Apostolic Brotherhood, one of the dissenting movements that sprang up in the 13th century among the poor. The membership lived communally, sharing goods and sexual partners. Muhammad is foretelling that in several years, when the pope declares a crusade against the Brotherhood, Dolcino will set up a fortified commune with several thousand followers near Novara. Muhammad speaks ironically because he foresees that they will be starved out and Dolcino will be burned at the stake.

70–75: Medicina, the town from which Pier comes, is in Romagna. Nothing is known of this character and there is no record of the crime that he foretells.

73–74: The plain to which Pier refers is the Po valley, from Vercelli in northwest Italy to Marcabò on the Adriatic, where Fano, La Cattòlica and Focara are also located.

76–90: The one-eyed tyrant is Malatestino Malatesta. See *Inf.* 27.46–48 and note. According to Pier's story Malatestino attempted to gain control of Fano by murdering Guido del Cassero and Angiolello da Carignano.

89–90: Focara is a mountainous promontory that was dreaded by sailors because of the high winds that swept down from it; vows and prayers were offered for safe passage.

91–102: The incident of Curio comes from Lucan. The civil war between Caesar and Pompey began when Caesar led his army across the Rubicon River toward

Rome, an act forbidden to a provincial commander. As he approaches Rome, however, Lucan's Caesar still entertains doubts until he meets the tribune Curio, who counsels: "Delay is ever fatal to those who are prepared." *Phars*. 1.269–85.

Dante takes Curio as a *figura* for division in the state. It matters not that by following this advice Caesar was laying the foundations of the Roman empire, which Dante believed was ordained by Providence. *Par*. 6.61–63; *Mon*. 2.3. The act that determines Curio as a *figura* is abstracted from this background. The providential-imperial background was implicit, however, when Dante himself used the same line from Lucan to urge the Emperor Henry VII to invade Tuscany. *Epist*. 7.16. Pertile finds this inconsistency – which he attributes to morality versus political expediency – shocking. Pertile 1997, 12.

103–11: The figure of Mosca recalls the beginning of the partisan violence between Guelfs and Ghibellines in Florence in the 13th century. Mosca de' Lamberti instigated the murder of a young noble by a family related to Mosca's, whom the young man had insulted by breaking his engagement to one of their young women. Mosca's declaration that the murder would put an end to the affair led to a century of bloodshed (*Cron*. 6.38) in which Mosca's once prominent clan was reduced to insignificance.

112–42: Bertran de Born was a 12th century troubadour, praised by Dante as the leading vernacular poet of war. *VE* 2.2.8. The most famous poem attributed to him, echoed in the opening lines of this canto, is a lament for the Young King. Hill/Bergin, No. 75. Henry Plantagenet, son of Henry II of England, was crowned during his father's lifetime and thereafter known as the Young King. He became discontented when his father would not give him any real power, either in England or in the part of France controlled by the family. Allying himself with the French king, he raised a rebellion in his father's French domains, in the course of which he was killed.

Dante probably took the story that Bertran fomented this rebellion from a traditional *vida* that has survived: "And he embroiled the father and son of England. . . ." Hill/Bergin, No. 71. These biographical sketches, which preceded a troubadour's songs in a songbook, often appear to be based on the songs themselves, here likely Bertran's lament for the Young King. See Toynbee 1914, 76; *Handbook of the Troubadours* 24–25, 189. (The same can be said of many of the biographical details supplied by the early commentators for characters in the *Comedy*.)

119–22: In Bertran's punishment Dante is repurposing a hagiographical motif. The decapitated martyr St. Denis was represented in art carrying his head (*e.g.*, portal of Notre Dame de Paris). St. Minias, the first Christian martyred in Florence, was supposed to have picked up his head after his decapitation and carried it across the Arno to the hill where the 11th century basilica dedicated to him, San Miniato al Monte, is located. *Cron*. 2.20. In Francesco Traini's great fresco of hell in the Pisan Camposanto, painted some decades after Dante's death, a headless figure holds his head by the hair.

132: "[S]ee if there be any sorrow like to my sorrow." Lam. 1:12.

137–38: Achitophel, a trusted adviser of King David of Israel, counseled David's son Absalom in his rebellion against his father. 2 Kings 15:12, 15:31, 15:34.

141: "Source": spinal cord.

142: "Retribution (*contrapasso*)." This is Dante's only use of the word *contrapasso* in the *Inferno* – his term for the exact retribution of divine punishment. He may have taken the term from Aquinas, who called the law of eye for eye *contrapassum*. *ST* 2–2.61.4; see *ED* 2.182. Giuseppe Mazzotta explains the form of the *contrapasso* here by noting that in medieval thought the unity of civil society (the "body politic"), as well as that of the church (the "mystical body") was conceived by analogy with the human body. Mazzotta 1993, 80.

Canto XXIX

The multitudes and their appalling wounds
    had made my eyes befuddled to the point
    that they were aching to remain and weep.
"What can you still be staring at?" said Virgil.
    "Why does your gaze still fix itself upon   5
    those wretched mutilated shades down there?
You have not done that at the other gulches.
    Consider, if you mean to count them all,
    twenty-two miles make up the valley's circuit.
The moon already is beneath our feet;   10
    not much remains of the time granted us,
    and there is more to see than what you look at."
"If you had given some consideration
    to the reason I was looking," I replied,
    "perhaps you would have let me stay there longer."   15
Meanwhile my guide was moving on and I
    followed behind him as I made this answer
    and added afterwards, "Within the hollow
I trained my gaze so closely on just now,
    I think the spirit of someone of my blood   20
    grieves for the guilt that costs so much down there."
My teacher answered, "You must not allow
    your thoughts to be distracted by him further.
    Look elsewhere now and there let him remain;

for I observed him at the foot of the bridge 25
    pointing at you with a fierce threatening gesture
    and heard him being called Geri del Bello.
You at the time were wholly taken up
    with him who once was master of Hautefort
    and did not look that way till he departed." 30
"Master," I said, "the violent death he met,
    which has not been as yet avenged for him
    by anyone who shares the shame of it,
makes him indignant, which I think explains
    why he went off without a word to me; 35
    and that has made me pity him the more."
Talking like this, we reached the point on the ridge
    where we could first have seen the farther valley
    down to the bottom, had the light been stronger.
Then, when we came above that final cloister 40
    of Devil's Gulches, so that the lay brothers
    within were now revealed before our eyes,
unearthly lamentations pierced me through
    and all their shafts were tipped with barbs of pity,
    making me clamp my hands upon my ears. 45
The suffering there would be, if all the sick
    in Valdichiana's hospitals from July
    until September, with Sardinia's
and Maremma's, were together in one ditch,
    would not surpass this; and a stench arose 50
    such as would come from putrefying limbs.
Then we came down upon the final bank
    from the long ridge, still turning to our left;
    there I could see more clearly down to the bottom,
to where the high Lord's minister, unerring 55
    justice, dispenses punishment to those
    that she records on earth as falsifiers.
It could not well have been more pitiful
    to see Aegina's entire people stricken,
    when pestilence hung so heavy in the air 60

that every creature, down to the smallest worm,
    died of it, and the ancient population,
    according to the tale the poets credit,
was then replenished from the race of ants,
    than to see, down the length of that dark valley, 65
    the spirits wasting in assorted heaps.
One lay against the other's belly and one
    leaned on another's back, while still another
    dragged on all fours along the dismal path.
Slowly we went along without a word, 70
    looking about and listening to the sick,
    who could not raise themselves. I noticed two
seated together, leaning against each other
    as a pan is propped against a pan to warm,
    both of them spotted head to foot with scabs. 75
I never saw a currycomb applied
    by a stableboy who knows his master's waiting
    or one who is eager to be off to bed
as vigorously as these applied their nipping
    nails to themselves because of the great frenzy 80
    of the itch, for which there is no other help;
they worked their fingernails beneath the scabs
    the way a scaling knife is used on bream
    or other fish with even larger scales.
"You that strip off your chain-mail with your fingers," 85
    my leader said to one of them, "and also
    make use of them from time to time as pincers,
tell us if any Italians are among
    those who are here, and may your fingernails
    forever serve you at your present task." 90
"We are Italian," one replied in tears,
    "both of us that you see here so disfigured.
    But who are you, who come and ask us this?"
"One who descends from ledge to ledge," my leader
    answered, "in company with this living man, 95
    and my intention is to show him hell."

At that their common abutment broke apart
  and they both trembled as they turned toward me,
  along with others who had overheard.
Then my good master came up close to me.   100
  "Ask of them anything you wish," he said.
  And so, since he desired it, I began:
"So all remembrance of you may not fade
  in the first world and vanish from men's minds
  but go on living under many suns,   105
tell me who you may be, and from what cities.
  Let not your foul and loathsome punishment
  make you reluctant to reveal yourselves."
One of them answered, "I was from Arezzo,
  and Albero of Siena had me burned;   110
  but what I died for did not bring me here.
It's true I told him, pulling his leg a bit,
  that I could levitate and fly through the air.
  He, with more curiosity than brains,
wanted to learn the trick; and just because   115
  I did not make him Daedalus, he had me
  burned by the one who held him as a son.
Minos, who can commit no error, though,
  condemned me to the last of the ten gulches
  because on earth I practiced alchemy."   120
And I remarked to the poet, "Was there ever
  a people as frivolous as the Sienese?
  Even the French surely do not come close!"
At which the other leper, who had heard me,
  added to my remark, "Except for Stricca,   125
  who knew the way to spend in moderation;
except for Niccolò, the one who first
  found the expensive fashion of the clove
  in the garden where such seed takes root; excepting
also the Club in which Caccia d'Asciano   130
  squandered his vineyard and extensive fields,
  and Abbagliato showed his common sense.

Now, so you know who seconds you against
    the Sienese, direct a searching gaze
    upon my face until it gives your answer: 135
then you will know the shade of Capocchio,
    whose alchemy counterfeited precious metals;
    you should recall, if you're the one I think,
how clever an ape of nature I could be."

Notes

1–36: The pilgrim keeps staring at the maimed troublemakers, hoping to verify whether his father's first cousin, Geri del Bello, is among them. Dante's son Pietro said that Geri was killed by a man of the Sacchetti family, "upon whom vengeance had not been taken for him at the time the author wrote. But afterward nephews of Geri killed one of the Sacchetti to avenge him." He added that some twenty years after Dante's death, the Sacchetti and the Alighieri families executed a formal act of reconciliation.

    The laws of Dante's Florence recognized that in cases of mayhem or homicide the injured party or his relatives had the right to exact proportionate revenge from the offender, and in the event of death from his relatives. See *ED* 1.141. No doubt Dante accepted intellectually the Christian doctrine of revenge: "Revenge not yourselves . . . for it is written: *Revenge is mine, I will repay*, saith the Lord." Rom. 12:19. He was also aware that, as the Mosca episode showed, blood feuds were rending the fabric of civic life in Italy. The pilgrim, however, seems not merely to pity his cousin but also to recognize the legitimacy of his claim on the family for vengeance. Virgil's sternly telling the pilgrim not to waste his thoughts on Geri implies a judgment against the legitimacy of such claims. This should probably be taken as resolving the conflict, but it is not easy to say whether Dante's emotions were entirely in accord with his intellect. Pertile considers the way that Dante ends the episode "deeply equivocal." Pertile 1998, 383.

8–9: The next canto will reveal that the circuit of the tenth gulch is 11 miles. These precise dimensions are meant to enhance the realism of the infernal terrain, but the proportions would quickly grow extravagant if taken literally.

10–12: As usual in hell, time is measured by the moon or stars. With the moon beneath the poets' feet, the sun is overhead, just past midday on Holy Saturday.

29: Hautefort was the castle of Bertran de Born.

40–45: The pilgrim's reflexive pity at suffering is tempered by Dante's ironic image of the tenth gulch as a monastery. Irony will be the keynote of the canto.

46–51: The pilgrim's closer view suggests the image that will continue to characterize the tenth gulch, that of a vast hospital. Hospitals were already common in the Middle Ages (Florence had 30 of them), although most of them were more what we would call hospices. Apart from a few large establishments, they ranged in size from a few beds to a few dozen, each accommodating several patients; and they provided more shelter than treatment. Hospitals were charity institutions, and their patients consisted almost entirely of the poor. A 13th century observer said that great courage was needed to tolerate the filth and stench of the patients. Mollat 90–91, 102, 135–51.

47–48: Pietro noted that Valdichiana was the marshy valley of a sluggish river where in summertime the air became corrupted with pestilence, *i.e.*, malaria. The Maremma was a marshy area along the Tuscan coast, also a breeding-ground for malaria, as was Sardinia.

52–54: The poets turn left and walk along the top of the final dike on the inside of the tenth gulch.

55–57: *The Falsifiers.* The final inhabitants of the eighth circle will not be major figures, like those of the last two gulches. They are all cheats of one of four sorts: alchemists, impostors, counterfeiters and liars.

58–64: The second simile describing the stricken sinners is based on one of the stories of Juno's wrath in Ovid. *Metam.* 7.523–659. The nymph Aegina gave birth to one of Jupiter's sons on an island named after her. In revenge, Juno sent a pestilence that killed nearly all living creatures on the island. To make amends, Jupiter replenished the population by changing ants into men. See *Conv.* 4.27.17.

73–84: The homely images of pans on a hearth and the cleaning of fish, like other kitchen similes in the *Inferno*, as well as the image of the stableboys, come from Dante's comic repertoire. The images set the tone for the rest of the canto.

79–84: Dante's two sinners are afflicted with an itching skin disease that results in scabbing and disfigurement. He calls it leprosy (124), but medieval people, like the ancients, did not clearly distinguish leprosy from scabies and other skin conditions. Isidore regarded scabies as a lesser form of leprosy, both being characterized by hardening of the skin with itching and scales. *Etym.* 4.8.10–11.

85–90: Virgil carries on the comic tone established in the preceding similes. This is the only time he employs the *captatio benevolentiae* ironically.

109–20: The first shade to speak is Griffolino d'Arezzo, who was burned as a heretic in Siena before 1272. The early commentator Lana said that after the jape about flying, Albero complained to his father the bishop, who denounced Griffolino to the Inquisition and had him burned as a member of the heretical Paterine sect.

120: The alchemists are falsifiers of metals. Buti distinguished between "sophistical" and "true" alchemists. Aquinas likewise assumed that most alchemists produced a counterfeit metal with the appearance but not the substance of gold. He left open, however, the possibility that chemical processes could produce real gold. *ST* 2-2.77.2. Dante's alchemists are charlatans who produce a material that counterfeits gold. Accordingly, they are punished with a skin disease that transmutes their appearance into a loathsome form while leaving their substance unchanged, the mirror image of their imparting a more noble appearance to a substance that remained base metal. An alchemical maxim held that lead is gold with leprosy. *ED* 3.605–06; see generally *DE* 12–13.

121–32: As examples of Sienese frivolity, Capocchio, the second alchemist, cites wealthy young men who deliberately squandered their money.

125–28: Stricca and Niccolò are generally thought to have been brothers, perhaps of the wealthy Salimbene family of Siena. References to their moderate spending are of course ironic. Cf. "except Bonturo." *Inf.* 21.41.

128–29: In the Middle Ages spices from the East Indies were one of the most coveted luxuries, affordable only by the wealthy; cloves were worth their weight in silver. Pietro said that Niccolò had capons stuffed with whole cloves. The garden where such seed takes root is frivolous Siena.

130–32: Little is known of Caccia d'Asciano, but Bartolomeo de' Folcacchiere, known as "Abbagliato" (perhaps "dupe" *ED* 1.9), had an administrative career in the late 13th century despite his dissipated youth.

130: The reference is to the Spendthrift Club, a group of twelve gilded youths devoted to conspicuous consumption who squandered their fortunes within two years in sumptuous banquets, after each of which the gold and silver serving pieces were thrown away. *ED* 1.699–700. Stricca and Niccolò seem to have belonged to the club, though Dante's text suggests otherwise.

136–39: Capochio was burned for alchemy at Siena in 1293. His final remark here claims a personal acquaintance with the pilgrim in life, and the early commentators asserted that they were fellow students.

Canto XXX

In the days when Juno was incensed, because
  of Semele, against the blood of Thebes,
  as she showed once and then a second time,
Athamas so completely lost his mind
  that seeing his wife approach with their two children,   5
  carrying one of them on either arm,
he cried, "Stretch out the nets, so I can trap
  the lioness and both cubs as they pass!"
  Then, reaching out with claws that knew no pity,
he snatched the one whom they had named Learchus,   10
  swung him around and smashed him on a rock;
  and she, still clutching the other, drowned herself.
And when the turn of fortune's wheel brought low
  the Trojans' arrogance, which braved the world,
  till king and kingdom were destroyed together,   15
the unhappy Hecuba, now a wretched captive,
  after she'd seen the slaughter of Polyxena
  and had with desolation recognized
her Polydorus washed up on the beach,
  howled like a dog in her demented frenzy   20
  because the grief had so unhinged her mind.
No maddened Theban, though, nor Trojan either,
  was ever known to savage with more cruelty
  even a beast, much less a human body,

than two pale naked shades did that I saw   25
    tearing around and biting as they ran,
    as would a hog whose sty was left ajar.
One rushed upon Capocchio, skewering
    the scruff of his neck with its tusks and dragged him off,
    making him scrape his gut on the rocky bottom.   30
The other from Arezzo, left there shaking,
    said to me, "That cruel sprite is Gianni Schicchi,
    and he runs rabid, mutilating others."
"Oh," I exclaimed, "now may the other's teeth
    not sink into your hide, let it not chafe you   35
    to say who it is before it rushes off."
"That one," he answered, "is the ancient spirit
    of shameless Myrrha, who became enamored,
    beyond all proper love, of her own father.
She came to consummate her crime with him   40
    having assumed a false identity,
    the way the one who just ran off contrived,
so he could gain the Lady of the stable,
    to impersonate the dead Buoso Donati,
    making his will and giving it legal form."   45
When those two rabid shades on whom I'd kept
    my eye had disappeared, I turned again
    to scan the other misbegotten souls.
I noticed one whose shape was like a lute's,
    or would have been, if he had had his groin   50
    cut from the part below, where a man is forked.
Dropsy, which makes one heavy from retention
    of fluids, producing parts so disproportioned
    the face no longer seems to match the paunch,
was causing him to keep his lips drawn back   55
    like one with fever, whom the thirst obliges
    to raise one up and curl one toward his chin.
"You that go free from any punishment
    in the world of misery – and I can't think why –
    look here," he said to us, "and meditate   60

on the pitiable state of Master Adam:
    all I desired and more I had in life
    and now, alas! I crave a drop of water.
The little streams that trickle down the green
    hills of the Casentino till they join   65
    the Arno, cooling and moistening their runnels,
are ever before my eyes, and not by chance,
    because that image parches me far more
    than the disease that withers up my face.
So the unbending justice that probes my soul   70
    draws from the place in which I sinned a motive
    to crowd my sighs more quickly into flight.
Romena lies hard by, where I debased
    the alloy stamped with John the Baptist's image,
    for which I left my body burnt up there.   75
Ah, but to see down here the wicked souls
    of Guido or Alessandro or their brother –
    that sight I would not trade for the Branda Fountain.
One is already down here, if the furious
    shades that go all about have told the truth;   80
    but what is that to me, whose limbs are bound?
If only I were lighter, by enough
    to crawl an inch in every hundred years,
    I would have taken to the road already
to seek him in this crowd of the deformed,   85
    although the gulch goes round eleven miles
    and is no less than half a mile across.
Because of them I live in this choice household,
    for they persuaded me to strike gold florins
    in which there were three carats of base metal."   90
"Who are the two unfortunates," I asked him,
    "lying there on the right against your boundary,
    steaming the way wet hands do in the winter?"
"I found them here – and they have not turned since –
    when I rained down," he answered, "on this gorge;   95
    I doubt they will for all eternity.

One is the lying wife who slandered Joseph,
    the other Sinon, the perjured Greek of Troy;
    they reek because they burn with a high fever."
And one of them, who took offense perhaps   100
    at hearing himself disparaged in those terms,
    thumped the great leathern belly with his fist.
The paunch reverberated like a drum;
    and Master Adam raised his arm, which looked
    at least as hard, and struck him in the face,   105
telling him, "Though I can no longer move
    because my body has become so heavy,
    my arm is free for such a job as this."
He answered, "When they dragged you to the stake
    your arm was not so quick, but the same arm   110
    was even quicker when you struck your coins."
The one with dropsy: "There you speak the truth,
    but you were not so scrupulous a witness
    when you were asked to tell the truth at Troy."
"If I spoke false, you falsified the coinage,"   115
    said Sinon. "I am here for one misdeed,
    and you for more than any other devil!"
"Remember, perjured soul, the wooden horse,"
    answered the one with the distended paunch,
    "and suffer that the whole world knows your guilt!"   120
"Suffer yourself, from thirst that cracks your tongue,"
    the Greek replied, "and from the putrid water
    that makes your belly a hedge before your eyes."
"As usual," the counterfeiter answered,
    "your mouth gapes only to reveal your pain: 125
    true, my throat parches while my belly bloats,
but look at you – you burn up, your head throbs;
    in fact you'd need no formal invitation
    to lick Narcissus' looking glass yourself."
Wholly intent on listening to them,   130
    I heard my teacher say, "Just keep on staring
    and I will soon be quarrelling with you!"

Hearing the angry tone he used with me,
    I turned to face him with a shame so deep
    it prowls around my memory to this day.   135
As someone who is dreaming of being harmed
    may wish within his dream that he were dreaming,
    longing for what he thinks does not exist,
so I, who could not say a word, was longing
    to excuse myself and I was doing so   140
    the whole time, but not knowing that I did.
"Less shame than that would wash away a greater
    failing than yours has been," my master said,
    "so lay aside your burden of remorse.
Imagine I am always by your side   145
    if it should happen again that fortune brings you
    where people are embroiled in such a squabble;
for the desire to hear such things is base."

Notes

1–21: Introducing the second class of falsifiers – the imposters, souls afflicted by madness – Dante begins with vignettes of madness taken from Ovid.

1–12: Juno took revenge for the infidelity of Jupiter with Semele, first by causing Semele's death and then that of her sister Ino (because Ino had raised Bacchus, Jupiter and Semele's son). She persuaded the Furies to visit madness on Ino's husband King Athamas. *Metam.* 4.416–562.

13–21: Hecuba, queen of Troy, was enslaved when the Greeks sacked the city. After being forced to watch her daughter Polyxena being sacrificed on Achilles' tomb, she saw the body of her son Polydorus, murdered by a neighboring king, wash ashore. She tore the king's eyes out, killing him, and then, her grief driving her mad, she began to bark like a dog. *Metam.* 13.404–575.

22–45: Benvenuto noted that the impostors falsified their own persons, so it is fitting that this alienation is involuntarily perpetuated in hell. They are driven mad and specifically infected with a rabid furor. Timeless folk belief holds that people infected with rabies run around biting other people. The hog whose sty was left ajar begins as a simile for the way the imposters run about, but Dante then seems to visualize the imposters as hogs, because they have tusks and the way one skewers Capocchio and drags him off suggests that they are running on all fours. Unlike their modern descendants, medieval domesticated hogs were slender and long-legged, hence better at running; and there are medieval illustrations of domesticated hogs with tusks like wild boars.

22–30: The oscillation between the pathetic and comic modes in the tenth gulch lies at the heart of the two opening similes. The emotions evoked by the classical scenes are subverted by the infernal scene to which they are compared. The Athamas scene retains Ovid's pathos and the Hecuba scene invokes the melancholy fall of princes theme dear to the Middle Ages and the Renaissance. See *Hamlet* 2.2.524–41. By contrast, Dante treats both the impostors and their victims satirically.

22–26: Athamas savaged a (supposed) lion cub and Hecuba a man. Dante, however, omits Hecuba's tearing out of the king's eyes, assuming a reader versed in the Latin classics.

28–33, 42–45: Gianni Schicchi was a mid-13th century Florentine knight. At the request of his friend Simone Donati, he impersonated Simone's recently deceased rich uncle Buoso. As Buoso, Gianni dictated a will that left the bulk of the estate to Simone, but included a bequest to himself of a beautiful mare from Buoso's stable. *ED* 5.65–66.

37–41: Consumed by her passion for her father, King Cinyras, with her nurse's connivance Myrrha took advantage of her mother's absence to gain access to his bedroom, assuming a false identity under cover of darkness. *Metam*. 10.298–502.

49–57: The shade with dropsy (edema) represents the third class of falsifiers, the counterfeiters, falsifiers of the coinage. Whereas the alchemist attempts to change the appearance of a base metal whose substance he cannot ennoble, the counterfeiter attempts to preserve the appearance of a noble metal whose substance he debases. This is reflected in their punishments: the alchemist has a skin disease that changes his appearance, the counterfeiter an internal disease that changes his constitution. Pietro Alighieri explained that as dropsy corrupts the body by improperly converting humors, thus changing into water what should become blood, so the counterfeiter corrupts money by diluting it with an admixture of base metal.

49: The sinner probably raises his head to look at the poets, a position that corresponds to "the bent-back peg-board of the lute." Heilbronn 52.

58–90: Little is known about Master Adam except what he tells us. He is one of the more complex characters in the *Inferno*: haughty, petulant, vindictive and self-pitying, he is also intelligent and he directs his psychological perception at himself. His title of Master signifies a university degree and Dante underlines his past affluence by having him crave a drop of water, echoing the rich man in the parable of Lazarus. Luke 16:24.

65, 73: A branch of the Conti Guidi (see note to *Inf*. 16.34–39) controlled the Casentino, a hilly region in the upper reaches of the Arno valley above Florence, from their castle at Romena there.

73–74: The gold florin, emblem of Florence's new financial power in the 13th century, became a well-known standard throughout Europe. The obverse of the 24-carat gold coin was stamped with an image of John the Baptist, the city's patron. Since a coin's value depended on its metallic content, the official stamp was the state's guarantee of the purity of the metal.

79–80: The information that the imposters, while they are running mad and savaging the other falsifiers, are also feeding them gossip (which might more naturally be assumed to pass from mouth to mouth) is to say the least curious.

91–99: The two remaining sinners represent the liars, falsifiers of words, the final class of falsifiers. Their punishment is fever, a *contrapasso* whose relevance is not apparent. The three are squeezed together as in a medieval hospital, where the norm was multiple patients to a bed. Lindberg 347; Mollat 149.

92: Despite Master Adam's self-importance, the pilgrim feels free to address him with the irony that he and Virgil use throughout the tenth gulch, here treating him as a geographical region.

97: When the patriarch Joseph was a slave in Egypt, the wife of his master Potiphar, failing to seduce him, complained that he had tried to rape her. Gen. 39:6–20.

98: After constructing the wooden horse filled with Greek soldiers, the Greeks sailed away from Troy, leaving Sinon behind. Questioned by King Priam, he swore by the gods that the Greeks had built it to placate a goddess and that if it were brought into Troy it would assure a Trojan victory. *Aen.* 2.57–198.

100–03: Sinon's resounding blow to Adam's belly displays Adam's disease. To diagnose dropsy, a doctor would rap the patient's abdomen to see whether it gave off a characteristic sound. Siraisi 125.

106–29: The patterned exchange of insults – with a tercet allocated to each (until Adam caps the argument with two) and repetition of the opponent's term of abuse to turn it against him – recalls the contemporary practice of exchanging insulting verses. Dante indulged in this exercise, known as a *tenzone*, in his youth. The speakers here combine strict form with the crude realistic terms of low comedy, and the result has an irresistible rhetorical vitality.

120: The world knows of Sinon's guilt because it is recorded in the *Aeneid*.

129: Narcissus' looking glass was a pool of water. *Metam.* 3.407–510. Adam's references to the *Aeneid* and the *Metamorphoses* show he is an educated man.

130–48: Such squabbles should be glanced at for education, not followed for their own interest with a kind of satisfaction. The series of insult sonnets that Dante exchanged with Forese Donati in his youth contained coarse vituperation in the guise of jocularity, which may have been a discomforting recollection to the mature poet. In any case the effect of this passage, somewhat like that of the Francesca episode in *Inf.* 5, is that Dante has inveigled the reader into a voyeuristic pleasure that he then condemns.

Canto XXXI

The self-same tongue first cut me to the quick,
    making my cheeks take on a deeper shade,
    and then supplied me with the medicine;
so I have heard the spear that once belonged
    to Achilles and his father caused a wound   5
    with its first stroke and healed it with a second.
Turning our backs on the valley of misery,
    we made our way without a word across
    the embankment that defines its inner side.
There it was not quite night and not quite day,   10
    so that my sight could not go far before me,
    but I heard a horn that sounded with such force
it would have made a thunderclap seem faint;
    it drew my gaze, which followed the sound's path
    backward to find the source, straight to one point.   15
After the sorrowful debacle in which
    Charlemagne lost the holy band of heroes,
    the blast from Roland's horn was not as terrible.
And shortly, having turned my head that way,
    I made out what seemed numerous high towers   20
    and asked, "What city, Master, is over there?"
"Because you try to penetrate the shadows
    from too far off," he answered, "it so happens
    you are mistaken in what you imagine.

You will see clearly, when you once arrive there,   25
    the tricks that distance plays upon the sight;
    spur yourself, therefore, to a quicker pace."
Then, as he took my hand with great affection,
    he said to me, "Before we come much nearer,
    so the reality may seem less startling,   30
know that those are not towers, but rather giants;
    and all of them are standing within the well
    up to the navel, stationed around its rim."
As when dense fog disperses and the sight
    little by little pieces out the contours   35
    of what was hidden by the thickened air,
so as I pierced this murky atmosphere
    while we came closer and closer to the brink,
    my misconception fled and my fear grew;
for as upon the circuit of its walls   40
    Montereggione has raised a crown of towers,
    here all around the bank encircling the well
there towered, up to half of their full height,
    the horrible giants, those whom even now
    Jove threatens from the sky whenever it thunders.   45
I could already see the face of one,
    the shoulders and the chest, much of the belly
    and both arms hanging down along his sides.
Nature, for certain, when she discontinued
    fashioning creatures of this kind, did well   50
    to take such instruments away from Mars.
If she has not repented for her whales
    and elephants, one who looks at this astutely
    will find her all the more exact and prudent;
for where the reasoning power of the mind   55
    is joined with malice and brute force as well,
    mankind is left with no defense against it.
I judged the face about as long and broad
    as the bronze pine cone at St. Peter's in Rome
    and all his other parts were scaled to match,   60

so that the bank, which formed a kind of apron
    from his waist down, still left so much exposed
    above it that three Frisians would have boasted
idly of being able to reach his hair;
    for I could see full thirty spans of him   65
    below the point where a man clasps his cloak.
"Raphèl maì amècche zabì almi,"
    the savage mouth, to which no softer psalms
    would have been suitable, began to shout.
"Slow-witted soul," my leader called to him,   70
    "stick to your horn and let that vent your feelings
    when anger or another passion moves you.
Grope at your neck and you will find the strap
    that holds it tied to you, confounded soul;
    see where it slants across your massive chest."   75
And then to me: "He is his own accuser,
    for this is Nimrod, through whose impious scheme
    the world no longer speaks a single language.
Here let us leave him and not waste our words,
    for every language is the same to him   80
    as his to others, which is known to none."
Then, turning left, we traveled on still further
    and at the limit of a crossbow's range
    we found the second, far more huge and savage.
Whose hand it could have been that shackled him   85
    I cannot say, but both his arms were pinioned
    – the left in front, the right behind his back –
with a single chain that wound its way around him
    from the neck down, so as to make five turns
    around the part of him that was exposed.   90
"Once this proud spirit longed to try his strength
    against that of supreme Jove," said my leader,
    "and this is his reward. He bears the name
of Ephialtes and performed great feats
    the day the giants made the gods feel fear.   95
    The arms he raised will never move again."

"If it were possible," I said to him,
  "I'd like to let my eyes take in the sight
  of the immeasurable Briareus."
He said, "Not far off, you will see Antaeus,   100
  who is not shackled and can speak, and he
  will set us on the floor of deepest guilt.
The one you want to see is far beyond;
  he is chained like this one and looks much the same,
  except that his expression is more fierce."   105
No earthquake yet, however turbulent,
  has made a tower shake as violently
  as Ephialtes shook himself just then.
Then was I more than ever afraid of death,
  and it would not have taken more than the fear   110
  had I not seen the chain that held him fast.
Proceeding onward then, we came upon
  Antaeus, who rose seven yards and more
  above the well, not reckoning his head.
"O you who once brought back a thousand lions   115
  fallen your prey within the fateful valley
  where Scipio later was left heir to glory
when Hannibal with all his troops turned tail,
  and through whom, had you joined the arduous war
  waged by your brothers, some still seem to think   120
the sons of earth would have emerged victorious,
  set us below, and do not scorn the task,
  down where the deep freeze locks Cocytus up.
Why make us go to Tityus or Typhon?
  This man can give what all down here desire;   125
  bend down then, and do not avert your face.
He can yet bring you fame in the upper world,
  for he lives and expects a long life yet
  unless grace calls him back before his time."
So said my teacher, and the other quickly   130
  stretched out his hands, the power of whose grip
  was felt by Hercules once, and grasped my guide.

When Virgil felt that he was being lifted
    he said to me, "Come here, where I can reach you,"
    and made a single bundle of us both.   135
The way the Garisenda looks, to someone
    who gazes up beneath the leaning side
    while a cloud in passing over makes it seem
to topple, was the way Antaeus looked
    to me who watched him stooping; in that moment   140
    I wished that we could take another route.
But gently on the floor that swallows both
    Judas and Lucifer he set us down;
    nor did he long remain in that position
but like a ship's mast bobbed upright again.   145

Notes

4–6: The spear of Achilles made a wound that only it could heal.

8–9: The poets have passed the last gulch and are crossing a wide ledge toward the central well that contains the final circle of hell.

16–18: The debacle of Roncesvalles is described in the Old French epic *The Song of Roland.* Informed by a traitor (who is punished as such in the final circle), the Saracens fall on the rear guard of Charlemagne's army, commanded by his nephew Roland. Charlemagne is called back too late by a tremendous blast from Roland's great horn, arriving in time only to wreak vengeance for the massacre of the flower of Frankish chivalry.

17: The "holy band" is made up of Roland and his paladins. The epic treats Charlemagne and his warriors as crusaders against the infidel, and those who died on crusade were considered martyrs. *See Par.* 15.148. St. Francis said that Roland and his companions were holy martyrs for the faith of Christ. Waley 28. Roland and Charlemagne appear among the defenders of the faith in heaven in *Par.* 18.43.

20–21: The pilgrim expects a city to bristle with towers because Italian cities of the 12th and 13th centuries actually did so. Noble families built towers to serve as in-town fortresses, necessary in the conduct of the frequent clan feuds. A large city could contain hundreds of these towers, which were up to several hundred feet high. See Waley 125–31. Because the towers were owned by the magnates and used in factional affrays, representative governments tore them down when they got control, as happened in Florence in the 13th century. See Vasari 2.6. The pilgrim's mistaken impression thus evokes the lawlessness and brutality of the powerful, which is appropriate for the giants. Pietro Alighieri said that the giants allegorically represent worldly lords who in their petulance and pride seek to go beyond natural limits.

40–45: The giants, sons of Earth, stormed Mt. Olympus in an unsuccessful attempt to overthrow the Olympian gods. Dante and early readers believed in the historical existence of giants, which was attested by scripture: "giants were upon the earth in those days." Gen. 6:4. The belief was confirmed by the periodic discovery of dinosaur or other fossils, which were taken for human. See note to *Inf.* 14.103–04.

40–41: Montereggione is a fortress near Siena surrounded by a circular wall crowned with fourteen towers at regular intervals.

42–45: The giants form part of the expected classical machinery of hell (see *Aen.* 6.580–84; *Phars.* 6.665; *Theb.* 4.534–35), but Dante gets Christian mileage out of them as well. The ninth circle is Satan's citadel, and the giants, its towers, share his sin because they exemplify pride (see Wis. 14:6) and rebellion against heaven, the sins for which Satan was cast down. *Inf.* 34 will show that he exceeds even their colossal stature. Augustine's commentary on Ps. 32:16, included in the *Glossa Ordinaria*, says "the giant is any proud man who raises himself up against God." The phrase combines biblical and classical traditions in a moral allegory.

46–81: Nimrod is the only biblical figure among Dante's hell-guardians, otherwise drawn from classical mythology; but paralleling him with the classical giants is based on Christian tradition. Augustine said that the giant Nimrod founded the city of Babel, who in his impious pride had his people erect a tower against the Lord so as to reach heaven. The Lord defeated their presumption by confounding their language. *Civ. Dei* 16.4. Dante elsewhere said that the giant Nimrod's attempt was to surpass his creator. *VE* 1.7.4. The classical giants' pilling of Mt. Ossa on Mt. Pelion made a contemporary of Dante's conclude that they were secular versions of the Babel story. Curtius 215.

59: A large bronze pine cone from ancient Rome was a medieval tourist attraction at St. Peter's. See Nichols 34. It is 11 feet, 8 inches tall (Kay 2002, 26) and may have been taller in Dante's time. *ED* 4.522.

62–64: With three six-foot Dutchmen standing on each other's shoulders, the one on top could reach up perhaps seven yards. Homely details like this and the pine cone are part of Dante's usual technique for making the marvels of the other world vividly present, but are unlikely to indicate exact size. The reach of the Dutchmen might suggest tht Nimrod was almost 50 feet tall, but the pine cone parallel would suggest something quite a bit bigger. Richard Kay, however, using Vitruvian proportions and some questionable assumptions, concludes that Nimrod is 116 feet, 10 inches tall. Kay 2002, 20.

76–81: When necessary, Virgil transcends his limitations as an ancient pagan and explains biblical history.

82–96: Ephialtes and his twin brother piled Mt. Ossa on Mt. Pelion; this is the chief of his great feats.

97–105: Statius describes "the immense Briareus" standing contemptuous against the armed might of heaven. *Theb.* 2.596–601. Briareus and Nimrod figure as examples of pride in *Purg.* 12.

112–45: Antaeus, son of the Earth, lived by hunting lions in North Africa, and as a latter day giant did not participate in the war. Overcoming him in wrestling was one of the twelve labors of Hercules. Each time he was pinned, Antaeus would draw strength from his mother Earth and rise invigorated. Realizing this, Hercules lifted him high in the air and crushed the life out of him. *Phars.* 4.593–660; *Conv.* 3.3.7–8. Virgil's speech to capture Antaeus's good will is unusually extended; the details all come from the passage in Lucan.

117–18: The Roman victory over Hannibal at Zama in 205 BC brought an end to the Carthaginian threat against Rome and glory to the Roman general Scipio.

124: Tityus and Typhon are mentioned by Lucan as inferior in strength to Antaeus, so Virgil's reference to them is another appeal to the giant's pride. *Phars.* 4.596–97.

136–40: The Garisenda is a leaning tower in Bologna built in the 12th century. It is almost 200 feet tall today and was a good deal taller in Dante's time. The vertigo Dante describes can be experienced by looking up at any tall building when clouds are racing past from behind you, because with part of your mind you perceive the clouds as stationary and the building as continuously falling toward you; but the effect would be especially striking at a leaning tower.

Canto XXXII

If I commanded hoarse and grating rhymes
    such as would suit the dismal cavity
    upon which every other rock bears down,
I could more thoroughly squeeze out the juice
    of my conception; lacking them, I feel   5
    some trepidation as I come to speak,
for rendering the bottom of the entire
    universe is a daunting enterprise,
    not for a tongue still crying *mama, dada.*
But may those ladies who once helped Amphion   10
    to wall in Thebes now lend my verse their aid
    and keep my words from straying from the facts.
O miscreated dregs, worse than all others,
    who occupy the place so hard to speak of,
    better had you been sheep while here, or goats!   15
While we were down in the darkness of the well
    deposited far below the giant's feet,
    I gazing up as yet at the deep shaft,
I heard myself addressed: "Look where you step!
    Take care in walking not to trample on   20
    the heads of miserable and weary brothers."
I turned at this and saw in front of me
    and underfoot a lake that from the cold
    appeared to be of glass instead of water.

In Austria the Danube never formed 25
    so thick a veil upon its flow in winter,
    nor did the Don beneath its frigid sky,
as there was here; for if Mount Tambernic
    had fallen on it, or Mount Pietrapana,
    even the edge of it would not have creaked. 30
As frogs, so they can croak, will squat with snouts
    above the water, in the season in which
    country girls in their dreams are gleaning still,
the grieving shades, blue-mottled, were encased
    up to the part where shame shows in the ice, 35
    making a stork-like clacking with their teeth.
All of them kept their faces turned below;
    the cold wrung testimony from their mouths
    as the sorrow in their hearts did from their eyes.
When I had gazed around me for a while 40
    I looked down and I saw two wedged together
    so closely that their hair was intermingled.
"Tell me who you may be," I said, "that clinch
    chest against chest." At that they bent their necks back
    and when they raised their faces up toward me, 45
their eyes, which had been only wet within,
    spilled over on their lips and the cold froze
    the tears between the lids and locked them shut.
No clamp could press a board against a board
    so tightly, goading them to butt each other 50
    like rams, they were so overcome by rage.
And someone who had lost both ears to frostbite
    said to me, while still keeping his face down,
    "Why stare at us so hard, as in a mirror?
If you desire to know who those two are, 55
    the valley the Bisenzio flows through
    was once their father Alberto's and then theirs.
They came from the same womb, and you could search
    all of Cain's Ring and not discover a shade
    more worthy to be set in gelatin, 60

not him whose chest and shadow let in daylight
    pierced by a single stroke from Arthur's hand;
    nor yet Foccacia; nor the one whose head
so blocks my view that I see nothing else,
    who bore the name of Sassol Mascheroni –   65
    you know who he was if you come from Tuscany.
And now, to spare myself from further speech,
    know that my name was Camicion de' Pazzi;
    I await Carlino for my vindication."
Then I saw countless faces turned by the cold   70
    bruise-colored, which still sets me shuddering now,
    and always will, at the sight of frozen ponds.
And while we kept on walking toward the center
    to which all heavy bodies gravitate
    and I was shivering in the eternal shade,   75
whether it was by will or fate or chance
    I do not know, but as I walked among
    the heads, my foot struck hard against one's face.
"Why do you trample me?" he screamed through tears.
    "Unless you come to heap on more revenge   80
    for Montaperti, why do you torment me?"
"Master," I said, "wait here for me a minute
    till I resolve a doubt concerning this one;
    then you can hurry me to your heart's content."
My leader stopped and I addressed the shade,   85
    who kept on showering me with violent curses:
    "Now who are you, who bitterly rebuke me?"
"Who're *you*," he cried, "who cross Antenor's Ring,
    kicking my face so hard it would be far
    too much to take if I were still alive?"   90
"I am alive, and it may profit you,"
    I answered, "if you want to be remembered,
    to have your name included in my notes."
"I want the very opposite," he said.
    "Get out of here and pester me no more –   95
    your flattery rings hollow in this sump."

I grabbed his hair then, at the scruff of the neck,
  and said, "You need to tell me your name now
  or you'll be left without a hair back here."
"Even," he answered, "if you snatch me bald,   100
  I will not tell you who I am or show you,
  not if you stomp my head a thousand times."
His hair was twisted already around my hand
  and I had yanked some bunches of it out,
  he howling like a dog with eyes cast down,   105
when someone shouted, "What's your problem, Bocca?
  The tune your jaws play doesn't satisfy you,
  you have to howl too? What the devil's wrong?"
"Now I don't want another word from you,
  black-hearted traitor," I said, "for to your shame   110
  I'll carry back a true report of you."
"Shove off," he answered. "Tell whatever you want;
  but if you make it back don't fail to mention
  the one who couldn't wait to shoot his mouth off.
Here he pays back the French bribe that he took,   115
  and you can say, 'I saw the traitor Duera
  down in the place where sinners are kept cool.'
If they should ask who else was there with him,
  you can see Beccheria there beside you,
  the one whose gorget Florence sawed in two.   120
Gianni de' Soldanier, I think, is further
  in there with Ganelon and Tebaldello,
  who opened up Faenza while it slept."
We'd passed somewhat beyond him when I noticed
  two that were frozen in a single hole,   125
  so close that one's head formed the other's hat.
The upper one was sinking his incisors
  into the lower where brain meets spinal cord
  the way a famished man devours bread.
Tydeus in his scorn and hatred gnawed   130
  upon the lifeless head of Menalippus
  as this one on the skull and the soft parts.

"You that display by such a bestial sign
    your hatred for the one on whom you feed,
    tell me the reason," I said, "on this condition: 135
if you have just cause to complain of him
    once I know who you are and his offense,
    I will repay you in the world above,
unless the tongue I speak with shrivels up."

Notes

1–12: Dante needs additional help from the Muses to describe the bottom of the pit, the ground zero of evil where the sinners keep company with Satan himself because they are the traitors, his fellow-sinners.

3, 74: The pilgrim is now close to the center of the earth, which in Dante's scheme is the center of the universe, the point toward which all heavy bodies tend. See note to *Inf*. 34.76–111.

10–11: Amphion, aided by the Muses, built the walls of Thebes by playing his lyre, the stones rising into place under the compulsion of the music. See Horace, "Ars poetica" 394–96. Thebes consistently appears in the *Inferno* as the city typifying violence, treachery and horror. See *Inf*. 33.89 and note.

16–21: Surprised to hear himself addressed, the pilgrim looks down and sees the frozen lake. In appealing to the pilgrim's human brotherhood, the speaker invokes what these sinners betrayed in life.

22–30: The frozen lake is Cocytus, formed by the rivers of hell, which pool here at the bottom. *Inf*. 14.112–20. Its freezing will be explained in canto 34. The tradition of ice in hell goes back to the 3d century *Vision of St. Paul*, where sinners are punished with ice and snow. See Eliott 635, 637. In medieval visions, sinners are chased into an icy river by demons or frozen in ice or immersed to different depths in an icy lake. Morgan 29, 32. Aquinas asserted that the damned will be punished by alternating fire and ice. *ST*, Suppl. 97.1; see *Paradise Lost* 2.596–603. Dante has reserved ice for the ninth circle because the traitors extinguished all human empathy in pursuit of self-interest. In the twilight of Cocytus the emotional freeze they adopted in life is reified.

36: Brunetto Latini asserted that the stork was mute but made a "great tumult" by clacking its beak. *Tresor* 1.160.

37: The pilgrim is in Cain's Ring, the outermost of four concentric zones of Cocytus, reserved for those who betrayed their blood kin. The sinners in this zone have the privilege of keeping their heads down. This allows their sorrow the vent of tears, which do not freeze in their eyes.

40–51, 55–60: These brothers are the happily named Alexander and Napoleon, sons of Count Alberto of Mangona, who controlled a valley north of Florence. The father left only a sliver of his domains to Napoleon, creating implacable hatred between the brothers that led to three decades of struggle in which they finally killed each other. See *ED* 1.98–99.

47–48: Others think that the freezing tears lock the brothers' lips together in a parody of a kiss, inciting their rage.

54: With the sinners' heads turned down, the pilgrim must look at their faces reflected in the glassy lake, where the speaker also sees him. The speaker may also imply that the pilgrim is one of them.

55–66: Throughout this canto the sinners reveal each other's identities and crimes to the pilgrim with sarcastic relish. Their speech exhibits the coarseness and cynicism of hardened criminals in a maximum security penitentiary.

60: The reference to the brothers being set in aspic initiates a series of ironic jailhouse euphemisms.

61–62: When King Arthur went abroad, he made his nephew (or incestuous son) Mordred regent. Mordred reported the king dead and had himself crowned. When Arthur returned, they fought in single combat and the mortally wounded Arthur drove his lance through Mordred's body so hard that a ray of sun appeared through the wound. See *ED* 3.1032.

63: Foccacia was a member of the Cancellieri family of Pistoia. Feuds among branches of this family divided the city and gave rise to the Black and White factions of the Guelfs. *Cron.* 9.38. When the Black Cancellieri killed a leading White in 1293, Foccacia, a violent White, retaliated by killing a relative who was a Black *capo*. *ED* 1.784–85.

65–66: Some early commentators said that Sassol Mascheroni killed his young nephew for his inheritance; others said the victim was a cousin.

67–69: Camicione de' Pazzi was said to have killed a relative named Ubertino. *ED* 4.354. He awaits Carlino de' Pazzi, another relative, whose crime will make Camicione's pale by comparison because Carlino took a bribe to betray the Florentine Whites to the Florentine Blacks (*Cron.* 9.53) and so his place will be in the next zone.

70–72: Here we enter the Ring of Antenor, the zone reserved for those who betrayed their country or party, a worse crime for Dante than betrayal of family. Note, however, that in the troubled political situation of medieval Italy, loyalty to party could involve betrayal of country (really city) and vice versa.

76–111: The pilgrim is arrested by a blurted reference to Montaperti, the battle in which the Florentine Guelfs were massacred by a Ghibelline force. See note to *Inf.* 10.22–27. Bocca degli Abati, a Florentine Ghibelline turned Guelf, cut off the hand of the Florentine standard-bearer when the enemy attacked. Seeing the standard fall, the Florentine troops lost heart, and the battle turned into a rout. *Cron.* 7.78.

88: Antenor was a Trojan prince. In accounts through which the Trojan war was known to the Middle Ages, when his advice to make peace with the Greeks was not taken, he betrayed the city. See Moore 190; *ED* 1.296.

97–105: Dante no doubt thinks that the pilgrim's violence toward Bocca is righteous. Some modern readers may wonder whether a hard and passionate man embittered by exile too easily identifies his own resentment with the rigor of divine justice, of which he sees himself as the instrument. Justin Steinberg concludes that under applicable principles of law the pilgrim's use of inquisitorial torture here is an abuse of discretion. Steinberg 81.

116–17: In 1265 the French forces of Charles of Anjou, moving south against Manfred, the son of Frederick II, had to cross a river guarded by Manfred's allies. They crossed without opposition, and it was said that Manfred's ally Buoso da Duera, the local governor, had been bribed to let them pass. *Cron.* 8.4; see note to *Inf.* 28.15–18.

119–20: Tesauro dei Beccheria was a churchman. When the Ghibellines were chased out of Florence in 1258, he was charged with plotting to bring them back and was decapitated. *ED* 1.553. He would not actually have worn armor; the way Bocca describes his fate is another jailhouse euphemism.

121: When Manfred was defeated at Benevento, the Ghibellines under Guido Novello still held Florence. *Cron.* 8.13. The people rose against them and Gianni de' Soldanieri, from an old Ghibelline family, switched sides to gain power. This gave the populace control of towers from which to throw rocks, forcing Guido to retreat. *Cron.* 8.14–15. The Ghibellines never regained power in Florence.

122: Ganelon, a frequent medieval *exemplum* of treachery, betrayed Charlemagne's army to the Saracens, leading to the death of the hero Roland and his companions at Roncesvalles. See note to *Inf.* 31.16–18.

122–23: Tebaldello de' Zambrasi was a Ghibelline of Faenza. He opened the city by night to the Guelfs of Bologna so they would attack his rivals, Bolognese Ghibellines in Faenza; but they also pillaged the city and massacred unarmed inhabitants. *ED* 5.1162–63.

124–32: The two figures in this grisly tableau will be the subject of the next canto. The reference to Tydeus, one of the Seven against Thebes, acknowledges Dante's source for this incident in Statius. *Theb.* 8.716–66. Tydeus was struck in battle by a spear hurled by Menalippus, in whom he was able to sink his own spear before collapsing. Dying, he asked his comrades for the head of Menalippus and shocked them by chewing it until he was covered in brains and blood.

135–39: This time the pilgrim makes a more canny offer to report to the world above – he will gratify the cannibal's hatred by reporting his grievance against the one he gnaws on.

Canto XXXIII

Raising his mouth up from his savage meal,
    the sinner wiped it on the hair that clung
    to the head, the back of which he'd devastated.
Then he began: "You want me to renew
    a desperate sorrow that already grips   5
    my heart to think of, much less talk about.
But if my words must be the seeds that ripen
    to infamy for the traitor that I gnaw,
    my talk will flow as steadily as my tears.
Who you may be and how you've gotten down here   10
    I do not know, but you appear to be
    Florentine, surely, from the way you speak.
First you must know I was Count Ugolino
    and this one is Ruggieri the archbishop:
    now hear why I'm this kind of neighbor to him.   15
How, as the outcome of his treacherous schemes,
    I trusted him and was taken prisoner,
    then put to death, there is no need to tell you;
what you cannot have heard about, however
    – the brutal circumstances of my death –   20
    that you shall hear. Then judge if he has wronged me.
A narrow loophole in The Coop, the tower
    now known because of me as Hunger Tower,
    in which I'm not the last to be confined,

had shown me through its chink repeated moons 25
    before the night I had the troubling dream
    that ripped in two for me the veil of the future.
This one appeared to me as lord and master,
    hunting the wolf and wolf cubs on the mountain
    that shuts off Lucca from the Pisans' view. 30
Ranging in front of him he had dispatched
    the Gualandi and Sismondi and Lanfranchi
    together with lean hounds, well-trained and eager.
After a short pursuit the father and sons
    seemed to be tiring, and I seemed to see 35
    the sharp incisors tearing at their sides.
When I awoke before the break of day
    I heard my children, who there there with me,
    whimpering in their sleep and asking for bread.
You must be heartless if you feel no sorrow 40
    now, when you realize what my heart foreboded.
    What do you ever weep for if not this?
They were awake now, and the hour approaching
    when usually our food was brought to us,
    each was left apprehensive by his dream; 45
and then below I heard them nailing shut
    the exit from the dreadful tower. I looked
    into my children's faces without a word.
I did not weep, I had so turned to stone
    inside. They wept; my little Anselm said, 50
    'You stare so strangely, father! What's the matter?'
And still I shed no tears and gave no answer
    all through that day and through the night that followed,
    till the next sun crept forth upon the world.
Then as a feeble ray of sunlight entered 55
    the dreary prison and I recognized
    by their four faces the expression of mine,
a spasm of anguish made me bite my hands.
    And they, who thought I did it out of hunger,
    stood up immediately and all exclaimed, 60

'Dear father, you would cause us far less pain
    in eating us instead; just as you once
    dressed us in this poor flesh, undress us now.'
I calmed myself to spare them further grief;
    that day and all the next we passed in silence.   65
    Why did you not split open, pitiless earth?
After we had arrived at the fourth day
    Gaddo fell down full length before my feet.
    'Father,' he said, 'why aren't you helping me?'
There he expired, and as you see me now   70
    I saw the other three drop one by one
    between the fifth day and the sixth; and I,
blind by now, groped for them and called their names
    for two days after all of them were dead.
    After that, fasting overpowered grief."   75
When he had said this, with his gaze grown grim
    he seized once more the wretched skull in his teeth,
    which gnawed the bone as hard as any dog's.
Ah, Pisa, the disgrace of all who live
    in the fair land that hears Italian speech,   80
    since neighbors have been slow to punish you,
now may Capraia and Gorgona move
    and form a barrier at the Arno's mouth
    so every living soul in you is drowned!
For though Count Ugolino was reputed   85
    a traitor for surrendering your forts,
    that was no cause for torturing his children.
Their tender years declared the innocence,
    O second Thebes, of Guccione, Brigata
    and the other two my song already named.   90
We passed on further, where the frozen pool
    roughly enshrouds another group, whose faces,
    instead of being bowed, are all turned up.
Their very tears serve to impede their weeping
    and rising grief, obstructed at their eyes,   95
    turns back within and swells the agony;

for the first tears emerging form a lump
    that, like a visor fashioned of rock crystal,
    fills the whole socket underneath the brow.
And though, as with a callus, all sensation   100
    had given up its residence in my face
    because of the deep cold, it seemed to me
that nonetheless I now could feel some wind.
    "Master," it made me say, "who makes this stir?
    Are not all exhalations quenched down here?"   105
"Soon you will reach," he said, "the place at which
    your eyes provide the answer to that question,
    seeing what makes this breath come raining down."
And one of the wretches in the frigid crust
    called to us, "Souls so cruel that the remotest   110
    posting has been assigned to you, detach
the hard veils from my eyes so I may drain
    the grief that saturates my heart a little
    before my tears freeze over once again."
"Tell me your name if you desire my help,"   115
    I said, "and then unless I disengage you
    may I be made to go below the ice."
He answered, "I am Brother Alberigo,
    the one whose orchard bore such evil fruit,
    and down here I am paid back date for fig."   120
"Oh," I exclaimed, "are you already dead?"
    "I have no knowledge about how my body
    fares," he responded, "in the world above.
This Ring of Ptolemy has the peculiar
    privilege that the soul quite often falls here   125
    before it is dispatched by Atropos.
And so you may with a more willing spirit
    scrape from my face the hard glaze of my tears,
    know this: the moment that a soul turns traitor
the way I did, a devil takes possession   130
    of its body and controls it afterwards
    until its time has fully come around;

the soul, however, plunges into this well.

    For all I know, up there one sees the body

    of the shade that's wintering behind me here;   135

but you must know, if you have just come down,

    for this is Branca Doria, and some years

    have passed since he was first encased like this."

"I think you play me for a fool," I answered,

    "for Branca Doria surely has not died yet: 140

    he eats and drinks and sleeps and puts on clothes."

"Up in the gully of the Nastyclaws,"

    he said, "in which the sticky pitch is boiling,

    not yet had Michael Zanche even arrived

when this one left a devil in his body   145

    instead of him, as did his near relation

    who in the treachery was his accomplice.

But now reach out your hand to me and open

    my eyes." I did not open them for him,

    and being rude to him was courtesy.   150

Ah men of Genoa, so far from all

    virtuous conduct and full of every vice,

    why have you not been cast forth from the world?

For with the foulest spirit of Romagna

    I came on one of you, who for his deeds   155

    in spirit bathes already in Cocytus

yet up here seems alive in the body still.

Notes

1–3: The sinner's wiping his mouth on the victim's hair before beginning to speak is, in its casualness, the most chilling detail yet.

13–21: Count Ugolino della Gherardesca was born near 1220 into the leading Ghibelline family of Pisa. He married his daughter to Giovanni Visconti, the head of the city's leading Guelf family, and in 1275, after Guelf power became dominant in Tuscany, he appears to have planned a Guelf coup with his son-in-law. After he was banished with other Guelfs, Pisa was defeated by Guelf Florence and a condition of the peace was that the exiles, including Ugolino, be readmitted. In 1284 Pisa was crushingly defeated in a naval battle with Genoa and was threatened with attack by a Guelf League formed by Florence and Lucca. In this crisis, Ugolino assumed power in Pisa as a Guelf, which appeased the Florentines; and he associated his grandson, the Guelf Nino Visconti, with him in the government. He further attempted to placate the Guelf League by handing over three Pisan castles to them, creating a rift with Nino.

By 1288 the Pisan Ghibellines were becoming more powerful again, chief among them Ruggieri degli Ubaldini, Archbishop of Pisa. Although the facts are less than clear, it appears that Ugolino negotiated with the Ghibellines to remove Nino from power and rule alone. In any case, Nino was forced to flee while Ugolino was out of town. The story reflected in Dante's account is that Ruggieri lured Ugolino back with a promise of an accord; he then told the people that Ugolino had betrayed Pisa by handing over her castles to her enemies. The enraged populace rose against Ugolino and he was imprisoned at the top of a tower with his sons Gaddo and Uguccione and his grandsons Anselm and Brigata. They were kept in the tower for over six months before their jailors sealed access to it, starving them. See *ED* 5.795–97; *DE* 839–40. Nino Visconti denounced Ruggieri to the pope, and the archbishop was imprisoned for life for his role in the murders. Dante knew both Nino and his mother, Ugolino's daughter.

It is not really clear why Ugolino and Ruggieri in are Antenor's Ring among the traitors to country or party. The only basis mentioned for Ugolino's treachery is his surrender of the castles. Villani saw that not as a strategic move but as his treacherously allying himself with Florence against Pisa (*Cron.* 8.47, 8.49); but Dante notes that view only as an allegation (85–86). No basis is mentioned for the treachery of Ruggieri, who does not appear to have betrayed either Pisa or the Ghibellines, though he betrayed Ugolino (16–18).

22–25: Dante's artfully told story (its artfulness may be gauged by comparing it with Chaucer's conventionalized condensation of Dante's version in The Monk's Tale) begins with a cinematic close-up that establishes time and place with evocative power. "The Coop (or Mews)" was a tower belonging to the Gualandi (32). The reference to future prisoners being confined there emphasizes the continuity of civic hatred in the Italian towns. The repeated (new) moons indicate the months of confinement (Bosco/Reggio).

26–36: Ugolino's dream apparently takes place toward morning, when dreams are likely to foretell the future. *Inf.* 26.7. He dreams of himself as an outcast from a city controlled by the Ghibelline families with the archbishop at their head. He is a wolf, a dangerous animal who poses a threat to the city and is hunted on a hill outside the walls. Ugolino's children appear first as wolf cubs being hunted, but wolf and cubs soon become father and sons. Ruggieri is the master of the hunt, his beaters are three leading Ghibelline families and his hounds are the mob he stirred up against Ugolino. The dream presents another image of cannibalism, one that inverts the scene in hell, where Ugolino gnaws Ruggieri like a dog (77–78).

37–39: The children are introduced as they whimper in their sleep for food, which also hints at the story that will unfold. At the time of his imprisonment, Ugolino was almost seventy, and his two sons imprisoned with him were middle-aged; his two grandsons were adolescents. All four need to become his sons and children – Chaucer made the eldest five years old – to evoke horrified pity for the barbarity shown to innocence. This emotion is first felt by Ugolino, through whose eyes we see the scene, and any pity he evokes is in his role as father.

45: Ugolino apparently infers the children's dreams from their whimpers.

46–75: From the nailing shut of the door to the final grim line, Dante tells the story with economy while achieving the maximum of horror. The attitude the reader should adopt toward Ugolino has been controversial. Traditional Italian critics have argued that the pathos of his paternal anguish is the key to the canto. More recent critics, some of them often zealous in slanging sinners, have rejected this appeal to the character's common humanity. Ugolino's sorrow for his children is certainly the focus of his narrative and denying the pathos of his situation appears willful. But the more pathetic Ugolino makes his tale, the more he succeeds in blackening Ruggieri's reputation. More important, by his own account the effect of his sorrow is to turn him to stone, incapable of offering comfort to his dying children. His narrative marks off the intervals of his rigid silence as if in anticipation of a word that never comes (he calls his children's names only after they are dead), and the childish reproach of the dying Gaddo (69) is deserved.

By contrast, the children attempt to comfort him. As Ugolino appeared to the pilgrim to be satisfying his hunger when he was actually expressing his hatred, he appears the same way to his children when he is actually expressing his grief. The children's offering themselves as food is the one detail of the story that strikes a modern reader as unnatural. Their speech is couched in the sort of sententious trope esteemed in the Middle Ages and the Renaissance. (Edoardo Sanguineti traces the body-as-dress trope from Seneca through the Christian fathers. Sanguineti 428.) Departure from an otherwise realistic narrative, however, can signal that something else is in play, and the children's offer can be understood as transforming the master image of the episode. Freccero sees it as an allusion to the Eucharist, the Christian sublimation of cannibalistic sacrifice. The children's self-sacrifice, proceeding from love, is the key to breaking the endless chain in which the last killing requires the next; but Ugolino can see in their suffering only a spur to eternal vengeance. Freccero 1986, 156–57.

75: The meaning that occurs first to most readers is that at the end of seven days Ugolino's death from starvation put an end to his grief. Since the 19th century many critics have argued that the line can equally well mean that Ugolino lived a while longer by eating his children's bodies. This does not appear to be the most natural reading, but it would bring the episode's pervasive imagery of cannibalism to a climax of horror and give added point to Ugolino's eternal revenge.

76–78: Virgil previously explained that fraud always gnaws the sinner's mind. *Inf.* 11.52. Here it does so with horrifying literalness. Pietro made this connection, remarking that Ugolino's death gnawed at the memory in the archbishop's brain. More generally, the image of cannibalism expresses the undying internecine hatred that devours the Italian cities and lives beyond the grave. In *Purg.* 6.83–84, Dante will say of the Italian cities that "of those enclosed within a single wall and moat, one gnaws the other."

79–90: It is probably best to think of this outburst as hyperbole induced by Dante's outrage at the torture of Ugolino's innocent children, an act so unnatural that nature itself should rise against it. Proscriptions and other forms of political retaliation in the Italian cities were pronounced against families as well as individuals, and Dante's own sons were banished and sentenced to death on his account. Nonetheless, a modern reader may be excused for wondering whether Dante is too ready to pose as an Old Testament prophet.

81: The neighbors would be Lucca and Florence, united in the Guelf League.

82–83: Capraia and Gorgona, islands in the Tyrhennian sea, were under Pisan control. Pisa is situated on the Arno, but was some distance from the seashore even in Dante's day.

89: Calling Pisa a new Thebes recalls the violence, madness and treachery of the dysfunctional ancient city, from the infanticide of Athamas to the parricide of Oedipus to the fratricidal conflict between his sons in the war of the Seven, with the blasphemy of Capaneus and the cannibalism of Tydeus, followed by the tyranny of Creon.

91: The poets cross into the Ring of Ptolemy (named in line 124), where treachery to guests and friends is punished. These sinners violated fiduciary obligations by betraying people whose benefactors they purported to be. Dante's name parallels biblical and classical examples of those who betrayed their guests. (1) Ptolemy was a captain of Israel. Plotting to take over the country, he invited Simon Machabeus and his sons to a banquet, where at his signal soldiers rushed in and put them to the sword. 1 Mach. 16:11–16. (2) After his defeat by Caesar, Pompey went to Egypt, seeking protection as a guest from Ptolemy, the boy king whose father had owed his crown to Pompey. Hoping to gain favor with Caesar, Ptolemy sent him Pompey's head. *Phars.* 8.536ff.

100–08: In Aristotle's meteorology, the heat of the sun makes dry exhalations rise from the earth, which become winds as they are carried obliquely by the motion of the heavens. Calm results when "cold quenches the exhalation." *Meteor.* 2.4–5 (359b25–361b30).

109–20: Brother Alberigo belonged to a leading family of Faenza and was a member of the order of "Jolly Friars." See note to *Inf.* 23.103–08. After a dispute with his cousin Manfredi, Alberigo pretended to make peace and invited Manfredi and one of his sons to a banquet. At the end of the meal he called for fruit and at this signal assassins rushed in and murdered the guests. The murder took place in 1285 and since the pilgrim is surprised at thinking Alberigo dead in 1300, he must have escaped punishment. *ED* 1.94–95.

115–17: The pilgrim makes an equivocal promise to induce the sinner's confidence, knowing that he will go below the ice to exit hell. It is not clear, however, why the promise would make sense to the sinner, who already believes that the pilgrim is going beneath the ice in the inmost ring of Cocytus.

120: Alberigo means paid back not "tit-for-tat" but rather "in spades," because dates were rare and expensive. See Mainoni 326.

121–33: The notion that a traitor falls into hell as soon as he sins, foreclosing the possibility of repentance (and saving appearances by leaving his body possessed by a devil), is unequivocally heterodox. Pietro defended his father from the imputation of heresy, arguing for the allegorical meaning that obdurate traitors despair of God's mercy and thus plunge from vice to vice, believing that their souls are already in hell. Modern sympathizers tend to stress that traitors have cut themselves off from all fellowship, so that they are no longer human.

Psychological justifications, however, do not explain the reality of the pilgrim's seeing the sinners' souls in hell, and the simplest way to read the text is that Dante is perfectly serious. This is puzzling because in his other departures from orthodoxy (the Elysian Fields, Beatrice as mediatrix of grace, the dead having aerial bodies and seeing the future) Dante had clear motives for tweaking theology. The even more flatly heterodox invention here appears gratuitous. Although it underlines the heinousness of this form of treachery, it does not apply to the even worse traitors of *Inf.* 34. Earlier visionaries, however, also meet people in hell who are still alive (Morgan 55) and see Num. 16:30; Ps. 54:16.

126: Atropos, one of the three Fates, cuts the thread of life.

134–47: Branca Doria, a member of the most powerful family of Genoa, was born in the early 1230s, putting him in his late sixties when the pilgrim sees his shade in hell. He was the son-in-law of Michael Zanche, Governor of Logodoro in Sardinia (for whom see note to *Inf.* 22.88). According to the story accepted by Dante, Branca, to gain control of Logodoro, invited Zanche and his followers to a banquet, where he had them murdered. He was said to have planned this with his nephew (the relative of lines 146–47). See *ED* 2.586–87. Like Alberigo, given the pilgrim's surprise at seeing him, Branca suffered no consequences for the crime.

151–57: The invectives against Pisa and Genoa in this canto complete the series of attacks on Italian cities in the *Inferno*: Florence, 16.73–78, 26.1–12; Bologna, 18.58–63; Lucca, 21.37–42; Pistoia, 25.10–15; and Siena, 29.121–32.

Canto XXXIV

"The banners of the king of hell come forth
    toward us and therefore look ahead and see,"
    my teacher said, "if you can make him out."
As when a dense fog rises or when night
    falls on our hemisphere, you may distinguish   5
    a distant windmill turning in the wind,
it seemed to me I saw a similar structure;
    and then to escape the wind I drew in close
    behind my guide, for lack of other shelter.
I'd come now – and I shudder as I write   10
    these verses – where the shades were totally covered
    and showed through as if they were straws in glass.
Some were recumbent; others stood erect,
    this on his heels and that one on his head;
    other were bent like bows, with face to feet.   15
When we had made such progress that my master
    was satisfied that it was time to show me
    the creature once so beautiful of face,
he stepped away from me and made me stand.
    "Look upon Dis," he said, "and on the place   20
    where you must fortify yourself with courage."
How faint and frozen I became then, reader,
    do not ask, for I will not try to write
    what language would be insufficient for.

I did not die nor yet remain alive;   25
    picture, if you have some imagination,
    my state, bereft of one and the other both.
The emperor of the realm of sorrow rose
    above the ice from halfway up his chest,
    and I would correspond to a giant's stature   30
more closely than the giants to his arms;
    you can imagine what the whole must be
    that bears proportion to such parts as these.
If once as beautiful as now he is ugly
    and if he raised his brow against his maker,   35
    well may all tribulation come from him.
Oh, what a great astonishment I felt
    when I made out three faces on his head!
    One of them, red in color, was in front;
the other two attached themselves to that one   40
    above the middle of each shoulder's slope,
    and all three joined together at the crest;
the one upon my right looked yellowish white,
    the left was in appearance like the people
    of the land from which the Nile takes its descent.   45
Beneath each face emerged two giant wings
    in the proportion fit for such a bird;
    never have I seen sails that size on ships.
They were not feathered but resembled rather
    those of a bat, and he was beating them   50
    so as to make three winds fan out from him,
keeping the whole of Cocytus frozen solid.
    From six eyes he was weeping and the tears
    trickled down three chins, mixed with bloody drool.
Each of his mouths was grinding on a sinner,   55
    the teeth disjoining sinews like a hackle,
    so that he tortured three of them that way.
To the one in front the biting was as nothing
    compared with being clawed, because his back
    was left at tines completely stripped of skin.   60

"The soul up there who bears the greater torment,
    his head inside while outside his legs thrash,
    is Judas Iscariot," my teacher said.
"As for the other two, whose heads are dangling,
    the one that hangs from the black snout is Brutus: 65
    look how he squirms but utters not a word!
The one who looks so muscular is Cassius.
    But night once more is rising and the time
    to leave has come, for we have seen it all."
At his request I clasped him around the neck;   70
    and he spied out the most convenient place,
    timing it so that when the wings were spread
he seized the shaggy flanks and clung to them;
    and then he let us down from tuft to tuft
    between the matted hair and the icy crust.   75
And when we came to where the thigh connects,
    right at the point where the hips' span is widest,
    my leader, straining now and short of breath,
swung his head round to face the other's shanks
    and grasped the hair the way you would when climbing,   80
    which made me think that we were going back
to hell. "Hold tight, for by this kind of ladder,"
    my teacher said, while panting from exertion,
    "we are obliged to part from all this evil."
Then he went out through a crevice in the rock,   85
    setting me down to sit upon its rim
    and with a careful step soon joining me.
I raised my eyes, expecting I would see
    Lucifer looking just as I had left him,
    and saw instead his legs projecting upward;   90
and whether I became bewildered then,
    those of dull wit may judge, who have as yet
    not grasped what point it was that I had passed.
"Get up," my teacher said, "and find your feet.
    The way is long and the route difficult,   95
    and the sun already rose an hour ago."

We found ourselves in no bright palace chamber
  but rather in a cavern formed by nature,
  uneven underfoot and lacking light.
"Before I tear myself from the abyss,   100
  Master," I said when I was on my feet,
  "say a few words to draw me from confusion:
Where is the ice? And he, how is he stuck
  head down like that? How, in so short a time,
  has the sun crossed from evening into morning?   105
He answered, "You imagine you are still
  beyond the center, where I clung to the hair
  of the evil worm that perforates the world.
There you remained so long as I descended,
  but when I turned around, you passed the point   110
  to which all weights are drawn from every side.
Now you have come beneath the hemisphere
  opposite to the one that vaults the great
  landmass, beneath whose zenith there was slain
the man born sinless and of sinless life.   115
    Your feet are resting on the little sphere
    that forms the other face of the Ring of Judas.
Here it is morning when it is evening there,
  and the one whose pelt provided us a ladder
  is still stuck just the way he was at first.   120
This is the side on which he fell from heaven,
  and all the land that previously emerged here
  drew back in fright behind a veil of sea
until it reached our hemisphere; and perhaps
  what does appear on this side, to flee him   125
  rushed upward, emptying this cavity."
There is a place as far from Beelzebub
  down there as the extent of that whole cavern,
  not to be found by sight but by the sound
of a little stream that trickles down from there   130
  out of the opening eaten in a rock
  by its winding course, which forms an easy grade.

We took this hidden path, my guide and I,
   to make our way back up to the bright world;
   and with no thought to stop for any rest   135
we climbed up, he in front and I behind,
   until at last I saw through a round hole
   some of the splendors heaven bears. And then
we emerged to look once more upon the stars.   139

Notes

1: Dante's first line is in Latin. It plays on the Christian hymn *Vexilla regis prodeunt* ("The banners of the king come forth") by adding the word *inferni*, changing heaven's king to the king of hell. The parody initiates the ironic treatment of Satan in this canto as the ape of God.

3–6: The pilgrim is seeing Satan in the distance. The vertical windmill was invented in Europe in the 12th century and was common by Dante's time. See Gimpel 24–27. The impression it makes on the pilgrim suggests that Satan will be a kind of towering mechanical device. What Virgil ironically likens to swaying standards and the pilgrim sees as the turning sails of a windmill will turn out to be Satan's flapping wings, the only thing that moves in the center of hell.

10–15: The poets have now entered the Ring of Judas, where those who betrayed their lords are punished next to Satan himself, who shares their sin. After the vividly dramatic narrative of the *Inferno* to this point, the presentation of the ultimate sinners is an anticlimax of silence and immobility, reflecting the idea that sin is the negation of authentic vitality.

20–54: Jacques LeGoff has commented on the extent to which the feudal organization of society resulted in the exaltation of fidelity to one's lord as the chief public virtue of the Middle Ages. Whereas the civic virtues of the ancient world required a man to be just, medieval man was required to be faithful, and faithlessness equaled wickedness. LeGoff 1988, 49–50.

    This dovetailed with the traditional Christian view that the sin of Satan was revolt against his rightful lord. The two concepts appear to have reinforced each other: the devil as rebellious vassal who attempts to draw others into his rebellion was an easily grasped paradigm of wickedness, and Satan played a more important role in the Middle Ages than he had in early Christianity. Here the image of Satan as the triune lord of hell is the final example of the *contrapasso*. Satan wanted to be God, and like the other inhabitants of hell he got his wish, though not on his terms. Forever silent and immobile, he is frozen in self-contemplation, whose inner dynamic is revealed by the tears that run eternally down his faces.

20: Dante does not use the name Satan, but "poetically," as Pietro said, calls him *Dis*, the classical god of the underworld. He is later called by the biblical names *Lucifer* and *Beelzebub*.

28–33, 55–58: The conception of Satan as a devouring giant has a long history. In Job 41:10–11 Leviathan is a great beast: "Out of his mouth go forth lamps, like torches of lighted fire. Out of his nostrils goeth smoke, like that of a pot heated and boiling." From the early Middle Ages Leviathan was identified with Satan. Morgan 14. In the art of the 12th and 13th centuries a conventional element of a Last Judgment is the Hellmouth, into which the damned are pushed by little devils. Hellmouth is a gigantic beast's head, at once the mouth of Satan and the entrance to hell. Typical representations appear on the facades of the cathedrals of Chartres, Amiens and Ferrara.

Closer to Dante's conception are full-length depictions of Satan in the 12th century ceiling mosaic of the Baptistery at Florence, which Dante would have known well, and in Giotto's fresco of hell in the Arena Chapel. In both images, Satan is a giant figure chewing a sinner whose legs dangle from his mouth, like those of Dante's Judas. Moreover, in both a huge snake emerges from each of Satan's ears; each snake also holds a sinner dangling from its mouth, for an overall effect much like Dante's.

30–33: Satan's immensity, like his ugliness, inspires awe. Richard Kay, using Vitruvian proportions and his calculations for the giants (see note to *Inf.* 31.62–64), concludes that Satan's height is well over a mile and a half. Kay 2002, 25. It is not clear how the pilgrim could make out the details of the following passage by looking up over three-quarters of a mile. It seems more likely that Dante simply meant to indicate an immense scale.

39–45: Dante was not the first to represent Satan with three faces; there is such an image in a 12th century carving in the church of San Pietro in Tuscania in Viterbo. Weir/Jerman 74. He would not have been familiar with contemporary Indian representations of Brahma *trimurti*, the three-faced; but as Hindu art uses multiple faces or arms to symbolize divine powers, Dante's Satan is a parody of the Blessed Trinity. This was clear to Pietro, who commented that "since God is the height of power, wisdom and love, so in Satan by opposition is the height of impotence, ignorance and hatred; and these are signified by his three faces." Pietro associated the three negative powers with the yellow-white, black and red faces respectively; other commentators have offered alternative identifications.

44–45: *I.e.*, the Ethiopians. Pliny and Lucan said that the sources of the Nile remained unknown but that it flowed into Egypt from Ethiopia beyond the cataracts. The passage in Lucan also mentions the complexion of the Ethiopians. *Nat. Hist.* 5.10; 8.32; *Phars.* 10.219–335.

46–49: Satan has the six wings characteristic of the Seraphim, the highest order of angels. Boyde 1981, 188. The wings, however, following popular art, have degenerated from feathered to bat-like.

48: *I.e.*, the triangular lateen sail, rather than a square sail. See Mainoni 318.

51–53: Like the minor devils, Satan is not only being punished, but is also God's instrument in punishing sinners, freezing Cocytus as well as chewing the three chief malefactors.

58–63: Treachery to one's lord was also the paradigm suited to Judas, always regarded as the blackest of sinners for betraying Jesus.

60: "At times" indicates that Judas's skin grows back so it can be clawed away again. See *Inf.* 28.37–42.

64–66: Brutus and Cassius are condemned for betraying Julius Caesar. In the republican tradition of Lucan, the assassination of Caesar was a blow against tyranny. Orosius, however, said that Caesar was "shamefully destroyed" (*Hist. Adv. Pag.* 6.17), and the names of Brutus and Cassius were "covered with shame throughout the Middle Ages." *ED* 1.862. Dante's overarching vision of a universal church paralleled by a universal state requires that Brutus and Cassius join Judas at the bottom of hell. As Judas betrayed the founder of the church, they betrayed the founder of the empire which, in Dante's belief, still retained its divine right to universal governance. The worst of sinners are those who attempted to thwart God's plan for the ordering of the world, secular as well as spiritual.

71–76: Virgil has darted in between one of the side pairs of wings.

73, 75: Dante has not previously called attention to the shaggy pelts of the devils, but they are a common feature of medieval representations.

74–75: It may seem too convenient that there is room between Satan and the ice for the poets to escape through, but Dante will explain that the earth avoids contact with him. See note to 119–26.

76–111: C.S. Lewis called the poets' passage through the center of the earth the first science fiction effect in literature. Lewis 141–42. In Dante's scheme, the closer one came to the center of the earth, the stronger the effect of what we would call gravity (a word that simply means heaviness). In fact, Newton's formulation shows that gravity is zero at the center of the earth because there is equal mass above and below. This passage is the climax of a pervasive trope in the *Inferno* (see note to *Inf.* 6.86) that attributes to the relative seriousness of sins a gravity that is physical as well as moral. Satan's ultimate sin has drawn him to the exact center of the universe, the point furthest from God.

82–84: Virgil's remark about the turning point passed by the poets will ultimately be seen to indicate that they are now set on the path to the mountain of Purgatory and, for the pilgrim, ultimately to Paradise.

104–05: Virgil has just said that night was beginning (68) and now he says it is morning.

112–18: Dante's terrestrial globe consists of two hemispheres, one containing earth's landmass and the other covered by water. Virgil does not refer directly to these, but describes them by reference to the celestial hemispheres that hang over them like vaults. The terrestrial hemisphere of land is centered on Jerusalem, "the umbilicus of our habitable earth," as *The Golden Legend* called it. *Gold. Leg.* 1.37. The watery hemisphere is centered on the antipodes of Jerusalem, at which – by a bold invention of Dante's that Virgil is about to explain – lies the mountain of purgatory, the sole dry land in that hemisphere. Having passed through the center of the earth, the poets must now climb an equivalent distance on the other side to come out at the foot of this mountain.

119–26: Virgil's account of Satan's fall constitutes Dante's original mythologizing at its most elaborate. The landmass that had emerged in the present hemisphere of water drew back in fright from the crashing Satan until it reached the present hemisphere of land, while some of earth's core, having no other escape, rushed up to the surface, creating the tumulus of Purgatory.

The mythologizing character of the explanation is clear from the fact that in his *Questio De Acqua Et Terra (Disputation Regarding Water and Earth)*, Dante attempted to explain scientifically why the dry land protrudes above the water. The efficient cause of the earth's emerging above the water, Dante explains, cannot be the earth itself, because that would imply it could raise itself, which would be contrary to its nature; rather the elevating force must come from the *primum mobile*, the ninth celestial sphere. He maintains that there is no rational way to determine why the earth emerged in our hemisphere and not the other; it was simply the creative act of God. *Questio* 59–76. (For Dante's similar mythological versus scientific explanations of the Milky Way, see note to *Inf.* 17.108.)

127–34: The cavern created by Satan's plunge extends from the center of the earth to its surface. The poets cannot see their way up in the darkness, but follow a stream that descends in a gentle spiral, mirroring the course they took down through hell. Dante offers no explanation of the stream here, but the *Purgatorio* will show it to be Lethe, which washes away the memory of sin from those about to enter heaven. Commentators suggest that the stream thus carries the sins down to the center of the earth, paralleling the rivers that carry the flood of human misery from the Old Man of Crete (*Inf.* 14) down to hell.

139: All three canticles of the *Comedy* end with the word *stars*, a repeated reminder of the beauty and order of the universe created and sustained by divine love. As the poets emerge from the underworld, Easter Sunday is dawning. By descending to hell on Good Friday and emerging on Easter, the pilgrim has followed in the footsteps of Jesus. Hawkins 100; Scott 174.

Works Cited

Abbreviations for books of the bible are conventional; biblical quotations are from the Douay-Rheims version, sometimes modified, but biblical names follow the more familiar King James spellings. Commentaries on the *Comedy*, including notes to translations, are cited *ad loc*. References to the early commentators Benvenuto, Boccaccio, Lana and the Anonimo are taken from the *Enciclopedia Dantesca* and the Dartmouth Dante Database. (References to Boccaccio in the notes are to his commentary unless the *Decameron* is cited.) When the works cited are foreign- or dual-language texts, translations in the notes are mine. Where translations and/or reprints are cited, the date of original publication appears in brackets when feasible.

Aen.	Virgil, *Aeneid*
Civ. Dei	St. Augustine, *City of God*
CLD	*California Lectura Dantis*
Consol. Phil.	Boethius, *Consolation of Philosophy*
Conv.	Dante, *Convivio*
Cron.	Villani, *Nuova Cronica*
De Animal.	Albertus Magnus, *Man and the Beasts*
Decam.	Boccaccio, *Decameron*
DE	*The Dante Encyclopedia*
EBDSA	*Electronic Bulletin of the Dante Society of America*
ED	*Enciclopedia Dantesca*
Epist.	Dante, *Epistoli*
Eth.	Aristotle, *Nichomachean Ethics*

Etym.	St. Isidore of Seville, *Etymologiarum*
Gold. Leg.	Jacobus de Voragine, *The Golden Legend*
Hist. Adv. Pag.	Orosius, *Seven Books of History Against the Pagans*
In Eth.	St. Thomas Aquinas, *Commentary on Aristotle's Nicomachean Ethics*
Inf.	Dante, *Inferno*
LCL	Loeb Classical Library
Metam.	Ovid, *Metamorphoses*
Meteorol.	Aristotle, *Meteorology*
Mon.	Dante, *Monarchy*
Nat. Hist.	Pliny, *Natural History*
Par.	Dante, *Paradiso*
Phars.	Lucan, *Pharsalia*
Purg.	Dante, *Purgatorio*
Rom. Rose	Lorris and Meun, *The Romance of the Rose*
SCG	St. Thomas Aquinas, *Summa Contra Gentiles*
ST	St. Thomas Aquinas, *Summa Theologica*
Theb.	Statius, *Thebaid*
Tresor	Brunetto Latini, *Li Livres dou Tresor*
VE	Dante, *De Vulgari Eloquentia*
VN	Dante, *Vita Nuova*

Abelard, Peter. *Historia Calamitatum (History of His Misfortunes)* in *The Letters of Abelard and Heloise*. Translated by Betty Radice. Introduction by Betty Radice. London: Penguin, 1974.

Abulafia, David. *Frederick II: A Medieval Emperor*. London: Allen Lane / Penguin, 1988.

Alain of Lille. *Plaint of Nature*. Translated by James J. Sheridan. Commentary by James J. Sheridan. Toronto: Pontifical Institute of Mediaeval Studies, 1980.

Albertus Magnus (Albert the Great, Saint). *Man and the Beasts: De Animalibus books 22–26*, Translated by James J. Scanlan. Introduction by James J. Scanlan. Binghamton, N.Y.: State University of New York at Binghamton, 1987.

Alighieri, Dante. *Convivio* in *ED* 6.679ff.

——. *Epistole* in *ED* 6.803ff.

——. *Fiore* in *ED* 6.965ff.

——. *Inferno* in *ED* 6.835ff. (Editions or translations of the *Comedy* with notes are listed under the name of the editor/translator/commentator.)

———. Lyric poetry. (Editions or translations listed under the name of the editor/ translator.)

———. *Monarchy*. Translated and edited by Prue Shaw. Introduction by Prue Shaw. Cambridge: Cambridge University Press, 1996.

———. *Paradiso* in *ED* 6.922ff.

———. *Purgatorio* in *ED* 6.879ff.

———. *Questio di Acqua et Terra* in *ED* 6.825ff.

———. *Vita Nuova* in *ED* 6.622ff.

———. *De Vulgari Eloquentia*. Edited and translated by Stephen Botterill. Introduction by Stephen Botterill. Cambridge: Cambridge University Press, 1996.

Alighieri, Pietro. *Il "Commentarium" di Pietro Alighieri*. Edited by Roberto della Vedova and Maria Teresa Silvotti. Introduction by Egidio Guidubaldi. Florence: Olschki, 1978.

The Apocalypse in the Middle Ages. Edited by Richard K. Emmerson and Bernard McGinn. Ithaca, N.Y.: Cornell University Press, 1992.

Apocalyptic Spirituality: Treatises and Letters of Lactantius, Adso of Montier-en-Der, Joachim of Fiore, The Spiritual Franciscans, Savonarola. Translation and Introduction by Bernard McGinn. Preface by Marjorie Reeves. New York: Paulist Press, 1979.

Aquinas, Saint Thomas. *Commentary on Aristotle's Metaphysics*. Translated by John P. Rowan. Preface by Ralph McInerny. Notre Dame, Ind.: Dumb Ox Books, 1995 [1961].

———. *Commentary on Aristotle's Nicomachean Ethics*. Translated by C.I. Litzinger. Forward by Ralph McInerny. Notre Dame, Ind.: Dumb Ox Books, 1993 [1964].

———. *Summa Contra Gentiles. Book Three: Providence*. Translated with an Introduction and Notes by Vernon J. Bourke. Notre Dame, Ind.: Notre Dame University Press, 1975 [1956].

———. *Summa Theologica*. Translated by Fathers of the English Dominican Province. 3 vols. New York: Benziger Brothers, 1948.

Aristotle. *The Complete Works of Aristotle*. Edited by Jonathan Barnes. 2 vols. Princeton, N.J.: Princeton University Press, 1984.

———. *Metphysics*. Translated by W.D. Ross in *The Complete Works of Aristotle, supra*.

———. ———. Translation of the medieval Latin text in Aquinas, *Commentary on the Metaphysics, supra*.

———. *Meteorology*. Translated by E.W. Webster in *The Complete Works of Aristotle, supra*.

———. *Nicomachean Ethics*. Translated by, W.D. Ross and J.O. Urmson in *The Complete Works of Aristotle, supra*.

———. ———. Translation of the medieval Latin text in Aquinas, *Commentary on the Ethics, supra*.

———. *Physics*. Translated by R.P. Hardie and R.K. Gaye in *The Complete Works of Aristotle, supra*.

Ascoli, Albert Russell. "Palinode and History in the Oeuvre of Dante" in *Dante Now* 155–86.

Auerbach 1929 – Auerbach, Erich. *Dante: Poet of the Secular World*. Translated by Ralph Manheim. Chicago: University of Chicago Press, 1961 [1929].

Auerbach 1944 – ——. "Figura," in *Scenes from the Drama of European Literature*. Translated by Ralph Manheim. Foreword by Paolo Valesio. Minneapolis: University of Minnesota Press, 1984 [1944].

Auerbach 1946 – ——. *Mimesis: the Representation of Reality in Western Literature*. Translated by Willard R. Trask. Princeton, N.J.: Princeton University Press, 1953 [1946].

Auerbach 1958 – ——. *Literary Language and its Public in Latin Antiquity and in the Middle Ages*. Translated by Ralph Mannheim. Princeton, N.J.: Princeton University Press, 1965 [1958].

Augustine, Saint. *The City of God*. Translated by Marcus Dodd. Introduction by Thomas Merton. Modern Library. New York: Random House, 1950.

——. *Confessions*. Translated by R.S. Pine-Coffin. London: Penguin, 1961.

——. *On Christian Doctrine*. Translated by D.W. Robertson, Jr. New York: Macmillan, 1958.

Baranski 1995 – Baranski, Zygmunt. "The Poetics of Meter: *Terza Rima*, 'Canto,' 'Canzon,' 'Cantica'" in *Dante Now* 3–42.

Baranski 2003 – ——. "Scatology and Obscenity in Dante" in *Dante for the New Millenium* 259–73.

Barolini 1984 – Barolini, Teodolinda. *Dante's Poets: Textuality and Truth in the "Comedy."* Princeton, N.J.: Princeton University Press, 1984.

Barolini 1992 – ——. *The Undivine Comedy: Detheologizing Dante*. Princeton, N.J.: Princeton University Press, 1992.

Barolini 1998 – ——. "True and False See-ers" in CLD 275–86.

Barolini 2006 – ——. *Dante and the Origins of Italian Literary Culture*. New York: Fordham University Press, 2006.

—— and Richard Lansing. *Dante's Lyric Poetry: Poems of Youth and of the Vita Nuova*. Edited by Teodolinda Barolini. Translated by Richard Lansing. General Introduction and Introductory Essays by Teodolinda Barolini. Toronto: University of Toronto Press, 2014.

Biblia Latina cum Glossa Ordinaria. 4 vols. Turnhout: Brepols, 1992. (The bible with marginal and interlinear glosses in a form compiled in the 12th century from scriptural commentaries of the church fathers and doctors.)

Bloom, Harold. *The Western Canon: The Books and School of the Ages*. New York: Riverhead Books, 1995.

Boccaccio, Giovanni. *The Decameron*. Translated by Mark Musa and Peter Bondanella. New York: Signet Classics, 1982.

Boethius, Ancius. *The Theological Tractates. The Consolation of Philosophy*. Translated by H.E. Stewart, E.K. Rand and S.J. Tester. New edition. LCL. Cambridge, Mass.: Harvard University Press, 1973.

Bonaventure, Saint. *Itinerarium Mentis ad Deum* in *Bonaventure: The Soul's Journey Into God, The Tree of Life, The Life of St. Francis*. Translated by Ewert Cousins. Introduction by Ewert Cousins. Preface by Ignatius Brady. New York: Paulist Press, 1978.

Bosco, Umberto and Giovanni Reggio. *La Divina Commedia*. 3 vols. Edited and with a commentary by Umberto Bosco and Giovanni Reggio. Florence: Le Monnier, n.d. [1979].

Boswell, John. *Christianity, Social Tolerance and Homosexuality*. Chicago: University of Chicago Press, 1980.

Boyde 1981 – Boyde, Patrick. *Dante Philomythes and Philosoher: Man in the Cosmos*. Cambridge: Cambridge University Press, 1981.

Boyde 1993 – ——. *Perception and Passion in Dante's Comedy*. Cambridge: Cambridge University Press, 1993.

Boyde 2000 – ——. *Human Vices and Human Worth in Dante's Comedy*. Cambridge: Cambridge University Press, 2000.

Brundage, James A. *Law, Sex, and Christian Society in Medieval Europe*. Chicago: University of Chicago Press, 1987.

Buti, Francesco da. *Commento di Francesco da Buti Sopra La Divina Comedia*. Pisa: Fratelli Nistri, 1858–1862.

Cachey, Theodore. "Cartographic Dante," *Italica* 87.3 (Autumn 2010): 325–54.

California Lectura Dantis. *See Lectura Dantis: Inferno, infra*.

The Cambridge Companion to Dante. Edited by Rachel Jacoff. 2d edition. Cambridge: Cambridge University Press, 2007.

Capellanus, Andreas. *The Art of Courtly Love*. Translated by John Jay Parry. Introduction and notes by John Jay Parry. New York: Columbia University Press, 1990 [1941].

Carruthers, Mary. *The Book of Memory: A Study of Memory in Medieval Culture*. Cambridge: Cambridge University Press, 1990.

Casagrande, Gino and Christopher Kleinhenz. "Alan of Lille and Dante: Questions of Influence," *Italica* 82.3–4 (Autumn/Winter 2005): 356–65.

Cassel, Anthony K. *Lectura Dantis Americana: Inferno I*. Philadelphia: University of Pennsylvania Press, 1989.

Chaucer, Geoffrey. *The Works of Geoffrey Chaucer*. Edited by F.N. Robinson. Boston: Houghton Mifflin, 1957.

Chiavacci Leonardi, Anna Maria, ed.. *Inferno con il commento di Anna Maria Chiavacci Leonardi*. Milan: Mondadori, 1991.

Cicero, Marcus Tullius. *De Finibus Bonorum et Malorum*. Translated by H. Rackham. LCL. London: Heinemann, 1914.

——. *On Duties (De Officiis)*. Translated by Walter Miller. LCL. Cambridge, Mass.: Harvard University Press, 1913.

——. *De Senectute, De Amicitia, De Divinatione*. Translated by W.A. Falconer. LCL. Cambridge, Mass.: Harvard University Press, 1923.

Cioffi, Caron Ann. "The Anxieties of Ovidian Influence: Theft in Inferno XXIV and XXV," *Dante Studies* 112 (1994): 77–100.

Clanchy, M.T. *From Memory to Written Record: England 1066–1307.* 2d ed. Oxford: Basil Blackwell, 1993.

Cogan, Marc. *The Design in the Wax: the Structure of the* Divine Comedy *and its Meaning.* Notre Dame, Ind.: Notre Dame University Press, 1999.

Compagni, Dino. *Cronica delle cose occorrenti ne' tempi suoi.* Introduction and Notes by Gabriella Mezzanotte. Milan: Monadori, 1993.

Crompton, Louis. *Homosexuality and Civilization.* Cambridge, Mass.: The Belknap Press of Harvard University Press, 2003.

Curtius, Ernst. *European Literature and the Latin Middle Ages.* Translated by Willard R. Trask. Afterword by Peter Godman. Princeton, N.J.: Princeton University Press, 1983 [1948].

Damian, Saint Peter. Letter 31 ('The Book of Gomorrha'), in *Peter Damian: Letters 31–60.* Translated by Owen J. Blum. Washington, D.C.: Catholic University of America Press, 1990.

Daniello, Bernardino. *L'Espositione di Bernardino da Lucca Sopra La Commedia di Dante.* Edited by Robert Hollander and Jeffrey Schnapp with Kevin Brownlee and Nancy Vickers. Hanover, New Hampshire: University Press of New England, 1989.

The Dante Encyclopedia. Edited by Richard Lansing. New York: Routledge, 2010 [2000].

Dante for the New Millennium. Edited by Teodolinda Barolini and H. Wayne Storey. New York: Fordham University Press, 2003.

Dante Now: Current Trends in Dante Studies. Edited by Theodore J. Cachey, Jr. Notre Dame, Ind.: University of Notre Dame Press, 1995.

Dante's Inferno: The Indiana Critical Edition. Translated and edited by Mark Musa. Bloomington, Ind.: Indiana University Press, 1995.

Davis 1957 – Davis, Charles T. *Dante and the Idea of Rome.* Oxford: Clarendon Press, 1957.

Davis 1998 – ——. "Simoniacs" in *CLD* 262–74.

Di Scipio, Giuseppe and Aldo Scaglione, eds. *The Divine Comedy and the Encyclopedia of Arts and Sciences.* Amsterdam: John Benjamins, 1988.

Doob, Penelope Reed. *The Idea of the Labyrinth from Classical Antiquity Through the Middle Ages.* Ithaca, N.Y.: Cornell University Press, 1990.

Duby, Georges, Xavier Barral i Altet and Sophie Guillot de Suduiraut, *Sculpture: The Great Art of the Middle Ages from the Fifth to the Fifteenth Century.* New York: Rizzoli, 1990.

Durling, Robert M., ed. and trans. *The Divine Comedy of Dante Alighieri, Vol. 1: Inferno.* Introduction and notes by Ronald L. Martinez and Robert M. Durling. New York: Oxford University Press, 1996.

Elliott, J.K., ed. *The Apocryphal New Testament: A Collection of Apocryphal Christian Literature in an English Translation.* Oxford: Clarendon Press, 1993.

Emmerson, Richard K. "Introduction: the Apocalypse in Medieval Culture" in *The Apocalypse in the Middle Ages* 293–332.

Enciclopedia Dantesca. 2d ed. 6 vols. Umberto Bosco, director. Giorgio Petrocchi, editor-in-chief. Rome: Istituto della Enciclopedia Italiana, 1984.

Ferrante, Joan M. *The Political Vision of the Divine Comedy*. Princeton, N.J.: Princeton University Press, 1984.

Fosca 2011 – Fosca, Nicola. "*Inf*. II.96: 'sì che duro giudizio là sú frange'," *EBDSA*, 5 March 2011.

Fossier, Robert, ed. *The Cambridge Illustrated History of the Middle Ages*. Vol. 3: 1250–1520. Translated by Sarah Hanbury Tenison. Cambridge: Cambridge University Press, 1987 [1983].

Foster, Kenelm and Patrick Boyde, ed. and trans. *Dante's Lyric Poetry*. Commentary by Kenelm Foster and Patrick Boyde. 2 vols. Oxford: Clarendon Press, 1967.

Foucault, Michel. *The History of Sexuality, Vol. 1: An Introduction*. Translated by Robert Hurley. New York: Vintage Books, 1990 [1976].

Freccero 1986 – Freccero, John. *Dante: the Poetics of Conversion*. Edited by Rachel Jacoff. Cambridge, Mass.: Harvard University Press, 1986.

Freccero 1991 – ——. "The Eternal Image of the Father" in *The Poetry of Allusion* 62–76.

Gardiner, Eileen, ed. *Visions of Heaven & Hell Before Dante*. New York: Italica Press, 1989.

Gilson, Etienne. *Dante the Philosopher*. Translated by David Moore. London: Sheed & Ward, 1948 [1939].

Gimpel, Jean. *The Medieval Machine: The Industrial Revolution of the Middle Ages*. New York: Penguin, 1977 [1976].

Glossa Ordinaria. See *Biblia Latina cum Glossa Ordinaria*.

Goetz, Hans-Werner. *Life in the Middle Ages*. Translated by Albert Wimmer. Notre Dame, Ind.: University of Notre Dame Press, 1993 [1986].

A Handbook of the Troubadours. Edited by F.R.P. Akehurst and Judith M. Davis. Berkeley, Calif.: University of California Press, 1995.

"The Harrowing of Hell," Play 37 from The York Corpus Christi Plays 2011. Clifford Davidson, editor. University of Rochester Middle English Text Series – A Robbins Library Digital Project. http:\ \ d.lib. rochester.edu/teams/text/davidson-play-37-the-harrowing-of-hell

Hassig, Debra. *Medieval Bestiaries: Text, Image, Ideology*. Cambridge: Cambridge University Press, 1995.

Hawkins, Peter S. *Dante's Testaments: Essays in Scriptural Imagination*. Stanford, Calif.: Stanford University Press, 1999.

Heilbronn, Denise. "Master Adam and the Fat-Bellied Lute ("Inf." XXX)," *Dante Studies* 101 (1983): 51–65.

Hertzman, Ronald B. "Dante and the Apocalypse" in *The Apocalypse in the Middle Ages* 398–413.

Hill, R.T. and Thomas G. Bergin, eds. *Anthology of the Provençal Troubadours*. 2d ed. Revised by Thomas G. Bergin. 2 vols. New Haven: Yale University Press, 1973.

Hollander 1969 – Hollander, Robert. *Allegory in Dante's Commedia*. Princeton, N.J.: Princeton University Press, 1969.

Hollander 1996 – ———. "Dante's Harmonious Homosexuals (*Inferno* 16.7–90)," *EBDSA*, 27 June 1996.

Hollander 2000 – ———and Jean Hollander, trans. *Dante Alighieri: Inferno*. Introduction and notes by Robert Hollander. New York: Doubleday, 2000.

Hollander 2013 – ———. "Inferno IX.58–63: *sotto 'l velame de li versi strani*," *EBDSA*, 20 October 2013.

Horace (Quintus Horatius Flaccus). *Satires and Epistles* [together with Persius, *Satires*]. Translated by Niall Rudd. Notes by Niall Rudd. London: Penguin, 1979.

———. "Ars Poetica." In *Satires and Epistles, supra*.

Huizinga, Johan. *The Waning of the Middle Ages: A Study of the Forms of Life, Thought and Art in France and the Netherlands in the XIVth and XVth Centuries*. Translated by F. Hopman. Anchor Books. New York: Doubleday, 1989 [1924].

Iannucci, Amilcare. "The Harrowing of Dante from Upper Hell" in *CLD* 123–35.

Isidore of Seville, Saint. *Etymologiarum sive Originum*. Edited by W.M. Lindsay. 2 vols. Oxford: Oxford University Press, 1911.

Jacoff, Rachel and William A. Stephany. *Lectura Dantis Americana: Inferno II*. Philadelphia: University of Pennsylvania Press, 1989.

Kantorowicz, Ernst H. *The King's Two Bodies: A Study in Medieval Political Theology*. Princeton, N.J.: Princeton University Press, 1957.

Kay 1994 – Kay, Richard. *Dante's Christian Astrology*. Philadelphia: University of Pennsylvania Press, 1994.

Kay 2003 – ———. "Vitruvius and Dante's Giants," *Dante Studies* 120 (2002): 17–34.

Kieckhefer, Richard. *Magic in the Middle Ages*. Cambridge: Cambridge University Press, 1995.

Kirshner, Julius and Karl F. Robinson eds. *Medieval Europe*. University of Chicago Readings in Western Civilization, vol. 4. Chicago: University of Chicago Press, 1986.

Kleinhenz, Christopher. "Iconographic Parody in *Inferno* XXI" in *Dante's Inferno: The Indiana Critical Edition* 325–39.

Lane, Frederic C. *Venice, A Maritime Republic*. Baltimore: Johns Hopkins University Press, 1973.

Langland, William. *Piers Plowman*. Translated by E. Talbot Donaldson. Edited by Elizabeth Robertson and Stephen H.A. Shepherd. New York: W.W. Norton & Company, 1990.

Lansing 1976 – Lansing, Richard H. "Submerged Meanings in Dante's Similes (*Inf.* XXVII)," *Dante Studies* 94 (1976): 61–69.

Lansing 1981 – ———. "Dante's Concept of Violence and the Great Chain of Being," *Dante Studies* 99 (1981): 67–87.

Lansing 2009 – ——. "The Pageantry of Dante's Verse," *Dante Studies* 127 (2009): 59–80.

Larner, John. *Italy in the Age of Dante and Petrarch 1216–1380*. London: Longman, 1980.

Latini, Brunetto. *Li Livres dou Tresor*. Edited by Francis J. Carmody. Introduction by Francis J. Carmody. Berkeley: University of California Press, 1948.

Lazar, Moshe. "Fin' Amor" in *Handbook of the Troubadours* 61–100.

[*Lectura Dantis*] *Inferno: Letture degli Anni 1973–76*. Casa di Dante in Roma. Rome: Bonacci, 1977.

Lectura Dantis: Inferno. Edited by Allen Mandelbaum, Anthony Oldcorn and Charles Ross. California Lectura Dantis. Berkeley: University of California Press, 1998.

Lectura Dantis Neapolitana: Inferno. Edited by Pompeo Giannantonio. Naples: Loffredo, n.d. [1986].

Lectura Dantis Scaligera: Inferno. Edited by Mario Marcazzan. Florence: Le Monnier, 1971.

LeGoff 1988 – LeGoff, Jacques. *Medieval Civilization 400–1500*. Translated by Julia Barrow. Oxford: Basil Blackwell, 1988 [1964].

LeGoff 1990 – ——. *Your Money or Your Life*. Translated by Patricia Ranum. New York: Zone Books, 1990 [1986].

Lewis, C.S. *The Discarded Image: an Introduction to Medieval and Renaissance Literature*. Cambridge: Cambridge University Press, 1994 [1966].

Lindberg, David C. *The Beginnings of Western Science: the European Scientific Tradition in Philosophical, Religious and Institutional Context, 600 B.C. to A.D. 1450*. Chicago: University of Chicago Press, 1992.

Link, Luther. *The Devil: the Archfiend in Art from the Sixth to the Sixteenth Century*. New York: Harry N. Abrams, Inc., 1996.

Livy (Titus Livius). *The Early History of Rome (The History of Rome from its Foundation, Books 1–4)*. Translated by Aubrey de Sélincourt. London: Penguin, 1960.

——. *The War with Hannibal (The History of Rome from its Foundation, Books 21–30)*. Translated by Aubrey de Sélincourt. London: Penguin, 1965.

Lorris, Guillaume de and Jean de Meun. *The Romance of the Rose*. Translated by Charles Dahlberg. 3d edition. Princeton, N.J.: Princeton University Press, 1995.

Lucan (M. Annaeus Lucanus). *The Civil War (Pharsalia)*. Translated by J.D. Duff. LCL. Cambridge, Mass.: Harvard University Press, 1928.

Macrobius, Ambrosius Theodosius. *Commentary on the Dream of Scipio*. Translated by William Harris Stahl. Introduction by William Harris Stahl. New York: Columbia University Press, 1952.

Mainoni, Patrizia. "L'Orizzonte Economica Medievale Nella *Divina Commedia* E Nei Principali Commenti Del Trecento" in *The Divine Comedy and the Encyclopedia of Arts and Sciences* 315–38.

Mazzoni 1977 – Mazzoni, Francesco. "Il Canto V Dell' *Inferno*" in [*Lectura Dantis*] *Inferno: Letture degli Anni 1973–76*, 97–143.

Mazzoni 1986 – ——. "Canto XI" in *Lectura Dantis Neapolitana: Inferno* 167–210.

Mazzotta 1993 – Mazzotta, Giuseppe. *Dante's Vision and the Circle of Knowledge*. Princeton, N.J.: Princeton University Press, 1993.

Mazzotta 1998 – ——. "Ulysses: Persuasion versus Prophecy" in *CLD* 348–356.

Modern Critical Views: Dante. Edited with an introduction by Harold Bloom. New York: Chelsea House Publishing, 1986.

Mollat, Michel. *The Poor in the Middle Ages: an Essay in Social History*. Translated by Arthur Goldhammer. New Haven: Yale University Press, 1986 [1978].

Moore, Edward. *Studies in Dante (First Series)*. New York: Haskell House, 1968 [1896].

Morgan, Allison. *Dante and the Medieval Other World*. Cambridge: Cambridge University Press, 1990.

Najemy 1994 – Najemy, John M. "Brunetto Latini's 'Politica'", *Dante Studies* 112 (1994): 33–51.

Najemy 2007 – ——. "Dante and Florence" in *Cambridge Companion to Dante* 235–56.

Nichols, Francis Morgan, ed. and trans., *The Marvels of Rome (Mirabilia urbis Romae)*. 2d ed. New York: Italica Press, 1986.

Noakes 1986 – Noakes, Susan. "The Double Misreading of Paolo and Francesca" in *Modern Critical Views: Dante* 151–66.

Noakes 1998 – "From Other Sodomites to Fraud" in *CLD* 213–224.

Orosius, Paulus. *The Seven Books of History Against the Pagans*. Translated by Roy J. Deferrari. Washington, D.C.: Catholic University of America Press, 1964.

L'Ottimo Commento della Divina Commedia. 3 vols. Arnoldo Forni, 1995.

Ovid (Publius Ovidius Naso). *The Art of Love* in *The Erotic Poems*. Translated by Peter Green. Notes by Peter Green. London: Penguin, 1982.

——. *Fasti*. Translated by Sir James G. Frazer. Revised by G.P. Goold. 2d edition. LCL. Cambridge, Mass.: Harvard University Press, 1989.

——. *Heroides. Amores*. Translated by Grant Showerman. Revised by G.P. Goold. 2d edition. LCL. Cambridge, Mass: Harvard University Press, 1977.

——. *Metamorphoses*. Translated by Frank Justus Miller. Revised by G.P. Goold. 2 vols. LCL. Cambridge, Mass.: Harvard University Press, 1977, 1984.

Pagliaro, Antonio. "Canto XIX" in *Lectura Dantis Scaligera* 617–68.

Pelikan, Jaroslav. *The Christian Tradition: A History of the Development of Doctrine* 5 vols. Chicago: University of Chicago Press, 1971 et seq.

Pertile 1996 – Pertile, Lino. " 'ANCOR NON M'ABBANDONA' (*Inferno* 5.105)," *EBDSA*, 24 August 1996.

Pertile 1997 – ——. "Dante Looks Forward and Back: Political Allegory in the Epistles," *Dante Studies* 115 (1997): 1–17.

Pertile 1998 – ——. "Such Outlandish Wounds" in *CLD* 378–91.

Pertile 2003 – ——. "Does the Stilnovo Go to Heaven?" in *Dante for the New Millenium* 104–14.

Pertile 2007a – ——. "Introduction to *Inferno*" in *Cambridge Companion to Dante* 67–90.

Pertile 2007b – ――. "Virgil is not angry. A note on *Inferno* 27.21," *EBDSA*, 13 December 2007.

Peters, Edward, ed. *Heresy and Authority in Medieval Europe: Documents in Translation*. Philadelphia: University of Pennsylvania Press, 1980.

Peterson, Thomas E. "Ovid and Parody in Dante's 'Inferno'," *Annali d'Italianistica* 25 (2007): 203–16.

Pézard, André, trans. *Dante: Oeuvres Complètes*. Commentaries by André Pézard. Bibliothèque de la Pléiade. Paris: Gallimard, 1965.

Piponnier, Françoise and Perrine Mane. *Dress in the Middle Ages*. Translated by Caroline Beamish. New Haven: Yale University Press, 1997 [1995].

Pleij, Herman. *Colors Demonic and Divine: Shades of Meaning in the Middle Ages and After*. Translated by Diane Webb. New York: Columbia University Press, 2004 [2002].

Pliny the Elder (Gaius Plinius Secundus). *Natural History*. Translated by H. Rackham *et al.* 10 vols. LCL. Cambridge, Mass.: Harvard University Press, 1949 *et seq.*

The Poetry of Allusion: Virgil and Ovid in Dante's Commedia. Edited by Rachel Jacoff and Jeffrey T. Schnapp. Stanford, Calif.: Stanford University Press, 1991.

Russell, Jeffrey Burton. *Lucifer: The Devil in the Middle Ages*. Ithaca, New York: Cornell University Press, 1984.

Sapegno, Natalino. *La Divina Commedia*. Edited and with a commentary by Natalino Sapegno. Milan: Riccardo Ricciardi, 1957.

Scartazzini, G.A. *A Companion to Dante*. Translated by Arthur John Butler. London: Macmillan and Co., 1893.

Scott, John A. *Understanding Dante*. Notre Dame, Ind.: Notre Dame University Press, 2004.

Shaw, Prue. *Reading Dante: From Here to Eternity*. New York: Liveright Publishing Corporation, 2014.

Sherberg, Michael. "Coin of the Realm: Dante and the Simonists," *Dante Studies* 129 (2011): 7–23.

Simmons, R.E. and J.M. Mendelsohn. "A Critical Review of Cartwheeling Flights of Raptors." *Ostrich* 64 (1993):13–24.

Simonelli, Maria Picchio. *Lectura Dantis Americana: Inferno III*. Philadelphia: University of Pennsylvania Press, 1993.

Sinclair, John D., trans. *The Divine Comedy of Dante Alighieri: I Inferno*. Comment by John D. Sinclair. New York: Oxford University Press, 1961 [1939].

Singleton 1954 – Singleton, Charles S. *Dante's Commedia: Elements of Structure*. Baltimore: Johns Hopkins University Press, 1954.

Singleton 1977 – ――, trans. *Dante: The Divine Comedy, Inferno*. Commentary by Charles S. Singleton. Princeton, N.J.: Princeton University Press, 1977.

Siraisi, Nancy G. *Medieval & Early Renaissance Medicine: An Introduction to Knowledge and Practice*. Chicago: University of Chicago Press, 1990.

Smith, Robinson, trans. *The Earliest Lives of Dante*. New York: Haskell House, 1974 [1901].

Southern, R.W.. *The Making of the Middle Ages*. New Haven: Yale University Press, 1953.

Statius (Publilius Papinius). *Silvae, Thebaid* and *Achilleid*. Translated by J.H. Mozley. 2 vols. LCL. Cambridge, Mass.: Harvard University Press, 1928.

Steinberg, Justin. *Dante and the Limits of the Law*. Chicago: University of Chicago Press, 2013.

Stoneman, Richard, trans. *The Greek Alexander Romance*. Notes by Richard Stoneman. London: Penguin, 1991.

Sumption, Jonathan. *The Age of Pilgrimage: The Medieval Journey to God*. Mahwah, N.J.: Hidden Spring, 2003.

Toynbee 1901 – Toynbee, Paget Jackson. *Dante Studies and Researches*. London: Methuen and Co., n.d. [1901].

Toynbee 1914 – ——. *Concise Dictionary of Proper Names and Notable Matters in the Works of Dante*. New York: Phaeton Press, 1968 [1914].

Triolo, Alfred A. "Malice and Mad Bestiality" in *CLD* 150–64.

Valesio, Paolo. "The Fierce Dove" in *CLD* 63–83.

Vasari, Giorgio. *Lives of the Artists*. Translated by George Bull. 2 vols. London: Penguin, 1987.

Villani, Giovanni. *Nuova Cronica*. Edited by Giuseppe Porta. 3 vols. Parma: Ugo Guanda, 1990–1991.

Virgil (Publius Vergilius Maro). *Eclogues, Georgics, Aeneid, Minor Poems*. Translated by H.R. Fairclough. 2 vols. New and revised edition. LCL. Cambridge, Mass.: Harvard University Press, 1935, 1934.

Voragine, Jacobus de. *The Golden Legend*. Translated by William Granger Ryan. 2 vols. Princeton, N.J.: Princeton University Press, 1993.

Waley, Daniel. *The Italian City Republics*. 3d edition. London: Longman, 1988.

Weir, Anthony and James Jerman. *Images of Lust: Sexual Carvings on Medieval Churches*. London: B.T. Batsford, 1986.

Williams, Charles. *The Figure of Beatrice: A Study in Dante*. Cambridge: D.S. Brewer, 1994 [1943].

Biographical Note on Dante

DANTE was born in Florence in 1265 into a family in modest circumstances, though he claimed noble origins for his forebears. In his youth he became one of the leading lyric poets in Italy, along with his friend Guido Cavalcanti. In his late twenties Dante wrote the *Vita Nuova* ("New Life"), an autobiographical prose narrative that served as a frame for poems written earlier about a woman named Beatrice Portinari. He says he met her when they were both eight years old and she first greeted him in the street nine years later, transforming his life. Although, according to him, they had no actual relationship over the years beyond exchanges of greetings, she became his amorous obsession and his muse. When Dante was 20 he married Gemma Donati, a woman from a lesser branch of an important family, with whom he would have four children. Five years after his marriage Beatrice died. Following her death, Dante entered into intensive studies in philosophy and theology and got involved in politics.

Florence, like other Italian cities, was riven by violent factional strife. The long-running struggle of the Guelfs (allied with the pope) and the Ghibellines (allied with the emperor) had ended with the Guelfs victorious. But Florence was then plagued by a violent struggle between the Black and White factions of the Guelf party; Dante was allied with the Whites. In 1300 he was serving a two-month term as one of the seven priors who administered the city when the struggle came to a boil. The priors exiled the leaders of both parties. After his term ended, the Whites were recalled from exile, which antagonized the pope, who called in a French force to restore the Blacks to power. When this happened Dante was on an embassy to Rome to dissuade the pope from this course. He was sentenced in absentia to exile and then to death and he never saw Florence again. He spent almost 20 years in exile, partly as a guest of the lords of Verona and Ravenna. He died after returning from an embassy on behalf of the latter in 1321, when he was 56.

In exile Dante wrote most of his works, including an unfinished treatise of moral philosophy, an unfinished work on linguistics and literature, a book of political theory and open letters on the international political situation. In the last 15 years of his life he wrote his masterpiece, *The Divine Comedy*, which begins in autobiography and becomes by its end the single most universal and transcendent work in Western literature. T.S. Eliot said, "Dante and Shakespeare divide the world between them. There is no third."

PETER THORNTON grew up in New York City and attended a Jesuit prep school in Manhattan where the curriculum was still based on Latin and Greek. After graduating from Boston College, he originally set out to be an academic. He took a Ph.D. in English literature at Stanford and taught for several years at Bradley University in Illinois. Then, like his father and his three brothers, he decided to become a lawyer and has spent the rest of his career happily practicing law in Chicago, where he has been recognized as a leading practitioner. The intellectual rigor of the law, however, did not satisfy his hunger for poetry and he has spent decades translating Dante and Petrarch into English verse.